Prisoner of Hope

Norm Mitchell

CALUMET EDITIONS
Minneapolis

**CALUMET
EDITIONS**
Minneapolis

SECOND EDITION DECEMBER 2022
Prisoner of Hope (Book 2 of the *People of the Blood* series.)
Copyright © 2020 by Norm Mitchell.
All rights reserved.

10 9 8 7 6 5 4 3 2

Cover and interior design: Gary Lindberg

ISBN: 978-1-959770-94-7

Prisoner of Hope

For Julie

"…Russia is a magical place where the rationality of the West and the mysticism of the East merge into an Hegelian synthesis."

–Sister Anastasia

Glossary of Unfamiliar Terms for *People of The Blood*

ABWEHR –- German Military Intelligence-1920-1945. It had three sections, so Section IV is fiction.

ALEPH – Colchi creator God, with two separate aspects, TRIPLE GOD and GODDESS in constant fluctuation. Meeting of opposites.

AMINALA/AMINALUS – -The female and male portions of a person, expressed as a percentage, such as, 60/40.

ANDRONYI – -An Iskandarova word for their gift of projecting an image or images of events or memories. An accomplished Iskandarova working with the recipient's TVARSCH can send three-dimensional images of themselves.

APPARAT – -The official names of the Soviet secret police agencies, such as 'APPARAT NKVD'.

CHEKIST – Initially, a member of Nicholai Lenin's secret police, run by Feliks Dzerzhinski, father of Svetlana Feliksovna. Used here as a way to simplify this agency that was 'constantly changing its name, but not its tactics.'. The three most important were CHEKA, NKVD, and KGB. After the fall of the Soviet Union in 1991, the KGB became the FSB.

DASVIDANIYA – Russian for "Until we meet again" not "goodbye"'.

DHESTOVY – -Iskandarova word meaning "apartness." It leads to madness and death, as was the case with Penelope Farwell. She could not control her PYORDARSCH, thus knowing the time and place of her violent death.

GRU – Main Intelligence Directorate. I have simplified the Soviet / Russian military intelligence agencies and their many names since there is only character Pavel Chichikov involved by simply using its current name, since 2010. (Artistic license.)

GULAG – a network of slave labor camps in the remote parts of the Soviet Union, established by Lenin, but reached its peak horror under Joseph Stalin.

ISK/ISKA – Informal form of Iskandarov and Iskandarova

ISKANDAROV MAGIC – Iskandarov men have a natural scent that women, especially Iskas, find irresistible.

KULAK – A "rich peasant." Primary target of Lenin's war on the peasants, many of whom were killed or starved.

LAGPUNKT – In the GULAG, a temporary camp. It might be used for a single season or longer, depending on needs.

NKP – "Na Kon Phanom" a huge Royal Thai naval/air force base on the Mekong River and the Laotian border. Ashley was stationed there while in Air Force as an interrogator in the Seventies.

NOMENKLATURA – Soviet bureaucratic class.

OKHRANA – The Romanov Tsars' secret police fighting terrorism and left-wing revolutionaries (1866-1917).

POW / PW -Prisoner of War.

PROTUS – Life Force, Spirit, Soul.

PHYGYNAYA – A condition that drives certain Iskas, when fertile, to desperately seek out an ISK to become pregnant. Failing that, it lasts until they are no longer fertile. There is also a rumor these women run with the wolves. But highly attuned to people.

PYORDARSCH – Iskandarova word for gift of visions. The visions may be past, present or future.

RAF – British Royal Air Force.

STASI – East German secret police, refuge for some former Nazis.

THURNANE – Iskandarov term, loosely translated as "Elsewhere." This is where Ashley has several of his most important tests.

TVARSCH – Iskandarov world for the gift of intuition building to the collective and cumulative wisdom of the clan.

ULIMOS – What Iskandarovs call their clan and its world.

URKAS – Originated in the Gulag camps where these criminal gangs ran the barracks. Eventually became the Russian MAFIYAH.

USAAF – United States Army Air Force. Successor to Army Air Corps in 1942 and became U.S. Air Force in 1947.

VOR-URKA – "Thief," a "made man" in the Russian MAFIYAH.

ZEK/ZECHKA – Male / female prisoners in the Gulag. Deemed useful for first three months of their ten - to twenty-five-year sentence.

Ashley Cooper's Partial Iskandarov Family Tree

ISKANDAR—ILYRIANAA-ALIANNAA-ATHALIAA

THREE COLCHI PRINCESSES FOUNDED THE ISKANDAROVS.

MANY YEARS LATER IN 1885

SERGEI & SONIA ISKANDAROV—BIRTH

DMITRI SERGEYOVICH & SOPHIA SERGEYVNA (COUNTESS)

(AND ALSO, ILLYRIA AND FEODOR WITHOUT KNOWN ISSUE) — BIRTH

SERGEI DMITROVICH WHO HAS EIGHT CHILDREN WITH FOUR DIFFERENT WOMEN. FIRST, WITH GRAND DUTCHESS NADIA MYTROVNA ANDREYEVA, THEY BIRTH—OLGA AND VERUSHKA SERGEYVNA. (VERUSHKA IS ALSO KNOWN AS VERONIQUE LANDFEAR AND RONNIE COOPER.) SECOND, WITH LADY CHARLOTTE ELIZABETH STERNWOOD, THEY BIRTH—ASHLEY COOPER AND LATER, NATALYA SERGEVNA ISKANDAROVA. WITH HER HUSBAND JOSEPH POLINKOV, THEY BIRTH—TWINS SONIA AND MAGDA.

THIRD, WITH SVETLANA FELIKSOVNA, THEY BIRTH—ALEKSANDR AND IRINI POLINKOV. FOURTH, WITH MARIA CIVILLI IN CUBA, THEY BIRTH—ANGHELINA DELAVEGA AND ROSALITA CIVILLI. ANGELINA DELAVEGA OR CIVILLI IS THEIR GRANDMOTHER. COUNTESS SOPHIA ALSO HAD A DAUGHTER WITH HER HUSBAND, COUNT MIKHAIL KOLCHAK—*DOCTORAT* AUNT SONIA. BAYTA AND SAINTE XENIA, WHILE ISKADAROVAS, ARE FROM DIFFERENT BRANCHES OF THE ISKANDAROV TREE.

ONE

Friday, 4 June 1993, Moscow Airport

1.

For almost two decades, Ashley Cooper had been coming to Moscow's Sheremetyevo Airport. And with his diplomatic passport had zipped through the VIP lane to get to central Moscow. Once there, he had negotiated with Soviet and now Russian Federation officials. But today held a different purpose and he would soon enter a new hell in the "Real Russia"—an enigmatic place of mystery, danger, poverty and corruption. This time he was with his daughter, Annie; her being with him was priceless, even if she was why they had to use the regular customs line.

The throbbing and itching of his bandaged chest wound drew him back to the trauma of their near-death in an explosion the night before at the Repast dinner of their Iskandarov family in Paris. It had been a wonderful evening up to that point, which made the explosion even more heartbreaking. He had run yelling warnings to the people closest to the bomb and now vividly re-membered their faces just before their being blown apart.

Since landing, Annie had said little; her first serious boy-friend, Yuri, had died from injuries after the explosion. She had slept during the three-hour flight, but Ashley could not and felt, despite his pain, waves of fatigue washing over him. Since the explosion, there was a ringing in his ears, and he longed for it to end. His body ached and the pain in his right thigh—from the mutinous Russian soldiers he had fought in his extraordinary flight back in time—was worse. And so too was the throbbing in his left leg where Alex Dragovitch had nearly broken it many years ago in soccer at Lawrenceville. He now wanted to take another painkiller, but it was too large to swallow without water, and there was none to be had. He tried to utilize the pain to help him remain mentally sharp, but he was failing.

He briefly considered returning to New York. However, with their Iskandarov blood, failure to join their clan meant ultimate insanity and even death. He also felt in limbo—not yet the person he was meant to be, but also neither fully Ashley F. Cooper, Esq., Senior Partner at "The Firm of Gules, Argent, Orr and Drew" in New York City. In addition, Ashley felt ambivalent about being the Hidden One, part of a prophecy his grandmother Countess Sophia had issued during the twilight of Imperial Russia in 1917. While not knowing the responsibilities, it was an honor and the Iskandarovs would continue to test him progressively harder to prove his worthiness. The last test in Paris, in the Realm of the Spirits, had been life-threatening. His Iskandarov family in New York and Paris had prepared him and Annie as well as they could, but he knew that would not be enough. Beyond that, he held on tightly to hope and was becoming its prisoner.

They had been moving forward in the customs line for almost ninety minutes in the hot and smoky terminal where the foul air made his eyes water. This airport was not exotic—only seedy and tedious. Even worse, strong body odor, which assaulted his nostrils, came from everywhere along with other unpleasant but unknown stenches. The line felt like a horizontal Tower of Babel with most people moving roughly in the same direction while all obeying their customary line etiquette. Sullen and short Russians constantly jockeyed for position and cut in on the line or tried to. As tempers flared, the customs officials ignored it all as they examined documents in their leisurely bureaucratic manner. Ashley looked at the overhead clock whose hands seemed frozen.

Finally, they came to the head of the line. Ashley handed their papers to the customs agent—a short, scowling uniformed woman. She studied their passports, then languidly looked at their faces and back at their passport pictures and again at their faces. She examined their visa and the packet with their currency declaration and hotel reservation at Moscow's famous Metropol Hotel. Finally, she looked up and loudly said in Russian, "Cooper. No hotel reservation, step to side. Next."

Ashley yelled, "It is there."

The woman shook her head. "Next."

Ashley felt a hand on his shoulder, turned and there was a short, uniformed man, who said in heavily accented English, "Mister Cooper, you and young miss will come with me." The official's face betrayed no emotion beyond self-important resolve, which Ashley had often encountered here. His bowels knotted and his stomach churned. Not even in country two hours and already he had again fallen afoul of the dreaded and Kafkaesque Russian officialdom. There would be no way out without help, which they did not have.

They sat at a gray metal desk in the official's windowless office off a long corridor reeking of cigarette smoke and cabbage. A row of gray overstuffed filing cabinets stood behind the desk and overhead were several monitors. Behind them, stood two very tall armed soldiers with arms folded. The official sitting in his desk chair opposite them with their documents in hand, yawned before speaking, "I am Major Iganiev of UVIR, Department of Visas and Registration. You have no hotel reservation, so we cannot clear your entry into the Russian Federation."

Ashley had specifically checked that before leaving Paris. *This is a scam. But to what purpose?* Now ignoring everything else, he completely embraced his pain as he had been taught so he could fully focus on the major. "I have made reservations for my daughter and myself at the Metropol where I always stay."

The major's brow wrinkled. "You come to Moscow regularly?"

Ashley replied in Russian, "Yes, I am senior partner at most highly regarded New York City international law firm. Work often brings me here to assist your government on certain agreements and treaties."

"And which agreements might those be?"

Although Annie's Russian was good, as they had agreed, she did not want to let the major know so, she maintained a bewildered expression while understanding most of what was being said.

"You must know I am not at liberty to disclose such sensitive information. And even though I am here as tourist, I intend to continue my discussions with your leaders."

"That may be. First you must, of course, clear customs."

"I have already made appointments and have been asked to contact my principals when I arrive."

"Very well. Here is my phone. Contact them."

Ashley looked at his watch and shook his head. "Their offices are closed now."

The major went through Ashley's passport before looking up. "Very well. I see no Russian or Soviet stamps and, aside from recent entry and exit stamps for Netherlands and France, only entry stamp from Cayman Islands but no exit." He leaned forward.

"They are very casual about that in Caribbean. Besides, obviously I travel on diplomatic passport."

"And where might that document be?"

"In my safe in New York. Although, as I have told you, I shall be meeting with government officials presently, today I am just tourist and saw no point in abusing privileges afforded me by that passport."

"How very, ah, upstanding of you." He studied their currency declaration. "Why have you brought five thousand American dollars? Your visit to Cayman Islands suggests there is something more involved than what appears."

"What are you suggesting?"

"We detain many currency speculators who bring dollars to sell on black market."

"That is absurd. I have little use for roubles. What proof have you for your allegation?"

"Amount you have is more than allowed. We must detain you both while we have time to assess situation."

"I checked limit before leaving New York."

"We reduced amount yesterday due to increase in black market activity. Now, because of new development, I need to see second form of identification."

"I am important and busy man. I do not have time and so cannot be held responsible for your arbitrary changes that are not well publicized."

"You are responsible. You should have checked yesterday."

I don't believe a word this bastard says. But no point arguing with a corrupt bureaucrat. Ashley gave him his New York State driver's license and the major copied the information onto the visa.

Annie, having used her fake Vassar College student ID on their two flights, and being very upset gave it to the major, instead of her Chaplin School ID.

The major resumed his questioning in English. "Most peculiar young miss, this identification contradicts your passport and declares you are Anastasia Sergeyvna Iskandarova and are much older at twenty-two than you appear. What say you?"

Ashley calmly said, "Major, this is no more than an innocent mistake."

"Not in my country, Mister Cooper. Now, young miss, how say you?"

"I'm truly Anne Elizabeth Cooper as my passport says. I have my school ID right here with my name on it."

"Doubtless you do. I suspect were I to go through your wallet, I would find a number of identifications for you. And this puts the authenticity of both your passports in question. I need to examine them further to determine if they are lawful." He paused. "We do not like Iskandarovs here and it appears you Coopers, if that's who you truly are, are rather casual about which laws you chose to obey. And know that in the Russian Federation we are a people of laws."

Ashley calmly knew, as the charges piled up, this was merely a delaying tactic. The whole matter would be resolved when his enemies, known and unknown, arrived. *Annie's mistake really doesn't matter.*

"Now we have visa problems, possible currency manipulations and counterfeit identifications and passports. This will take some time to sort out. Meanwhile, we have dormitories for you and the young miss."

"Absolutely not, I won't leave my daughter alone."

"It would be improper under our extremely strict housing arrangements for either you to be with her or she with you. Have no fear. Our dormitories are perfectly safe. These are the only accommodations available to you."

I know from experience that if we are not officially in Russia, there's no point in calling the chowderheads at the American Embassy. "I demand you send my daughter back to Paris on next flight out."

"We have no facilities to make such arrangements."

Ashley thought about calling Sasha, his government contact. He's in Georgia and I don't have that number, but he's due back in Moscow soon.

The major said, "Only way I can get you on a plane to anywhere is if I deport you." He shrugged. "And now, young miss, you will shortly be escorted to the women's dormitories..."

Ashley stood. "No. I'm not letting her go there. It's not safe."

Mister Cooper, I assure you our female dormitory is heavily chaperoned. And we have a guard on the outside, so as to protect our valued women. They are not luxurious by your standards, but for the time you will be our guests, they will be adequate."

Iganiev inadvertently just let me know we won't be here long.

Ashley felt two big hands on his shoulders pressing him back into his seat. *With these two big mugs here, I've no choice,* "OK, Annie. But watch yourself and your possessions."

She sighed. "Whatever."

When she goes into this world-weary mood, she's trying to cover up that she's scared. That greatly troubles me, but I see no alternative. Ashley knew Rosalita Civilli had been teaching Annie self-defense. Something to be thankful for. He did not ask about their luggage, which he knew could easily get "lost."

"Excellent. It is settled." The major pressed his desk buzzer and two more soldiers, a man and a woman, came in. After finally being allowed to stand, Ashley hugged Annie and watched the woman lead her away before he followed the man through the corridors.

2.

The windowless men's dormitory had rough wood floors, cement walls and creaky metal bunk beds with bare mattresses. Hanging light bulbs swung from the noise of low-level airplanes. Although no one else was present, a gunmetal blue cigarette haze hung over everything. By the door, Ashley stashed his briefcase under a stained pillow on a lower bunk and lay down, trying to breathe while not inhaling too much foul air. Closing his eyes, he again thought about Paris. Last night, while sleeping, his mentor, sister Olga Sergeyvna's spirit visited him to finally end their bond. So, he could attempt a Blood Union with another Iskandarova. After she left, if that had not bad enough, Nick Stevens, his long-time arch enemy, arrived. Nick had unexpectedly told him a bomb was about to go off in Grand Duchess Nadia Mytrovna Andreyeva's Repast ballroom and Baroness Ulrika von Manteuffel, his grandfather Dmitri Sergeyovich's paramour, was the target. Ashley quickly dressed and ran to the ballroom. But now realized had he gone just a bit faster, he would have joined the baroness and the others in non-being. He did not know what had spared him—luck, fate or something he did not even know existed.

Can't trust Nick. He's not a swine like Dragovitch. No, he's a-dime-a-dozen bastard. I know I'll soon see him. With his stomach seeming like it was about to burst, he ran to the filthy and foul-smelling toilet, where, without a seat, he sat on the steel rim. Shortly, feeling as though his whole intestines and a significant amount of blood had filled the grimy bowl, he felt relieved but sat for another five to ten minutes, just in case, and devised a plan to get Annie back before the principals arrived.

After returning to his bunk, he found Cosette's pain pills in his briefcase. Tempted to use one, he decided to continue embracing the pain, so he could think clearly. Yuri, *Sabreur Bleu*, Annie's boyfriend and their protector in New York had told him in Paris they had friends in Russia. *Now would be an appropriate time for one of them to appear. God, I owe that young man so much. He's saved my life several times. And after the explosion, he died in bed with Annie, I think before anything serious had happened.* Ashley swore revenge on the killers of both the baroness and Yuri before falling into sleep and began dreaming.

* * *

Ashley again runs into the ballroom trying to save the baroness as the explosion erupts and he helplessly watches as everyone burns alive after the explosion.

On the stained wooden floor, Ashley was shaking and in intense pain. *Some damn plane sounded as though it were coming right through here.* Rising up, a man of indeterminate age stood a respectful distance from him. His shaved head was bent forward, with a black wool cap in his hands. His ruddy face was furrowed and creased, and his hands were gnarled and calloused. A thick, drooping salt-and-pepper moustache dominated his face, under which, some metal teeth glinted. His pants, held up by a coarse rope belt, looked clean but worn at the knees. His shirt must have had some color at one time, but it had long since been washed out. His shoes were scuffed and coming apart and he spoke Russian with a strange accent. "Your Honor, I am called Kaha Antonovich."

"Kaha Antonovich, why are you here?"

"I am Cartvelian. Brutal civil war now going on in Sakartvelo, which you know as Georgia. I come here as refugee. Russian bastards refuse to accept passport but will not return me. I have been here some time. And why, if I may ask, is your Honor here?"

Ashley felt uneasy about being addressed by this honorific, but this man was merely following tradition. "I am Ashley Cooper, American. Here with my daughter to sightsee in Moscow but we have problems. I am told they will be resolved in few days."

"I am certain major will not detain your Honor for long.

"Thank you for your optimism. Is there something I might do to help you enter Russia?"

"Do you have cigarettes?'

"I am sorry, but I do not smoke."

"No, your Honor. American or British cigarettes are true currency here. If you could buy carton at tourist store that would help us both. I know back way to get there but have no foreign monies."

He might just be the friend I need. "Lead on, Kaha Antonovich."

* * *

Shortly, they returned with a carton of Marlboros. "Your Honor, please excuse me, it is time for me to eat in cafeteria."

"Then I shall join you."

"No, please your Honor, I could not repay your kindness by taking you with me. I believe food would make you sick. I will return quickly." He bowed and left.

Ashley returned to his bunk. *I'm grateful to Kaha for sparing me further indigestion.* He took out a bar of Swiss chocolate bought in the duty-free shop and broke off several triangles. As he ate, Ashley felt somewhat better with something in his stomach and focused on what he called his Plan B. *I still have my doubts about the Iskandarovs and, especially, am skeptical about going insane or dying. After I've had a chance to meet with them, I may return to New York with a signed L'Enfant Bosnian Initiative and will be a shoo-in to become managing partner when Charles Drew retires. The Firm needs to be reformed and I'm the man who can do it.*

Appealing as that seemed, was that what he truly wanted? His stepmother Ronnie's comment at the recent start of his Iskandarov journey, "What else matters if you don't know who you truly are?" strongly resonated because he still did not know how to become his new self. Thinking again about his disturbing trip to the Realm of the Spirits, he realized that this was significant because for the first time, he had discovered his limitations and accepted help from Sainte Xenia, a pregnant angel, and this had to be a step forward in creating his new self. He also knew Annie with the zeal of the new convert would go with the Iskandarovs. Ronnie had been prepping her for years so he and Annie would soon be on separate paths. But now, he would try again to reason with the major before Kaha Antonovich returned.

* * *

Returning to his dormitory after another fruitless attempt with Major Iganiev, Kaha Antonovich had left, along with all his possessions. *If he had gotten into Russia, the relatively small amount I paid for the cigarettes had been money well spent.* He felt disappointed he would no longer have someone to talk to. And he would need to find Annie by himself. Following another visit to the toilet, he set out to locate the women's dormitory. After going past the cafeteria on his way through the corridors, he came to a steel door with "Females" in Cyrillic and tried to open it.

A woman's voice bellowed, "Halt." With clipboard in hand she ambled toward him, corpulent and overflowing her uniform. "What doing here? You not allowed. Show identification."

"I am trying to find my daughter."

"And what is name of daughter, pervert?"

Why does she call me a pervert? *Why am I being so reviled?* "I am American. Ashley Cooper. My daughter is Anne Elizabeth."

Without glancing at her clipboard, the woman shook her head. "Have no Anne Elizabeth."

"No, her name is Anne Elizabeth Cooper."

"Have no Anne Elizabeth Cooper."

"Wait. What about Anastasia Sergeyvna Iskandarova?"

She looked suspiciously at him. "No. Third time, no."

"Are you not even going to look at list?"

"Know all women under protection. You come, we see Major Iganiev. He knows how to deal with degenerate Iskandarov scum like you."

"I told you, I am American." I'm getting a much better picture of my kin.

Major Iganiev rose, shaking his head and motioned for the matron to leave. "You, now here three time, are becoming very much nuisance. You, and all men, are not allowed in female dormitory for rather obvious reasons. Job of matron is to protect women from unwanted advances. She is not permitted to either confirm or deny existence of any woman or girl. Have no fear, your daughter is safe. You, despite perverted reputation of Iskandarov, clearly, are gentleman. We do not always have such refined guests. Many unscrupulous men have told me mistresses are daughters. Most of girls are young enough. Therefore, we Instituted policy." He pointed toward his door. "I make this clear. One more incident, I will deport you."

Ashley cursed and headed back to the dormitory. Once there, he heard, "Your Honor, whatever is matter?"

He turned. "Kaha Antonovich, I thought you had left."

"No, had business to attend elsewhere. Will be leaving later. I am in your debt eternally, your Honor. He paused and studied Ashley before standing erectly. "Why, if I may ask, are you truly here, your Honor?"

"I am looking for mother and father."

"And?"

Ashley shook his head, "It is long story."

"We have time now, your Honor."

Ashley paused, studied him, and decided to tell him about his journey—which began in the spring of 1962 with the poisoning murder of Olga Sergevna, his Harvard Russian literature professor—and his lover, despite her being about thirteen years his senior. She was pregnant with his son, who also died. Then, since Ashley had recently discovered he was adopted, he told Kaha Antonovich generally about his Iskandarov tests and ended with the Paris explosion. He also emphasized Annie's importance in the journey while not speaking of her *pyordarsch*, which he was not allowed to reveal. "You know about Iskandarov, then?"

"Oh yes, sons and daughters of Great Iskandar in Sakartvelo, our ancestral homeland. You do look some like him with your
blonde curly hair and your Grecian nose. But your eyes are both
blue without a brown one."

"Who is Great Iskandar? No one will tell me."

"He was conqueror who swept over sacred mountains, down
into valley of Rakhsi River and into Hindu Kush. You know him
as Great Alexander."

Doubtless, some obscure chieftain seeking status started
this completely ridiculous story about Alexander the Great.

"I see your disbelief. His conquests were only yesterday."

Nothing to be gained by arguing.

"Your Honor, you are definitely brave and heroic gentleman. It becomes my duty to assist you in your release of daughter. But first, may I ask, how were you able to accomplish such
amazing feats?"

"I have been blessed with form of intuition, but it is so
much more. Sadly, it is not now functioning despite my stepmother Ronnie, no, Verushka Sergeyvna, who has been coaching
me on this and other matters for more than thirty years." *I have a
gut feeling that everything is about to go badly, and I've learned
long ago to trust my gut.*

"Thank you, your Honor. I know Verushka Sergeyvna. I
suspect she is here now, as she often is. I have heard of this intuition but thought it was no more than babushka tale."

I'm not surprised he knows Ronnie. That's good news.

"Now, would your Honor know father's patronymic?"

"Sergei Dmitrovich."

"Oh, bless me, your Excellency." The man hugged Ashley,
bringing with him the aroma of cheap tobacco and even cheaper
vodka. "My grandfather, Nikos Samsonovich, was batman to his
Excellency, Andrei Ivanovich Rittmeister Iskandarov, commander of Third Squadron, Light Hussars of Russian Imperial Horse
Guards during Great War." He beamed with pride, bringing himself to full attention as he spoke. "Your family is much revered
in Sakartvelo, as you must know. And here is how I repay your

Excellency. I will easily bribe matron with cigarette packet you were so kind to buy for me to get you into female dormitory. After I leave, walk down corridor slowly. Is that acceptable your Excellency?"

Ashley smiled as he nodded and watched Kaha leave.

Kaha Antonovich was sharing a smoke with the matron, who motioned Ashley to go in. *Focus now. This is it.*

The room appeared similar to the men's dormitory with the same smoky haze but also with an acrid, vinegary odor. Most women wore bland clothing, while a few, probably prostitutes, dressed provocatively. As an Asiatic girl wearing a short red silk robe approached, Ashley waved her off. She persisted and opened her robe, revealing her pubescent body before again covering herself. "I am Lala. What is matter, you not like?"

Her Russian accent sounded strange. *She couldn't be over ninety pounds.* "No, you are fine. I am looking for my daughter."

"Oh, why you not say you look for young girl? We had one today, but she gone." She gestured toward the door.

"What did she look like?"

"Pretty face, very nice girl tits, long legs, curled red hair. Not Russian. English maybe or American."

"What was her name?"

"I hear her called, Ah-nee, I think.

"What has become of her?"

"She left with very fancy woman after maybe hour from when she comes."

"Please describe this fancy woman."

"Again, British or American. Tall, short black hair, expensive foreign clothes, very nice mother tits. Old, but very sexy. Wife or mistress of important man."

While that sounds like Ronnie, I can't afford to assume it's her. There were a number of ladies in the terminal who could fit that description going through the VIP customs lane.

"Thank you. Where did she go?"

"What am I, *Intourist*?" She smiled, revealing several rotted teeth. "Not worry, you saw I am small like little girl and have my own private space. You flow me very nice." She reached her arms toward Ashley who backed away.

"No, thank you, I must find my daughter and make sure she is not here."

Lala counted on her hands. "Four old women in *douche*. Three mothers drying off. Everyone else here is here. You see her?" She moved her head around. "Oh, my mother and two aunts stand behind you."

"You have been most helpful." He gave her a twenty-dollar bill before turning to face three Khazak women.

"I am Kaleefa. Pervert, what are you doing giving money to virgin daughter? Speak now or we punish you badly." The three women wore minimal clothing, and all had sharp curved knives.

"I am looking for my daughter who was here and your daughter was helping me."

Kaleefa looked skeptical and spoke to Lala in her native tongue.

"Daughter says story is true. You lucky man, we would have cut your balls off before again making rounds of airport."

"Understood." Ashley exhaled before feeling several people behind him. He turned to see Major Iganiev, accompanied by two armed men, each over seven feet tall, the matron and Kaha Antonovich.

"I saw you on monitor. I warned you that you are not allowed here. And now, added to everything else, you are soliciting minor age prostitute." Iganiev turned to his guards. "Take him away, Vorkuta deportation protocol. And matron, you are in serious trouble as is this bothersome Georgian bandit."

Ashley spoke calmly. "I have friends who shall not be pleased you allow whores in your so-called well-chaperoned female dormitory. Look around. It is obvious. In truth, I paid Lala for information about my daughter, you corrupt son of a shit." One guard slugged him in the stomach, but he had prepared for it by tensing his muscles. As he had been taught in Air Force survival school, to prevent getting another one, he bent over and groaned dramatically pretending to be severely injured.

After being dragged through a door marked "No Admittance", the men left Ashley in a windowless cinderblock room. Ashley yelled after them, "Where is my daughter?"

One guard turned, "What daughter, pervert? You have no daughter. Anastasia Sergeyvna Iskandarova is well-known and expensive Georgian child prostitute and source of your many dollars. You tried to get her in country with fake Americanski passports. She is arrested and you never see her again." He slammed the steel door shut. While the door had a keyhole handle, it had no key.

Ashley sat and gathered himself together doing his customary yoga breathing. He knew he had done nothing wrong and would strongly resist being deported. Especially to Vorkuta, where his father, Sergei Dmitrovich Iskandarov, was held in the Gulag network of slave labor camps in the forties for political undesirables. *In this room, I'll meet whoever wanted me detained.*

He thought about the airport—the gateway to one of the world's most important cities always appeared to be the exact opposite of welcoming. From the air, it appeared an isolated and ugly scar on the landscape, all of it reflecting the paranoid insularity Joseph Stalin had bequeathed to the Soviet Union. And, partially, why that state no longer existed. *No, that was incorrect. The names may have changed but that paranoia and brutality continue.*

He knew, regardless who showed up, the ultimate boss was corrupt George Farwell, his father-in-law and powerful CEO of Western Petroleum, and Charles Drew, Gules Managing Partner. George always referred to his mother as "the grand dame" of her old Brooklyn family but never said much about his father. When fourteen, George went off to St. Paul's School in New Hampshire and even there could not completely escape from her orbit and had never fully developed as an adult man. He still chased after young women like the Civilli sisters, Rosalita and, especially, Anghelina, who worked for him.

In the Realm of the Spirits, Ashley had sworn to Countess Sophia that he would kill George for his many business sins. But worse than all that, George had repeatedly molested his daughter Penelope, who would later become Ashley's wife. One reason she slowly went mad and had recently killed herself. Given the opportunity, Ashley would gladly keep his word to Sophia.

TWO

Friday, 4 June 1993, in Limbo

1.

This is the third windowless airport room I've been in today. And being an interrogation room is the only one that makes sense. The other two are unreasonable.

The room's walls were a dingy institutional gray with plastic Russian cigarette holders and flattened butts littering the floor. Over an industrial drain, in the room's left-hand corner was a metal chair without a seat—bolted through the worn linoleum. Over it in a glass-fronted cabinet were whips, chains, and several forceps. He felt more horrified about the saws and sharp knives and the leather collar with sharp spikes on the inside. In comparison, the brass knuckles appeared almost humane. And, below the rest, syringes with long needles completed the collection. Ashley rose to examine the implements. They were in working order with traces of dried blood around the chair.

Obviously, this is meant to intimidate. But what else? Is this someone's idea of a nostalgic museum to when Stalin's notorious NKVD secret police ran passport control? To get his mind off this, he paced the room and estimated it to be about twenty-one feet square. And he smiled at the familiar gray interrogator's metal desk with another gray metal chair bolted to the floor about three feet from it. It reminded him of his interrogation room at the Na Khom Phanom Royal Naval Base on the Thai-Laotian border where he had been stationed during Vietnam. There was more blood around the bolted chair. Real or not? But certainly, a scary effect. He sat in the chair facing the interrogation desk, the cabinet looming in his peripheral vision. *I won't be sitting in this chair during interrogation.*

The room reeked of body odor, the nickel smell of blood and hot, and stale air, which prompted a fit of coughing. *Someone has gone to a lot of work in order to intimidate the victim.* He stood in the middle of the room, arms folded, feeling he now had an edge. *Once out of here, I'll immediately call Nadia Mytrovna Andreyeva, Prime Director of the Bleu Agency-Paris, about getting Annie, their fourth-generation leader, back. Nadia had warned us about the dangers of going to Russia, so she might not help. No matter, my friend New York Senator Al D'Amato still owes me. No one does righteous indignation on the Senate floor better. And I'll also involve my international law colleagues.*

* * *

The door opened and Alex Dragovitch, large and well-muscled in a red T-shirt, jeans and combat boots, entered.

Ah, first the muscle. "So, Drago, where's Nick Stevens?"

"Well, Cooper, you can't say I didn't warn you back in Paris about coming to Moscow."

"That you did. Are you now here to beat me to a pulp?"

"That depends on you. You maintain a good attitude and we'll get along famously. Bad attitude, well…you know the drill." He paused. "You don't look so good, dehydrated, probably diarrhea you got from the cafeteria slop they serve here. Tell you what. I'll take you down the hall to the guard's washroom where you can get cleaned up and then I'll give you a bottle of water before Nick arrives. And remember, this is a very secure place. No way out without the right key."

As Dragovitch escorted Ashley down the hall, he said, "You know, we've never really spoken very much. Tell me why you always came after me with such intensity in both in soccer and lacrosse. You're the only one in my eight years at Choate and Yale, who ever got past me. And you know, your wing was clear and could've scored the soccer goal in the fall of '62. Of course, your lacrosse goal was perfect."

"Thanks. You know, I was haunted by that missed goal for a long time and I've subsequently worked on my ego problem. The first time we met in soccer at Lawrenceville, you nearly broke my leg."

"But I've no memory of injuring you because you played the whole game."

Hell, I was just a skinny fourteen-year-old second former and you were a big fifth former. And that had been eating at me and the reason I had to score on you when I made the Harvard squad four years later. I really was driven in those days."

"Yes, you were. I remember you very well back then because you were so determined, especially for a wiry little kid."

"Thanks. And it's funny because the same day I got my revenge on you in soccer, the love of my life, my Olga Sergeyvna, was murdered. But now I know the two events were connected— life usually gives and takes in almost equal measure."

"That it does. Also, I'm sorry for your loss. I had no hand in it."

"I know. And thanks for your apology." Ashley headed for the washroom.

* * *

Back into the interrogation room, Ashley felt relieved to see a bottle of Vichy water with a clean glass on the table. While sitting in the interrogator's chair and finishing his glassful of water, Nick Stevens arrived wearing sunglasses, a black suit, white shirt, rep tie and black loafers. "Hey, Drago, thanks for the set-up. Our boy's looking pretty cushy."

"Yeah, he was in bad shape when I found him."

"Come on, Nick, don't be a weenie, take off your shades and expose your obviously delicate eyes to the blinding light, like Drago and me."

Nick removed them. "Happy now, Ashley?"

"Nick, was this Mickey Mouse scam your idea?"

"Ashley, I know you've been fretting about Annie. She's with Rosalita Civilli. Even if you were to get out of here, you'll have a tough time finding her."

"You mean Anghelina DelaVega, George's bodyguard?"

"Could be. I can't tell the diff between the two sisters."

No one is ever going to confuse Ronnie with 'Lita or even Anghelina. I'm almost certain Nick's lying. Lala had no reason to lie and, besides, Nick still has that same annoying Hoosier drawl he had at Harvard. "Don't be so sure. I know Moscow quite well."

"Could be, but first you would need to get out of here. And right now, that's very unlikely."

"Wait. I get it. This isn't about me. At some point, one of the Civillis is going to take Annie back to George while I'm stuck here in limbo. Civilli will probably tell Annie some plausible but fake tale about me. That's not going to work because Annie's stronger and smarter than you both think."

"Well, Sherlock, one small wrinkle. She's now in Russia illegally with no documents and she'll do as she's told. You know, after thirty-one years, you haven't changed, you always did like to excel and be the smart guy—in your own mind anyway. Well, you've done it again. You've excelled—in royally pissing off everyone. And they all want a piece of you." He shook his head. "And here, it's totally my call about your future." He pointed to the cabinet of horrors. "Those things are still in good working order. Drago, which one would you start with?"

"Oh, probably start with brass knuckles and work up from there as necessary. Then who knows?"

"So, should I be scared or something?"

"Drago. You want to fix this guy's attitude?"

"Not yet, I want to hear what he has to say...for a while."

"OK, Drago. Here I go. Nick, aside from last night in Paris, I haven't seen you since NKP. You were an Army Ranger with Long-Range Patrol Recon, LRRPs, right? I thought you were dead or a POW some place. So, you with the Company, the Agency, freelance, what?"

"Yeah." Nick laughed. "And you were a big deal interrogator at NKP. Okay. I'm not going to waste your time. First, I'll explain what the Vorkuta deportation protocol means. As far as Major Iganiev knows, or cares, you're on an old plane to Vorkuta, one of the worst places in Russia in the so-called Komi Republic. It's a frozen nowhere above the Arctic Circle, formerly part of the Gulag. And don't think this would a pleasant flight. Before you're let on the plane, those big guards will rob you of everything and your luggage before beating you up. The chances of getting back from Vorkuta are slightly better than nil. Hey, this could still happen if Drago and I don't like your attitude. And I guarantee, you get out of line, we're going to do some real, retro interrogation."

"Come on, Nick, you're slipping. You said last night you needed me alive. Which reminds me." He drank more water. "You know, I still don't know why you warned me about the bomb just before it went off. Perhaps you wanted me blown up as well?"

"You know, in your old age, you're getting a little paranoid. I admit had you been blown up, that would've made our lives considerably easier. But for the present, we have orders to keep you alive. Unless, of course, you're uncooperative." He smiled. "I'm sure your father-in-law George wouldn't be too broken up if we took care of you permanently. Probably get us a nice bonus too. But I know you like to play the hero and that's why I told you about the explosion. It's okay. You owe me one. But this doesn't mean we're going to be buddy-buddy all of a sudden."

"No, perish the thought. Why don't you stop wasting time and tell me what you really want?"

"Okay, a little recent history. You got pretty chummy with Anghelina DelaVega and told her a lot of things you shouldn't have. She's not just George's bodyguard but also his best agent. But then you were always a sucker for a pretty face. You warned me a long time ago Pen Farwell was a rich, spoiled psycho bitch.

And she damn sure was." He laughed. "That's why I dumped her. And then you go and marry her. Totally nutso." He shook his head. "Anyway, Anghelina has screwed you better than you ever did her."

"I never had sex with her. She's almost young enough to be my daughter. So, tell me why she and Rosalita body guarded us to Newark Airport?"

"Two reasons. First, they were protecting you from your other enemies. Like you said, we had orders to protect you. Second, Anghelina gave us your arrival time in Paris."

"So, Nick how much you getting paid? Perhaps we can come to an understanding."

"Not likely, Ashley. Your Iskandarov buddy killed my son Joseph. Way I see it, that's as good as if you'd killed him yourself. No, this is personal. I'm referring to that pompous little Iskandarov shit 'blue saber." He shook his head. "Geesh."

"You have proof, yeah?"

"All I needed. Just for grins, I poisoned him last night at the Repast."

"My daughter's pretty broken up about that. And his father, Minister Iskandarov, won't like it either. You're right. Now this is personal. I liked him very much and he saved my life a few times."

"In my book, we're even. We each lost one."

"Good luck, Nick. Remember, the minister's Georgian and they play by different and unpleasant rules."

"That big oaf doesn't scare me. Okay, if you're all finished with twenty-questions, Ashley why are you in Russia?"

"I'm looking for my real mother and father."

"Haven't you heard? They're both dead, long time ago."

"I don't think so."

"Interesting. Of course, you won't have much time to look for them. We've plans for you."

"And what might those be?"

"First, I've another option instead of the flight to nowheresville. You could simply fall between the cracks in the system, like your old man Sergei Dmitrovich Iskandarov. How do you feel about spending the rest of your life without seeing another human being? Think of it as being virtually buried alive." Nick scratched his nails against his lapel. "Know what I love? Idiots and Russia. I love idiots because they make my job so easy. Like you here on a diplomatic mission, who wasn't carrying his diplomatic passport. And Russia? I'll tell you, it's like a huge shopping mall where everything and everyone is for sale, cheap. We did all this with about five thou spread around." He laughed. "Hey, I really love this fucked-up excuse for a country." He moved to Ashley's right and lit a Camel. After exhaling, he spat a few loose strands of tobacco on the floor before inhaling and blew a thick smoke ring and watched it hang there. "But, there's a way out for you. You find your old man's Gulag diary and hand it over. Hey, magic. All your problems go away."

"And what if such a diary doesn't exist?"

"My employers insist it does. They know what a big ego your old man had."

"True, but then a whole bunch of people, the Iskandarovs, the Polinkovs and probably many others, have tried to find it. So, what if I don't?"

"That would be bad, Ashley, worse than even you can imagine. And that's where Anghelina comes in. She's going to keep tabs on you to make sure you're trying hard enough. She'll provide some incentives to keep you looking. The Cuban DI trained her very well to find people who don't want to be found and she, like a cat burglar, can find a way into anywhere."

I remember the first time I saw Anghelina DelaVega at The Firm. She would be a formidable opponent, if it came to that.

"Now, worst thing is for you to find the diary and not hand it over."

"If I want to play your game, how will I contact you, assuming I find this mythical diary?"

"You don't listen very well, do you? Anghelina will know your every move. She's your contact."

"And what really happens to me if I find the diary and hand it over to her?"

"Like I said, all your problems disappear. But if you fail or kill any of our people, we won't like that." He shrugged and moved around the room thinking with hands in his pockets. "You were warned by a whole bunch of people not to come here. I guess you don't like people telling you what to do. Makes my job so much easier."

"Tell me. Why not just leave this diary alone? If no one's found it after almost fifty years, it's unlikely anyone ever will. Again, assuming it even exists."

"You better hope it exists. Right now, it's all that's standing between you and some of my options."

"Perhaps, but I'm not buying you have Annie. Convince me."

"She's not stupid enough to leave the airport dormitory with someone she doesn't know. She and 'Lita, as she calls her, are pretty thick. Again, she'll do what she's told. The Russians think she's a Georgian child whore and she could be deported to that shithole of a county. Instead, I actually know the truth about her being an All-American virgin. And if she gets deported, all bets for her future are off. It's always kind of fun guessing how far a young babe will go to save her ass. What she'd be willing to do. You know?" Nick smiled.

Ashley knew Nick was ready for his ferocious reaction. But when he did not respond, Nick continued, "It might happen she gets pumped full of junk and sent someplace exotic, like one of the Muslin 'Stans, where she'd do anything for her fix and pretty young white virgins would bring a handsome price…"

Ashley remained seated, knowing a violent response was a sucker move. "What kind of sickos you working for, Nick? You obviously have the power to do any damn thing you want to me. I'm a player here and know the score. Annie's just, well, along for the ride. She's searching for some romantic schoolgirl notion. So, leave her out of this."

"Or what?"

Ashley shrugged. "Who knows? She's made some pretty powerful friends in Bleu, people who'll take it personally since she's under the personal protection of Grand Duchess Nadia, their Prime Director." Ashley stood and folded his arms.

"I'm impressed although not exactly shaking." He laughed. "Hey, I'm not saying my scenario would actually happen. Simply a possibility. Maybe, Farwell gets her for her alleged visions and, as a bonus, her lovely virgin pussy and beautiful rack." He puffed again and looked at his watch. "Okay, you're free to go. I have the missing documents for you to clear customs."

"That's it? Now I'm free?" Ashley did not move. "All this was just some time killer to allow your leader to arrive and get control of Annie? Well, I'm not convinced you have her. You were never a good liar"

"I've gotten better and because I played you for a sap, now you don't know where she is. Besides, this room is the perfect place to get someone's undivided attention. We've used it many times. The major's on our payroll."

As Ashley rose, he laughed. "I'm shocked."

"You're not as smart as advertised. Drago and I are the main event."

"I'm not buying that, Nick. Besides, you already let slip that several groups and not just George and Charles after me. Thanks for the tip."

"Hey, this was simply a preview of things that could happen if you stepped out of line while diary searching."

"Tell me why your employer Prometheus cares so much about this diary?"

"The diary is, right now, simply an inconvenience. Should it get out, well, Iron Cage's a problem, a dangerous embarrassment."

"An embarrassment? All that horrible suffering doesn't mean much to you guys, huh?" He shook his head. "What makes you think I care about blowing the lid off Iron Cage, anyway?"

"That's just the kind of thing a straight arrow like you would love to do. Even if you don't, Drago and I have been successful all these years by not being sloppy. We hate loose ends. Could be you want the diary to find out what really happened to your old man. That makes you a loose end."

"Don't you think we could've had our chat at the Metropol bar?"

"No, much more fun here. We needed to find out who we were really dealing with and how you'd react under stress. Haven't seen or really spoken to you since Harvard. Now I know you're the same freak you were then."

"That's funny. I was about to say a similar thing about you, Hoosier boy. And I know now why you hate me so much."

Nick thrust his face right in Ashley's. "Nick, the veins are bulging in your forehead, just like your old man when he threatened my father, probably the dumbest bad cop in the history of bad cops." He laughed and sat down.

"You don't know anything about my dad. Get back up and fight, damn you."

"Get a grip, Nick. Sit down. If I whip your ass like I did back then, Drago will have to intervene, and I sense he doesn't want that. Right, Drago?"

"Back off, Nick," Dragovitch said. "You're supposed to be a pro."

Nick mumbled with arms folded in the victim's chair.

"So, how much time do I have to find this damn diary?"

"I can spot you forty-eight hours to begin. Don't even ask for more."

"Why not?"

"Look, for all my people know, you're still in Paris with Nadia and Annie helping to clean up after the explosion. This gives you a chance to get ready."

"OK. Tell me though, Iron Cage is almost fifty years old. Some of your LRRPs buddies in Laos probably wound up as unreported POWs. Why're you involved in suppressing it?"

"I remember a special buddy from college, Jay Collins, my favorite running back. We called him 'three yards and a cloud of dust.' Jay was built like a tank. He could have done any number of things, safe things, even the Pros. But he believed. So, he volunteered for LRRPs. He knew if captured, if he were lucky, he'd be killed immediately, or at least after interrogation. He also knew he might wind up in a POW camp or worse. And that's just what happened."

"How do you know?"

"I've seen aerial recon photos with his serial number made of a bunch of small stones on the ground some ten years after Vietnam."

"So, I'd think you of all people, would want the truth about Iron Cage to come out. You might even help…"

"No. Let me tell you what would happen if Iron Cage somehow got out." He puffed again on his Camel, angrily threw the butt on the floor and stamped it out. "Some morons will have a field day making the governments involved look bad. It'll be a huge story. Maybe even, 'the Crime of the Century'. Or 'the Scandal of the Century'. And there'll be a lot of hoopla and hype for a while. All those newscaster pretty boys with blow-dried hair will peer into the TV camera with serious expressions and ask, 'How could this possibly happen?' They'll demand answers and accountability for the abduction of our troops. And in the end, a lot of people, who otherwise accomplished a great deal, will have their reputations destroyed. Then the media will grow bored and move on, leaving a trail of wrecked lives like slug slime. Or even worse, it'll remain covered up because these same people love Stalin, who killed tens of millions of his people while Hitler's the big bogeyman with six million Jews. I know Iron Cage is an end, not a beginning. Won't be good for any of my buddies. Because any still alive, once all the hoopla starts, will be conveniently found dead. That's the bottom line. You know, you're not on the side of the angels here."

Ashley had not thought about this and was genuinely troubled. There was a cost of taking action and POWs would likely die. On the other hand, there was a cost for not acting and the same POWs would eventually end up dead anyway. But by exposing Iron Cage, his father Sergei Dmitrovich and Harvey Jacobs, his best friend Randell Speers's father would be honored, along with the rest of his father's "Lost Souls" and all the abducted Allied troops. He had to find the diary. *And it's obvious if I hand it over, someone will kill me and destroy the diary because revealing Iron Cage would destroy George's reputation. There's only one monument to the victims of Stalin I'm aware of—a small one in Charlottenburg, Berlin. This will be an appropriate time to create another monument. And I know just the place.*

His thoughts were interrupted by a buxom blonde woman making a grand entrance and while she spoke sternly to Nick and Dragovitch, Ashley lingered by the desk and recognized Lana van Rouene. It was not long ago that he had been in bed with her in New York before all this madness broke open. He felt both relief and fear. She was playing the ambassador's grieving widow by wearing an expensive and well-tailored black suit with black hose; the mourning veil of the matching hat partially obscured her eyes which he knew would be heavily made-up. Beneath the veil her sensual mouth was embellished with red lipstick. She said, "You two, time to leave and close the door. I'll call you if I need you again. Drago, put your eyes back in their sockets."

After they left and closed the door, Lana came over with her black briefcase and placed it on the interrogator's desk. *Dobra-heh dehn, Kitzi.*"

Ashley responded, *"Preveht.* Lana, why are you here?"

She said in Russian, "I am no longer Lana van Rouene. Here, I am Svetlana Vladimirovna Palaeologa. My husband, Ambassador Linus, was killed and Iskandarov did it. Our son is safe. Oh, I am positive you know he is our son. And I wish to continue with you. Perhaps, even get married."

"Perhaps." He had told several people back in New York that given the opportunity, he would break off with her. She had embarrassed him by telling her husband and many others about their affair. It was quickly all over The Firm and even Annie found out about it, which galled him. But he loved that Annie called her "Lana van Booben." Lana removed her hat and put her jacket on the table, revealing a tight, low-cut ivory blouse. *Damn, she looks almost too good to resist. But I must. For the present, anyway.* She stood with legs slightly parted and eyes shining. "Since we have not seen each other for some time, I thought reminder of what you have been missing would be appropriate. Only eyes today, but when you come to me…" She frowned, "What, you do not like me anymore? You are not even trying to undress me with eyes."

"No, it is me. I cannot focus on you because Annie is missing."

"I am terribly sorry. I do not have her. I have many contacts here. After I unlock these doors, we can find her."

"Thank you. But, right now, you and I have many unresolved issues."

She touched his face. "I know. And they shall be resolved in future." She whispered in his ear, "I wanted your Iskandarov seed and I gave you my mother's tea to ensure I became pregnant."

"My seed is not miraculous. And after-effects of tea were terrible."

"I apologize but knew I must act quickly before you left New York. Besides, I have great faith in your seed which is working. No matter—I have proposition."

"I am listening."

"With your brains and my contacts, we can create new and superior Russia." She came over and hugged him. "Oh, *Kitzi*, give up this journey of yours. Stay with me. If you go to Iskandarov, you shall be descending into pit of madness you cannot even begin to comprehend or imagine. I know you have to meet Iskandarov. They are evil. Do not say you have not been warned. I shall always be near. There has been blood feud between our clans for more than five hundred years. I wish to make peace."

"Why?"

"Feud is medieval and stupid. I look to future, not past."

"Interesting. Tell me more."

She smiled broadly. "You know name 'Palaeologus'?'"

"While it is familiar, I cannot say I do." Of course, I know it. I want to hear her interpretation.

"It is name of final Byzantine royal family who ruled empire for last two hundred years." Her voice reflected pride. "My ancestor, Saint Constantine XI, was killed defending Constantinople against Turk. In earlier battle, Constantine's brother, Iannis, had been wounded and was sent away on Genoan merchant ship to Sakartvelo to recover and remained until after fall of Constantinople, when he planned to retake city and empire from Turk. Tragically, he was betrayed and murdered. His son, Andreas, focused on gaining power in then splintered Sakartvelo, seeing that the time was not right to defeat Turk. Ultimately, his name was Russianized to 'Polinkov'."

"That is pretty fantastic story."

"But true." She crossed her hand over her heart. "And nothing at all compared to absurd myth Iskandarov tell."

"About Alexander?"

"Such nonsense." She laughed. "As I said, there is much bad blood between Iskandarov and Palaeologus. Now with Russia again free, think of remarkable things two clans could accomplish, if united in common purpose."

"And what do you propose to accomplish?"

"More later." As she put on her jacket, she said, "When you meet Iskandarov, you may say I overlooked attempt to kill me in interest of making peace." She opened her briefcase and put a file on the table. "Proof is here. You may examine later."

"All right, assuming proof is compelling, how shall I contact you?"

She replaced her veiled hat. "As I said before, I shall be near."

"OK."

"All right, I take you to office of Major Iganiev."

As Ashley followed her from the room, he wondered if she was trying to revive her mother Svetlana Feliksovna's genetic experiments. At this point, he did not know enough about the results, but according to the Iskandarov diaries he had recently studied, her mother had tortured and abused both his parents and sister Natalya. After unlocking the *No Admittance* door, she put her arm through his and pressed against him, chatting as they walked. *She's manic and it's as if she stops yakking, I'll disappear or something.*

Kaha Antonovich appeared but ignored Svetlana. "Excellency, I called Madame Natalya Sergeyvna who arrived about fifteen minutes ago. In meantime, I will fetch luggage and put in car. Here is your briefcase."

Ashley opened his case and put Svetlana's file inside before relocking it. "Thank you, Kaha Antonovich, for everything. Did the major punish you?"

"Excellency, despite threats, he would not dare cause trouble with me."

A woman's voice speaking loudly in Russian interrupted their conversation. "...if you have sent him to Vorkuta and he is injured, I shall see you disgraced and demotion for corruption. You have no idea how serious this shall become."

Whoever was speaking had, even in anger, a very refined Russian accent.

Iganiev replied, "How dare you speak such slander of senior UVIR officer. I demand immediate apology from both you and Minister Iskandarov."

Arriving at the major's office door, Ashley waited to present his papers, amused at who was leaning over Iganiev's desk—a tall and slim black-haired lady in a well-tailored dove-gray suit and black hose and heels. "Iganiev, we know all about your Vorkuta deportation protocol. No such apology shall be offered. Under our laws you may only deport person back to whence they last came, in this case, Paris. Obviously, robbery, assault and battery are never permitted. I persuaded several of your soldiers to turn on you. Expect Monday very unpleasant call from Minister Iskandarov. Oh yes, Monsieur Cooper, *avocat*, shall also make very compelling witness and is half-brother to Minister Iskandarov. And, unlike you, comrade major, we Iskandarov consider family more important than state."

After disentangling from Svetlana's arm, Ashley said, "Major, I now have complete documents and am leaving with my daughter." He handed in his papers as she watched. *I remember her from the Paris Repast.*

Iganiev took both Ashley and Annie's documents, gave them a brief look, stamped and handed them back. "Enjoy my enormous and dangerous country, Mister Cooper. It is time for me to have late lunch. You will be gone when I return." He picked up his hat and left.

"Monsieur Cooper, you may call me Madame *Prinkipia* Natalya Sergeyvna." She shot a contemptuous sneer at Svetlana. "You are not needed nor wanted here."

Svetlana returned the look before facing Ashley, "So, *Kitzi*, we shall be in touch."

"We shall see."

She smiled and left.

Natalya Sergeyvna shook her head, as though mystified.

"Where is my daughter, Natalya Sergeyvna? I am not leaving without her."

"Mademoiselle Ani is safe. Do not worry."

"And who, Madame, might you be this time? You seem to have abandoned Baroness Heida from the Repast last night."

"I was on assignment then. Again, I am Madame *Prinkipia* Natalya Sergeyvna Iskandarova, Special Assistant to his Excellency, Minister Aleksandr Sergeyovich Iskandarov." She extended her slender hand, which Ashley gently shook.

"Now, Monsieur Cooper, follow me to my car." She put on her large dark glasses and asked, "Do you know where your luggage is?"

"Yes, Kaha Antonovich has it and shall be waiting at your car."

"Very good. He is most reliable."

Ashley with his briefcase walked beside Natalya Sergevna through the airport. Her silver BMW 735i sedan with diplomatic plates was parked in front of the terminal entrance, its lights flashing. Grimy working men partially surrounded it, staring in amazement. Natalya Sergeyvna said, "Do not be concerned, these men are largely harmless. They have come this afternoon to begin their second job as cab drivers in order to survive."

Natalya Sergeyvna opened the trunk and Ashley loaded his suitcase and briefcase before smiling, "Thank you for all your assistance, Kaha Antonovich."

"Excellency, I am very pleased I could help such fine gentleman as yourself."

"May we offer you ride into Moscow, Kaha Antonovich?"

"Thank you, Excellency. I must get to hospital to see my son."

Natalya Sergeyvna said, "Please sit in back and no smoking. Agreed?"

"Of course, *Prinkipia*. I will likely sleep."

As he opened the passenger door, Ashley realized that he had accepted help for a second time today and it felt so right. His stepfather David Cooper always said, "A man must know his limitations." And his father Sergei Dmitrovich had written, "Adversity is how we grow and mature and learn true wisdom." Ashley winced from pain as he entered her car. "Natalya Sergeyvna, does Kaha Antonovich understand English?"

"Not that I am aware..."

"Good, we'll speak English to keep our conversations private."

"But he would never betray a confidence."

"I know. Natalya Sergeyvna, my friends call me 'Ash'."

"Very well then, Ash. I notice you are not particularly good at following instructions."

"Of course, Madame *Prinkipia* Natalya Sergeyvna. But, as an American liberal, I absolutely loath titles and as my grandfather Dmitri Sergeyovich wrote in his diary, 'The superior will requires no titles. Such as *Prinkipia* or Princess.'"

"Very well, Ash. I shall be mentoring you and I surmise you are going to be a great deal more difficult than I imagined."

"Natalya Sergeyvna, as a good Iskandarova, you must relish a good challenge."

"Of course, I do. But I sense you shall soon challenge my limits."

God, this woman is impossible. She must really believe she's a real princess and everyone must cater to her. Well, at least my fantasy about my sister and mystery woman is over.

"Before I forget, I have heard you have a shrapnel wound in your chest. It is best if you refrain from those French pain pills. If you are not careful, they can become addictive."

"Yes, I know. I've been extremely careful with them. Do you have a better idea?"

"Perhaps I may be able to help you later. Baroness Ulrika was a longtime friend and mentor to me. And I greatly miss her. I learned early this morning you tried, at the risk of your own life, to save her. For that I am in your debt and why I wish to help you."

I know this woman had a horrible childhood, so I'm not surprised she's so mercurial. If I can get past her arrogance, this might just be fun.

"Thank you. But what can you tell me about my daughter?"

"Only that she is safe. What more do you need?"

"A great deal more." He looked out the window as they left the airport.

THREE

Friday, 4 June 1993, Moscow

1.

After leaving the airport, Natalya Sergeyvna focused on her high-speed driving on the boulevard to Moscow, apparently with no concern about being ticketed. Kaha Antonovich, curled up in the backseat was snoring. After noticing her kid gloves, Ashley dozed as well until he felt the car slowing.

"Good, you are awake. Right now, though, I need to focus on these rutted narrow streets."

Ashley looked out at the grimy streets of a Moscow district he did not even know existed. Soon, they were stuck in traffic, which seemed unusual, given the obvious poverty of the area. The other stopped cars seemed to belch even more black smoke than when moving. And he was grateful the car's air-conditioner kept most of the stink on the outside. A ragged man knocked on Natalya Sergeyvna's window looking for a handout. She curtly waved him off. "I cannot give to one without giving to many more."

"Just like New York."

A breeze blew away enough smoke to reveal the problem—a huge Soviet dump truck stalled in the middle of the street. With the hood up, both steam and oily smoke shot upwards. Around the truck, several workmen were loudly arguing. Another worker waved cars around it when he thought it was safe for them to drive on the sidewalk.

"Natalya Sergeyvna, as an Iska, do you have *pyordarsch*?"

Natalya Sergeyvna gasped, angrily stared at him and leaned in closer so as not to wake Kaha Antonovich. "Monsieur Cooper, that is a most rude question. Whether I have it or not is too intimate for you to even know about, like asking me the size of my brassiere. No, even worse. You should not even know such a thing exists. Further, it is not appropriate to ever mention such things before our retainers. And as for Iska…"

Ashley whispered, "I meant no offence. Olga Sergeyvna had it and she explained a great deal about it. Because she knew one day, I would have a daughter blessed with it."

"I have heard many stories about our unorthodox sister Olga Sergeyvna. It is obvious your daughter has it. In Paris, her aura was extraordinarily strong."

"You must know I've been mentored by both Olga and Verushka Sergeyvna and understand more than you assume."

"Although Verushka Sergevna is a senior Iskandarova, she has spent extraordinarily little time in Russia. She was always more Parisian and now appears almost American. I do not trust her knowledge of such matters. As for Olga Sergeyvna, not to speak ill of the dead, but she never spent any time in Russia. And even more than her sister, I believe Olga Sergeyvna told you a lot of stuff and nonsense, which I shall try to rectify."

Well, she's back in form and this time there's no mystery why she's royally pissed about nothing. An apology won't be forthcoming. But just then she was breathing on me with lovely apricot breath.

She continued staring at him as her expression gradually softened and she almost smiled. "How silly of me to react like that. This has been a most trying day for me as well as you. I thought some plain truth about our half-sisters might be appropriate. I am now curious about what you know and what you think you know."

"Here, there are many things I don't understand."

"Yes, this is Iskandarov reality and not just the theory you have been exposed to in New York and Paris. Be patient. This requires time."

"Are you saying the journals I've read are…unreliable?"

"They were a good introduction. But I would take what you read with several grains of salt. I believe that is the idiom. They were, after all, personal reflections."

"Interesting point and you're right. I must get up to speed as soon as possible."

"That shall not happen quickly because this shall be far more complicated than anything you have ever done."

Ashley was silent as Natalya Sergeyvna drove around the truck, which seemed ever larger than he thought, and deftly maneuvered on and off the crowded sidewalk.

She said, "You would think these workers would know enough to keep water and oil in that monster."

"Indeed. Please tell me about your English?"

"Very few people in Russia speak English, except those who come into direct contact with foreigners. I also speak French and German, although not as well as I would like."

"I don't think anyone ever truly masters a foreign language without really living it. Your English is quite good but very formal. Who taught you?"

"Our mother Charlotte. I was unaware that my English was formal. I suppose that is because I speak it mostly in formal business situations. But, perhaps, with you, I could be a bit less formal?"

"That would be very nice."

A few blocks past the truck, Natalya Sergeyvna slowed down among the once elegant nineteenth century townhouses, which had been divided into smaller units and had not been washed in a long time. Everything on the buildings' outside had long been vandalized and some even had unpainted plywood doors. People, some in costumes he could not identify, leaned out from most of the windows to catch a breeze and speak to neighbors. Had her car not been sealed for the air-conditioning, Ashley knew he would be smelling cooked cabbage and other odors he probably could not recognize. The streets were littered with a wide variety of trash and the multi-ethnic people seemed sullen and aimless, carrying their meager possessions in well-worn but sturdy reusable white plastic bags. Turning a corner, as she now sped past, there was a violent brawl between two street gangs of different ethnicities, seemingly Christian and Muslim by their clothing and manner.

"Kaha Antonovich, please awake. We have achieved your destination."

Kaha sat up, rubbing his eyes, "Thank you, *Prinkipia*, this is correct place, Cartvelian clinic for our patriots wounded in current war."

"I know."

Ashley turned around, "Kaha Antonovich, I wish you well and hope your son fully recovers. And, I again thank you for your help."

"You are most welcome, Excellency. Now, I must go and will find my way back to airport later."

"Of course. I hope we meet again."

"Most likely, sir, most likely." Once outside, Kaha Antonovich bowed to the car, lit a Marlboro and walked briskly toward a building cleaner than the others and went inside.

Natalya Sergeyvna did not drive away because Ashley said, "I've an awfully bad feeling about this. I think I should go in and check on him."

"No. Absolutely not."

"You don't care about him then?"

"For someone supposed to be a brilliant legal mind, you can be incredibly obtuse. Firstly, I know you don't speak or understand Cartvelian. You couldn't even gain entry. Secondly, even if you could, your presence would be an insult to Kaha Antonovich, implying he can't take care of himself. Thirdly, he's strong and resourceful. And fourthly, I, as I'm able, volunteer there to help our wounded patriots. I promise you he's in no danger."

Well, I'll be damned. I never thought she would get her kid gloves soiled in such a place.

"And finally, I care greatly for him." She turned to him. "You have a reputation for being the bear in a china shop."

"True. I'm trying extremely hard to learn many things in an unfamiliar environment."

"Yes, this is far from the Russia you have visited all these years. But now where do you need to go?"

"Even though I believe Ronnie, Verushka, has my daughter, I must find her. Please drop me at the Metropol Hotel."

Driving, she asked, "Is that where *tvarsch* is telling you?"

"It's presently not working. I was told Annie was with Rosalita Civilli. And that hotel is the logical place to begin. I'm on good terms with the manager who knows everything going on in Moscow and is in my debt."

Ah yes, Rosalita— one of Sergei Dmitrovich's Cuban daughters whom I have never met. Do you believe this information?"

"Only partially. Nick Stevens never tells the complete truth. I'm convinced Annie's at the Metropol where she knows we have a reservation, so she'll do her best to get there."

"Since you said she's safe, do you know where and with whom?"

"I know she is with Verushka Sergeyvna and Rosalita, presumably, at the Metropol." She picked up her car phone and said something Ashley did not understand before refocusing on her driving.

Confirmation Lala was right. Ashley said, "We have many issues of more personal nature to discuss now that Kaha Antonovich has departed. And we shall speak Russian so there are no misunderstandings."

"You are most careful."

"Aside from threats we know of with Polinkov, I must remain vigilant against those we do not know. I now know, thanks to Major Iganiev, that Russians hold Iskandarov in contempt."

"True. With fall of Bolsheviks, we are now striving to regain some of our former prominence. Actually, our rise began under Gorbachev, but it has long way to go."

"Good to know. Now, when you were young, did you know I even existed?"

"Yes. Mummy, that is, Charlotte, told me all about you and she maintained correspondence with Verushka Sergeyvna for many years."

"Thanks to your *Andronyis,* I have recently learned great deal about your horrible childhood. Did you ever resent me for not being with and protecting you?"

"I probably did, especially after Svetlana Feliksovna branded me. But, on whole, I was more curious about you. And I thank you for speaking Russian and I am also impressed that you speak it quite well with just slight accent, as Kaha Antonovich told me. This is a large plus for you. Right now, I sense strain you are still under and also your pain. And later, as I said, I might be able to offer relief."

"I would appreciate that. Ears are still ringing, not as badly as they were, now annoyance more than anything."

"My sympathy. Now that we are alone, I am, of course, your full sister and we may drop any pretense. Please remember we must always maintain formality before our retainers. My friends call me Nata. As I said, I wish to help you as much as I may."

"Thank you. I know I have lot to learn to become Hidden One."

"That shall be determined by you through number of tests. Ash, because you lost *tvarsch* at airport, please tell me how long were you without it?"

"I think the explosion caused it."

"Possibly. *Tvarsch* should not fail you, regardless. This means it is low level and needs to be strengthened."

"Curious. It has helped me most of my life and I was able to get through Realm of Spirits successfully."

"I was unaware you had done that. Although that is test of courage more than anything else. And *tvarsch* is part of Iskandarov Quadriga, along with faith, intellect and courage."

"I know Quadriga very well. But how can I improve *tvarsch*?"

"That is extremely complicated. There are numerous causes. I would need to know why before being able to potentially help you. I can offer no guarantees." She looked at him. "Wait, your aura is weak and that is reflection of your gifts. You are out of balance and that can be extremely difficult to resolve."

"What does all that mean?"

"I regret to tell you that unless your condition is resolved, you shall fail in your most important test and, even if that does not kill you, you shall never be truly Of Iskandarov. And you might even lose your daughter to us, assuming her Ceremony goes as planned. But I shall do all I am able to rectify your problem."

"Ceremony? I do not understand."

"Your daughter is seventeen in three days and, as is Iskandarova custom, she shall have hers then. I may tell you no more."

"Why?"

"Telling you now would only complicate your situation. Knowing your problem, I am sorry I did not arrive sooner at airport. As I have said, I had particularly important, but unpleasant, undertaking to attend to."

"I am sorry about that and I know you shall tell me all about it when you are ready. While airport delay was grueling, I learned about plans of Nick and Drago."

"This would be Nicholas Stevens and Alexandr Dragovitch, agents of George Farwell then?"

"Yes."

"I need to know what those plans are."

"I can tell you that Nick told me daughter of Sergei Dmitrovich, Anghelina DelaVega, is working for Farwell now. And she is going to be keeping watch on me about father's diary. Plus, I do not know how far and well this penetration goes into Iskandarovs. Now you know why I must be careful."

"I understand fully."

"Also, it is my understanding that even if *tvarsch* were functioning, it would not work with you."

"I did not know you knew such facts as that. But you are correct. I can also assure you if Anghelina's contamination has spread deeper into our ranks, we would absolutely know by now.

I realize I must earn your trust." Natalya Sergeyvna had to fully concentrate on her driving in the comparatively heavier traffic of central Moscow until the huge Metropol Hotel came into view.

Ashley loved its elegant art nouveau style and the roof's stained-glass atrium. Unlike the airport, it was supremely welcoming. *First goal achieved. Reach the Metropol.*

2.

Natalya parked her car near the hotel's main entrance, as a large man in a blue suit came out to stand near the vehicle. Ashley asked, "Who is this?"

"Bleu security. To make certain no one plants bomb or tracking device while we are inside."

"I thought I would get reservation, clean up and begin search for Annie."

"No need. You shall leave luggage in boot. Now, come with me."

As they entered, the doorman greeted Ashley warmly in Russian. And Ashley replied as if they were old friends.

"You are known and welcomed here. Impressive."

"Not really. I have been coming here several times annually for almost twenty years. They are good people."

"Yes, indeed. I come here on occasion, but being woman, I do not receive such treatment."

"I am sorry. I shall speak to manager about this."

"Oh no, please do not. I do not wish to create problem for you. I am most used to way Russians treat women. It shall not change any time soon. I am content."

"Should you change your mind…"

"Thank you. Not likely."

"I know why I am here but why are you?"

"Your daughter is here. Follow me."

They went through the bright, polished marble lobby under multiple chandeliers among crowds of rich Russians, foreigners, a few international celebrities and businessmen in three-piece suits of varying colors and quality. They easily found Rosalita

Civilli—dark, tall and toned like her sister, Anghelina—in the largely pallid Slavic crowd, standing by the thick Ionian column nearest Registration. Ashley was surprised by her shaved head and, coming closer, saw her blue and green eyes. However, he knew Anghelina had a contact lens she sometimes used to impersonate her sister and remained skeptical and vigilant. But what most puzzled him was her starched white linen robe.

Natalya said, "Oh yes, hello again, Rosalita."

Natalya said she didn't know Rosalita. Or was this an innocent mistake? Was Natalya in league with this woman who could be working for George as well? *Here I am with two women I barely know, and this feels like a trap. I need a plan quickly.*

"Hello, Mr. Cooper, Madame Natalya Sergeyvna. Please come with me."

Ashley said, "Wait. Why are you here and where're we going?"

Rosalita winked. "I'm charged with protecting someone."

Yes, she's vague because the lobby is probably bugged. I must take this chance that I'll see Annie. But even if George Farwell's in the same room with Annie, I can, at least, verify his demands. Also, I'm the only person who could find Sergei Dmitrovich's diary, assuming it even exists, which gives me a bargaining tool.

He remained careful in the elevator and following the two women down the long corridor, paid just enough attention to his surroundings to be able to find his way back. *I'm too exhausted to form a plan, so I'm going to trust these two women.* He began to feel better as they reached the room's door.

When Rosalita knocked twice, Ronnie, also wearing a similar white robe, opened the door. "Welcome, Ash, Nata, Raisa, please come in."

The elegant blue room had two king beds and Ashley asked, "Verushka Sergeyvna, where's Annie and why the white robes with you and Rosalita?"

"Here Rosalita is Raisa and we are wearing them because Annie's preparing for her seventeenth birthday. She's currently about to begin fasting, praying, and meditating in the next room."

"I must see her. I've been so worried. I…"

"I know and you may have a brief reunion, but we have a rigid schedule to keep for her preparations. She was never in great danger because I was already near the airport and Kaha Antonovich told me where to find her. I took her, so she couldn't be used against you."

"Why didn't Kaha Antonovich tell me this?"

"This was an impromptu test for you—how you'd react in very adverse conditions. But also, for you to find out what plans Nick and Drago had."

"I could've been deported to Vorkuta or worse."

"There's no worse place than Vorkuta. Kaha Antonovich was observing you. And you had *tvarsch.* That should've been enough."

"My *tvarsch* wasn't working. But Kaha Antonovich was an immense help. Also, there was a Khazak girl named Lala, younger than Annie, who perfectly described you as Annie's rescuer."

"Yes, I saw her in her short red robe and *phygynaya* sensed something about her. I'll revisit her when I return from Annie's Ceremony."

"Good, I think she deserves a chance. She also has her mother and two aunts with her. The mother told me Lala's a virgin and a trap for perverts, whom the three women guard against. So, they may not want her taken away by a foreigner."

"I'll still try a rescue. I know of a school here in Moscow for rescued girls. They do miraculous work."

"Great. Now, I must see Annie."

"Patience please. Still not your strong suit, I see. Why wasn't *tvarsch* working?"

"I don't know. I can't focus on anything until after I've seen and spoken with her."

Ronnie sighed, "All right, but again keep it brief because we'll barely beat the forty-eight-hour deadline on the seventh to complete her preparations."

"What the hell is going on here? This is way too much for a seventeenth birthday. I've her surprise birthday party set here for the seventh."

"Ash, that's nice, but this is extremely important for her. And you'll be pleased with the results. Please, I'm not allowed to say any more."

"Why not?"

Natalya put her hand on his shoulder. "I know you are frustrated with a *tvarsch* failure. But gathered here under our Iskandarov Truth, I swear to you we all are speaking truly. I noticed back in the corridor how you seemingly shed a thousand kilo weight and almost immediately looked better. Patience, Ash, we three are your friends, not your enemies."

"I know. I…"

"Ash, come." Ronnie led him to a door and whispered, "Ten minutes, max."

Ashley eagerly entered a small room with dim lighting. Annie in a black gown, ran and hugged him. "Dad, I'm so glad you're here. I thought I might never see you again."

"I was worried sick about you. I tried to rescue you once I could bribe my way into the female dormitory. I had help from a young girl…"

"Lala. There were some rough women in there and she, her mother and aunts sat on my bunk to protect me until Aunt Ronnie arrived."

"I'm so grateful they did."

"I've had a chance to compose myself since my rescue. I know you'll get a similar opportunity. I sense your pain and feel your fatigue. Cosette and I had a long talk in Paris early this morning. She's right. As an Iskandarova, I'll lose many people close to me. I must learn to control my emotions. I miss Yuri terribly, but what freaks me out is my vision, my *pyordarsch,* was correct. I mean, in the past, I was watching other people's lives. But there I was in the vision with someone special whose death I had seen but still didn't know the reason. That's what I haven't yet come to terms with. And thank you for not sending me back to New York. I would've liked to spend more time in Paris with Nadia and Cosette, but I knew you'd need me here."

"I'm enormously proud of the courage you've displayed on this trip. But, what's all this about a Ceremony?"

"Don't forget on the seventh I'll be seventeen and, I hope, an Iskandarova. I've been preparing my whole life for this. Well, actually, for the last four years. I told you that grandpa, that is, the Colonel, and Aunt Ronnie would often take me to for dinner at *El Meson* in the west Village. Then afterwards, he would meet with Major Maria Civilli. And Aunt Ronnie and 'Lita would take me to another room to teach me about being Iskandarova. When I started, I was still a little girl and I didn't have *pyordarsch*. They wanted to prepare me for when it arrived. I never knew exactly where it was all going but they told me to have faith. Anyway, the first time *pyordarsch* hit me, I was really scared and ran to Mom. You remember she totally freaked out. At Countess Sophia's plaque in the Iskandarov mausoleum yesterday, she told me why I'd been chosen as Bleu's Fourth-Generation Leader. Earlier, Great-Aunt Nadia also confirmed it when she said during our meeting that we should be informal and speak as equals. That was why she had a responsibility to protect me and I accepted she did. I wish you could've seen your face during that. You looked so completely lost. But when I saw the blue dress, I'd done my homework and already knew what it meant. And now I must become an Iskandarova to be successor to Aunt Ronnie. There was probably a pool of hundreds of young women and men. And they chose me."

"I'm not surprised. I'm also glad to know I wasn't the only one who was being asked to take things on faith. I'm curious about one thing. When we were in the car after the Colonel's funeral, you told me about your visions and how uncomfortable you were with them."

"Any Iska with *pyordarsch*, regardless how long she's had it, who says she isn't freaked by it, is lying. It's that powerful."

"Amazing. But why did Ronnie bring Rosalita into it?"

"Lita has *pyordarsch*, so she was the expert. Aunt Ronnie has been my Iska coach."

"I think I understand, but help me—what does Ronnie have?" *I know this but Annie might expand on it.*

"*Phygynaya,* which is very strange. She's highly attuned to people's emotions."

"Oh yes, I know that well."

"Dad, I don't think I'll be returning to New York and the Chaplin School. There's no longer anything there for me. And you may decide differently, but I don't think there's much at The Firm for you either."

"You may be right. I am, at this point, undecided. I'm soon going into the lion's den and I may not survive. Or, as I was warned today, I could simply disappear. I'm not concerned because I've faith I'll be all right." He paused. "I really understand what you're saying about New York and why. But I would ask you to remain open to the possibility of going back."

Ashley expected an argument, but Annie said, "I'd love to talk to you more and we will, but now I need to prepare myself, so, I'll say, 'Annie Cooper says goodbye.' And hopefully the next time you see me, I'll be Mademoiselle Anastasia." She kissed his cheek and returned to her single bed sitting in full lotus.

Well, it's official, I'm on the cusp of losing my little girl.

Rosalita was standing outside. Ashley said, "Nick Stevens told me you had Annie somewhere under an assumed name."

"I'm not surprised at his lie. I'm body guarding Annie, not working with Nick, although my sister is. Anghelina and I had a parting of the ways after we left you at Newark Airport. And that's why I shaved my head—in penance for her treachery. I'll not grow my hair until she recants."

"Being highly competitive sisters, your falling out was inevitable."

Ronnie came over. "Come, Ash, we have a nice spread to celebrate your homecoming with caviar, Tvishi, which is a very good Cartvelian wine, assorted finger sandwiches, fresh fruits, and nuts." She took him into a large red room with Louis XV furniture and a panoramic view of Moscow.

Ashley went to the window. "There's St. Basil's Cathedral, the Kremlin's towers with stars, Red Square and GUM Department Store. I've been to them all, a short walk from here. But never from this height. Thank you all."

Seated at an ornate round table with the food and drink in the middle, Ronnie said, "You're most welcome. Now sit and relax. We may speak safely here because the room's been swept, and we have counter measures in place."

Ashley drank a large glass of water before he carefully placed chopped onion and lemon juice on the caviar's cracker, then he savored a long sip of wine "Very nice. It's too bad Annie can't be enjoying this with us."

"Ash, in a few days she'll, hopefully, have a sumptuous banquet in her honor." Ronnie raised her wine glass in toast to Ashley and then said, "Last year, sweet sixteen, should be Annie's last birthday. Birthdays are for children because they have their child names, like, for example, Ashley." She smiled. "When Annie becomes Anastasia, she'll celebrate her saint's name day instead."

"So, if I become Sergei Sergeyovich, I'll do the same. Please tell me why seventeen is so important?"

All were silent until Natalya spoke, "The three Colchi princesses who lay with Iskandar were triplets and seventeen. And that's all you're permitted to know."

"Something has been bothering me for a long time. Today, we have three of Sergei Dmitrovich's daughters present. As his son, I must know why all the mystery is around female training, while mine has been completely out in the open."

Rosalita answered, "While your training is exceedingly difficult emotionally and physically, your *tvarsch* is fairly simple. But as I'm sure you remember about your wife, Penelope, our visions and other gifts can be turned against us unless we're properly prepared."

Ronnie added, "If you marry again, your wife, at her discretion, may reveal all or none of these secrets."

"Good to know." The Iskandarov, in some ways, appear medieval and yet in Russia, where women have traditionally been treated as little better than chattel, Iskas seem to be quite liberated.

Natalya leaned forward. "Your daughter has a mandatory vow of silence for the remainder of her forty-eight hours. I shall start by telling you the significance of this Ceremony and my experience. My life changed from horrible to being free as I never had been because after that I had the confidence and strength to defy Svetlana Feliksovna and she never dominated me again."

"Those *Andronyi* images I received from you a while back were pretty horrifying."

"Yes, but you must begin to know the truth."

Rosalita added, "Mr. Cooper, Annie couldn't be safer anywhere on earth than where we're going. My mother came with my sister and me when we were seventeen and it was incredible."

"I'd assumed only Iskas were allowed in." He paused. "Lita, please call me 'Ash'. We're all siblings here."

Lita nodded. "Ash it will be. My mother, obviously, was extremely controversial. But she was given a waiver and all three of us were profoundly changed."

Ronnie said, "Sister Olga Sergeyvna, of blessed memory, and I went through this." She crossed herself in the three-fingered Orthodox Christian manner. "And I wouldn't be here today had I not done it. I assure you it'll make Annie stronger and happier."

"I really wish I could be at the Ceremony."

"There will be many women there," Ronnie said. "You, as a male, are never even allowed into the *haram* area where the Ceremony takes place—a forbidden area to you."

"And where will this take place?"

Natalya said, "In Sakartvelo."

"I trust you all but Kaha Antonovich said there's a civil war raging there."

Ronnie said, "That's true. But we shall be very well protected and have been for an extraordinarily long time. Don't worry. It's in a part of the country that has been spared heavy fighting."

Natalya continued, "The fortress where we are going was begun in the first century A.D. and finished in the fourteenth. Like most construction at that time, it was based on conditions and money. But it was never conquered, even after many armies attempted sieges and attacks. It remains eternally free Cartvelian land. Renovations began in the seventies and continue today."

Ronnie stood. "Ash, we're not taking Annie away from you. Have no fear, she'll always be your daughter and your journeys will still cross from time to time."

Rosalita looked at her watch. "Please excuse me. It's time for Annie's first full body massage."

"Please excuse me as well. I need to visit the washroom." Ashley rose and watched Natalya leave. *Something's going on. Damn, she even gave me a dirty look as though I'm cheating on her.*

Alone, Ronnie came over and passionately hugged and kissed him. "I've wanted to do that since you arrived."

"Me too. Our time together at your cottage was fabulous. But..."

She placed her index finger lightly on his lips. "I know. This was our goodbye kiss."

"Got it. Now, what just happened?"

"As senior Iska, I'm in charge of your homecoming. And gave the other ladies the signal I had to speak to you alone."

"Natalya seemed to know you'd kiss me and gave me a really dirty look as she went to the bathroom."

"She's very jealous and doesn't like me because I tease her."

"So that's it. She also has a low opinion of you, thinks you're too westernized and not a true Iska."

"Oh, I know. I actually like her quite well. She is kind and generous although she can be very tough when she needs to be. Also, she is, at her core, very eastern and feels all Iskas should be as well."

"What does that mean?

"I'll only say that's one reason for Bleu-Russia breaking with Bleu-Paris. My first act, when I succeed Nadia Mytrovna will be to heal the rift."

"Long overdue. I'll support you any way I can."

"Thanks. You must be patient with Nata because the two of you must join together. You have what she needs, and she has what you need. Only then can you begin to assume leadership of the Iskandarov."

"That'll be a tall order. But why is she always testing me? She says I'm not a true Iskandarov."

"Ash, don't you realize that when the time is right, you're auditioning to be the father of her children? Oh, the tests will continue because you're going to a place not even most of our clan has ever been. You're the next step in our evolution. But you can't do this alone. You need her. Don't forget that and don't rush her. She'll come to you only when she's ready."

"OK. Tell me, she wants my children, Svetlana Polinkova may already be pregnant and even you wanted one or two. What gives? I'm not even sure I want to get married again."

"Thanks for being candid. You're obviously overwhelmed right now. As for the children, you produced a nearly perfect daughter." She smiled. "At least, when she becomes a full Iska Lady. And you did so with a deranged Iska. And Olga Sergeyvna, of blessed memory, told me you finally broke your bond in Paris." She crossed herself. "And thank you for not making this any harder than it had to be. About your full sister, Natalya Sergeyvna, you can trust her completely." She paused. "She can also be truly *formidable* when sets her mind to something."

"Yes, I've noticed."

"But given her horrible childhood, it's amazing she's not completely insane. After breaking free of Svetlana Feliksovna, she had a fairly happy marriage that resulted in her twin girls and the death of her Polinkov cosmonaut husband." She sadly shook her head. "Be patient with her, despite her bravado, she's…"

"I know. I'll be careful. But honestly, I don't know how I feel about her."

"I understand that. She must seem very alien to you. Now, you should be proud of your daughter and have no fears about our safety. Again, the place's incredibly secure."

"Of course. I wouldn't even be here if not for you."

"I'm immensely proud of you for doing all the heavy lifting. And I'll see you in a few days. I'll call the others back now. We'll need to leave soon, flying down on one of brother Aleks's private jets. Have no fear, they're French and not Soviet."

He reached into his blazer pocket. "Good. Here are Annie's documents, all stamped and approved." He then told her what Nick and Dragovitch wanted him to do.

"Good to know. Remember, if you fail any test, your *tvarsch* will turn on you and drive you mad just like it did with Pen and her *pyordarsch*. Giving all you have and even dying in the process is better than failure."

Shocked by her candor about the tests, he could only nod.

Once everyone finished their meals, the Iskas kissed each other according to their custom before Ronnie and Rosalita excused themselves and went into Annie's room.

Natalya told Ashley they should go back to the main room. A few minutes later, Annie, in her black robe now with a dark veil, proceeded in single file into the room between Ronnie in front and Rosalita.

Natalya stood near Ashley as they stopped and turned, bowed at the waist before saying in unison, "All hail you, great father," and silently left the room.

Ashley said, "I still don't fully understand this Ceremony and lavish preparations."

"It's quite simple really. Iskandarov men are strong and powerful. Iskas must be as well, but in a totally unique way."

"Seems logical, I suppose."

"Since Lenin's coup d'état in 1917, we Iskandarovs have been playing an extremely dangerous game by staying here and not going abroad. We were condemned by the regime for merely existing. We became the people Russians came to fear because they didn't, indeed couldn't, understand our Cartvelian and Iskandarov ways. Eventually, under Monster Stalin, the people were ordered to fear, denounce and persecute us."

"But Stalin was Georgian. Why did he hate you?"

"He was allied with Polinkov. We'd been aristocracy. And he'd spent a large part of his life trying to kill us before assuming absolute power. As I said earlier, even before the 1991 Overthrow, we'd been gradually coming back into the light, especially brother Aleks. He inherited part of his power from his mother and my tormenter, Svetlana Feliksovna. But it's dangerous to be in public and we may again become targets. Natalya is my Iska name. As a girl, when I was called by name, it was 'Little Princess' or my *zechka* number. Except by Mummy, who called me 'Lassie.'" She grimaced. "Yes, I've heard all the dog jokes. But I loved that name. It made me feel special."

"As well it should. I appreciate you for telling me the unembellished truth about what I'm trying to join."

"It certainly isn't for the weak or fainthearted. And that's why we test Seekers like you. We may appear heartless and cruel, but should you be successful in the future, you'll be glad we were so rigorous. This is obviously a physical discipline, but also spiritual, religious and psychological."

"You sound like you would love to go with them to the Ceremony. I've a reservation here and I'll be fine. Go. Thank you for your assistance at the airport."

"You're most welcome, but I decline your offer. As your full sister, it's my obligation to mentor and test you, as it would be yours when I turned seventeen had you grown up here."

"But why do I need more testing and mentoring?"

"Did not Olga Sergevna, of blessed memory, test you before she began your tutelage?" She crossed herself while speaking.

"Yes, but why test me at all? I'm Iskandarov. Why do you insist I'm not?"

"While the blood of Iskandar may flow in your veins, that alone doesn't qualify you to be Iskandarov. You are not yet there. Just like in school, there is a final test that will, in large measure, determine your fate."

"Nata, what's next for us?"

"Dinner and then your meeting tomorrow morning before I leave for the Celebration."

"Who am I meeting?"

"Later."

"You do seem upset."

"Verushka Sergeyvna as Senior Iskandarova was within her rights to speak to you alone. But I'm Annie's aunt and I came to know her quite well in Paris, and absent my obligation to you, as you intuited, I would've loved to have gone with her today. I was receiving extraordinarily strong non-verbal signals from Verushka Sergevna who didn't want me along, even though that would be customary. She seemed very proprietary about you. In fact, I smell a trace of her perfume on you. This suggests you two have been intimate in the past and again recently."

"Nata, you're most perceptive, but she merely gave me a goodbye kiss. My relationship with Ronnie, as I know her, over the past thirty years has always been rather complicated. In the summer after Olga Sergeyvna died, Ronnie mentored, protected and helped me recover from her death. She's a dear friend and that's all you need to know." He paused. "Again, you could catch the flight to Sakartvelo. As I said, I'll be fine here. Nick and Drago have given me forty-eight hours…"

"No. You have other enemies right here in this hotel who want you dead."

"Why? What have I done now?"

"You bring the L'Enfant Bosnian Treaty. They cannot defeat it but believe if they kill you, the treaty dies as well."

"Absurd. Another person would come in my place."

"And they would kill that person as well. These are the unknown persons. Here, we cannot properly protect you from the numerous weapons they might use. I know the safest place for you to be."

"Good. My stepfather, David Cooper, taught me to be a good negotiator. So, I know about people, again, I can almost taste your sadness and it bothers me."

"I'm sorry, you're wrong. I'm quite content. Compared to most Russians, I've an exceptionally good life."

"Remember, we're still under our Truth. I had an exceptionally good life in New York but wasn't truly happy. My journey has given me purpose and through it all, even just seeing Annie restored my spirits. When she was little, we were very close, but at adolescence, we became estranged. So, having recently had her back in my life, I couldn't imagine anything worse than losing her again."

"I believe what you just told me. But you are solitary. You have spent much of your life alone, am I correct?"

"In a spiritual sense, yes."

"But this solitude is quite painful, and you seek intimacy as the cure. Let me be very candid. Even though I'm your full sister, I may not be the one you seek. Therefore, when you come with me, our relationship shall be strictly platonic. Are we clear?"

"Why do you find me unworthy besides not being, in your estimation, an Iskandarov?"

"You possess what I call the 'Devil's Trio.' That is, you are handsome, rich and powerful."

"I don't understand. I've always understood, as do most people, those to be positive attributes to women. So please explain further."

"Very well. Men like you shall, in time, attempt to dominate me. And I shall never again submit to anyone. We then argue, which leads to fighting and, ultimately, my being alone."

"I'm sorry. Were any of these Iskandarov?"

"Yes. Apollon. And a Polinkov."

"Really?"

"Truly. He was mostly very nice." She shook her head. "He was murdered for his efforts."

"I'm sorry. But were any of them your full brother?"

"You're my only full brother."

"Perhaps, as your full brother, I could be different. Like your Polinkov husband."

"I didn't say he was my husband."

"It seems perfectly obvious to me he was the father of your twins."

"Perhaps you are different, but that remains to be seen. Enough, this isn't the place to discuss such intimate matters. Now, do you accept my condition for coming with me? Am I clear?"

"Extremely. But no, I don't accept your terms. I still have a question. Why did you send me *Andronyis*? And especially one about Ronnie and me."

"I never sent you anything about any of your half-sisters."

"Interesting." It now seems so obvious. That particular Andronyi was all part of Ronnie's recent seduction plan at her cottage. "Then why did you send the others?"

"You're my brother and I've acknowledged you as such. I wanted you to know about that part of my life. It doesn't logically follow from that I wish to be sexually associated with you. Now, are you clear on my terms?"

"You assume I only have a sexual interest in you, which may not be accurate." *What a relief. I'm not ready to commit to her.* "I need you to trust me."

"Perhaps in the future. Patience is a great virtue. I can't confide in any non-Iskandarov, man or woman, whom I've only known for a few hours."

Well, at least I know her fear of intimacy is why she's using the excuse I'm not of the Iskandarov. Which gives me an idea. I did notice she has recently tried to make her English less formal and that's progress. "As you said, you've known about me for a long time. I've only known about you for a brief time. I need to know more about you."

"You may ask me a single non-sexual question."

"Let us go to our genesis, the French Embassy Reception. You spoke to me in a language I didn't understand before you retreated and then you came back before retreating again. And this went on most of the evening, what I call your 'indecisive dance.'"

"Simply, I was curious about you and wanted to learn more. But, as you must know by now, the time was not then right. And the language was Cartvelian, which all Iskandarov must learn." She smiled ever so slightly. "Come, shall you join me."

He nodded. Damn, that makes sense, knowing what I know now. I also swear to beat my tvarsch problem. And when I do, I'll decide whether to join the Iskandarov. And that will determine whom I marry—my sister, Lana or someone else not yet on the scene.

"It's nothing short of a miracle, given your unknown enemies, you made it up here alive. Of course, I was armed and from the way Rosalita spoke, she must have been as well. No matter, we can't risk your life by leaving the way we entered."

"Yes, of course, I was so distracted by Annie I hardly even took notice of my surroundings."

"Very understandable. However, I have a plan."

FOUR

Friday, 4 June 1993, Moscow

1.

After Natalya explained her plan, Ashley smiled. "Of course, Nata, when the Metropol was built in 1899, Tsar Nicholas II ordered clandestine passageways be built so the *Okhrana,* his secret police, could eavesdrop on foreigners and subjects. These were expanded by the Chekists. For a long time, I thought this was nothing more than rumors. Then, about ten years ago, I was taken through them because I had to leave the hotel undetected. I remember a few VIPs and KGB using them and it was a KGB agent who led me through the dimly lit passageways to the VIP exit."

"You're a man of many stories."

"The hotel arranged the whole thing with the KGB. For the record, I was with him no more than ten minutes and we barely spoke."

"Of course, then you were ignorant of your true heritage and, for that matter, Bleu. We have this suite on long-term lease. The passageway is right behind you in that empty closet. Go down to the VIP exit and I'll be there in my car. Once in, keep going until you find the black spiral stairs. At the bottom, the VIP door is on the left. But you should be armed, just in case. I have my Bleu service Beretta, but it wouldn't be good in close quarters. My back-up, also in my purse, is a Russian PSM Security Forces Pistol, known as 'small but lethal.' And that's your most effective protection, especially since you're dressed like an American. Your slacks, polo shirt and deck shoes, and, even your blazer are all a dead giveaway."

"Ha, you made a pun."

She slowly shook her head, irritated. "It is now 15:35. I'll be at the exit in ten minutes. And here's my small gun."

"Ten minutes." He entered the well-lit passageway, slightly more than two people wide, and was surprised. What had once been used for espionage was now largely a fashionable way for people to get to and from their assignations. Many wore thick terrycloth Metropol robes as they hurried along, while some wore little or nothing. It was hot and smelled of a plethora of perfumes, after-shaves and scented soaps, partially concealing other less pleasant ones. Numerous *No Smoking* signs did not stop the smokers. Fortunately, no one was smoking the foul-smelling Makhorka tobacco or drinking cheap liquor to get even drunker. It almost felt like a party atmosphere and some attractive women gave him the eye, but what caught his attention were the men in suits, presumably FSB secret police. Were they looking for him, someone else or just patrolling? Eventually, as the line slowed for some unknown reason, people pressed against him. And while it was very pleasant to be sandwiched between two slightly drunk women making lewd suggestions along with a third woman going the other way, he knew one of them could also be an assassin and felt extremely vulnerable before the line began moving. He finally reached the black spiral staircase and descended the lighted cast iron steps, just wide enough for one person. About one floor down above him, he heard a man's heavy footsteps moving quickly down. When he stopped, so did the other footsteps. Ashley hurried to the next level, drew his pistol and left the stairs. The footsteps again stopped. *Had whoever it was just gone down a flight or two? Or was I being followed?* He waited five minutes until smelling patchouli, he saw an Arab man and woman coming down speaking what he assumed was Arabic. He followed them, listening for footsteps other than the man's and the woman's heels on the steps until again hearing footsteps above him. He looked up, but despite the lighting, could not see anyone. The couple slowly made their way down and he followed one floor up, so he would not be stuck between floors. After the couple left the building, Ashley came down and was met by another man in a suit just like the FSB men upstairs.

"Your passport, please."

Ashley handed it to him, and the man studied it. Looking up, he quickly drew his revolver and fired off four shots over Ashley's shoulder and he heard the sound of a body falling down the stairs. "Ah, you are American who is being threatened. Follow me, please."

Once outside, two men in worker's clothes with large metal baseball bats came running toward him. The FSB man again quickly shot both men, wounding them. They both proceeded to Natalya's car. "Madame Iskandarova, here is your friend."

"Thank you, Ivan. Good day." The man saluted and then handcuffed the two workers before Ashley got in the car

2.

Once Ashley again settled into the comfortable passenger seat, Natalya said, "What took you so long and why do you reek of perfume? Perhaps, I should've accompanied you?"

"When was the last time you were in the passageways?"

"It's been some time. Why?"

Ashley told her about how the passageways had changed since the fall of the Soviet Union. And finished by asking her about Ivan.

"Oh, not his real name because he, like many other FSBs in Moscow, is on brother Aleks's payroll. I asked him to protect you and I'm most pleased he did."

"Are those two dead?"

"Don't know nor do I care. They probably are wounded and soon shall be guests of the Moscow Constabulary." She, seemingly ignoring her driving, was openly studying him. *Damn. I haven't come all this way only to end up as a hood ornament on some*

Russian truck. Fortunately, Natalya's fast reflexes always avoided disaster. And, for one who praised patience, she certainly did not practice it behind the wheel, continuously honking at miscreants.

"Ash, you are a mystery and amaze me. But right now, I believe I am seeing you at your worst. You need to rest. I can almost smell your fatigue over the perfume. But now, hear my confession. I thought I'd met Rosalita before. But it was the other sister, Anghelina. When I arrived at the airport, I noticed she had a very bright aura and black hair. As is customary, I introduced myself and she nodded, not telling me who she was because, as an agent on assignment, she appeared to be waiting for someone. I asked her whether she had seen you. She told me to try Major Iganiev's office. I told her I knew the way. We kissed and I left."

"And you're only telling me this now? That's particularly valuable information I needed to know."

"But whatever for?"

"It's conclusive proof she's actually working with Nick and was probably waiting for him or Drago, and confirms what Nick told me." *Why is she playing dumb on this?* "And Anghelina is never to be underestimated. She's slightly crazy and quite lethal. But I'll be damned if I'll go searching for the diary only to have it burned in front of me before I'm killed as a loose end."

"I apologize. Yes, of course. You shall be protected. You may rest shortly."

"Thanks. But I'll be fine."

"In that case, I wish to introduce an extremely sensitive subject. I believe the American idiom is 'the elephant in the room.'"

"We may as well clear the air about Lana van Rouene."

Yes, that *muzhik* cow was in the interrogation room with you?" She looked over at him. "You understand this term, *muzhik*?"

"It's a term you aristocrat use for 'peasant.'" He paused. "I assure you, she's no peasant. Svetlana Palaeologa…"

"Palaeologa? Merciful God, she's Polinkova. No more than a peasant with airs. I don't suppose you noticed her thick *muzhik* ankles while she was displaying her enormous udders."

"No, not really. In New York, we don't place so much weight on someone's origins."

"Of course not. Your class simply dismisses them as *nouveau riche*. But for a woman with such vulgar large bosoms, you are the perfect democrat, no?"

"True, we were involved. However, I never looked down on her. And I wouldn't have in any case. I know better. She was highly accomplished and had been married to a venerable gentleman."

"But when you came into Major Iganiev's office with that cow, what am I to think of a man who would allow such a creature anywhere near him? Except to assume that man knows nothing at all."

"Do I detect some jealousy?"

"Jealousy? Of that creature? I hardly think so."

"She claims descent from the Byzantines."

"Only if the Byzantines were cattle."

"My missing *tvarsch* couldn't tell me who she really was"

"If you were a true Iskandarov *tvarsch* would tell you everything you need to know."

"Stop the car. I'm getting out. You've insulted me for the last time, and I don't have time to play your ludicrous games. I'll go back to the Metropol and you won't be inconvenienced any longer"

"If I do so, I guarantee you should be dead in short order."

"I know my way around Moscow. I've been here many times before."

"Yes, but then you were Ashley Cooper and not a target for the anti-Balkan peace lot. And the person you heard on the stairs most likely would've followed you, absent Ivan to kill you outside for maximum effect."

Oh my God, why did I say such a stupid thing? I'd be screwed if she stops.

"Even after you have been so rude, I don't wish to leave you on the street." She paused. "However, if that's what you want..."

"I remain Ashley Cooper and I don't require assistance from you."

"You're wrong. You're no longer Ashley Cooper, but you aren't yet who you need to be. Hence, your interim name, Ashlei, which I saw on your nameplate at the Repast in Paris."

Yes, there I was called Ash-lay not Ash-lee.

"Bleu has been protecting you since you were an adolescent. As a Bleu agent I'll not stop my car because I'm charged with protecting you for the near future. And I add, if you should seek our father's Gulag diary by yourself, you'll fail."

"From whom do I need help?"

"When, and if the situation arises, we shall speak again."

She wants to go with me. No way, it'll be far too dangerous. "Am I your prisoner then?"

"Of course not. The *muzhik* who accompanied you to the major's office is definitely the same person with whom you had your affair in New York City. I know because we've been monitoring her for a long time. You may resume your affair with her, if you wish, but you need to learn a great deal more about her before you do. And once you know, she may not seem quite so alluring. Furthermore, *tvarsch,* which I assume was then working, should've alerted you with whom you were dealing. At a minimum, you should've known she was Polinkova."

"T*varsch* didn't tell me anything substantial, except to be cautious. But she did proudly tell me that her mother was Svetlana Feliksovna, originally of the NKVD."

"Wait. I think I perceive one problem with *tvarsch*. You're using it like an *avocat*, seeking a level of proof for the courtroom. Did no one teach you how to use it properly?"

"Olga Sergeyvna tried, but she couldn't tell me fully and I didn't know enough to entirely appreciate or understand it. Despite using it since I was thirteen, I've only known its proper name from Ronnie for a few weeks."

"I don't know how this could happen, but it gives me hope for a solution."

"Really? I could use some good news. There's another item. Lana gave me her peace proposal. She's willing to overlook the attempt on her life in order to begin talks with you…"

"Typical. Peasant wenches develop special cunning to survive. They use men like you as you use Kleenex. I speak for the Iskandarov. We've no interest in talking to Polinkov about the weather, much less anything more serious."

"She gave me her written proposal."

"Have you examined it yet?"

"No, haven't had time. I will. If it's compelling, I'll show you. If not, we'll say no more, and based on what I know, I'm skeptical."

"Good. Our Polinkov wounds are still far too recent. You've no idea of the horrors Svetlana Feliksovna inflicted upon me, our mother and father and all her other victims."

"You're right. I'm too tired to think clearly. I apologize for being such an idiot."

Natalya smiled. "Sometimes, the obvious is so apparent as to become invisible. But I thank you for your apology. I know how hard that is for you."

"I'm getting better. Recently, I've even learned to accept help."

"Bravo."

He heard her sarcasm. *She doesn't laugh at anything. Perhaps, she's just being a Russian.* "Now, let me be very candid, Nata. You seem so normal, so mentally healthy you made me forget about your horrible childhood. So, my stupid comment."

"Now that we're in no risk of being bugged, I can now tell you your appointment tomorrow shall be with brother Aleks. I also know you're here, in part, to convince him of the rightness of your L'Enfant Bosnian Peace Initiative. And as you claim, you're a skilled negotiator. This initiative is obviously causing great consternation. Have no fear, my studio's safe and you'll be as well."

She turned her focus on the road and honked at a pedestrian, who jumped back toward the curb. "Bloody Russians think they own the streets. Now, I still don't understand why you left Paris in such bad condition."

"Nadia told us we were too exposed in Paris after the explosion and we could catch our enemies in Moscow off balance after we secretly left. Also, Nadia knew about Annie's Ceremony."

"Now I understand."

3.

Natalya's car vibrated as she slowly drove over the parking area's uneven and missing cobblestones past a decrepit horse stable. Parked at the stone curb, she asked Ashley to get out before opening the car's trunk so he could quickly grab his luggage. She explained that *urkas*, thieves, in the district were very quick and brazen. Although he thought her silly and even paranoid, when he left the car, several shady men came toward him as he quickly pulled out his luggage. Natalya looked over the other parked cars near her building with great concern while setting the alarm and locking her car. Despite her high heels, she walked rapidly on the cracked concrete and readied a cylindrical key. At the building's steel door, she used the key as an *urka* with a tattooed face approached her. She calmly opened the door and held it for Ashley, who swung his hard-sided briefcase at the man's face and solidly connected with his nose. The man held his hands to his face as blood sprang through his fingers. Ashley wheeled his suitcase into the building and slammed the door behind him. His chest wound throbbed and a sharp pain from exertion pinched his side.

As they waited in the spartan lobby for the antique birdcage elevator, Natalya Sergeyvna said, "I've never seen anyone use an attaché case as a weapon."

"That was a skill I developed as a kid waiting for the bus to the Buckley School. We used our book bags to both block and hit. It was all in wholesome boy fun."

"Perhaps. I'm impressed by your quick reaction. The *urka's* tattoos are Gulag criminal and he is extremely dangerous. Had you not struck him, he would've killed you and attacked me."

"Don't you the appreciate humor in this?"

"You're like our mother and her English humor. Nearly drove me crazy. I don't understand how you joke in the face of danger."

"It keeps me sane."

"You think you're sane?" She said this with a straight face, and he wondered if he could ever get a laugh from her. "Now, this is the back of the building. The front is actually quite beautiful, but it needs a good wash, which it hasn't had in a long time. The last workers who tried had most of their equipment stolen while they were cleaning it."

"I'm not surprised. I've heard similar stories before."

"Yes, this is modern Russia, the result of Mikhail Sergeyovich Gorbachev's *glasnost* or openness." She laughed mockingly. "Thieves not only crave our possessions, but feel they have the right to them."

"Yeltsin's doing nothing about this?"

"He has much bigger problems."

"I know."

"Have no fear. My studio's safe."

As the elevator lifted, Ashley recognized the heavy-duty metal gate at the foot of the stairs as a second deterrent. And it reminded him of the lobbies in the lofts in New York City's Chelsea District. "Where are we?"

"In one of the twelve *Okrugs*, districts, with boring geographical names. I favor the traditional Orthodox name, Saint Sergius Parish. Downstream from the Kremlin and south of Moskva River."

"I've been in the district before."

On the fifth and highest floor, Natalya unlocked her steel door and ushered Ashley ahead of her into a central atrium, a high-ceilinged beige space partitioned into rooms with twelve-foot-high walls painted in different pastels on all the walls. *This color variety is very unexpected.*

Hanging from suspended metal racks near the far wall were many large paintings on silky materials, moving in a breeze. "Are these your creations?"

"Yes, I prefer to work on silk. Let me escort you to your room, so you may rest. Supper will be in about two hours, around eight."

"Thank you. Great."

His room had scarlet walls, a queen-sized bed with a white duvet and a large window, from which he could see the Moskva River.

"Bathroom is next door to the left, which has only a shower. When you awake, shorts and a shirt will suffice for tonight. Excuse me, I must paint now."

Ashley felt relief to be away from Natalya Sergeyvna. Atop his thick pillow was a new black silk sleep mask to ward off the White Night. This time of year, and this far north, twilight only briefly interrupted daylight. His whole body ached, and his ears still rang. Exhausted, he stretched out on the bed wearing the mask. Relieved in the quiet room, he decided the bed was even better than his usual one at the Metropol.

4.

Feeling rested, Ashley needed to form a plan for dealing with Natalya and, like many, did his best thinking in the shower. Wrapped in a large blue towel, he went down the hall to the bathroom, where he found a pale-yellow metal shower with red stars on the white porcelain controls. Soviet plumbing required his full attention to keep from being either scalded or frozen without warning. After several minutes, he found the point of equilibrium and cautiously entered.

His father, Sergei Dmitrovich, had written, "Little Nata, although she appears frail and delicate, is pure Iskandarova." Since I really don't know what pure Iskandarova means or looks like, she could be anyone. Even someone replacing the real Natalya after Svetlana Feliksovna killed her. Also, she's certainly not an easy person to like. But she'd told me she had had a particularly important, but unpleasant, undertaking today and that could've accounted for her mood. However, she also seems erratic because while she was jealous of Lana, Ronnie and Rosalita, she has no interest in me. Perhaps, she's crazy after all, which is understandable given her horrendous childhood. A charm offensive tonight will answer many questions, including her validity. But to do that I need to embrace, not fight my pain.

While he missed Annie and hoped she really was safe in Sakartvelo, he knew there was nothing he could do and moved on to something he could. He felt refreshed after brushing his teeth, shaving, and changing into a dark blue polo shirt, khaki shorts, and deck shoes.

As he left his room, he smelled lilacs and roses mixed with sandalwood incense and heard Rimsky-Korsakov's *Scheherazade* playing softly. He found Natalya in her studio, painting, with her back to him, intently working on what appeared to be an angel's wing. He stood quietly, studying her while his expert eye determined her to be around 5'10 and one hundred and thirty pounds. She wore jeans, running shoes with small Union Jacks on the backs, a grey smock and a blue baseball cap, all covered in many shades of dye and wax, especially scarlet and royal blue. He noticed, for the first time, some gray in her short black hair. Given her position, why had she not colored it?

She spoke without turning. "Ah, hello, you're here. I've some good news. I reviewed your medical records. You're one chromosome removed from being slightly autistic and have *petit mal* epilepsy. While this isn't true of all who have these, for an Iskandarov, it not only means you have *tvarsch* but it's much stronger than I realized."

She has my medical records? No, control yourself. "I never realized that connection. And my friend Rand was right."

She turned toward him. "Then I am extremely glad I told you. And this person you mention would be your good friend Randell Speers, the Episcopal priest, yes? I'd like to learn more about this religion."

"I think you mean 'denomination'. I'm certain we'll get around to discussing it. Rand told me this one day after tennis at our club in the city."

She turned back to her angel. "Supper shall be ready shortly. Would you care for a drink?"

Ashley smiled and replied, "I would. I couldn't help noticing you're wearing a Los Angeles Dodgers baseball cap."

"Really? I had no idea. I just liked the shade of blue. Now, after a difficult day, you need a proper full-measure drink. I've a carafe of some fine Polish vodka in the refrigerator. And since you are no longer on Fifth Avenue, fill the glasses to the rim."

"Good idea. But where's the kitchen?"

"Just to your left, look for the orange lamp."

"Certainly." After going about fifteen feet through an archway, he found the kitchen, where several earthen pots filled the room with exotic and inviting aromas. He opened the white Red Star refrigerator and poured vodka into two French café wine glasses he found on the counter. He brought the two full glasses to Natalya, who turned from the angel wing and took one to offer "*Vashe zdorovie.*"

Ashley raised his glass and responded, "To your health as well." They downed their glasses in a gulp and Ashley felt the delightful burn. "Now, please tell me about the building."

"This was the town house of Boris Sergeyovich Prince Iskandarov before the Bolshevik coup. This floor was his ballroom, which the previous owner remodeled to her needs. I've further changed it, while leaving the floor plan only slightly revised."

"Impressive. I'm quite curious. Please tell me about your art. I've never seen anything like it. It appears simple and yet quite sophisticated."

It's an ancient technique, batik from Java. It was popular in *avant-garde* circles before and after World War I. I discovered it about five years ago. I begin with a section of silk and using that pen over there." She pointed to a large black object to her right. "I use the hot wax to cover areas I don't want dyed. Once the wax hardens, I paint dye where I want. When the dye dries, I plunge the whole thing in hot water to melt the wax and then reapply it again and so on." She made a casual circular motion with her hand and resumed painting.

Listening, he moved to see her better and studied her high cheekbones, aquiline nose, large mouth, dark eyes, set deep in a heart-shaped face, and olive skin with small wrinkles around her dark red lipstick and eyes. With her dark glasses gone, he noticed she wore mascara and eyeliner to make her eyes appear even larger and more mysterious, as though she were veiled. And only. He said, "Your art's truly incredible. I note you're very fond of naked women and angels."

"I should ease your fears. I am neither a lesbian nor religious fanatic, but naked women are the epitome of God's creation and I adore angels. My nude here is Mother Russia on her back in the White Night as two angels blow their trumpets to wake her from slumber."

"And why exactly are the angels waking Mother Russia?"

Natalya tilted her head coyly. "The interpretation of art lies with the beholder." She studied him for a second. "I suppose you hear this quite often, but you bear a strong resemblance to a more vigorous Ashley Wilkes from *Gone with the Wind*."

"Yes, I've heard that once or twice."

Natalya looked surprised. "Ah yes, you are having the joke with me. Very well. I don't understand why you rush your speech in English, which should easily roll off your tongue. You don't do it when you speak Russian."

This is so ingrained in me, I do it without noticing. "I'm a New Yorker, and we, by our nature, are impatient people. That's why we speak quickly."

"Interesting. As you noticed, being a person of infinite patience, I think before speaking."

"Major Iganiev said patience would benefit me."

"The former major shall have abundant time to practice what he says in a horrible prison in the Far North."

"Couldn't happen to a nicer guy."

"What?" She paused. "You are having another joke with me. I don't know how to take this, this humor of yours."

"Take it for the innocent fun it is."

"I'll attempt to do that. But now, my turn to be the elephant in the room. Because of my aura, you think me an imposter, largely, because it's different from yours. Also, I don't resemble either of my parents. And yet I promise you I'm the daughter of Sergei Dmitrovich Iskandarov, or, if you prefer, First Lieutenant Spencer Talbott, USAAF and Lady Charlotte Elizabeth Sternwood."

"I've been troubled by this. When I saw you in the first *Andronyi*, I thought you'd have red hair like my daughter and was surprised you didn't. And then, there's…"

"I understand your confusion. Over generations our genes have mutated. You resemble Iskandar and I'm what's known as pure Iskandarova. That is, I resemble Athaliaa, youngest of the triplet Colchi princesses who birthed our dynasty. When I was young, I felt badly to not have red hair. But as I've learned about Iskandarovas, I realized I'm as I'm supposed to be, like Olga and Verushka Sergeyvna. My aura's different from yours but was harmonious with both of our parents. And that's most important."

"What do you mean, 'harmonious'?"

"We were highly compatible because my aura was a blend of both my parents' auras and is different from any Iskandarova auras with which you're familiar. That's also because I'm different." She paused. "I suspect you and Penelope had incompatible auras because you had a child but no union."

"Possibly. Pen's aura was always there, just strong enough to be alluring, but no more. When she was an adolescent and, in her twenties, it was irresistible. Annie was born after a difficult pregnancy and that began fading her aura. By the time she died, it was virtually gone." Ashley shook his head. "While you've told me some interesting information, you've not proven you're whom you claim to be."

"Ah, you heard me say I'm different and now you think I stole your *tvarsch*."

"It had crossed my mind."

"What will it take to convince you of whom I am? Of course, it would be most inappropriate for me to reveal my scars and branding. I could ask you the same question, and I'll not accept solely seeing your passport. I know all too well how easily they're forged. I declare Iskandarov Truth for the duration of your stay and swear I'm as represented, Natalya Sergeyvna Iskandarova." She crossed herself.

"Under Iskandarov Truth, I'm Ashley Finlayson Cooper. Is that good enough?"

"Yes, I accept you are whom you think you are. But again, you're simply Ashlei."

"I'd like to believe you..."

"You can't be certain of me and, of course, *tvarsch* wouldn't help you. As I said in the car when I was uncertain you were listening to me, even though you've been to Moscow before, you are like a traveler to your country who has seen New York City and Washington, DC, and thinks he has seen America."

"True, I've tried to prepare myself."

"But you've no way of even imagining what's to come. T*varsch* is a gift and even a luxury on which you've become far too dependent. We'll focus on this after I return from your daughter's Ceremony."

"All right, going back to auras, I didn't know our mother, not being Iskandarova, had one."

She looked at him quizzically before saying, "Right then, you never actually met her, only her spirit visiting you when you were young. Yes, she has a strong aura, and, like mine, closer to the violet end of the spectrum. Unlike Iskandarov's, which are more to the red. Of course, I never saw her in her prime, but despite her dreadful treatment in the Gulag's mines and at the Institute, her physical beauty and optimism continually shone through. And although Svetlana Feliksovna claimed to be my mother, I knew Charlotte, who had been reduced to a household slave, was my true mother because I didn't resemble Svetlana Feliksovna in any way. Svetlana Polinkova's clearly her mother's daughter—coarse, vulgar and bosomy."

Nata's loosening up a bit, or perhaps, it's me. I can't contain my chest pain too much longer. "Now, please, tell me about Iskandar."

"No, not yet. I've something more important. You're clearly a gentleman of good character—when rested. I received a full report on your ordeal at the airport from our mole. I'm told you handled your interrogation with great courage."

"Bleu has a mole in George Farwell's operation?"

"Obviously, I'm not going to reveal who. For you, ignorance is the best and safest defense."

"Wise thinking. However, I know George very well. Once the diary has been delivered, he will also want the mole. And, right now, I don't like my chances in interrogation."

"I remind you that you have many friends here, known and unknown. I was giving you what you call 'the worst-case scenario.' There are many more optimistic outcomes."

"One more question about the French Embassy Reception the last time I was in Moscow. You were there with a rather large, tall gentleman."

"Minister Iskandarov. I sometimes substitute for his wife and my half-sister, Princess Rini, whom you spoke with at length in Paris."

"What else do you do for him?"

"I work with him as circumstances demand. Sometimes, there's much to be done and sometimes, nothing. Then I paint. I also handle situations, such as yours, which require special intervention. I enjoy Aleks's absolute trust and I don't sleep with him."

This revelation startled Ashley. *Does she sleep with anyone?*

"I see your reaction. It's all right. I'm happiest on my own because I've art to fill my life." She turned and studied the wing. "Yes, for now, it's complete." She turned and said, "Ashlei, excuse me. I've been somewhat distracted all day, but why did you not tell me of your wounds?"

"As you said, you already had a lot on your plate."

"Come now, I saw you wince when you entered my car and before the lift arrived. Do you now trust me?"

"Yes, but I don't see…"

"I've struggled with this all day, but in the end, you are my full brother and I can't let you suffer. This is something I was not yet going to reveal, but I trust you not to share this to anyone else. Agreed?"

"Agreed."

"Go to your room, remove your shoes, shirt and short pants, lie on your bed, put on your mask and call me."

"I feel it's only fair to warn you I'm not wearing underwear."

"Thank you for your warning. But since this is not sexual, it really doesn't matter. I'll wear my Ceremonial gown."

"You kept your Ceremonial gown after all these years?"

"I'll wear it tomorrow and for a long time to come. My gown is a great honor."

"Understood."

Ashley lay naked on his bed. He called Natalya, heard her and kept his eyes shut under the mask, knowing this was also another of her tests.

"Please lie still. This is going to hurt a bit." Then she ripped off his chest bandage, along with some hairs, which really hurt but he felt warm hands first on his wound and then his legs and whole body. Through leaks around his mask, the whole room seemed filled with white light. As the light eased into his mask, his pain subsided, and he felt lighter and lighter until he realized he was floating. *I can't remember feeling as relaxed, calm and pain-free in my life and, as a result, I also feel my erection such as I've not had since adolescence. Was this planned or accidental?*

He heard Natalya leaving the room as he slowly floated back onto the bed. If she has that kind of power, what else can she do? I must be extremely cautious, although I'm also tremendously grateful. What have I gotten myself into? He put his hand on where his chest wound had been and only a small scar remained.

5.

Later, when he reentered the kitchen, Natalya, at the sink, motioned him to sit at the large rough-hewn table. She washed her hands with an easy grace. She had changed into cut-off jeans, a sleeveless shirt with a deeply scooped neckline and no brassiere. A slight bit of mahogany nipple poked over the scoop's edge. He smiled when he caught a glimpse of the black hair of her armpits; it reminded him of *Olga, and it had been most erotic.*

"Please don't think I'm trying to be seductive. I'm not. Being safe, this is how I dress comfortably this time of year. I find wearing a brassiere still uncomfortable because of my whippings as a girl. Svetlana Feliksovna designed the knout lashes to wound in such a way they never properly heal. And, no, I don't know how she did that and wish to terminate this subject."

I've been around enough to know when a woman's being seductive and she's clearly not. Rather, she's testing me yet again to discover if I can resist ogling her. I'll use this time to alleviate her fears. "I don't know how but you certainly cured me. And you'll tell me your secret when the time's right. Now, as long as we're talking about pain, I've two questions about your wounds."

"As I said, I don't wish to speak further on this topic." She closed her eyes. "Oh, very well. You may ask, but if I regard your question as too personal, I'll not reply."

"In your *Andronyi*, I saw your three Cyrillic C branding for *Stalin, Svetlana and Soviet*. But what's the significance of it happening on your fifteenth birthday?"

"The date has no significance. She wished to make me a sexually and politically repugnant Iskandarova. Thus, I'd remain her sex slave. As usual with her, it was all about her power to do anything to anyone, justified because, in her mind, she was doing it for the people."

"Thanks for your candor. Secondly, I'm curious why you've not had plastic surgery."

"I've known Baroness Ulrika von Manteuffel for some twenty-five years or so. In the event, she told me she kept her long neck scar as a badge of honor. A reminder of all she had endured from the NKVD and triumphed over. I do the same." She paused. "I also have a most secret third reason."

She brought the vodka carafe when she sat at the table. For no apparent reason, she crossed herself as Ronnie did earlier. I'm surprised by that because she doesn't appear to be a religious person. But she has a small gold Orthodox cross around her neck, which was hidden before. Just like Olga's.

"Tell me about the squiggle on your Orthodox cross."

"Squiggle? This is a letter in the Cartvelian alphabet. That's all you need know at this point." She shook her head. "Squiggle, indeed."

Refilling their vodka glasses, she said something in Russian he did not understand After clicking, they emptied them. "That was the toast of 'The Order of The Orange Light.' Stop, I know you're trying to think of a joke for this."

"You're incorrect. What's The Order of The Orange Light? And why orange?"

"In the psychology of color and some folklore, orange is creativity and joy, also, a sense of general wellness and emotional energy. Orange is also controversial. You either love or hate it, no middle ground. In other words, the creative process."

"I never knew colors have their own psychology."

"Of course, they do. Everyone has a favorite color and colors they hate. The latter because it has negative connotations. Now, The Order had artists and writers from across Russia. I'd characterize them as going as far as they could without being sent to the Gulag. In *Moskva*, a group of them gathered around this table for years to discuss politics, philosophy and their works, which, even with their least controversial, never had full Kremlin sanction. The Order began way before the Khrushchev Thaw of 1956 and continued for many years. When I was a girl, I used to sometimes sit on the floor and listen to them." She beamed with pride. "Boris Leonidovich Pasternak sat in the very chair where you now sit. Dmitri Dmitrievich Shostakovich and Yevgeny Aleksandrovich Yevtushenko and Mikhail Afanasyevich Bulgakov often sat here until the small hours of the morning." She waved her hands in an encompassing gesture. "And those are only the artists with whom you are familiar. There are others we

hold dear such as the Cartvelian poets Bulat Okudzhava, Bel-
la Akhmadulina and Aleksandr Galich. They were all important
during that time." She held up her finger. "Can you recognize
this and when it was composed." She paused for a few moments
before reciting:

> This girl comes from New York
> Yet she does not belong to it.
> This girl is running past neon lights
> away from herself.
>
> To this girl the world seems odious-
> a moralist who has been howled down.
> It holds no more truths for her.
> Now the 'twist' alone is true.
>
> Everything strikes her as false,
> everything--from the Bible to the press.
> The Montagues exist, and the Capulets,
> but there are no Romeos and Juliets.
>
> Wanders, as if from bar to bar,
> wrapped in thought, unsocial,
> and the city spreads underneath
> in all its hard-hearted beauty.

"Although I've heard this before, I don't recall the poet. I
would guess Yevtushenko. And with his reference to the Twist
dance craze, this is from the early sixties."

"Very good. Some lines from Yevtushenko's *Girl Beatnik.* I
know many condemn Yevgeny Aleksandrovich for becoming too
friendly with the regime. But a writer or artist has a primary obligation of surviving to tell the truth and, as long as the majority of
their work remains honest, I think they may be forgiven."

"Are you speaking academically or, perhaps, as one who
has been criticized?"

"Good question. I should say some of each. I learned from
my mentor long ago, the human soul needs art. Some need to produce it and some need to consume it. And both are equally valid,

and regardless of what regime has power, this truth may never be denied, at least, for long."

"I envy you your art. I wish I had something similar."

"Is not international law enough for you? There are few more heroic undertakings than working for that better world."

Ashley shrugged. "Progress is so gradual and frustrating. In addition, when peace has been achieved here, it's lost there. Very easy to become discouraged. With your art, you see results in a relatively short time. That's what I envy."

"My art is only for my amusement and that of my clients. Unlike me, what you do has consequence and great meaning."

"Perhaps. How did you come to own this flat?"

"It belonged to my mentor, Bayta, a wonderful Iskandarova *Kyria, a Lady,* who had never been blessed with children. She was like a mother to me and I like a daughter to her. In her will, she bequeathed the flat to me and I moved in before the authorities discovered she was dead—an old Moscow custom. She was also a significant poet and hostess of The Orange Light. She never told me, but I know her beauty attracted many of the artists. I also believe she was intimate with many of them." She blushed slightly as she rose and began busily stirring pots on the stove, tasting and adding ingredients.

Her maidenly blush was deliberately cute. Clever. "What can I do to help?"

"You'll be in charge of vodka and wine." She looked at her empty glass. "I need a refill and you should open the wine. There's a corkscrew in the drawer over there."

After opening the wine, Ashley watched as she became completely involved in her cooking. Her dampened face, chest and arms glistened in the light, which Ashley found her naturalness reassuring and felt himself relaxing even more happy to be with such a surprising woman. *Yes, there were women in New York, both before, during and after my marriage, beautiful, independent and sophisticated, who tried to spin their webs around me. But I knew their games and tricks. However, none of them remotely had this woman's passion. Perhaps, that passion is the unifying characteristic of the Iskandarovs. What I previously took as her obnoxious arrogance, I now recognize as her expectation of excellence in herself and others.* He momentarily closed his eyes. *I need to watch my alcohol consumption but still keep pace with her. I must also be on guard, despite her protestations, for a jealous lover lurking somewhere.*

Now, when will my half-sister, Anghelina, begin her Gulag diary incentives? No, she'll not find me here. In New York, she told him she would mercy kill him if things became too bad. But she would be the judge of that, and her assessment might not agree with his. Her madness could become uncontrolled at any time which frightened him.

But he began to forget all this as the vodka took effect and standing close to Natalya, he became entranced by her unfathomable black eyes. They were, at once, knowing and yet held a deep sadness from her hard life. *I'll be patient. All would be revealed here in the East at an appropriate time."*

She finished her vodka. "Dinner smells ready. We're having traditional Cartvelian food with Tvishi wine, which we had earlier. It's still popular in Russia, unfortunately because it was Monster Stalin's favorite." She placed a tray with many small plates before him: fried eggplant with walnut sauce, pork sausage, meatballs and cornbread with walnuts, pepper skin stuffed with walnuts and what appeared to be corn porridge, something similar to lasagna, lamb, pork, turkey and chicken in various sauces and two types of bread. *The Cartvelians really love walnuts. Walnuts remind me of little plaque-encrusted brains.* He deeply inhaled the collective aromas, which comforted him. "My mouth's watering."

"Good, break off some bread and begin. Don't wait for me."

Uncomfortable starting without her, he waited

After sitting, she asked, "Tell me what you know of the Sakartvelo?"

I need to focus and concentrate on her question, not eyes. "Ah, let me think." He took a deep breath. "Sakartvelo, known as Georgia in the West, in the South Caucasus located between the Black and Caspian Seas. Joined the Russian Empire voluntarily for protection against Muslims in, I believe, 1801. Also, the birthplace of Stalin. That's substantially all I know. But ask me about Russian history some time."

"That's adequate, but now, please indulge me by listening to my history lesson. It is as well where Jason and the Argonauts sought the Golden Fleece with the help of Colchi princess Medea. We have ancient ties to the Mediterranean peoples and are located in the Caucasus Mountains, original home of the Caucasian race. For thirteen hundred years until the seventh century A.D., we were in continuous contact with the Greeks, who also, in the fourth century, converted us to Orthodox Christianity. In the seventh century, Muslim Arabs and then Turks conquered us and remained our masters for five hundred years. For slightly more than a century, we maintained an independent kingdom, until the thirteenth century, when the darkness of the Mongols' Golden Horde began another five hundred years of misery, murder, rape and slavery. In the eighteenth, we again fell under the Turks for about fifty years before regaining independence. As you mentioned, in 1801, we voluntarily joined Russia. In 1918, we had three years of independence. And now, we are again independent."

"I'm sorry—such a sad history."

"Our culture has survived great adversity, which made us stronger. That's one reason why we test those who would join us."

"Yes, when you are its defending edge, this gives such people a much stronger attachment to their culture."

Her brow wrinkled. "I don't understand."

"Alexander of Macedonia, Napoleon of Corsica, Hitler of Austria, and Stalin of Georgia were all born far from center of their cultures yet carried them far and wide."

"Interesting." She sipped her vodka. "Permit me to warn you of Minister Iskandarov, who has an almost maniacal hatred of Muslims. As do many from the Sakartvelo for an obvious reason. Now, Minister Iskandarov always compiles extensive dossiers on those he is going to meet. One of my projects was the collection of your information."

"That hardly seems fair."

"Life's not fair. I thought I'd tell you some facts about brother to help prepare you."

"Why would you do that for me?"

"I've an intense sense of justice and fairness."

"But the minister's also your employer."

"He enjoys a good discussion with a worthy opponent. So, I shall tell you, most candidly, he'll, under no circumstances, agree to the L'Enfant Initiative."

Natalya's candor felt like a slap across his face. "Why not?"

"As you know, Russia's support of Serbia proved one of the precipitating causes of World War I. That tie emphatically remains. Brother Aleks should be delighted if Serbian Ethnic Cleansing of the entire Balkans continued unabated. Hence, I wish you success."

"I've always relished a good challenge."

"Quite." Her slight smile soon disappeared but not from her eyes. "That's why I told you."

"We shall see then." I'm confident Minister Iskandarov can be made to see the unreasonableness of his position. He smiled. "Tell me about yourself."

"Why? There's no mystery about me. I'm as an open book. What do you wish to know?"

"Everything."

"Then after dinner, you may explore my flat as fully as you desire, and no doors shall be locked. I'll not make the mistake God made at Eden about the Tree of Knowledge. I'm going to trust you to know what's private and what's open to discussion."

She cleared the table, put the dishes in the sink and poured the last of the wine before going to the refrigerator. She returned with a lacquered black tray with a red teapot and two small cups and two nut and raisin crème caramels.

Ashley found the desert extraordinary and complimented her on her cooking. But she was totally absorbed in the preparation and serving of the extremely sweet tea.

After Ashley put the pots in the refrigerator and she finished washing the plates, they returned to the table and he said, "I don't like the idea of being Ashlei. What am I not getting?

"That's for you to discover. But then, you, at almost fifty, are most unusual. You should have had your manhood Ceremony at eighteen to become Of the Iskandarov and fulfilled the Covenant before you began Harvard University. No, I don't know any particulars of the men's Ceremony. Had you done so, Olga Sergeyvna could've completed your knowledge and would probably still been alive today." She crossed herself. "And she would, had she not decided to get pregnant with you. No. On second thought, she should've left you completely alone. You, with no background, weren't ready for the training she gave you and also because she couldn't tell you everything you needed. Honestly, I've never been able to fathom why our grandfather, Dmitri Sergeyovich, decided you were to be the Hidden One. Or why we even require one. I've heard many explanations, but none make sense."

"Verushka explained it in the context of Grandmother Countess Sophia's prophesy that the momentous events couldn't begin until my stepfather David Cooper died. I feel very ambiguous about our father's Gulag diary for reasons I can't share right now."

"As you spend more time with us, things shall become clearer. But only if you commit to us." She sipped her wine. "Candidly, I don't think you're deeply committed at all. As I said earlier, you're like a visitor, a tourist."

This is getting spooky. How does she know about my Plan B to return to The Firm with a signed L'Enfant Treaty? Then all would be forgiven and with the Gulag diary still hidden because both Charles Drew and George Farwell would be satisfied. L'Enfant's my project and I must see it through. "I don't know what you mean."

"Yes, you do. And you've an especially crucial decision to make. But now isn't the time." Supporting her head with one hand on the table, she looked at her wine glass before finishing its content and began:

"And every evening my only friend is mirrored in my wineglass
and like myself, is subdued and dazed by the tart and mysterious liquor."

Ashley, uninvited, continued,

"And nearby, sleepy waiters hang about beside the adjoining tables, while drunkards, with rabbit-like eyes, shout: In vino veritas. And every evening at the appointed hour, or is this only a dream that I see? The figure of a girl swathed in silk—"

Natalya closed her eyes.

"Moves across the misted window. And slowly passing among the drunkards, always unescorted breathing perfumes and mists, she sits down alone by the window."

He smiled adding:

"Her resilient silks, her hat with its black plumes, and her narrow hand adorned with rings exhale an air of ancient legends. Entranced by this strange nearness, I look through a dark veil and see an enchanted shore and an enchanted distance."

Her words sounded a little slurred as she finished.

"Hidden mysteries are entrusted to me, someone's sun has been committed to my care; and the tart wine has pierced all the convolutions of my soul. And the drooping ostrich plumes wave in my brain, and blue fathomless eyes flower on a distant shore. A treasure lies buried in my soul and the key is entrusted to me alone. You are right, you drunken monster; I know: truth lies in wine."

Natalya threw her head back and laughed. "Yes, we know even more truth lies in vodka. Now, why did not Alexandr Alexandrovich Blok, a Russian, not know this?" She laughed even harder as tears began to wet her cheeks. Her laughter was so contagious that Ashley laughed too as if it were the most brilliant and funniest line to ever escape human lips. It felt almost like a laughing climax growing to a peak before slowly sputtering out to silence. After a few minutes, he looked into her eyes and moved his fingers out to her as she did the same. When they touched, he felt an electricity between them. *This is insane, I can't be falling in love with someone I just met today.* No, he looked deeply into her eyes until he realized he had known her since his adolescence when he received *tvarsch*. She was his full sister and yet, they were so dissimilar. Nonetheless, he knew the time had come. He paid attention to the music—Alexander Borodin's Polovtsian *Dances*. He rose and walked around the small table until he stood over her. She rose to meet him. They touched their lips tentatively, a bit too chastely for Ashley, so he kissed her deeply, loving the apricot taste of her mouth. And she kissed back harder, pressing her breasts against his chest. Her eyes, joyful and yet seductive, closed and her left hand held his neck. He was becoming aroused in a way he had not been in many years. He felt the ridged scaring on her back but did not remove his hand. She reopened her eyes and pulled away. Ashley kept his hand on her back. "You're so beautiful."

"I'm not beautiful."

"Don't you know beauty, like art, is in the eye of the beholder?"

"I wager you tell that to all your girls." But her eyes said, *You are the one I have been waiting for*.

"Never mind them. You're the special one with your bright aura, your amazing eyes, and your whole wonderful being."

"Thank you, Brother. I am, right now, by all means, not rejecting you. In truth, I have waited patiently for this time. And now that it has happened, we must part for now. Our time is not yet at hand. Have no fear, it's close. When it arrives, we shall be magnificent together. But, now, we must say goodnight and dream the most wonderful dreams of all that shall be ours in the future. Good night, dearest Brother, good night."

"Good night, Sister Natalya."

She walked unsteadily to her room and the light under her door remained on for several minutes. He assumed their time would be right when she entered *phygynaya* and would be fertile. But when would that be? Later tonight, later this week, or even next month? She said when the time was right, it would happen. Standing shakily, inebriated from the vodka but too stimulated to sleep, he further explored her studio, guided by the White Night, which came through the large open windows above. As he passed through, her ghostly silk batiks again swayed in a light movement of air. An Alexandr Blok poem, as it had been long ago with Olga Sergeyvna, had been their breakthrough. Of course, the wine and vodka helped Natalya relax to the point where, surely being used to hard drinking, she still might pay him a surprise visit tonight. *Wishful thinking—don't get your hopes up.*

He came to a closed door with a small sign saying *Family* in Cyrillic. Going into the light blue room, thirty photographs were arranged in three neat rows on the walls. It began with their grandparents, Countess Sophia and Colonel Dmitri in their regalia, then Charlotte and Spencer in their respective uniforms. There were several of Olga and Verushka as teenagers and older, Aleks and Rini upon graduation from Moscow University, Natalya in a black robe for her Ceremony and a snowy one afterwards. Also, one of her in a school uniform with a very attractive, well-dressed lady, who must be Bayta. There were several with Natalya as a ballerina both in toes up poses and performing with others on a large stage. Natalya, late-term pregnant, smiled with her Polinkov husband and then both with their young twin girls. And pictures of her husband in his cosmonaut space suit and officer's uniform. In a black and white picture Bayta wore a silver fox fur over an elegant dark gown. But he knew from her expression, a combination of a mischievous smile coupled with come-hither eyes, this was an inside joke. Finally, there was a tall woman wearing dark glasses in a white nun's habit both with Natalya and Bayta and by herself. This had to be his mother, Charlotte Sternwood. The rest of the people he could not identify. But as he was leaving, he found a familiar face, Princess Xenia

Iskandarova—both by herself and with her husband and a boat-load of children on a placid lake. Cosette had told him in Paris no pictures of Xenia and her family remained, having all been destroyed. And yet, somehow, Natalya had obtained these.

On the door of the next room he read: *Hell—The Personal Collection of Colonel Svetlana Feliksovna Polinkova.* He took a deep breath before going in. The room was covered in pictures of naked men and women, most of whom were pregnant. He only recognized Sergei and Charlotte, Natalya and Sainte Xenia. He also noted that Svetlana Feliksovna appeared twice, once pregnant, presumably with Aleks and Rini and once with a young Natalya. They were both naked and she was squeezing Natalya's right breast in a very proprietary way and Natalya's left breast showed very clearly her roughly three-inch diameter branding. *I wonder why such a private woman keeps and even displays such a photograph.* He was shocked that all the Mongolian guards were castrated and looked a second time to make sure he was right. He left the room shaken and felt great gratitude that he had not ex-perienced the Institute. *Heaven* was posted on the next door and he eagerly went in. It had been sound-proofed and painted silver, with only a red yoga mat in the middle of the floor. Beyond med-itation, he had no idea what its purpose might be.

He felt sleepy, returned to his room and undressed. In bed, he felt he had done the absolute proper thing in agreeing with Natalya to stop when they did. She had her reasons and he had his. He smiled as sleep swept over him.

FIVE

Saturday, 5 June 1993, Moscow & Novo Ogarevo

1.

Ashley awoke about half-past seven, a bit hungover but feeling wonderful because Natalya had come to his bed. She had whispered for him to keep his mask on before straddling him and vigorously driving to an intense mutual, if muffled, climax. It had been strange and wonderful. He understood about the mask. *She could be bold enough to come to me but still be insecure about her branding and whip scars.* Her whispering and the hushed climax, in the privacy of her own studio, seemed unusual but whatever a lady wants in bed he knew to give her. He had desperately wanted her to stay but before he could say anything, she kissed him and slipped away. *Clearly, not ready for such togetherness.*

Afterwards, he felt deeply and pleasantly tired, raising the duvet so he could again relish her divine scent. But he would not rush an encore because her quick departure had to be interpreted as a message to proceed slowly. And he fell asleep wondering how they would handle this in the morning. As a veteran of many mornings-after, he knew her most likely morning response—denial.

Rising from his bed, he thought, But now, I've got to get control of myself. I can start by reading Svetlana Polinkova's peace proposal. That's certainly tiresome enough to calm me down. After reading it, he saw no reason to go forward. Wrapped in his blue towel, he headed for the shower to regretfully wash off her lovely scent and get focused on his meeting with brother Aleks.

Surprised to see Natalya in her white Ceremonial robe, he cheerily said "Good morning, Nata, I checked Svetlana's proposal and there's nothing of interest there."

"I don't think it appropriate, based on a single kiss, for you to feel you can parade around here almost naked."

"But it's based on so much more than that."

She came closer. "I don't understand what you're saying. Please explain. I... Wait, I smell an Iska on you."

"Naturally," he said, laughing. "Since you came and had your wicked way with me last night."

"Brother, I confess I was tempted to do as you say, but I quickly fell into deep wonderful sleep. And when I awoke, I was glad I hadn't because I usually don't engage in meaningless intercourse. In the event, do you not think I know my own scent? This is not it."

"What? This is crazy," he said, half expecting her to smile and reveal that she was joking. Then who was that with me last night in this fortress, a succubus?"

She stared at him and he watched pain drain color from her face. She spoke quietly "I have no idea beyond the unmistakable scent of another Iska." She turned away. "I don't wish to believe you betrayed me and yet I sense something awful has happened."

"Come on, don't be coy, you can admit it was you. There's no shame and I remind you we're both bound by Iskandarov Truth."

"I speak the truth."

"As do I."

"I don't know whether I am angrier that some Iska seduced you behind my back or she defeated my vaunted security." She breathed deeply. "You don't know what this means. Some other Iska has claimed you as her own."

"What the hell is going on here?"

"It's a warning for others to leave you alone."

"This is insane. Are you seriously saying some Iska came in here and had her way?"

"It would appear so."

"Don't I get any say in this?"

"If you commit to me, then that voids her claim."

"How much time do I have to commit?"

"Why do you care? I'm perfectly aware, as we have discussed, you can't truly commit to me. And I understand, to a degree, why you can't."

"You're so calm. If what you say is true, it's a kind of rape. Wouldn't you be more incensed?"

With her eyes full of tears, she said, "I suppose I must be used to these ungodly horrors."

"Well, I'm not used to them. If this is one of your tests, it's an outrage."

"There's only one thing to do and that's to calm down. Now, please go shower. I can't bear her scent on you. I'll be in my Heaven Room."

Numb, Ashley went toward the bathroom. Surely, this woman's propriety knows no bounds, even to the point of self-delusion. She'll deny what really happened forever. Unless what she says is true. In any case, our relationship is in ruins. After she drops me off at Aleks's office, I'll probably never see her again.

2.

After another challenging shower, Ashley returned to his room and hearing nothing, assumed Natalya remained in her sanctuary. *I was too hard on her. She's a proud woman who wishes to maintain she's not the type to enter a man's bed without invitation. And yet, at the same time, I've realized I can't live without this woman, quirks and all. The people who told me we had to get together can't all be wrong. Now, if there were another Iska claiming me, she would make herself known and, at least, leave me a clue.*

While getting into his suit pants, he noticed a fountain pen on a notepad in the middle of the polished bureau. One the notepad was written:

Ashley, you once asked me what my Iskandarova
gift was. When I told you I did not know, I broke our
Iskandarov Truth, but I had good reasons. You may
also remember I told you I was particularly good
at finding people who do not wish to be found. My
gift is I'm highly attuned to people and especially
to Iskandarovs because of our auras. That was how
I found you and I immediately knew you did not
have tvarsch and this will greatly complicate your
searching for our father's diary. In fact, without it,
you are virtually worthless. But I am skeptical the
diary even exists. No matter. Frankly, your lack of
tvarsch does not matter, whether you find the diary
or not, you will be killed at some point. And that is
where I come in. You remain under my protection.
I have promised a mercy killing if you ever faced
the unendurable. George Farwell has an incredibly
gruesome and horrific fate in store for you.

Second confession. I'm in phygynaya right now. I
know you've encountered this before with Ronnie
Cooper. I wasn't to be denied and I am certain I am
pregnant. I loved your cock, which was the only part
of you actively involved. I look forward to a rematch
with all of you participating, Now, I have a new plan.
I will do my best to help you escape death because
I want more babies with you. I will be keeping tabs
on you and Natalya, if you need her help. The sooner
you find the diary, the better for both of you. The
clock begins ticking the day after tomorrow. Use your
time wisely. Love, Anghelina.

P.S. Very careless of Natalya to leave those large
windows over her studio open at night.

So, Natalya was right. This is crazy. Why me? Anghelina
never showed me any interest in New York but I sense she would
have done this absent my affair with Lana. And why, for reasons
unknown, does she want to humiliate Natalya. Also, if, as her

note claims, she was in phygynaya, she could indeed be pregnant. He folded her note and put it in his pants pocket.

Coming into the kitchen without his tie and suit jacket, Natalya was sipping pensively from a steaming mug of coffee. She handed one to him before looking up. "I know who did this. Since it can't be Rosalita in the Caves, it has to be Anghelina DelaVega. She and her sister are the only Iskas I know who, being Cuban DI trained, have the ability to get past my security. Of course, I stupidly left the tall windows in the atrium open and I'm certain she simply rappelled down. When I saw her at the airport, I read her and didn't like what I found. She's clearly wicked enough to want to humiliate me in this way and, from the way you described your encounter, you as well."

"You're right, as usual. I found her note." He took it from his pocket and handed it to Natalya before sipping his coffee. She read it twice then handed it back and he returned it to his pocket.

"This is even worse than I imagined. She says you're under her protection. First, are you aware of this?"

"We briefly discussed it back in New York."

"Do you think she has the power to enforce this?"

"I would never underestimate her."

"Agreed. Again, did she formally proclaim her protection?"

"It just came up in conversation."

"You now have a dilemma. If you deny her claim, she'll likely revoke her protection. And the next time she comes to visit, she may kidnap or even kill you. We'll of course, do our best to protect you, but there can be no guarantees."

"I'll have to take my chances."

"We need you alive. I'm curious. You can't commit to me because of your desire for a signed L'Enfant Treaty. You've substantially given up most of your past life and yet you cling to this last shred."

"There are many reasons, too many to…"

"You still fear me, do you not?"

"Your magical healing scared me. If you can do that, what else can you do?"

"From my perspective, I don't feel I may trust you. Only your commitment shall solve that."

"Round and round we go. For what it's worth, I do love you."

"I know. And I love you as well. We're meant to be together. I can also believe since she and I are physically similar, you with your mask on could think Anghelina was me, assuming you've never been intimate with her before."

"The thought never crossed my mind."

"I can't blame you for this happening. I'm to blame for leaving open windows to release the heat. Also, this is my punishment for being vain and boasting of my superior security and I accept that."

"I knew something was wrong and I should've removed my mask to check."

"Absent *tvarsch*, your actions are no longer an issue." She sipped her coffee. "When you told me of your affair with Svetlana, that, truthfully made me less eager to become intimate with you. However, by comparison, that was an abstraction. I can't drive Anghelina's scent from my nostrils and don't know if I ever shall. Weighing all the other factors, if we try to be intimate, she shall always come between us. Although such refusal of you breaks my heart." Tears streaked her mascara.

"Nata, we can work this out. I promise you."

"No. It's for the best. I'm the wrong mentor for you. You'll find someone better."

"But you said you were honor bound to mentor me."

"Perhaps, I may still do that, but it would be most difficult. I ask you to release me from my oath."

"For the present, we should do nothing to change our situation."

"True." She finished her coffee. "Come, we must leave after we finish our toilet."

They stood and hugged.

"Nata…"

She placed a finger on his lips before leaving.

Alone, Ashley let his tears flow. *I must commit to her but how can I when I don't yet know what I want, her or L'Enfant? Can't have both.*

Ashley finished dressing and silently followed Natalya to the lift, their luggage in tow. He focused on the metallic sound of the gears, the squeal of the gate and the sound of the lift hitting bottom.

Once in the car, he saw that Natalya's eyes were still red and wet, before she shook her head and turned to focus on the road. Despite the rain, Natalya put on her dark glasses to shut him out. Realizing there would be no conversation, Ashley sat, deep in thought. *Our tenuous relationship's shattered. The only question being how long? Anywhere from five minutes to eternity. Again, I find myself in limbo, stuck between my old life and the person, as Nata said, I'm becoming. While I'm uneasy about my new identity, I want to end my old self on the best possible terms by getting L'Enfant signed for The Firm.* Most of all, this is my project and I want to see it through. Finishing everything I began has been deeply imbedded in me since I began at age six, school at Buckley. Again, I recall *Ronnie's question at her cottage.* 'If you don't know who you are, what else matters?' Ronnie, I still don't know, and, without Nata, I may never. But now, I need to compartmentalize this and *move to focus on Aleks.*

* * *

As they approached a tall, whitewashed wall topped with rolls of concertina wire and imbedded glass shards, the black iron gate swung open and two armed sentries came to attention. The gate had a Cyrillic gold plaque, *People's Institute of Genetic Research.* He felt the car bump along the cracked and potholed concrete driveway and did not like Natalya bringing him to this horrible place where his parents had been tortured. She stopped under the dacha's roofed entrance. A man in a blue suit came out and took Ashley's suitcase from the trunk. Ashley turned and Natalya was staring straight ahead leaning close to the steering wheel, her pallid hands clenching its top half.

"Nata, come back, please." With no response, he left the car, briefcase in hand and did not look back. When he came near the front door, he watched her drive through the gate. *Well, she's gone and there's nothing further I can do. I must focus on implementing Plan B and this meeting is key. Wow! My tvarsch has returned. Did Nata suppress it or had someone or something else?*

3.

He walked with the blue-suited man in tow to the dacha's ornate baroque facade, which had been freshly restored. Once the door opened, a butler welcomed him as "Monsieur *Avocat* Cooper" and introduced himself as "Feodor." He escorted Ashley through an ornate foyer with a ceiling of angels and cherubim. The anteroom, in the process of being restored, had drop cloths everywhere. Down a hallway to the right, the walls and ceilings remained a dull institutional gray. Turning to the left, he came into an enormous dining room with a long banquet table.

Next to it, another man taller than Ashley stood with dark and curly slicked-down hair, wearing a neatly trimmed van dyke. A well-tailored black suit minimized his large stomach. As with any negotiation, Ashley focused first on his eyes, which shone clear and confident. He came over, embraced Ashley in an all-consuming bear hug and kissed him on the lips and cheeks. Speaking with a slight English accent, he said, "Mr. Cooper, good to meet you. I'm Aleksandr Sergeyovich Iskandarov." He bowed slightly. "Terribly sorry about that nasty business yesterday. Had I not been in Sakartvelo…"

Ashley, still recovering from the kiss, said, "It's all right."

"That's quite sporting of you." He motioned for Ashley to sit at a smaller table about ten feet from the larger one and held up a silver coffee pot.

While Aleksandr poured, Ashley sat with his briefcase next to his feet. "I apologize about all the clutter. We're still restoring this place after the previous owner." His voice sounded vaguely familiar, but Ashley could not place it. Adding cream, Aleksandr smiled, "I think in a spirit of fraternalism, we should call each other by our first names. I'm Aleks."

"As you doubtless know, I'm Ash to my friends." He still thought it curious that this man had not chosen the usual Russian diminutive of Alexandr, "Sasha" Or, perhaps he had. *I wonder if Sasha, my Moscow phone contact, actually exists.*

"I didn't eat very much on my flight from the Sakartvelo and I'm starved." He rang for Feodor who brought in two large cut crystal bowls of mixed fruits.

As they ate, Aleks said, "I love British English, in large part, because my tutor, educated at Oxford, was a devout English Communist. In my professional capacity as Foreign Affairs Minister for the Near South, I've had to learn American English. So, really, all that remains is the accent and the odd word."

"Then I don't expect your assistant, my Gules Russian contact, Sasha, will join us because he doesn't exist. Very clever, by the way, but his Russian accent was a bit over the top."

"Vell, of course, dahling, it vas me." He laughed. "I learned a long time ago, always give a client what they expect and want."

"So, given your position, for what areas are you responsible?"

"Balkans and all the way east to the gates of China. I originally secured my position because my mother vouched for me. I could be the primary foreign affairs minister. But being a primary minister remains a dangerous position often leading to death. I prefer to work one-on-one with people at various levels of government. Exchanging favors. That sort of thing."

"You're a freewheeling agent then?"

"Plus, I have my duties as Prince of the Iskandarov as well."

"Thank you for trusting me with all this information."

"Of course, I feel as though I've known you for a long time. After all, I've been keeping tabs on you since even before you joined Gules, Argent and Or as an associate back in the seventies. You've a most impressive résumé and your senior partnership was well earned."

"Thank you again." This is curious, he seems to accept me at face value. No tests.

Ashley served himself scrambled eggs with caviar, three assorted sausages, and buttered rye toast from a buffet table. Although hungry, he ate sparingly.

Aleks piled three times the amount of food on his plate than Ashley had taken, and with mouth full, asked, "Has our Nata made you as comfortable as possible? I wanted you to stay here, but she insisted upon her studio."

"She made me feel right at home. She's a very good cook."

"I feel it only fair to warn you that she employs a cook, who starts her dishes. But now down to cases. As Nata must have told you, my government, in all likelihood, can't support your L'Enfant Initiative."

"Then why are you meeting with me?"

"We both know this isn't the only reason you're here. No matter. Your reputation for fairness and brilliance precedes you. I understand that this initiative is important to you and your government and I wished to have a fair hearing before I made a final decision."

"Thank you, Aleks. You're a fair man as I suspected."

"Not always easy in the current environment. I'm pleased *tvarsch* has recently returned to you." He smiled. "Also, in the interest of full disclosure, Nata called me early this morning with her report."

"What time?"

"When she first awoke. Around seven."

Good, Aleks knows nothing about our dispute. I may tell him about it later. "You know, I was literally lost without *tvarsch*. Since you must have it as well, have you ever lost it, like I did?"

"Never." He paused, deep in thought. "Ash, there are forces here in Russia that can be immensely powerful and disruptive. They used to be everywhere and even common. But in the West, they've almost disappeared. Magic, both black and white, for example."

"Are you saying it was magic that blocked *tvarsch*?"

"I'm simply saying when you try to discover how it happened, cast a broader net than you normally would."

Aleks was proving to be a sophisticated and complex man, who had learned, probably in childhood, how to say something seemingly neutral and mean something different or even the opposite. Ashley would have to start listening to him even more carefully. "Good advice."

Aleks smiled. "Do you like the theater, Ash?"

"Yes, my wife and I went regularly during the season."

"Now, let us suppose there were a blizzard in New York, and you were late arriving at the theater for an unfamiliar murder mystery, and you're pulling for the most appealing character. At the end of the play, it's revealed that he's the villain. How would you feel?"

Ashley, ready for this question, smiled. "I know the Serbs and Croats were once one tribe, but when Diocletian divided the Roman Empire into east and west, the dividing line ran right through their tribal lands. In time, the eastern group, the Serbs, looked to Constantinople and, ultimately, Moscow for their inspiration, choosing Orthodox Christianity and the Cyrillic alphabet. While the western group, the Croats, favored Rome and ultimately Germany for their Catholicism and alphabet. These differences, as time went on, resulted in mounting bad blood between the brother tribes. Then, in the fifteenth century the Ottoman Turk conquered Bosnia and made it a Muslim stronghold by originally forced conversions of many of the Bosnian, Croatian and Serbian nobility. In a relatively small space we have Roman Catholic, Serbian Orthodox and Muslim all living and fighting a three-sided power struggle for domination right in the heart of the Balkans. A region that Churchill said, 'Produces more history than they can consume locally.' Then during World War II, the Croatian *Ustashe* allied with the Germans attempted to kill all the Serbs with a ferocity that scared even the ardent Nazis. So, clearly the Serbs felt justified to return the favor in the current war. And today, despite how we may personally feel about the players, who all have blood-soaked hands, we must maintain a semblance of peace in the Balkans before the war spirals out of control as it did in 1914."

"You know your history." They ate for a while without speaking because Aleks appeared to be in deep thought. After clearing his plate, he said, "Let's adjourn to my study, where we may continue undisturbed."

He led Ashley to a light and airy bookcase-lined room with a spectacular view of formal gardens and a tall hedge beyond. On the high ceiling, naked Rubenesque blondes frolicked in the clouds. Feodor appeared with a silver samovar and Aleks prepared tea, sweetened with marmalade, served in silver-handled crystal glasses.

For the next two hours, Ashley, without notes from his briefcase, made what he considered the presentation of his career, despite his own reservations about the Initiative. When he had finished, Aleks asked, "Yes, you have made some excellent points. And in rebuttal, I have only one question—tell me why Russia should be concerned if there's a general war in the Balkans or if it spreads into Europe?"

"Who is to say it will only spread to Europe? Conflict, like water flowing downhill, will always seek the easiest route. Or, in this case, the most unstable region. Western Europe is very stable politically and so I would suggest to you the most vulnerable region, on your doorstep, after the Balkans, is Eastern Europe and the Caucasus. There's a brutal civil war going on in Sakartvelo. Don't forget, there's the Nagoro-Karabakh War where Armenians and Azeries are slaughtering each other with already tens of thousands of dead. Either of these could provoke a larger conflict."

"Ash, I have to disagree on both accounts. First, the Cartvelian war is over creating a non-Communist and non-Russian leadership. As for the nasty Nagoro-Karabakh War, we're supplying both sides and we've managed to limit its media exposure."

"The Great Game raises its ugly head," said Ashley.

Aleks looked at him seriously. "I do not mean to minimize the brutality, but they're part of the long ongoing Christian-Muslim struggle. If we were supplying only Armenians, then someone else, like the Chinese, would be supplying the Azeris and it could easily escalate and engulf the entire region."

"Let's move to another scenario. Muslims in the former Soviet republics, in solidarity with their Bosnian brothers, might seek to revenge themselves on Russia, the Serbian protector. We're already seeing unrest in your south and that could easily escalate. Then there's Afghanistan. There, the recent Soviet occupation created the seeds of Muslim extremism. It's not beyond imagination the recently victorious *Mujahedeen* might feel the need to help their Muslim brethren by attacking Russia, guerilla or terrorist style. And, if the Soviet Army's performance in Afghanistan was any indication of its mettle, that could be a huge problem for your government in Moscow."

Aleks rose. "You're plainspoken as expected. I respect a man who speaks his mind. Always interesting to see a problem from a completely unfamiliar perspective. I'll take this under advisement. I'm not saying I'll endorse this initiative, but I may not impede it, either." He shook his head. "I know you were attacked yesterday, coming out of the Metropol, by three hotheads who felt you were betraying our little Serb brothers. It seems there's always a constituency for violence on virtually any question affecting the Russian state these days." Aleks went to a bookcase. "I greatly admire *Profiles in Courage* by your president, Mr. John F. Kennedy. I've always been impressed by the chapter on Kansas Senator Edmund G. Ross who did not vote to impeach your president, Mr. Andrew Johnson, even though it cost him his career and virtually everything else." He tapped his forehead. "Perhaps, like him, I'll risk all to produce a greater good."

"Aleks, one thing I've never understood is why the country of Georgia has two names. In fact, I don't even know why we call it 'Georgia' when we already have a state called that."

"Sakartvelo is where St. George slew the dragon, hence the name. Since you aspire to join us, you need to know a great deal more about the country and, especially, its language, which often comes in very handy for speaking privately. Nata in her report told me you know truly little about the country, which surprised me. I would have thought Verushka Sergeyvna would've instructed you."

"While I obviously knew the country existed, my primary focus since forever has been Russia. But again, why the name?"

"I suggest you ask the Swiss. They call their homeland 'Helvetia.' It's a country's right to name itself. As a Cartvelian patriot, I'm proud to call it the Sakartvelo."

"Point taken."

"Now let's speak of the other reason you came to Russia to find your family roots."

"Like a typical naïve Yank?"

Aleks grinned, "One thing that I can guarantee is that you have a motherload of family. But first it's necessary for you to understand the secret you Americans and your allies call 'Iron Cage'"

Ashley leaned forward.

"The defeat of the German Sixth Army at Stalingrad was, as every Russian schoolboy knows, the reason Hitler lost World War II. In truth, only Hitler's inability to use the tremendous Russian and ethnic hatreds against the Stalin *clique* cost Germany the war. Despite what some of his own senior officers and experts, like our grandfather Dmitri Sergeyovich, were telling him, the fool made the Germans more hated than Stalin." He shook his head. "Due to Stalin's own stupidity, the cost of victory was appalling. Russia lost twenty-one million civilians, more or less, in addition to almost fourteen million troops in the so-called 'Great Patriotic War'". As the war ended, the Red Army simply kidnapped some six-hundred-eighty-thousand refugees and displaced persons, including some twenty thousand Allied POWs or anyone else in their path, and sent them to slave in the factories or mines of the Gulag. That, of course, does not count all those hundreds of thousands of Soviet POWs who involuntarily traded German brutality for Chekist murder or Gulag mercilessness. Most of the Russian units who had fought for the Germans were either killed at the point of their forced repatriation or sent directly to the Gulag. Stalin saw it simply as a form of reparations for his trouble, as though only he had suffered."

"I'm furious and still can't believe the Western Allies would simply abandon all those POWs."

"Ever since your government intervened in the civil war here following World War I, it has been your official policy not to negotiate for soldiers captured by the Communists."

"But what about Korea and Vietnam?"

"What of them? I've personally seen the files. Some POWs did return after both wars, but hardly all. POWs from Korea and Vietnam were shipped to the Gulag, including POWs captured in Laos and Cambodia. And your government couldn't complain about that either because, prior to the Cambodian Incursion, officially you had no troops in either country." He gulped his tea. "You may not realize how especially vulnerable your military was in 1945 after the end of the war in Europe. Another war still raged against the formidable Japanese Empire that possessed mostly undefeated large and elite units in China, Korea, Manchuria, and Southeast Asia. Even without the Japanese navy, hostilities could have lasted into 1948 or perhaps longer. According to the most reliable estimates, invading the Japanese Home Islands, which wouldn't necessarily end the war, would cost millions of American and Allied casualties. This is based on experience with island fighting, especially Iwo Jima and Okinawa. Then more fighting these other forces on the Asian mainland, which would've been even more ghastly and expensive. You had a theoretical, but untested, atomic bomb. Some of the scientists working on the Manhattan Project theorized its detonation could ignite the whole atmosphere. Understandably, there was a great reluctance to even test it. As an insurance policy—you needed the goodwill of the Soviets to fight in Asia because the Japanese feared them for being as relentless as they were. In the final analysis, what were some twenty thousand or so Allied POWs in comparison to many millions more Allied casualties?"

"Put that way, it makes infinite sense. Of course, the Soviet intervention ultimately led to Communist China, North Korea, North Vietnam and Pol Pot's Cambodia. Unresolved problems even today."

"No roses without thorns. Sadly, by the time you knew that your bomb worked, it was too late to get your POWs back because of the intense war fatigue of American public opinion. Without a credible threat of war against Stalin, your POWs were doomed." Aleks took a deep drink of tea. "As you must know, Sergei Dmitrovich Iskandarov was one of the unfortunates." He gulped more tea. "Sergei Dmitrovich was my father as well."

"Of course. I recall in either his diary or letter, Sergei made a cryptic reference to 'Aleks, Rini and little Nata'. I assumed you and Rini were his children with Svetlana Feliksovna, which makes us half-brothers. And I'd be interested in anything you have to say concerning our father."

"You sound as though you've seen the relevant diaries of our father."

"I've seen them from the twenties through the seventies, but there is a gap from after his meeting with his father at Luftstalag III-B, near Furstenberg, Germany in 1944 until he emerges from the Icebox at Vorkuta. I've also seen the Gestapo report from Luftstalag III-C near Alt Drewitz, obviously a forgery, of Sergei's execution there in 1945. This period of 1944 to 1946 is important to me because that's when he again became Of the Iskandarov and I'd like to see how he did it. From the first letter he sent me, I'm confident his Gulag diary contains the information I need."

"First Lieutenant Spencer Talbott, navigator / bombardier of the B-24 *Jezebel* was sent to Vorkuta in May of 1945. He was there only until the fall of 1946. My mother discovered his existence and went with alias 'Chichikov' to find and bring him to the Institute. That's all I know on that score."

"Svetlana Feliksovna appeared to me in an enhanced *Andronyi* with Nata, who was branded by her on her fifteenth birthday. I also saw her presiding over Nata's rape, whipping and playing The Game in humiliating and executing Mongolian guards and, I assume, other undesirables."

"I was there as well. The three of us were forced to participate in The Game on a rotating basis. And those executions were fairly frequent. Remember, the current *apparat* FSB has had many names since the founding of the Cheka by Feliks Dzer-zhinsky. It's hard to remember them all but I know the important ones—Cheka, NKVD, KGB, and FSB. The rest I call Chekists."

"Makes sense. What else can you tell me about your mother?"

"Very well. Svetlana Feliksovna's mother, also named Svet-lana, was a maid to our grandmother, the Countess Sophia. If I'm not mistaken, she's briefly mentioned in Colonel Cooper's diary about Odessa. Her husband was an officer in the Red Partisans. Svetlana Feliksovna, born in 1915 was sent to live with her aunt outside Kiev. In 1920, our grandfather, Dmitri Sergeyovich, be-fore leaving Russia, killed the elder Svetlana and other house servants as Red spies—such were the times." He took another gulp of his tea. "So, after the Second World War, Svetlana Fe-liksovna, the daughter of a powerful commissar, was looking for a replacement for her dead hero husband, a tank officer killed at Kursk, Soviet Union in 1943. She was then not quite twen-ty-eight and just beginning her rise to power with direct assign-ments from Stalin. You should know that she was a large, wide-hipped woman who, in your measurements was six feet three inches tall, around a hundred and ninety pounds and quite strong. Most people she met were physically intimidated by her, not least of all because she had large, pointed knockers that were at eye level for many shorter people, such as Stalin, who was about five feet, four. Also, she appeared quite attractive, even in her later years, in an unrefined peasant sort of way, as compared to our elegant, refined Aunt Verushka. When the war ended, Svetlana Feliksovna not enthused by any of the choices she had amongst her peers, began looking through Chekist files for what amounted to a male concubine. She came across Sergei's Chekist file. As far as the *apparats* and Svetlana Feliksovna were concerned, he was a Russian aristocrat, an Enemy of the People. She also knew about the Iskandarov and wanted to gain continuous access to our seed. She demanded the Chekists give him to her and they did."

"I'm confused. I can understand Svetlana Feliksovna want-ed revenge on the Iskandarov for her mother. But why did she need our father's seed? I believe it's not the magic bullet it's supposed to be. And I also know several well-educated ladies who are convinced it is."

"Like the Dracula myths of Transylvania, the Cartvelian peasants attributed great power to the seed of the Iskandarov."

"But why? There must be some historical basis for such a belief."

"Who can understand the peasant mind? My mother, even though of an aristocratic family, the Palaeologus, had never known any royal trappings. In the event, she was little more than a peasant herself, susceptible to babushka tales and the like."

So, Svetlana Polinkova's story was true."

"I'm sorry, but I didn't quite hear you."

"Oh, yesterday at the airport, Svetlana Polinkova told me about her background. And her desire for peace with the Iskandarovs."

"It sounds very much like her. As you doubtless know, she's a cunning bitch." Aleks laughed. "As for her peace proposal, well, that would be a thousand time harder to sell me on than L'Enfant. And I know her very well because she's my half-sister. Different father."

I begin to appreciate how Svetlana Feliksovna further complicated the relationship between the Iskandarov and the Polinkov. I also realize how this conflict between them is simply the Serbo-Croatian-Bosnian Conflict in miniature. And a prime example of Orthodox Time, where, 'Nothing is forgotten, and nothing is forgiven.' Moreover, for the first time I really understand the difficulty of peace in the Balkans or here. "Aleks, there's something about the Palaeologus I don't understand. Since, after the fall of Constantinople in 1456, in 1472 Sophia Palaeologa married Grand Prince Ivan III of Muscovy and brought the Byzantine Imperial trappings with her. Why didn't the Polinkov ally with Muscovy?"

"It's complicated. The Polinkov regarded Sophia as a heretic because in her upbringing, she was more Italian Catholic than Byzantine Orthodox. The pope had sent her to Muscovy to convert it to Catholicism. Once there, she converted to Orthodoxy. But that was not good enough for the Polinkov. Because, as only the niece of the last Byzantine emperor, she had no legal right to bring Byzantine trappings with her. And in doing so, to the Polinkov, she had corrupted the pure Muscovite court, which made her actions illegitimate." He shook his head. "But really by then, it didn't matter because in 1213 our ancestors, who were close to the powerful Cartvelian Queen Tamar, helped soundly defeated the Polinkov at Gori the year she ended her twenty-nine-year reign. Gori, not far from Tbilisi, ironically, was also where Stalin was later born. The Sakartvelo was subsequently invaded by the Mongol Golden Horde and the first Iskandarovs escaped to Russia and became allies of Kiev then Muscovy and, finally, Russia. An alliance that lasted until 1917, with the abdication of Tsar Nicholas II."

"Amazing story. I get the extraordinarily strong impression the Polinkov are certainly brutal but for the most part, not very smart. I'm simply amazed that an impoverished clan that could have regained some power by allying with Muscovy actually looked down on them."

"Indeed. Now, we were discussing Svetlana Feliksovna. She went to the Gulag in Vorkuta, a truly hellish place, far northeast of here, replete with a sign over the camp entrance, *Work in the Soviet Union Is a Matter of Honour and Glory*."

"Just like *Work Makes Free* at Auschwitz."

"Beyond your interest in our father's Gulag diary, how do you feel now that you've learned more about it?"

"I'm uncertain, at this point. My interest in this is largely about my father. And I'm not in disagreement with Nick Stevens, who interrogated me and said its release would only result in a media frenzy with nothing accomplished. After all, most all of the principals are dead. But, on the other hand, I'm outraged that our men were abandoned so cavalierly, especially when I can easily put a face on one of the victims." He shook his head. "Nick is convinced the Gulag diary exists. In addition, George Farwell has a team that will force me to search for the diary. And they threaten to kill me whether I find it or not."

"Dear brother, I thank you for your candor and I'm most familiar with Nick Stevens. You forget that you now enjoy what you Americans refer to as 'home field advantage'. Simply say the word and Nick and associates will be canceled."

"But George, and who knows who, would only send another."

"Then to kill a snake, cut off its head." Smiling, Aleks drew a finger across his throat.

"That's the problem. As I'm sure you appreciate, George remains virtually untouchable."

"Farwell is obviously much more protected in New York than he would be if he came to Russia. As I said, here we hold the advantage. Have you formed a plan yet?"

"I've some ideas I would like to follow up on and then we'll talk again." Ashley sipped his tea. "Now you were saying about Vorkuta."

"Yes, it was designed to strip away any shreds of decency and humanity from the inmates, called *zeks,* politicals as opposed to the *Urkas* who helped run the camps. The *zeks* had precious little by the time they arrived there. Svetlana Feliksovna, as you said, sent our father for a six-day stint in the Icebox—after ten days, you developed tuberculosis and never got out of the hospital until you died or were killed. Stalin copied the idea for the Gulag from Hitler's death camps. But he knew that while Hitler's Jews made soap, his class enemies could be made to produce more than that. Vorkuta and the Icebox were the sixth ring of Hell. Svetlana Feliksovna had simply to threaten sending Sergei to the seventh, Butuguchak for Operation Borodino in order to gain his co-operation for whatever she needed. Both knew he would never return from there."

"I'm sorry, you speak as though I should know this, but I'm unfamiliar."

"Truly? I'm greatly surprised. Borodino was Stalin's extremely primitive and brutal program to build our first atomic bomb. *Zeks* were sent to open-pit mine the necessary uranium. Most died of radiation sickness in three months. So hellacious was the place that some *zeks* volunteered to serve in the ore treatment plant, where most died within a month. Today, the area around Butuguchak remains highly radioactive." He sadly shook his head.

"I never had any idea." Ashley did not disguise the disgust in his voice. "But what did Svetlana Feliksovna do to Sergei that was so horrendous? You mentioned she was attractive and wanted his seed."

"Perfectly logical, but sadly, wrong. First of all, our father was an enormously proud man whom Svetlana Feliksovna had broken. Something no one had ever done before, neither the SS nor the Gestapo, not really even the Chekists. When he emerged from the Icebox, she reminded him that this was personal. She would do anything to break him in their test of wills and she held all the high cards. In winning, Svetlana Feliksovna made a key mistake. Spencer Talbott went into the Icebox, but Sergei Dmitrovich Iskandarov emerged."

"You've lost me."

"Spencer Talbott, pragmatic American democrat, might've come to terms with Svetlana Feliksovna sooner and, thus, no Icebox. But Sergei Dmitrovich, the Russian aristocrat, felt it deeply humiliating for him to even have to speak with Svetlana Feliksovna, whom he regarded as an unclean peasant wench."

"Given his upbringing and beliefs, now I understand."

"She knew this as well and went out of her way to torment, persecute and humiliate him. Also, the political component as well. The Polinkov had pre-Revolutionary ties to Stalin and many other prominent Bolsheviks, including Cheka secret police founder, Feliks Dzerzhinsky, illegitimate Svetlana Feliksovna's father. The Polinkov's rapid ascendancy after the Revolution matched the decline of the Iskandarov."

"So, what happened to the Iskandarovs after the Revolution?"

"Some of those who remained were exiled to the barren soil of Kazakhstan, where many perished. Those who resisted, either at home or overseas, were largely sent to the Gulag. After the war, our fortunes were at their nadir. Our great leaders, Dmitri Sergeyovich had disappeared, and Countess Sophia Sergeyvna was completely exhausted. Future Grand Duchess Nadezdha

Mytrovna Andreyeva had not emerged from the shadow of Sophia. We also had no one to turn to. You Americans had yet to grasp the evilness of Stalin's regime. The Germans were disgraced and decimated. The British were in no position to help us, even had they so desired, which they did not, after being burned by their intervention in our civil war in 1919. In addition, no new leaders had yet appeared on the scene. Olga Sergeyvna was estranged from her mother and Russia. Verushka, still with the Grand Duchess, was deeply involved in her studies." He gulped tea. "Our father had a brother, Alexei Dmitrovich, always a shadowy figure, who was then in exile in Iran. Therefore, the mantle of leadership of the Iskandarov cause fell to our father in the Gulag, where it proved virtually impossible for him to exercise much leadership. A prudent person would have left him there to die. But Svetlana Feliksovna became blindly driven by the idea that our father's seed would empower a new generation of Polinkov with the power of the Iskandarov to become masters of the Soviet Union." Aleks smiled. "I know what you're thinking. But recall the crude state of Soviet genetics at that point, under the complete influence of the charlatan Trofim Lysenko."

"It's all so amazing and ridiculous, it has to be true."

"Svetlana Feliksovna counted on her ability to shape me ideologically into a good Communist and Polinkov. But as an adolescent, my Iskandarov side had come to the fore and my stepfather Pavel Chichikov used to sometimes administer severe beatings." He shook his head sadly and paused, looking pensive. "We've been speaking for hours and it's like only a few minutes have elapsed. Therefore, we have to be brothers. I first noticed you were not eating very much, although you appeared hungry. Then you appeared a bit distracted during our conversations, although you focused quite well with only an occasional slip, which, had I not been alert, I wouldn't have caught. Ash, as your brother, you can trust me to be circumspect. I know all the signs of woman trouble. What happened between you and our sister?"

Ashley studied him intently before telling him virtually everything. When he finished, he sat—drained and tearful.

"You're a brave man to let it all out like that in front of me. But you've made me feel your pain and I thank you again for your candor. I think it most fortuitous sister will be away for the weekend and have time to reflect. And, so will you. You've succeeded in your primary mission and I now ask you to enjoy my hospitality for the weekend."

"Thank you. Time to think is just what I need."

"If you will excuse me, I've some pressing matters to attend to. But in my absence, I've something for you." Aleks walked over to one of Natalya's large batiks mounted on the wall and after sliding it over, opened a wall safe and took out a white envelope, yellowed with age and bearing a red wax crested seal. "It's for you from our father with the seal of the Iskandarov." He handed it to Ashley. "He wanted only you, initially, to see it. I gave him my word and I've not seen its contents. No one has. I assume it contains the information you need to know about our family. Therefore, it will be most helpful in our further discussions. Go ahead and open it. You'll not be disturbed. If you require anything, ring for Feodor."

"Thank you." This isn't the first time my father has left me a letter and I remember the one Maria Civilli gave me a long time ago. No. It was only last Tuesday. I will try to put all the various parts since then together logically and then formulate a plan for the diary and the Iskandarov. He looked up and realized he had been ignoring Aleks standing there and asked, "Tell me, your voice is familiar, but I can't recall from where."

"Yes, long time ago. Bangkok and the Polinkov."

"You were the Englishman who saved my life?"

"Cheers." He smiled and left, leaving Ashley in stunned silence.

SIX

Saturday, 5 June 1993, Novo Ogarevo

1.

Ashley Cooper remained in Aleks's study in his comfortable chair trying to recall Bangkok. But all he could think about was Natalya's kiss. *Oh my God, it's because it's still fantastic even though we've kissed a thousand times before. But how is that possible when the first time I ever saw her, outside an Andronyi, was yesterday? I also sense had we made love last night, it wouldn't have worked because, as she said, our time wasn't yet right. She also said our time is near and I believe, since we are meant to be together, it'll happen.*

He could now only recall a few details about Bangkok in the early seventies and sensed that something was blocking him. Besides, being jet-lagged, his presentation to Aleks had taken most of his mental energy and with his adrenaline fading, he could no longer keep his eyes open. But with eyes shut, his thoughts—Annie being away, Nick Stevens's threats, Svetlana Polinkova's unwelcome reentry into his life, Anghelina's dehumanization of him last night, and the ongoing riddle of Natalya—all mixed together incoherently.

He hears a faint hum, looks up at the ceiling and just below it, an egg spins rapidly, becoming larger until a blue falcon breaks the shell and swoops down. Ashley finds himself inside the falcon, seeing through the raptor's sharp vision and he senses that the same force that had blocked his memories and *tvarsch* has done this as well. After adjusting to flying and curious where he is headed, he enjoys the ride.

Ashley sees Bangkok's wide Chao Phraya River, with its mix of colorful and commercial boat traffic, as the falcon circles the Mandarin Oriental Hotel on the riverbank. Ashley had stayed there in 1973. As the sun begins to set, the falcon lands on a balcony over the hotel's original nineteenth century entrance. Looking down, about twenty feet away, is himself as he was —an Air Force captain in Hawaiian shirt, shorts, sandals and wide-brimmed planter's hat. *On leave, I wasn't allowed to wear any part of my uniform, but with my short hair and bearing, I knew very few people would be fooled by my civilian charade.* Next to the captain, Lucy, his contracted companion for his stay, is wearing a tight green cocktail dress and sandals. She is petite and slim with dyed red hair. They are standing by one of the four tall palm trees in the garden, umbrella drinks in hand. Ashley remembers waiting impatiently for three of his brother officers and their companions to come down for their night of fun and adventure. Even though Ashley cannot hear them, he remembers Lucy, in her good English, telling him the history of the hotel and about all the famous authors—from Conrad to Michener—who had stayed there. The distracted captain does not notice a man in traditional Thai apparel approaching and, without a word, shoots him. *What the hell is Sainte Elizabeta doing?* Lucy screams. Before the assassin can fire again, a tall man in a black silk shirt, shorts and sneakers, runs past where the captain lies and shoots the assassin twice in the chest, knocking him backward onto the lawn. People run in all directions. The man, standing over the assassin with his foot on his gun hand, says something before squatting down and shooting him in the face. Before leaving, he stops to look at the captain. *I still remember the intense pain before my body began to shut down and the feel of a finger checking my neck pulse.* As the man leaves, Ashley recognizes a much younger Aleks. Lucy kneels beside the captain as a crowd gathers around them. Ashley sees a dark gray cloud rise from the assassin's chest, while a white blur enters the captain's, who is soon breathing again. Ashley recognizes the blur as his guardian spirit, Olga Sergeyvna. She had told him in Paris that he had briefly died and her lifeforce, her *protos,* had saved him. An ambulance arrives and takes both men and Lucy away and only the captain's glass and his planter's hat remain on the lawn. *Two days later, I was medevacked to the military hospital at Da Nang, Vietnam. After all this time, I still don't know who the assassin was or why he shot me.*

The falcon flies away. I never realized until now but the vision I had before joining the Air Force in 1970 was a shorter and garbled version of what I just experienced. And when I told my fiancée, Monica, about it, we argued and broke up and she ultimately married Randell. Looking back, it's now obvious I was fated to marry Pen, my first Iska.

The falcon speeds into the clouds and soon they are nearing an unfamiliar and sizeable city also with a river running through it. Crossing the river, on the left side of a wide boulevard, he sees a small park. On his right is a very large square with several government buildings. There is a huge demonstration with strange flags, unintelligible banners and men fighting and arguing. Turning right, he flies over brightly painted wooden houses, numerous ancient churches, a synagogue and two clock towers as he hears sporadic gunfire. The falcon circles over a pink building with a multi-colored tile roof, three large-shuttered windows and a wrought-iron balcony. And behind it is a café with seven large tables. Swooping down, he sees there are many Iskandarovas in white robes and he recognizes several of them. When all look up, they interrupt their drinking and eating to cheer and chant, "All hail wonderful blue falcon." *Why can I now hear, unlike Bangkok?* He sees Natalya trying to appear happy toasting with friends. *Did she cast this spell on me?*

After circling a few more times, the falcon lands on Annie's table. In her new white robe, she is now Anastasia, drinking vodka and eating, after her lengthy fast, traditional Cartvelian food like Ashley had at Natalya's. *As far as I know, today is June fifth, two days before her seventeenth birthday. As Ronnie had ex-plained, her Ceremony should still be going on in the Caves and she should still be in her black robe. She certainly appears more mature and confident.* She is speaking with an elderly woman next to her in a motorized wheelchair. Then laughing with others, she offers the falcon a morsel of meat before, again to cheers, it flies off. *I've lost my little girl.* Tears cause his eyes to lose their focus. Once recovered, the café is gone, and he hears, "Iskas have owned and run café in Tbilisi for as long as anyone remembers, and it is pleasurable part of profoundly serious Ceremony. She now has her Iskandarova name, *Kyria* Anastasia, although pat-ronymic remains to be determined by your actions. Blue falcon has always flown from Caves to café to announce to Cartvelian people Iskandarovas have admitted new member into sisterhood. She is well, and, like all Iskas, has been changed for better by Ceremony. What you are seeing is near future. Now, focus to organize your communication."

Back in his chair, Ashley is sweating and feeling nauseated. When he tries to stand, vertigo pulls him down and he awkward-ly slumps as his brain aches. He dimly notices a middle-aged woman floating over to his chair before he feels something liquid and warm pressing against his face, and as it spreads through his body, he feels much better also thanks to a sensual tingling. *Could this be Olga's protus? No, she never got to middle age.* The *pro-tus* goes from one pleasure point to another as Olga sometimes did. But this woman knows far more places to give him a quiet ecstasy and leaves him at peace and asleep.

When he awakes, he sees a naked middle-aged woman with good-spirit eyes in a slightly wrinkled face smiling back at him. Her long, wavy copper hair covers her weighty breasts and con-tinues to her wide hips. Standing before him, he sees her strong blue aura, like Nata's, framing her face. "Ashley Cooper, greet-ings. I am Elizabeta Mikhailovna Iskandarova. You may call me Bayta." She smiles. "You have discomfort after flights. Not un-common reaction for first time aloft."

"Did you…?"

"I sent you my healing warmth."

"It was so maternal, as though I were baby, and you were nursing me. But first, I want to thank you for saving Nata's life from Svetlana Feliksovna."

"You are most thoughtful."

"Tell me why you are here."

"I have come to speak about you and Nata. You were doing so well and then…"

"I believe what happened was for best."

"I have always heard Americanski are optimistic. But I think you underestimate seriousness of situation. I thought falcon flight would remove two of your anxieties and help you think more clearly."

"It did. And I know Nata loves me."

"Of course, in her own awkward way."

"I strongly believe there remains hope for reunion."

"That is your task, if you are strong enough, mentally and physically."

"I feel I am…"

"You are not. You must fully commit to her. That is only way."

"Yes, I know I must choose between L'Enfant and her. But right now, that is nearly impossible. Getting treaty signed shall be the crown of my lengthy legal career."

"But is that more important than Nata?"

"You, especially, should be aware how I struggle over this."

"I am. That is also why I blocked your *tvarsch*, which you rely on too heavily. And I shall help you, as much as I am allowed, to find resolution. And I know you have question for me."

"Why is your aura blue and not white?"

She looks at him strangely. "White is for living. And besides I am different."

"That was what Natalya said. How ?"

"*Je suis une sorcière*. Sorceress in English. While alive, I practiced healing and white magic. As you now know, I still do. I consider Realm of the Spirits to be home, although I do drift between there and here."

"I do not recall seeing you in Realm."

"I was there. We all were, silently cheering you on. We were all impressed with your courage, especially against Svetlana Feliksovna's persona from your subconscious, who she used to attempt to draw you into her hellacious cabin…forever." She shook her head. "I should also tell you there are many spirits who visit here, site of their martyrdom on regular basis, especially on their anniversaries."

"Are any of them dangerous?"

"Number of them are irritated about not having proper burial. Scary, perhaps, but no, not dangerous. Now, I also cast spell to put your *aminala*, female part of you, into my falcon, so you could observe what you needed to."

"I thought Natalya wanted revenge and had cast spell."

"Oh no, Nata is good girl and would never do such thing."

"All right, but why did you put my *aminala* in falcon?"

"Had your male *aminalus* gone in, you would have been detected by Iskas and punished severely."

"Thank you. Very clever. Now, while it is obvious why you sent me to Bangkok, why could I not hear anything?"

"I wanted you to comprehend all crucial details and not be distracted by any sounds."

"And what about Tbilisi?"

"Capital of Sakartvelo. You flew over Mtkvari River, Pushkin Park and Freedom Square on your way to café."

"Why were all Iskas there in midst of war? I was concerned about their safety."

"It has been tradition for over one hundred and fifty years that new Iskas go there after Ceremony at Caves. Have no fear, they are safe everywhere. Aleks can elaborate."

"I still do not understand why you are here."

"In addition to explaining flights, I have come about my daughter, Nata."

"But Charlotte Sternwood is her mother."

"True, but to be successful, Iska girl needs three mothers—birth, challenger and mentor. Of course, mother could have dual roles, such as birth and mentor. That was not true with Nata. Charlotte is her biological mother, Svetlana Feliksovna her challenger and I am her mentor mother, who saved her. It was my contacts that led to enrollment in Kirov Ballet's preparatory school and, most importantly, getting her away from Svetlana Feliksovna. I also threatened to place strong curse on Svetlana Feliksovna if she refused to let Nata leave."

"And I assume you also taught Nata your art."

"Correct. I know your fear of Nata but consider only way she could escape from Svetlana Feliksovna permanently was to learn my art. Prior to that, I had failed her twice. First was her branding because I was in Paris with Bleu. When I returned and saw what that bitch had done, I put strongest curse I knew on Svetlana Feliksovna. And I have sanction to use strongest power that exists in Cosmos for this purpose. I condemned her for all eternity to lowest depths of Hell. It was this knowledge, before she died, that caused madness. I could have easily fixed Nata's scars and branding, but she declined on several occasions."

"Understood. I hate to even ask about second time."

"This actually happened before her branding and still haunts me. I had spent day with her and when we arrived back at my general's dacha, he was unexpectedly there, and, because he was feeling amorous, Nata had to go home. That was night Chichikov raped her."

Even though I saw the result, that's something I'm not looking forward to hearing about. Bayta's face had softened, and he appreciates her aged beauty. "I know what Cosmos means to me, but what does it mean to you?

"It is everything and much larger than you can comprehend. You shall spend your life trying to come to terms with it. And to do that you must become warrior. You are clearly hero but that shall not be enough, something you shall soon discover. Also, you cannot do this alone. I sense I am scaring you because of my powers. Have no fear. I am not here to punish you in any way. I shall never harm you as long as you become Of Iskandarov. And once you become warrior, you shall protect Nata from all our en-

emies. "You once had Olga Sergeyvna, your bond-mate and spiritual protector. We have drifted together. She told me all about
you. Almost all, very favorable. She has now passed to another
dimension, so I shall be your protector until you no longer need
me. And that shall be when you and my daughter are one. Now,
to repair Nata's relationship, there is crucial issue you missed.
Svetlana Polinkova and Anghelina Iskandarova are younger than
Nata, and because you have given each baby, you have insulted
sister, making her feel like spinster."

"That was not my intention."

"I know. Remember, the Way of the Iskandarova is procreation before pleasure. And she has not yet been able to procreate
this month. Be patient."

"Now I understand her 'meaningless intercourse' comment.
But…?"

"She fears once you have real power as Iskandarov leader,
you shall abuse it."

"But why? I have never abused any power I have had."

"Oh, this is extremely complicated. Nata's *pyordarsch* pre-
dicts when you attain power you do so without her. Your great
fear of what you call incest and, most importantly, your continued attraction to Svetlana Polinkova means you never have Blood
Union with Nata and also you share power with Svetlana. Nata
shall accept no other lover and dies without having any perfect
children, which is worst possible Iska fate. Am I clear?"

"Is that future for Nata and me? My daughter's *pyordarsch*
predicted Yuri Aleksandrovich's death and we did all we could to
protect and save him—to no avail."

"Do you honestly believe I should be here were this already
preordained? It is not too late, if you act properly in next week.
But even if you reconcile but you do not fully commit to each
other, your union shall fail."

"We must succeed then."

"However, you know something important but do not understand it."

"It's about her kiss."

"Very good. But you cannot discover more because you presently do not have nearly enough understanding. And you cannot discover answer without her. Although she does not know answer either."

"If you are attempting to be obscure, you have succeeded admirably."

"Spoken as true *avocat*. That type of logical thinking shall not be sufficient to solve your problem. You need imagination. Would you have believed before today you could fly in falcon through time and space?"

"Since being in Realm of Spirits, I believe flight in falcon was real and why I had vertigo. But since we were not in either realm, where were we?"

"What is *tvarsch*?"

"Um, the collective wisdom of the Iskandarov."

"Very good. But where does it permanently reside?"

"No idea. I never even thought about it."

"In *Thurnane*, Elsewhere in our language, which exists for those able to find it. As one of our poets once wrote 'It is neither here nor there but elsewhere instead.' That was also where you were in Grandfather Dmitri Sergeyovich's body in 1917. You know wound in your leg was real and you shall encounter this place again."

"Yes, that wound was often painful until Nata cured it. OK. You make good case."

"You once knew how to think freely with my friend Olga Sergeyvna. That was what I spoke about when I told you of something important you had forgotten, and you wanted to show me how smart you were by answering Nata's kiss was answer. No one has ever doubted, for even moment, and including Nata, your superior intellect. You have failed to apply Olga Sergeyvna's most important lesson after all these years. You cannot let other people define your achievements. Had you applied her lesson at Harvard, you would have enjoyed much happier life. And that is also factor with Nata. If you had been in balance, you would have been confident enough to eagerly accept Olga Sergeyvna's teachings."

"What do you mean by my being 'in balance'?"

"What is this kindergarten?" She shook her head. "*Tvarsch*, now that it has returned shall answer all if you let it. You've been blocking it for many years. That is also why you failed in Realm and had to be rescued by Sainte Xenia. Iskandarov have no use for *avocats*. That is your old life, not your new one."

"I feel as though I am speaking to Delphic Oracle."

"And that is bad?"

"No, only confusing."

"Confusion exists only with ignorant people. Again, you have *tvarsch*, which should be sufficient. We still have much to discuss. Svetlana Polinkova is temptress and witch. Mad like her mother and if you so much as kiss her again, you shall be doomed to her, like your father was to her mother. And her rule, with or without you, if not defeated, shall weaken, if not destroy, our clan."

"Understood. Back to Nata's *pyordarsch*. How can I prevent this outcome?"

"Start with knowledge that Svetlana Polinkova is powerful sorceress like Cartvelian Medea. Her seduction and ruination of so many men were, and remain for both, nothing but play of children. And she can easily enslave you, should you underestimate her. It was only ignorance of your heritage that spared you in New York City. Even then, she gave you enough of her mother's tea to kill normal person because she had decided you were too important to us to be allowed to live."

"Then I shall be on my guard."

"While it is to your credit you do not take Hidden One role seriously, you must begin, and soon."

"But I have no idea what it even is or what I am supposed to be doing."

"I shall only say you shall never learn this by yourself."

"I would like to return to something you said earlier—what is this great power you used against Svetlana Feliksovna?"

"As with all things Iska that is something I cannot reveal. You were not listening carefully. I do not currently have power. It becomes available to me when needed." She smiles. "Now, there is something else you need to know. I was one of triplets born to mother Gmella Ivanovna Iskandarova, sorcière. When I was girl of twelve, she decided I would be her successor. After she taught me, I gradually became stronger than she. And this was my trade-off with being able to have children. This was not Iskandarov Curse. I may say no more."

"Since your mother had children you must be *grande sor-cière*."

"How do you even know such term?" She loudly shrieks and shatters glass as Ashley covers his ears, closes his eyes and shakes his head.

When he recovers, "Please, do not do that again." His empty silver tea glass holder has shards in the bottom. "*Tvarsch* knows this. I did not know whether *grande sorcières* actually exist or were myths."

"I am impressed. You are more advanced in some areas than I knew. There are only few of us at any time. Remember, every-thing you require is within you." She floats away and disappears with a *Das vedanya*.

2.

Hearing Aleks's return, Ashley awoke, feeling refreshed and confident. But where's father's letter? I'll look later. And Bayta said, "Das vedanya." that is, until we meet again and not goodbye.

As Aleks entered his study, Ashley said, "You know, I had a remarkably interesting visit from Bayta after you left."

Aleks looked at the shattered tea glass. "No doubt Bayta also did that. I can't tell you how much of my glass and china she's destroyed. Feodor will bring in another samovar and glass-es. I remember Bayta. She spent time with Nata while Rini and I were usually someplace else. But I did have some good chats with her. Very smart, attractive woman and a long-time Bleu agent with a clever alias, she became mistress to many powerful people in the military, *apparats* and Politburo. She was born in Odessa in the early fifties, came to Moscow, hoping to be a fashion model. She achieved that through the contacts she had made at her Ceremony. But, because even Soviet fashion designers didn't design their best clothes for real women, she had to bind her impeccable knockers to fit into the clothes. Even though being a model gave her status, she still had to make ends meet. She became a pin-up model, all very modest by Western standards. While the regime was publicly puritanical, these pictures of her were popular with our armed forces. She made even more money doing candid photos for party poohbahs. That is, she'd pose however the client wanted. That's how she came to be Khrushchev's off-and-on mistress starting in 1956 and going past 1964 when he was ousted and became a 'non-person.' Although, since the KGB was monitoring everything he did in 'retirement,' she came mostly to talk with him. And she continued until his death in the fall of 1971. After Khrushchev was denied the honor of being buried in the Kremlin Wall, he was buried at Moscow's Novodevichy Cemetery. This hadn't been announced to the public, yet the cemetery was surrounded by armed troops. But she was able to go with a group of artists and writers who stood with the Khrushchev family. It's also rumored she helped get his memoirs out of the country that became *Khrushchev Remembers* in the West. The information she received from her clients helped Bleu more quickly rebuild its network destroyed by Pavel Chichikov during the second war."

"Now I understand what happened in Bangkok. Since Bayta was Bleu, she learned through pillow talk with someone in the KGB that I was going to be assassinated. She contacted you to track down the killer. Who was he anyway?"

"A former Nazi and Stasi agent, Heinrich Sassen, in the pay of the Polinkov. Bayta also told me she was going to send you a warning, which she hoped *tvarsch* would receive."

"Oh yes, I received it, but it was garbled, and I didn't take it as a warning, but an omen. And that led to a breakup with my fiancée Monica."

"Pardon my candor, but whoever she was, she had to be a better choice than Penelope."

"No offence taken. Since then, losing Monica has haunted me from time to time."

"I'm terribly sorry and now I remember what happened. For all her gifts and talents, the one thing Bayta didn't know how to do was sending an *Andronyi*. So, she asked Nata to send it for her. But Nata in 1970 was fifteen and although she knew in theory how to do it, she'd never actually sent one. She wanted to help you and had a personal stake in your survival. But she found that in practice, it's an extremely tricky thing to do." He smiled. "And I suppose even had you fully received the *Andronyi,* there wasn't much you could've done."

"You're right, even if she had resent it in 1973, when she would be an Iska and more experienced, I wouldn't have gone to Bangkok or anywhere else. Because regardless where I went, this Sassen would've followed me. So, I'd probably stayed safe on the base. Anyway, thank you again for saving my life. I'm deeply in your debt."

"Not at all. Besides, I've heard how you tried to help my son Yuri after the Paris explosion. And I was also impressed that you searched Nadia Mytrovna's apartments for the bomb. And knowing Yuri died peacefully in the company of your daughter, the girl he loved, is invaluable. We're more than even."

"Please tell me more about Bayta. Especially, how such a powerful woman died."

"It's an amazing story. There was a prominent KGB colonel, a past assassin, alias Raskolnikov, in bed with Bayta, and he had let slip the plot against you. Later, when he realized what she had done, he denounced her as a spy and swore he'd kill her. But her cover was so perfect, and she was in such demand that no one believed him, and after a while of his rantings he was nicknamed Inspector Javert."

Ashley laughed loudly. "I love it, first, Raskolnikov, from Dostoyevsky's *Crime and Punishment* and then, the cop who obsessed over capturing Jean Valjean in Victor Hugo's *Les Misérables*. The KGB are quite well read."

"Precisely. After twelve years, Raskolnikov, with several failed kidnapping attempts, was ordered to stop. In 1985, Bayta, nearly sixty, with her beautiful snow-white hair, was still in demand sexually. The colonel called her to make peace. She agreed and went to his dacha not far from here. And during a post-coital cigarette, he pulled out a long knife from under his pillow and stabbed her, thinking he'd killed her. She rose, the knife still in her, and spelled him to levitate and catch fire internally. He died screaming until only cinders remained. She cast another spell, producing a fireball that became progressively larger until it consumed the whole building, and she happily fell into the purifying flames. When she was a spirit, after telling us her story, she said that at sixty, she had lived long enough as a courtesan. Also, she knew what Raskolnikov was up to when he called her the last time. Her period of transition had come."

"I assume this Raskolnikov was Polinkov."

"I can see why you'd say that, but his real name was Mikhail Mikhailovich Ausmankarov. She told me he confessed to killing many people, using a drug that mimicked a heart attack. She said later he'd bragged about hundreds of killings, including, among others, perhaps Nikita Sergeyovich and Olga Sergeyvna. He felt he should be a great hero, but she had reduced him to a laughing-stock."

"Amazing. She had the power to cause a man to destroy himself. But why didn't he just use his drug on her?"

"He wanted everyone to know he had brutally killed her to restore his credibility. But Bayta bested him by burning down his dacha and making the cause of death unclear."

"When I saw her, she had copper hair and not the white hair you remember."

"Now, Ash, I know you're all caught up in the metaphysics of being an Isk. But I'm a realist, a rarity. And that's the reason everyone wants to kill me and thinks the clan will then fall apart. My *forte* is business and finance, hence my position at the ministry. I have no interest in metaphysics. I do make an exception for Bayta because, well, I love and admire her. She may take any form she had in life and her copper hair was from her most successful time."

Feodor quietly arrived with the samovar already steaming on a hand-carved wooden cart. Ashley rose to fill his new tea glass and said, "She's a very interesting spirit and must've been even more so alive."

"Was she ever." Aleks went over to the samovar. "Did you see her pictures in Nata's photo gallery?"

"Yes, in an elegant strapless gown and two more modest ones. I thought the first was some inside joke."

"Precisely. Her picture in the gown and fur is the first one of a thirtieth birthday series she sent out to appropriate people, including Secretary Khrushchev, whom she seduced the following year, 1956. It was a jest because she could never accompany any of her men to formal occasions. And this was to show what, had she been invited, what she would have worn. It was also to remind these men of how beautiful she still looked at thirty. Here's the fun part, her silver fox fur is covering the deep scoop in the front of her gown. In the second picture, she has bared her lovely knockers and the photographs continue until she is completely naked."

"Was this successful?"

"Her modeling career shot up like a rocket as men and even women responded positively. She helped women to realize they were not past their prime at thirty."

"That's incredibly interesting. She sent me in a blue falcon to Bangkok and Tbilisi." Ashley recounted his adventures.

"Even though Bayta is a grand sorceress, not even she can isolate your female aspect and put it in a falcon from a thousand miles away and travel to the past and future. Besides, why a blue falcon? Since you're American why not an eagle?"

"Tradition. For some hundred and fifty years, falcons have flown from the Caves to the café to announce a new Iska. And after the flight, I had terrible vertigo. No dream."

"Hmm. Was anyone at the café?"

"Yes, there were many Iskas, including my daughter, her aunts, cousins, and I also saw Nata and Cosette from Paris. They were all celebrating. Even an older woman in a motorized wheelchair."

"Please describe the café for me."

He gave Aleks a complete description of the Iskandarova's café.

"Have you ever been to Tbilisi before?"

"No. Not even close. I knew it existed, but that's it. Even in Russia, outside Moscow, I was only in St Petersburg once."

"You must have seen pictures of Tbilisi when you were doing research."

"No. Why is this upsetting you so much?"

"Because your tale is too fantastic. It simply can't be."

"Why not? My two trips could go back to 1973 or forward because *tvarsch* knows there's no time or space in what Bayta called *Thurnane*."

"That loosely translates as Elsewhere. I'll concede your *tvarsch* is getting much stronger. But that's the least of it. You're telling me things you couldn't possibly know."

"Perhaps, but, thanks to *tvarsch,* I've been seeing fantastic things and events most of my life. Tell me, have you ever been to the Realm of the Spirits?"

"No, because it doesn't exist. Again, merely folklore and nonsense."

"Oh, it's real all right. I've been there and barely made it out before the portal closed."

"And whom did you think you saw?"

"I was summoned by Countess Sophia. I saw her and Prince Dmitri, my wife Pen and Princess Sainte Xenia. Then there was Svetlana Feliksovna and Ovals, who threatened and nearly killed me when I was at Harvard. Bayta told me she was in the Realm, but I didn't see her."

"Ash, you're highly intelligent and, doubtless, have a vivid imagination. You created that in your mind."

"I was not only there, I could feel being on the stairs and smelling the dampness, the rot, and hearing the demon voices, walking in the pitch dark and my confrontation with Svetlana Feliksovna was terrifying beyond imagination."

"And what language did you use to speak to everyone? Russian, English or French?"

"In the Realm, we used mental images and thoughts. After my blue falcon ride, Bata and I spoke Russian like I did with Olga in Paris." He went back to the samovar. "Hmm, could it be that because of your Polinkov blood, your *tvarsch* is not as strong as mine?"

"Brother, like me, you are half-Iskandarov. I'm no less Iskandarov than you. That's the absolute worst insult you could have thrown at me. In olden days, our men fought duels after being slandered like that. And I'm not talking pistols at twenty paces. No. They fought with sabers, slashing until one died." He laughed. "Had you going there, didn't I?"

"You certainly did."

"Yes, I'll forgive you because you're new to all this. But hear what I'm saying. Since our blood is stronger than most any other, by the time we reach adulthood, ours has driven out all the inferior."

"Aleks, I apologize. Like you, I'm looking for any possible answers to these mysteries, and especially, I try to rely on faith because my best friend Randell is an Episcopal priest."

"You a religious man?"

"I go to services, say prayers for dead friends, take communion regularly."

"Yes, that's all well and good, but do you believe?"

"In God, yes."

"And how do you perceive Him?"

"The eternal and all-powerful creator of everything."

"As you must know the Iskandarov are closely tied to the Russian and Cartvelian Orthodox Churches. And the latter since the fourth century A.D. Would you have difficulty converting to Orthodoxy?"

"I don't know. I would need to study your dogma in greater detail. And I'm having difficulty with the Fates aspect. But, if I had a compelling reason, I would."

"Fair enough. I know there's something else which is part of your reluctance to join us and, don't try to deny it—because we're Fascists.

Ashley reluctantly nodded.

"Permit me to clarify. As you know from the diaries, we've been anti-Communist since 1917, but after the horror of Hitler and his Nazi zealots, we became more liberal. If we ran this country, we'd have a parliamentary system like Britain. But we would also have a strong executive…"

"You refer to an old idea that Russians want a strong leader, because the country has historically suffered under weak leadership. Your idea sounds like Fascism with window dressing."

"I thank you for your candor, but the executive would be constrained by the legislature, like in the U.S. system. We might even bring back the tsar as a symbolic head of the state, above politics, like the British."

"A noble goal perhaps."

"That was the way Russia was heading before the war began in 1914. We're working hard to make this a reality, but we also know it'll take time. Like Churchill said, 'The Americans will always do the right thing, after exhausting all the alternatives.' Similarly, the Russians will go down many dark alleys before arriving at the right solution." He laughed. "On a happier note, I've started the process for L'Enfant, but should you wish it to stop it, I can do that anytime in the next five days."

"I really appreciate that."

"You know, you've made me curious about Bayta's visit. What was most important for her?"

"While almost everything she said and showed me was important, I would say she seemed most concerned about Nata and me getting back together so we can have our union."

"These women seem to feel if there's a single man on the loose, we, in short order, are all doomed." He shook his head and smiled. God bless them anyway. When we were talking before, as I said, you were telling me things you couldn't have known."

"I've explained as best as I can."

"But the most disturbing thing was your accurate description of King Mirian III's café."

"And who was he?"

"The Cartvelian monarch who converted to Christianity in 337 A.D. The house and café were built about 150 years ago on a site we had occupied for mostly military purposes for millennia. Except during the Golden Horde, when we had to relinquish it to the Tatars. We keep the café low profile, not anywhere a tourist would likely go and definitely not in the guidebooks. It has been owned and run by Iskas since the building's beginning."

"The secret's safe. I didn't mention that when I passed over Freedom Square, there was a large demonstration going on there with mostly men arguing and fighting. I also heard quite a bit of gunfire. I was concerned about Annie's safety."

"Be assured, Annie couldn't be safer anywhere than with those Iskas. I've seen a group of them in their white robes walking into an area where two factions were shooting each other. Before they walked through, the gunfire ceased, and men doffed their caps or even went down on their knees."

"Amazing. Although I'm not surprised. Now, who was the elderly lady in the wheelchair?"

"She's Sergei Dmitrovich's sister, Aunt Sonia Dmitrievna. She was born with crippled legs and decided to die to the world. She has been at the Caves since finishing her formal education, leading an extremely productive life as the scholar of our clan. You'll meet her when you go there. And I'm confident you'll find her charming as she interrogates you about your history, as she hopefully will do with Anastasia." He gulped his tea.

"Aleks, why do you pace in a circle like that? It's like you're trying to cast a spell on me."

"By Jove, we've really been messing with your head." He laughed. "Actually, it helps me think. Also, there are no Iskandarov warlocks."

"How come?"

"Early on there were, but they died out."

"Why?"

"I don't know. Never given it any thought."

"Might be something to look into. Now, I know not all Iskas are witches, but why would any sane man knowingly want to marry one?"

"No idea. Rini isn't one. It happens quite often and the men I know seem to enjoy it. Moving on, I don't expect you've had much time to read our father's letter."

"If I can find it, I'd appreciate some time to read it."

"It's on the floor beside your chair."

Ashley picked it up. "Before I read it, I'd like to know how our father was killed."

"It happened here in the banquet hall where we had breakfast. Svetlana Feliksovna had planned, with Nata's help, a welcome home banquet for 'the Hero of Camp David." He was to receive an important medal from Brezhnev, a full pardon for his crimes and a substantial government pension. After the medal presentation, he was going to make a speech extolling the great virtues and wonders of the Soviet Union. But before the speech, Svetlana Feliksovna fatally shot him in front of all the dignitaries."

"Wow. I can't say I'm surprised. I didn't think she would be stupid enough to kill him in front of witnesses. When was this?"

"In the fall of 1976. Her arrogance proved to be a great victory for Sergei Dmitrovich. In his martyrdom, he finally brought down this most horrendous woman because, under Brezhnev's orders, she was sent to a mental hospital and was soon on the wrong end of torture, which helped to drive her mad. She never got out and is buried somewhere on the grounds in a mass grave and, as you claim, is now in Hell. You also need to understand she was the last powerful Stalinist and had become an embarrassment to the Brezhnev regime. Our father gave Brezhnev the perfect excuse to get rid of her. And, I've heard Brezhnev had been trying for some time to do this without alienating most of her supporters."

"Did she have that many?"

"Yes. Stalin had been her mentor and she was a symbol of socialist upward mobility to all those Ivans who thought Stalin was a genius."

"Yes, I've seen the old pensioners many times in Red Square still demonstrating for Stalin's rehabilitation and never for Khrushchev's. Why?" Ashley sipped his tea.

"No need. When Khrushchev delivered his secret speech at the Twentieth Party Congress in February of 1956 about the crimes of Stalin, it was quickly leaked. The so-called Children of the Twentieth Congress gradually took power until one of their own, Mikhail Gorbachev, began his reforms. That is the Khrushchev legacy and Bayta played her part."

"While I know about the secret speech, I had no idea of the rest. Thank you. But

you've been testing me throughout our conversations going back to L'Enfant, haven't you?"

"Not precisely, I was interviewing you and I suspect you'll learn more about why we do this in the near future."

"Call it what you will. Brother, you are a real son-of-a-bitch."

"Oh, I've been called much worse by better men than you." Ashley stood and they both laughed and hugged.

"I'm not yet ready to leave Sergei Dmitrovich's murder. There must have been some other way Brezhnev could have gotten rid of Svetlana Feliksovna."

"Afraid not. As I said, it was the ideal circumstances. Had our father killed her, he would've been sent, if he were lucky, to a very northern prison. No, *tvarsch* was working perfectly because he knew what was going to happen and didn't try to escape or even resist." Aleks looked at his watch. "It's right around four. I again have some calls to return, so let's meet in the dining room at seven. This extra time will give you a chance to read the letter, freshen up and change for dinner. After dinner, we'll take full advantage of our ladies' absence to have some old-fashioned Saturday night bachelor fun." Aleks smiled wickedly.

"I'm game. See you at seven." I wonder how the Russian version of this would be different from the American. I also sense Aleks is smart enough not to invite prostitutes to the party. Ashley opened the envelope and read:

5 August 1976

My son, we are descendants of the Colchi, a tribe
of the Caucasus Mountains, who were vassals of
the Armenians. We paid them tribute and they left
us, substantially, in peace. Perhaps our tribe could
have gone on in obscurity for millennia. However,
Iskandar, whom you know better as Alexander the
Great, conquered the Armenians. In turn, as the
vassal of a vassal, he demanded specific tribute from
us because he knew our history. Therefore, our chief
sent his three seventeen-year-old virgin daughters,
Ilyrianaa, Aliannaa and Athaliaa, to Iskandar's
court. When they returned, they were all pregnant
by Iskandar himself and birthed a boy and two girls.
They later intermarried and, each with the blood of
Iskandar, produced many more children. That is why
we are called the Iskandarov.

Iskandar, who was regarded as a god by many, had
given the young ladies instructions on what to do next
when they returned. He, as you probably know, had
spent time in Egypt where he adopted many of their
customs. From earliest times, Egyptian pharaohs had
practiced brother and sister marriage. You may recall
Cleopatra, the last of the Greek Ptolemy Dynasty
Iskandar founded, married her brother before her
involvement with Caesar and Anthony. Iskandar
continued this tradition with his successors to our
south, the Greek Seleucids, as did the Hindi to our
east. The Seleucids enforced this pronouncement on
our tribe's nobility for several hundred years. After
that, selective breeding had become traditional and was
continued voluntarily. Sexual relations between parent
and child were and are strictly forbidden. We continue
the tradition because it has, overall, served us well.

When there is no sibling to marry, and in some cases,
where there is, we are allowed to enter into dynastic

marriages. That is, marriages to enhance the House of Iskandarov—what my first marriage to Nadia Mytrovna was all about, although she had some Iskandarov blood. With my dearest Charlotte, we formed a dynastic union with the Sternwood Tradition. You and Natalya are the fruit of the merging of two great Traditions. In both you and Nata your Iskandarov and Sternwood bloods are in equilibrium, perfect for renewing the bloodline of the Iskandarov.

Now to the second matter. You are also here to find my diary from the Gulag. Be aware I wrote it and, as of this date, it exists. I copied an early version, which I gave to Binkie only about the Lost Souls before I was sent on my mission to Camp David. If still alive, Binkie will know where it is. If not, I am certain she left detailed instructions with a trusted confidant. In the event this letter should fall into the wrong hands, I cannot tell you where your mother is. Use tvarsch to locate her. I left the original diary with an old and trusted friend, which he continued to update. And you know very well who this is.

Ashley had had a conversation with Randell Speers less than two weeks ago. Randell's real father, Captain Harvey Jacobs was the pilot of the B-24 *Jezebel* on the Ploesti Raid. He, Spencer Talbott, and co-pilot Mac Goodwin had been shot down on One August 1943. Because he did not survive the raid, Randell never knew Mac. But Ashley had seen Captain Jacobs's name on the Gestapo list, slated for execution at Alt Drewitz, proving he had survived to be caught up in Iron Cage. But had he survived the Gulag and did the diary still exist? *Tvarsch now remains annoyingly silent.*

Those who keep Iron Cage secret are old, rich and powerful men, who sold their souls long ago to get where they are. Now all they have left of importance

is their bogus reputations. If those are destroyed, they
have nothing. Therefore, they can go to the Devil.
Expect no mercy from their henchman and give none
either. I long ago made peace with my tormentors.
They stripped me of everything I had ever owned.
It was only then I found out who I truly was. And I
knew then, that, indeed, in my darkest hours, I had
triumphed. I have achieved everything I was meant
to. I may now die without regret or fear. I have
looked the Devil in the face and spat in his eye.

May God in His mercy bless and protect you. And
may we meet again one day, as is promised.

Your loving father, Sergei

P.S. VL-19-5

Aleks had been correct; Sergei knew what Svetlana Feliksovna had in mind. Four of his children, Aleks, Rini, Ashley
and Nata were then grown up and married. Charlotte had safely
disappeared and so his life's work was done. Sergei Dmitrovich
really was a hero, not of the Soviet Union but of the world. When
Ashley would finally meet his mother for the first time, she could
fill in the rest of Sergei's life. Ashley wished he could have met
him, but in 1976 he was getting married to Penelope in New York
and had no inkling this great man even existed. He said a prayer
for the repose of Sergei Dmitrovich's soul and, while he did not
know whether this did any good, it certainly did not hurt, so he
would keep on saying them. As much as he tried, beyond the obvious V for Vorkuta, the rest of the postscript made no sense. At
least, it was a place to start.

Exhausted from this rollercoaster of a day, Ashley asked Feodor to take him up to his bedroom. Ashley was surprised by the
king-sized bed in the middle, the spacious bathroom, the study
area in one corner and the view of the formal gardens and tall
hedges possibly forming some sort of maze. He sensed something was amiss, but he was too tired to pursue that. Instead, he
lay on the bed in his sleep mask and fell asleep.

SEVEN

Sunday and Monday, June 6 & 7, 1993, Novo Ogarevo

1.

Early on Sunday morning, badly hungover Ashley Cooper hears an unfamiliar sound. He sits up as he lifts his sleep mask and discovers he is still dressed on top of his huge bed. In the White Night, Bayta stands just beyond his feet. "Good morning, are you aware you are sleeping in Svetlana Feliksovna's bedroom?"

"I sensed something was amiss with room. Why did Aleks put me here?"

"Courtesy, it is best bedroom in Institute. Also, test of *tvarsch*."

"I am certain you did not come here to discuss this."

"I have just left Nata at your daughter's Ceremony. While Annie remains in fasting, prayer and meditation, it is also time for Iskas to gather in small groups, usually no more than six, to discuss triumphs and problems. While I cannot be too specific, they are in someone's bedroom with large bottle of vodka to loosen tongues. I saw Nata wailing and cursing you to heavens."

"Is this supposed to be something good?"

"Ultimately, I asked her what she wanted, and she told me that she was foolish to have left you here, where Anghelina could easily find you or Svetlana Polinkova who knows way around Institute. And there are other women in area as well. And none of them would ask you for commitment. Just sex. Thus, by time she returns, you would have returned to New York City with your signed L'Enfant Treaty and one of, as she put it, vamps."

"Then she does not know me at all."

"She knows you better than you know yourself. Are you ready to act like adult and not some ignorant adolescent?"

"What do you mean?"

"Although she would have loved to fall into bed with you, she did not want you thinking she was that kind of girl. But she overcompensated and now fears she has driven you away—forever. After her rant, I reminded her she was Iska *Prinkipia* and she should begin to act like one with duties and responsibilities. She shook her head and said she was tired of all this and wanted to break free. I told her she was acting like schoolgirl defying mother by wearing lipstick. The time to be real woman has come. At this point, she began crying and could not stop until she fell over backwards and said she was fool before passing out."

"Shall she be all right?"

"She has done this before at Ceremonies. But because of you, this time is different."

"What can I do to help her?"

"You shall soon face most profound test. If you succeed, you shall have what she needs. That is beginning."

"Because she has what I need?"

"Precisely. She knows that and is why she shall be coming back...soon. I must take my leave and shall be absent for period. I have done what I may. *Das Vedanya*." She disappears.

2.

After a restless sleep, Ashley went down to the breakfast buffet, filling his plate with Polish sausage, scrambled eggs with caviar, pumpernickel toast and French coffee. When Aleks, also hungover, joined him and after some pleasantries, Ashley said, "This is exceptionally good coffee. But now, please tell me more, aside from the sex, about our father's time here."

Aleks gulped his coffee and took a bite of toast. "Svetlana Feliksovna and Chichikov kept our father under constant pressure to exploit his feelings of disgust and abandonment. In a country where seemingly nothing else worked, the *apparats* mastered, to use the American idiom, brainwashing. During the day, our father worked at a secret facility on a unique project with Chichikov, who indoctrinated him before and after work. Svetlana Feliksovna did so at night, usually, along with a post-coital cigarette. His trip to the American Embassy proved decisive."

"I don't know about this."

"You don't know? Silly me. One day, as a special reward for early completion of his project, Chichikov told our father he could walk unescorted around Moscow for the afternoon. The American Embassy was not far from the facility. Svetlana Feliksovna had authorized this, knowing he would go there. She always gave her special victims what they thought they wanted. He stopped outside and…"

"How do you know all this?"

"Father and I discussed it at some length, and I've seen the Chekist surveillance dossiers. I also have silent films from 1954 of the whole thing. There's an official transcript for you to follow along."

"Then I must see it."

"Feodor will make it all ready."

"The rain hasn't stopped so, an excellent time to delve into this."

"After you finish breakfast everything should be ready."

* * *

About a half hour later in the annex to Aleks's study, everything was ready, and the curtains were drawn. He dimmed the lights and standing close to the screen watched the watery colored film. Two men walk along what he recognized as the quay of the Moskva River. He studied Sergei's fine curly hair, his tall, slim build, his gait, and the way he sometimes held his right hand opened and rigid, just as Ashley did. His heartbeat faster at finally seeing his father in motion. The two men parted company.

Ashley rewound the projector to focus on Chichikov. He seemed surprisingly small, a good foot shorter than Sergei Dmitrovich, yet powerfully built—a full handlebar moustache obscuring his mouth. Nor did Ashley miss Chichikov's slightly slanted brown eyes and shaved head. Shooting this man would not have been easy because he looked as though bullets would only bounce off.

Sergei Dmitrovich walked through Moscow stopping at store windows until he came to the American Embassy. He looked at it, started to go in but continued walking. Returning, he walked slowly back and forth. He started to enter, stopped, turned, and looked around, at one point facing the camera. After a shoddy splicing to a grainy black and white film, Sergei Dmitrovich walked into the embassy. He went from one office to another, meeting with men who became progressively older. Ashley focused on the officials' expressions and gestures. Finally, when Sergei Dmitrovich entered a large office, Ashley recognized the sitting man—Ambassador Linus van Rouene. When van Rouene stood up at his desk and clearly dismissed Sergei Dmitrovich, Marine guards came in and took him away. The final frames were of van Rouene theatrically wiping his hands.

On his way to his comfortable chair to read the *apparat* MGB transcript, Ashley noticed a picture he had not seen before—Stalin with a young vivacious woman—and picked it up and read the dedication on the back. The woman is Svetlana Feliksovna on her thirtieth birthday. *Wow! She was an absolutely beautiful woman, at least physically. And it's strange Aleks would have a picture of two people he despised.* He shook his head as he sat. The folder marked with security warnings bore the MGB seal. Opening it, the musty scent caused him to sneeze. Likely no one, except Aleks, had seen it in a long time. He read the Russian and that his father was referred as SDI, Sergei Dmitrovich Iskandarov.

At the front desk, Sergei asked to see the ambassador and is told that he does not become involved in the daily business of the embassy. Sergei knew he had little time and insisted on speaking to this man's superior. The first man, Edwards, reluctantly agreed to hear what Sergei had to say. After listening to the story, Edwards was skeptical. Why was Sergei wearing a suit issued by the MGB? He replied it was the only suit he had. Besides, he is a *zek*. Was that not proof this was not a trap? As they both knew, the MGB were not stupid. Edwards took him to another official.

After hearing his story, the new man, Stafford, demanded some identification. Sergei gave him Spencer Talbott's service number, rank and unit. But Stafford asked for more proof. Sergei had nothing beyond that. He told the man to contact his associates in New York. Stafford asked what that would prove. Sergei conceded the point because to everyone at The Firm, he was dead and buried. He countered that since the Chekists are so thorough, his lack of proof was proof of his veracity. Stafford said there was something in that and called in his secretary to find what information they have about USAAF First Lt. Spencer Talbott. When the secretary returned, Sergei learned he has been posthumously promoted to Captain. He told Stafford that he had kept a diary of his time at Vorkuta and Stafford can send someone to Charlotte to release it. Stafford again declined. What would such a thing prove? Sergei responded it would blow the lid off Iron Cage, for one. Stafford showed no interest in pursuing either the diary or Iron Cage.

Ashley reread the paragraph making certain he translated it correctly. Sergei, presumably for the first time, had told Stafford, who had to be a member of George Farwell's Prometheus Group, about his Gulag diary and Iron Cage because he thought that would get him asylum. Ashley went back to the beginning of the transcripts looking for a date for the interviews—15 September 1954. *Tvarsch tells me that when Svetlana Feliksovna confirmed his betrayal, she began his Camp David training in early 1955, which would either get him killed or, as happened, buried alive in prison. So why did my father, knowing the bad results at the embassy, not keep quiet about Iron Cage in Maria Civilli's interrogations after Camp David? Since Sergei wasn't stupid, there had to be a particularly good reason for his actions.* Ashley shook his head. His mother, if still alive, might know.

Ashley resumed reading about a third man, Morrison, who, after hearing Sergei's story, briefed the ambassador's assistant, Miller, who brought him to the special ambassador. The transcript continued in English:

> SDI: Lin, Lin van Rouene. It's me. Spence, Spence Talbott.
>
> SAvR: I've no idea who you are. Now what do require of me?
>
> SDI: Lin, we were associates at Gules before the war.
>
> SAvR: I have no idea what Gules is. Now, again, what do you require?
>
> SDI: Lin, I demand asylum.
>
> SAvR: Ah, I see, you're trying to trick me, aren't you? Just another MGB agent out to create a diplomatic incident for us. Leave. Now!
>
> SDI: No. Not until you've heard my story.
>
> SAvR: No, Miller told me quite all I need to know. (Marine guards enter) Sergeant, have your men immediately escort this imposter from the embassy premises.
>
> SDI: Damn you, Lin. You're still pissed about Deborah, aren't you? She came on to me and at the time I didn't know she was your wife. Like you, I was then new at The Firm. Just remember, the MGB will kill me for sure. Or send me back to the Gulag. And it's going to be on your head, you chicken-shit excuse for a man.

As he closed the file, Ashley knew Deborah had been the ambassador's first wife who unexpectedly disappeared. Obviously, van Rouene felt safe in his refusal of asylum. The American government still did not negotiate for Soviet-held POWs, even if they had the initiative to show up at the embassy in Moscow.

Yes, it all makes sense now. Lana told me in New York she had married the ambassador because he had done a favor for Svetlana Feliksovna. And this was it. Too bad Nick Stevens already killed van Rouene and his men from the Moscow Embassy. I wonder what other skullduggery Lana, the ambassador and his men were involved in?

3.

Later, Aleks and Ashley went to the local Russian Orthodox church, Saint Vladimir the Healer. Ashley now remembered the liturgy's power from when he and Olga Sergeyvna attended services in Boston in the sixties—part of his passion, at that time, for all things Russian. But dealing with the Russians over the last twenty plus year had dampened that.

During the service, he fell under the spell of the liturgy. He had time to meditate about his situation and the knowledge that if he joined the Iskandarov he would not only have to change his name but also join the Orthodox Church. But any religion that allowed mysticism in the form of mad monks such as Rasputin seemed worth further study. Also, with Sainte Xenia's intervention in the Realm of the Spirits, he now sensed she had much greater power than he had imagined and also that he could only fully access that power through Orthodoxy.

After church, Ashley asked Aleks, "Tell me about Saint Vladimir."

"He was a local prince who ruled all the lands around here before and after the Great Famine of 1601 to 1603 that killed an estimated two million people. This occurred during 'The Time of Troubles', a period of anarchy and joint Polish and Lithuanian invasions of Russia. This was the result of the death of Feodor I without issue in 1598. He was the idiot son of Tsar Ivan the Terrible and last of the Rurik Dynasty. We call Tsar Ivan *Grosni*, which means dread, much more accurate and sinister than terrible. The ascension of Michael I, founder of the Romanov Dynasty in 1613 restored stability. Vladimir, allied with Michael, was awarded these lands and more. Vladimir was ultimately a saintly fellow and did a great deal to heal the people and the lands after the chaos. After Vladimir's death, Michael wanted to reward his ally with sainthood."

"And he was Iskandarov?"

"This was the beginning of our power base in Russia. Before the Troubles, our power had been in the south."

"Interesting. I sensed the Institute was owned by our clan before Svetlana Feliksovna took over."

"Yes, the last Iskandarov owner was a direct descendant of Vladimir, although this was not his original house. My mother didn't know much but she knew the house's history, which became the ultimate humiliation as virtually all the Iskandarov sent here also knew it. You look troubled, brother."

"I'm trying to recover a memory but can't recall what or why."

"I get that sometimes. Perhaps, it'll soon come to you."

"Likely. Now, there's something I don't understand. I was surprised you go to church regularly after our conversations yesterday."

"I even surprise myself. Well, this afternoon we're having English Sunday Lunch—roast beef, Yorkshire pudding, veggies, brown gravy, and extra special bitter to wash it down. Then later, a single malt from the Isle of Skye."

"Sounds great, especially, the malt.

* * *

At 3 p.m., on the table where they had breakfast, there was a big Union Jack centerpiece and Ashley asked Aleks about it.

"Oh, it's my little joke. But no one seems to get it. I was certain you would."

"And I do. But let me ask you...before seeing our father's film, I saw the picture of Stalin and your mother. I don't understand."

"Well first, it's a reminder my mother had once been a real human being. And secondly, because there's a wonderful story that goes along with it."

"I'm listening."

"She had just graduated first in her class at NKVD school in 1937. As was customary, Stalin would have a brief meeting with the honoree, give them a medal and a pep talk and they'd be on their way to their assignment. Most people who were sent to Stalin were terrified. After all, he literally held the power of life and death over everyone. Moreover, it was considered a horrible thing if he knew you existed. Most Soviet citizens in those days just wanted to be as anonymous as possible. Svetlana Feliksovna wasn't most people. Because of her smile, you can't see she was angry most of the time and spoke in a very loud voice. Given her brutal upbringing, she also didn't care a damn about people. At this stage of her career, she knew she was special and could probably kill Stalin and get away with it and that made her exceptionally brave."

"Was she delusional?"

"Probably. You decide after my story. She barged into the office. Stalin's secretary, a tubby little man, followed outraged in her wake. But he was dismissed. Stalin was seated at his desk and Svetlana Feliksovna sat on the edge, displaying her beautiful crossed legs. Uninvited, she reached into his cigarette box, took one between her red lips and said, 'Light me.' Stalin looked at her a moment and burst out laughing. I remember this part verbatim. 'Comrade Svetlana Feliksovna, you are very bold young woman.' Without missing a beat, she responded, 'Match!' Stalin again laughed and lit her cigarette. She inhaled deeply and exhaled all the smoke through her nostrils while he lit his own. Stalin asked her why she didn't fear him because everyone else came in in trembling. He could have her shot or locked up in the Lubyanka or exiled to the Zone, what he called the Gulag. She shrugged, 'You would not do that. You know this and so do I.' He replied, 'And, Comrade Svetlana Feliksovna, how do you know this?' She laughed, 'We both know who father was and Organs love me.' He smiled his crocodile smile, 'You think Organs would defy me if I ordered your immediate execution?' She shrugged, 'No, not directly.' She again took a deep drag on her cigarette and stared at him. He, in return, shook his head, 'This is not usual graduation meeting.' She told him she was a scientist, a biologist and that she had a way of making the Soviet people a race of supermen. Stalin immediately asked her how she planned to reach this lofty goal. She told me that his tone was neither dismissive nor enthused. She told him ten million rubles would suffice. He laughed, 'Comrade Svetlana Feliksovna, sum that large will do many things.' She presented her plan in great detail for remodeling the Institute. Stalin countered that he could get *zeks* to remodel it much cheaper. She said that *zek* labor was not delicate and precise enough for such a scientific facility. Stalin then refused but made a counteroffer. He would assign her to a secret and special unit within the *Apparats*. 'Your job would be, along with several other specially chosen comrades, to ensure that Sword of NKVD remains sharp.' She asked if she would be spying on her comrade officers. He asked if she had a problem with that. 'Absolutely not.' He told her she would have clearances to go everywhere and anywhere and to interview anyone, including him. She could tell he really meant it, but because she realized Stalin was her ally, she would never investigate him, unless he turned on her. Then she would kill him. As a reward, when she did an excellent job for him, she would have her Institute. This was the period just before the war with Germany, and Stalin had to make certain there were no unreliable persons in the highest ranks of the Military, Party or State. She asked when she would have her facility. He asked her if she trusted him. She replied that she trusted no one. Stalin laughed and said he wished he could clone her for an entire army. He guaranteed she would have her facility after victory in the coming war because he knew she would be a terror. She was about to leave when Stalin said there was one more thing. Again, I know the exact conversation. 'I have another man and we had similar conversation. He is almost as bold as you. I want two of you to marry because as team you would be three times terror.' She thought it over for a few minutes before agreeing. She was then invited to dine with Stalin that evening and they began their affair. A week later, she married the commissar, the one killed at

Kursk. In case you were wondering, my mother told me that story so many times, it's almost now like I was there with her, sitting on a chair watching."

"Well, you certainly painted a picture for me. I do take issue with one fact. During the Great Purges of the late thirties, the Manchurian Command was left alone and most of the great Soviet officers, including Zhukov, came from there."

"Again, you know your history. Mother actually advised Stalin not to purge the military at all. He refused but, fearing the Japanese who wanted Siberia, he spared that one command. And when the Germans invaded in 1941, they were facing Party hacks commanders and hence the horrible slaughter of the Soviet troops."

"I've decided my question about her killing Stalin is moot. Had she killed him and taken over, she would've been just as bad, if not worse, than Stalin."

"That's a story for another time. Mother dragged Rini and me—never Nata—to Stalin's Kremlin office on many occasions. He liked us and we were always treated well by our Uncle Josif. Mother never spoke of her husband and there were no pictures of him in the house. It's possible the memory of him was too painful for her, although I greatly doubt it. I believe they were more of a team than a marriage. And knowing her as I did, I wouldn't be surprised, given her affair with Stalin, if they hadn't even lived together. In the event, they were the terror Stalin had predicted. Stalin was exceptionally good at reading people and then placing them where they would do him the most benefit. He knew that someone like Svetlana Feliksovna wouldn't be bound by any conventions—Soviet or otherwise. People like her seldom are. He also knew she would be absolutely ruthless in dealing with 'spies, counter-revolutionaries and wreckers.' In the meantime, he quietly had many of the Iskandarovs, either here or abroad, rounded up. They were sent to a special camp where their treatment was rather good. Then, when this Institute opened, she had a good supply of, as she put it, 'subjects.' Our father was not rounded up for a while after the war because he was still listed as Spencer Talbott on all the official documents. There was her *muzhik* tea that could cause a man to remain aroused for hours so, she could collect as much Iskandarov seed as she wanted."

"We know her experiments were failures."

"You can no more extract what makes us unique than you can throw a snowball from here to the Kremlin."

"Yes, of course."

After dinner, Aleks and Ashley sat under the patio awning watching the rain, telling tall tales and jokes as they became drunker on the single malt and enjoying Ashley's secret vice— Cuban cigars. After Aleks went up, Ashley saw an *Andronyi* about Natalya and her sister Iskandarovas and smiled.

4.

Monday morning, Ashley awoke with a terrible hangover and the sun in his eyes. He rose to close the curtains and looked out on the formal garden and the high shrubbery. *Tvarsch* hit him hard with "explore the Maze." He shakily put on khaki shorts, a white polo shirt, and deck shoes, and stumbled down to breakfast. Not seeing Aleks, he asked Feodor in French, seemingly the only language he spoke, where Aleks might be.

"Difficult to say, Monsieur. The prince has not emerged from his chamber. He will not be among the living for some time. And even longer, if he is dead." He smiled slyly and raised his eyebrows. "*Alors*, would you like what the prince normally eats on such occasions."

Ashley nodded and was soon eating scrambled eggs and caviar, some greasy sausage, flat champagne and strong tea. Ashley soon felt some reflux. He knew a brisk walk in the maze, even if he became lost, would be a superb hangover remedy.

Outside, his head still throbbing, his sunglasses protected him from the overly bright sun, and he heard someone to his far right mowing the lawn. The wonderful smell of fresh cut grass reminded him of Quaker Mount and made him feel better as he walked the gravel paths of the formal garden. He paused at a monument with statues of his grandparents, Dmitri and Sophia. He knelt, getting his knees wet, to say a prayer, and hoped to receive a vibration from them but felt nothing.

He headed toward the maze about twenty feet away and remembered Feodor told him that if he became lost there to scream like a banshee. Feodor kept things light and Ashley needed that lightness after he read a gold Cyrillic plaque fastened to a black pole:

UNDER BEAUTY OF THIS GARDEN ARE MASS GRAVES OF OUR ISKANDAROV MARTYRS MURDERED BY COLONEL SVETLANA FELIKSOVNA POLINKOVA. THEIR IDENTITIES ARE KNOWN ONLY TO THEMSELVES AND TO GOD. MAY WE ALL MEET AGAIN IN THAT BETTER PLACE.

He paused, said another prayer for all the dead under his feet and went through the Maze's entrance to its tall greenery and pebbled paths. Initially, the path was narrow, and he put his hands on both sides of the hedges. Sudden hand pains made him realize the hedge was holly bush—definitely not something one could power though without being completely cut up. He stared at his cut and bloody hands. *Yes, Aleks was wrong, this blood is what makes us unique.* He licked the blood off before continuing among all the beautiful flowers lining the paths. Their aromas relaxed him. He breathed in deeply in this quiet, idyllic spot as he walked. As the path widened, a light caught his peripheral vision and shining in the sun, there was another gold plaque:

4 JULY 1947 AT THIS PLACE, EVAHN IVANOVICH PRINCE ISKANDAROV, WAS MURDERED MOST FOULLY. MAY WE ALL MEET AGAIN IN THAT BETTER PLACE.

Tvarsch showed Evahn, a human torch, screaming as he burned to death, and Ashley could smell gasoline and feel his unbearable burning flesh. He held on to the plaque to support himself as his stomach churned and his head spun. Despite this horror, he eventually recovered and continued walking, getting lost in several dead ends, but he had to continue because this was clearly another test. He stopped when he saw a fifteen-foot wooden cross to his left with another gold plaque:

7 JULY 1947 XENIA IVANOVNA PRINCESS ISKANDAROVA
BECAUSE SHE HEROICALLY MAINTAINED OUR RELIGIOUS
TRADITIONS, WAS MURDERED MOST HORRIBLY AS WARNING
TO OTHERS NOT TO DEFY MAJOR POLINKOVA. MAY WE ALL
MEET IN THAT BETTER PLACE.

Tvarsch revealed naked Xenia, full-term pregnant, and he felt the railroad spikes, which nailed her hands and feet to the cross, and a rounded black iron bar hammered into the cross under her large belly supporting her weight while binding her thighs so she could not give birth. Ashley felt her pain intensifying as she tried to give birth to her son. Pyotr, fighting to be born, caused her increasing pain to pass unbearable until it abruptly decreased because the fight abruptly ended. Pyotr was dead and Xenia's brokenhearted suffering surpassed even that of being on the cross. Without her baby, she lost her will to live and soon all pain stopped when she died.

The bastards killed her physically and emotionally. Knowing that Xenia was now an angel and a saint helped subdue Ashley's pain. Looking down, he could make out most of his breakfast on the gravel with some staining on his damp, sweaty shirt. *These plaques are confirmation of Svetlana Feliksovna's ghastly experiments in Iskandarov-Polinkov breeding. My father's mission to Camp David makes perfect sense and I feel even more respect for him. He risked his life and freedom for the chance to help Charlotte, whom he loved, escape from Hell.* Sainte Xenia, still on the cross, smiled down upon him with sublime peace. He smiled, but not for long. Upon rising, he came to a bench plaque:

5 JUNE 1948 NATALYA IVANOVNA ISKANDAROVA, OF BARREN
STOCK, WAS MURDERED ON THIS DATE. MAY WE ALL MEET IN
THAT BETTER PLACE.

Tvarsch saw her many Mongolian guards raping her as she lay bound and spread-eagled on this bench, Mongolian guards raping her before horribly stabbing her to death. He sensed she was why Svetlana Feliksovna had all the guards castrated so as not to interfere with her "experiments." Could his Natalya be a namesake, even a replacement for this Natalya? He looked down, the remainder of his breakfast and some of his dinner lay at his feet, especially, the tomatoes, with only green bile down his chin and his wet shirt. He sat silently on the bench and, despite his revulsion, sensed he must stay to learn who and what he was becoming. Taking a deep breath of the flowers, he felt almost calm. *These flowers have been selected for their calming scents and I wonder what else?*

Later, lost after several dead ends on narrow paths, he saw only holly on all sides until the glimmer of another plaque caught his eye and led him back to a wider path:

TO ALL ZEKS AND ZECHKAS KILLED IN MAZE, THEIR IDENTITY KNOWN ONLY TO THEMSELVES AND GOD. MAY WE ALL MEET IN THAT BETTER PLACE.

As he read this, he saw first a tear splattered on the plaque, followed by more, and soon he could not stop. Although he knew none of these people, he felt great empathy for his kin to have suffered so terribly. He had been extremely empathetic with Olga Sergeyvna, but after she was murdered, that part of him had receded. He closed his eyes, thinking about the *zeks* and *zechkas* hunted down here for sport and intense rage crowded out his tears. *I shed tears of pain for all. Rage will only make me do something stupid. I must regain my composure.*

Sitting on another bench, he felt proud to be associated with these people. In a place of intentional and almost unimaginable cruelty and terror, the Iskandarov retained their faith when most others in the Soviet Union had lost theirs. Because the Iskandarov posed a real threat to the regime, they were persecuted, but in the end, they triumphed.

After walking further, he felt heavy and lethargic as he thought of Natalya. *That damn witch is just toying with me. If I can't focus, she would be all I can think about. Why can I not feel this way about someone not my full sister? Surely, there must be someone else I could love. Yes, I've been intimate with my half-sisters, Olga and Ronnie. I'm certain if I rely on tvarsch, it'll lead me to Nata's bed. Therefore, I must ignore it and rely on my rational self. But that would lead to Svetlana Polinkova. And how* can I now be intimate with the daughter of the architect of this horror? I'm lost between two women. No, three with Anghelina. He sat and raised his face to the warmth of the sun, letting his mind go blank and again Natalya entered his thoughts. To counter this, he thought about being Of the Iskandarov, which was a package deal and not a Chinese buffet. Annie genuinely believed in becoming an Iskandarova and she, with the zeal of the new convert, would never leave these people. People? More like these martyrs who now surround me had such faith. Something I never had to any great degree.

After Olga died, he eventually found and loved the ritual and majesty of the Episcopal service. But faith? He was trained as a lawyer. Facts were what mattered, not intangibles. His father had great faith and that was what held him together during his darkest days—of which he had many. Slowly and tentatively, Ashley processed all the information that had been thrown at him since that long-ago letter from David, telling him he was adopted. The Countess Sophia had told him that he must become a warrior to be Of Iskandarov. Clearly, fighting was more important than lawyering to the Iskandarov, but he had no idea how to become one. Right now, Natalya was right, he was nothing, no one. No longer Ashley Cooper but not yet arrived…at what? Sergei Sergeyovich? No, that was not whom he wanted to be. But he aspired to be whom? Natalya again consumed his thoughts, especially her eyes with their knowing and sadness, eyes reflecting the unimaginable horrors she had seen and experienced here. Eyes that seared his soul and in which he could become lost forever. She had looked at him critically, as no one ever had, and asked, "Are you worthy enough to be my brother, my lover?" No, he had to drive such ideas from his head. He could never be incestuous with his sister. The taboo remained too strong because he remembered seeing the results of incest—sometime in the mid-fifties driving through Appalachia with David and Patricia on the way down to Georgia for a Cooper Family Reunion. Iskandarova Natalya would have no such qualms about incest. But growing up, he always wanted a sister and she was strong because she had persevered through everything to become a ballerina at the Kirov. She was scarred by her ordeal, just as their father had been. There was no one who could take Ashley's place as the Hidden One. Not even Aleks, whom he sensed would never really be ready to lead the clan because his power lay outside it.

I've not suffered as Aleks and Rini, Natalya and our father and mother had plus all the martyrs here and in the Gulag. So, I'm not worthy to be an Iskandarov. As punishment, I feel the hedges are closing in from both sides and the path has disappeared. Oh my God, I feel all alone as the holly smothers me. I'm doomed. I should've stayed in New York. I've no business being here. The holly's now pressing all over me and I feel as though I'm being cut with a thousand razors and I can't breathe. I'm dying and can't fight this alone. No. Wait. I can because the blood of Iskandar flows in my veins and I'm Iskandarov and I embrace the pain. I'm also not alone here among my kin. As they're teaching me, I'm learning to become a warrior.

And then he was back on the path with cuts. I realize having merely kissed Nata, if I can't commit to her, I'll be completely lost and lonely for the rest of my life. And that will daily feel like being trapped in the holly. And to think I almost named Annie, Holly.

Moving as *tvarsch* navigated through the twists, turns and dead ends of the Maze and when the paths again became narrower, he received more cuts all over. But he ignored them. The floral aromas soothed him as he walked, and he began to make sense of what had just happened; this was all part of his transition and he understood why it had to happen here.

6.

Ashley smelled pipe tobacco and Aleks did not seem surprised to see him and said, "Hello, Ash. We really have to stop meeting like this."

Despite himself, Ashley laughed, and his spirits rose.

"Had I known you were coming in here, I would've advised against breakfast. You really look a fright, old man." Aleks laughed heartily. "You've been here for a while. I wager it was Princess Xenia who did the damage to your shirt."

"Well, while it has all been intense, because I know Sainte Xenia, she resonated most. But her husband's flaming death and the other Natalya's rape and murder were equally horrible."

"Let me tell you more about our other martyrs."

As they walked, the Maze felt like the warm inside of his brain and Ashley suddenly blurted, "I sense you killed Chichikov. When was that?"

"*Tvarsch* is getting stronger. I killed Pavel Chichikov years before Bangkok. I'll let Nata tell you the details. It was strange though, I thought Svetlana Feliksovna would punish me severely for what I'd done to her paramour. But she displayed no emotion and, in her self-absorbed manner, truly did not appear to care. There's a tie to Bangkok, though. As I said before, the man I killed there was Heinrich Sassen, a Stasi operative. He had replaced Chichikov as Svetlana Feliksovna's paramour and primary operative. He killed most of her enemies, real or perceived, outside the Institute."

"So, why was I her enemy? I didn't even know she existed."

"As far as she was concerned, you were her property because your parents were her slaves. That's why she sent Stashinski and Richardt Frank to kidnap you on Quaker Mount back in 1962. And subsequently, the attempt to wound you in Bangkok and have you brought back here."

"Wound? I remember distinctly, while I was in the falcon the assassin was trying to kill me."

"You survived, and I'd wager, even without my intervention, you would've survived as well."

"Why are you telling me this only now?"

"After you experienced what happened in Bangkok, I thought it would be perfectly obvious to you. I also know Sassen's orders to wound and incapacitate."

"Why?"

"After the 1962 kidnappings failed, in 1972 Svetlana Feliksovna resumed them because Nata, as an Iska at seventeen was no longer a child and could get pregnant. This was after she tried unsuccessfully to block Nata's Ceremony and Kirov and absent Bayta and her protection, she would've. Because you were too well protected on the military bases, it took a year to get everything set. After successfully kidnapping you in 1973 and getting Nata fired from the Kirov, you would've been ordered to mate with our Nata. Svetlana Feliksovna told me that had either of you refused, she would've tortured you both together until you agreed. But, since that was what you two wanted, I don't think that would have been necessary. You both would've been the genesis of Svetlana Feliksovna's race of superior Communists. And once Nata was pregnant, Bayta could've done nothing. Abortion was never an option because that is abhorrent to all Iskandarovs."

"What a wonderful and horrible existence with Nata and your mother. Now, I saw what happened in Bangkok—the bullet slowed down as the air seemed to curve and it went down closer to my heart. So, I think my protector, Sainte Elizabeta, whose presence I sensed but did not see, wanted me dead."

"She knew you were in danger of being kidnapped. And she decided, not having any good choices, it was better you be killed quickly than to become a slave. And absent my intervention, Sassen's second shot, probably to your leg, would've incapacitated you and you'd be here."

"Right. But Olga Sergeyvna's intervention undid the harm of Sainte Elizabeta's decision."

"Well, Olga Sergeyvna wanted you alive. By Jove, why didn't you tell me about Sainte Elizabeta the other day?"

"Well, you were acting like a complete atheist asshole and wouldn't have believed it. But thank you for your intervention."

"Think nothing of it, old son-of-a-fart." He laughed. "Tell you what. I've already received death threats about the L'Enfant Initiative. If anyone shoots me over that, you can kill them. Then, we'll really be even."

Ashley felt uncertain about Aleks's seriousness. "The odds of that happening appear absurdly long for one of the best-protected men in Russia."

"Life is cheap here, brother. Now, I'll tell you more about Chichikov. The irony was he taught me how to use a pistol. He also taught me to hunt and fish and we went camping. The life of a GRU agent wasn't easy. I emphatically make no apologies for his crimes. He was a profoundly lonely and scared man, an ignorant, yet cunning, peasant, caught up in an unending cycle of unimaginable terror. Where today's tormentor, through no fault of their own, could well be tomorrow's victim."

"But if it hadn't been for him, my mother…"

"No, brother. That's the point. It would have been someone else—purely anonymous, interchangeable cogs in a giant mechanism producing terror, just as machines produce shoes." He puffed on his pipe. "Had not the revolution of Lenin and Stalin so completely destroyed Russian society, my mother would've been a peasant's wife. Despite her high rank, she remained a peasant, hobbled by peasant superstitions and beliefs, and is why she insisted on having our father's children, rather than foisting it off on some underling. In peasant culture, the more children a woman has, the greater her status." Aleks chuckled. "Of course, there can be no doubt she was totally crackers. A fact she acknowledged."

"How so?"

"She bragged to me on several occasions that in her village, she would've been ostracized. Because, as she put it, she had always seen and thought differently, which she prized as 'revolutionary consciousness'. It was madness all the same. So, she was drawn into Stalin's orbit as naturally as metal to a magnet."

"You're certainly giving both of them the extreme benefit of the doubt."

"You think this is easy for me? I hate, detest and loathe my mother. And while I can never forgive her..."

"I get that. What can you tell me about her?"

"As a child, she was heartbreakingly beautiful and an orphan, living with her aunt and uncle in a village outside Kiev. The Civil War was over, but times remained exceptionally hard. What I'm about to tell you is something I've verified with *tvarsch* because she would neither confirm nor deny it. And it's not in any documents I've seen. One afternoon, when she was about eight, her uncle lured her to a hut with a promise of food. There was no food, only twelve men. They passed her around like a vodka bottle, each, in turn, raping her. When the morning came, they tossed her out. Her aunt soon collected her. While she carried the unconscious child home, a commissar stopped her and asked what happened to beautiful Svetlana. The aunt told him and went home. A day later, the uncle and his comrades were rounded up along with the aunt. All tortured and executed."

"Even the aunt?"

"Especially the aunt. She had failed to protect the child and so she, reportedly, had her eyes gouged out before being executed. After that, Dzerzhinski had Svetlana Feliksovna brought to Moscow not as his daughter but as a Hero of the Revolution, raped by *Kulaks*, the so-called rich peasants. At least that's what they were declared after the fact. In truth, those Polinkov were poor as dirt. Of course, this all fit in with the Party's war against the peasantry. She was raised by a trusted Chekist aide because Dzerzhinski knew, by then, he was dying. Under this tutelage, she learned everything a successful woman commissar needed to know. Especially, being skillful enough to always be one step ahead of Stalin and smart enough to stay in the background. For most, becoming Stalin's lover was ultimately a one-way ticket to the Gulag. Like Scheherazade, she charmed the murderous sultan and convinced him of the need to punish the Iskandarov as Enemies of the People. After the war, she had free reign to carry out her plan here."

"Why did she hate the Iskandarov? They hadn't raped her."

"She felt, as all Polinkov do, that we had somehow robbed them of their birthright."

"Sounds delusional. Stalin knew what she was doing here?"

"No, he didn't want to know. If her scheme backfired, it would be on Svetlana Feliksovna and not him."

"How long did the Institute function?"

"It began in the spring of 1946 and the worst excesses lasted until the mid-fifties. After our father left for Camp David in 1955, she lost interest. Because, after 1953 when Stalin died, she understood the shift in the political winds. Therefore, she cleverly supported Khrushchev in his fight for control. And became, reportedly, his mistress for a few years until Bayta replaced her. Then, Svetlana Feliksovna's reward was to continue her projects with a generous state subsidy to expand the Institute. Like Stalin, Khrushchev didn't want to know what went on here. She turned the Institute into a resource for gathering information about the remaining internal and overseas Iskandarovs and other Enemies of the People. But her excesses continued, on a lesser scale, well into the seventies. She was then sending out teams and such, like Stashinski and Frank. By the way, Stashinski, whom you called Ovals, never had sanction to kill you, only to scare you and keep you off balance prior to your planned kidnapping."

"What finally happened?"

"When Svetlana Feliksovna learned that her property, as she called father, produced two girls—Anghelina and Rosalita— with Cuban Maria Civilli, she was incensed. Initially, she maintained the girls were her property because they had been conceived with her seed and demanded their return. Angelina DelaVega, Maria's mother, wrote to her to go to blazes. Later, as I've said, Svetlana Feliksovna shot our father and that was the end of her Institute. I released every non-Iskandarov working here, leaving our guards and Rini, Nata, Bayta, Feodor and our retainers. Thus, we began making it over to what you see today."

"You know, I'm not sure I could stay in this place. After just a few hours, I feel drained."

"Not an uncommon Maze reaction. Rini hates it here. Nata spends most of her time at her studio. For me, it's safer than Moscow. Therefore, I am here quite often. Rini stays here, I think, primarily out of her love for me. I understand this in larger terms. This estate, confiscated by the Polinkov, now again belongs to us. That's our victory over Svetlana Feliksovna. Were we to abandon this place, Svetlana Polinkova and her allies would take it over in a heartbeat. And our victory would be lost."

"I understand." However, the Polinkov peace proposal might be the best overall solution. I understand Svetlana Polinkova and can deal with her. Arranging peace between these feuding clans would my gift to both. Wait, that's how Nata's pyordarsch becomes reality. Wrong again, Ash. "Tell me, though, aren't you scared about telling me all this about Iron Cage and such? Everyone else seemed too terrified to say anything about it."

"Doubtless so. Since the Soviet Union no longer exists, who cares? Who can be embarrassed? Certainly not Russia, which bears no responsibility for the acts of the previous regime, which, I believe, is in our Federation constitution. Certainly not me or Yeltsin for the same reason. Therefore, primarily only the American, British and French Governments should like to conceal this matter. In addition, I suppose there are some die-hard Communists who should like to suppress it, as well. But you, you've a right to know what happened to our father and why."

"I get the impression you feel there are other culprits at work here as well."

"I do. I've seen copies of documents, which I intend to share with you, indicating Charles Drew was the partner in your law firm assigned to making certain our father never reappeared. He reported to a 'Mr. Phillips'."

"Yes, Charles has consistently misled me about anything related to my father. Any information on whom Mr. Phillips might be?"

"Your father-in-law, Farwell, seems a very good possibility."

"No surprises there. Are there others?"

"Yes, however, circumstantially, there is one who appears very plausible."

"And whom might that be?"

"I'm sorry, Ash, but it's Colonel Cooper."

"David? Surely, you're joking. That's ridiculous."

"I know how you must feel…"

"You have no fucking idea how I feel."

"Yes, you're right. But please, hear me out."

Ashley regained his composure while exhaling loudly. "Fine, go ahead."

"Hasn't it struck you as strange that Colonel Cooper asked his protégé to go on what he must've known to be a one-way mission? Exceptionally effective way to dispose of Spencer Talbott."

"An exceptionally good question. One I've been scared to ask myself."

"As I say, the evidence for Colonel Cooper's only circumstantial. I want you to be aware that your Gulag diary quest may raise issues you truly do not wish to face. I thought it advisable to prepare you for the possibility that your stepfather could be involved."

"I appreciate that. I think David redeemed himself for any alleged sins by working so hard to get Sergei released from prison. And there's always a lot of politics involved in anyone's promotion at The Firm—from even becoming an associate, and then associate to partner, and partner to senior partner. Nothing unusual there. That last step is the tricky one. I never asked David about his making senior partner. He certainly had the qualifications but that alone wasn't enough. Clearly, no one makes senior partner without George's blessing. In my own case, I'm certain I made senior partner to keep me from coming here and learning my heritage."

"I now grasp why L'Enfant's so important to you—a peace offering to the powers-that-be. Now, I've a question for you and I'm not looking for an immediate answer. Why do you feel the need to even return to your firm? It sounds like a real snake pit. Are we so much worse?"

"Everyone's treated me very well here, even, to a degree, Nata. And, of course, the Iskandarovs have saved my life several times. So, I'm in our clan's debt. That, in part, is why I'm going after the diary. And yes, the luster of the Firm has begun to fade."

"Fair enough. I need to fill in one more chapter in our father's saga. After Camp David, Svetlana Feliksovna, having no further use for our father, was perfectly willing to let him be buried alive in an American prison. She even went so far as to tell us he no longer loved us. But *tvarsch* caught her in the lie." He grinned. "She sent a General Rianovski to negotiate an arrangement with the American government to not release him under any circumstances. Sadly, the Americans proved only too interested in complying. This was during Grand Duchess Nadia's first attempt to get him released when the deal quite suddenly fell apart.

"Ronnie told me she, as Madame Veronique Landfear, David and Angelina DelaVega Delgado did the negotiations with Henry Baker representing my government."

"True, but Nadia Mytrovna as Bleu's Prime Director was always in charge. Also, I'm told Colonel Cooper had to use every ounce of influence, persuasion and threat to achieve our father's release. And if you're wondering, not even Colonel Cooper could've shortened Sergei's captivity by so much as five minutes."

"How do you know all this?"

"I've used my position to locate every file extant concerning our father, Svetlana Feliksovna, Pavel Chichikov, Stashinski, Frank and Sassen, among others."

"There's something else I'd like to know. I must know the name of the architect of my protection over the years."

"Along with Nadia, your Uncle Alexei Dmitrovich. Actually, our father's half-brother. In the late thirties, at the height of Stalin's terror against the Iskandarov and Russia in general, Alexei successfully led a group of Iskandarov to Iran, where they waited out Stalin. They returned under Khrushchev's thaw. But during the war, he was in Washington at the French Embassy…"

"He was Pen's real father, not George."

"Correct. Alexei's a long-time Bleu officer and lives in the Cartvelian Mountains but travels extensively. He married the daughter of a Don Cossack chieftain in Iran and had many children with her, who are now scattered throughout the Caucasus, Russia and the Middle East."

"Is he still alive?"

"Yes, very much."

"I want to meet him."

"Brother, that would be difficult."

"Why?"

"He's back in the shadows again. By that, I mean that he is in the process of negotiating some particularly important and delicate matters. But rest assured, once he has returned, you'll be on his calendar."

"Thanks. Now, tell me about Iskandar."

"Personally, I think it was probable some Colchi warlord started this tale to give extra prestige to his clan."

"Aleks, why are you debunking this when I know you believe it?"

"Oh? At the end of the day, what difference does it make if we are descended from Alexander or some obscure Colchi chieftain, who was probably influenced by him? We've accomplished a great deal and are destined for more greatness." He paused. "Remember back in classical Greek times, Medea, who helped Jason find the Golden Fleece? She was not just a Colchi princess, but also a sorceress. Nata is merely following tradition."

"Right. Nata said I have the Devil's Triangle—handsome, powerful and rich. I'd say she has her own Devil's Triangle—princess, sorceress and temptress."

"I see you're feeling better now." Aleks checked his watch. "Well, I must be heading back. I've an important call coming in. But before that, I need breakfast."

"Good. I'll go back with you."

"No stay. It's a beautiful day. There's still much the Maze will teach you."

Confident of his ability to navigate the Maze, Ashley said, "See you in a while. Brother, in all your files, do you have a map of the Vorkuta camp?"

Aleks turned. "I don't have any maps. Nor can I recall ever seeing one because only Chekists have maps of the Gulag and they're reluctant to share, even with me." Aleks disappeared around a corner before Ashley went deeper into the Maze, *tvarsch* guiding him.

EIGHT

Monday, 7 June 1993, Novo Ogarevo

1.

In another section of the Maze, Ashley Cooper heard Maurice Ravel's Bolero, which became gradually louder. *I don't know what Ravel had in mind, but I imagine one of the legendary caravans leaving from the grand mosque of Timbuktu, capital of the Mali Empire, where the Mansa set out on his hajj pilgrimage to Mecca. The caravan of elephants and camels stretched for miles to show his immense wealth as it moved regally and leisurely across North Africa. He also brought his favorite wives, concubines, courtiers, soldiers and especially, drummers. But it's also a damn earworm and I won't be able to get it out of my head for at least a week*

He stood before the entrance to a large grass area surrounded by a tall hedge—the center of the Maze. But surprisingly, a few feet in front of him by a bench was a Soviet PKS tripod-mounted machine gun, which Ashley recognized as a staple of the North Vietnamese Army, its fresh coat of silver paint reflecting the sun. *Why would Aleks keep such a painful reminder? Strange man indeed.*

As he stepped onto the grass, he felt extremely disappointed to see Svetlana Polinkova, not Natalya. *Ah yes, a real Maze has a Minotaur at its center and here she is.* He decided he would be cordial but careful. She was reading and sunning herself on one of several large lawn chaises with four-inch pillows, wearing only bright red panties. He had not seen her toned arms and legs, flat stomach and sloping breasts in a while. *Her display is for my benefit because she knew from bugging us, I'd be here. She was never very subtle.* A red portable radio was the source of *Bolero*, next to a red and black satchel beside her chaise. She looked up and smiled. "*Dobraheh dehn, Kitzi.*" She continued in her refined Russian. "I am delighted to see you, but you look pale as whitefish and your cuts and shirt…"

Ashley responded, "*Preveht.* I did not expect to find you here."

She smiled gleefully. "I am trespassing because I know of old gate in far wall. Remember, I grew up here and come often. I am not on good terms Aleksandr. He is half-brother but wants to shoot me. But come, I need sunscreen on my back." She handed Ashley the tube, rolled over and he rubbed the oil into her warm, smooth skin. "That feels delightful. If you are good boy, I may let you rub more oil on my tits." She laughed. "I believe you are doing this because you have forgiven me for manipulating you to get me pregnant in New York."

"Oh, I knew what you were doing, but you had me so aroused with your mother's tea, I did not care. Today, I most certainly do." He continued applying the lotion. "Now that I have finished, roll back over."

She smiled and rolled onto her back. As he slowly ran his hands over her abdomen, she laughed, "Naughty boy." But soon said, "What are you doing?"

"Satisfying my curiosity. Lie still." Sergei Dmitrovich had written that he'd used this method to discover that Nata's babies with her cosmonaut husband would be inferior. I thought this technique would at least reveal whether Svetlana was actually pregnant. And I feel a vibration. "You are pregnant. But do you not realize, like Aleks, he shall mature to become good Iskandarov?"

"Then you want me to abort baby?"

"I sense you shall kill him eventually."

"We shall see about that. All right. Why are you here?"

"*Tvarsch* guided me. Iskandarovs rejected your peace proposal."

"You most certainly did not come here to only tell me that. I am not surprised. They wish to continue slaughtering us."

"Do not try to play victim. That never shall work with me. Now, what is name of my son?"

"Pyotr."

"Why?"

"First husband of mother killed at Kursk in 1943. Why?"

He remained silent as he rose. She wore no make-up and for the first time he noticed a slight slant to her eyes, no doubt, the result of some Tatar bloodlines. And he remembered the old adage, "Scratch Russian and you find Tatar." A result of the Mongol Golden Horde's long and brutal rule.

She rose and softly ran her hand across his jaw, while slightly shaking her breasts, trying most unsubtlety to distract him from her eyes. She said, "Honestly, all I want is you. Not quite all, I want to get away from madness of feud over death mask of Iskandar your family long ago stole from Palaeologus."

Ashley knew from lifelong experience that when someone said "honestly", they were usually lying. "Come on, stop playing victim. Iskandarov bought mask legally and saved Palaeologus from certain death had they remained in Constantinople. Because, after conquest, Turk slaughtered all Byzantines they could find, with a much more horrible fate for royal Palaeologus."

"Perhaps but charged them ransom for king to sail to Sakartvelo."

"Are you saying Palaeologus lives then were not valuable? Do not forget virtually everyone was trying to escape Constantinople. Iskandarov easily could have found other passengers willing to pay even more."

"How do you know so much about this?"

"How come you know so little? Enough of this. You said you wanted to go someplace else. Where would that be?"

"We shall decide together. In short term, my dacha is short distance from here in beautiful forest. Seems logical place for us to go. What is harm?" Although she maintained her calm and cool persona, her constant brushing of her hair away from her face betrayed her nervousness. His presence here meant a lot to her. Ashley also remembered his attraction beyond the obvious— her brains and confidence like Olga Sergeyvna. But as a Polinkova, she lacked any type of aura. *Should I even be talking to this sworn enemy of the Iskandarov? Especially, in this place where her mother had slaughtered so many of my kin. I could leave but I need to know more about her and the Polinkov. Having heard Aleks's version of history, I now have a chance to hear hers.*

"I realize you have been already negatively influenced by Iskandarov. I am no different than I was in New York, only now, I have competition."

"And who is this competition?"

"Madame *Prinkipia* Natalya, as she so grandly styles herself. I know she wants you to make her many babies."

"Natalya? I certainly think not." *I don't owe Svetlana any truth.*

"Do not be so certain. She knows you relish challenge, but you are most reluctant to mate with your sister. I, and most normal people, understand that. Incest is, after all, universal taboo." She leaned forward. "Besides, since I am pregnant, we would just be having fun when you join me at my dacha. I also understand Iskandarov women, especially sorceresses, once they have been intimate, exert extraordinarily strong influence over their husbands. Your expression says you think this is just some babushka tale. Well, think about your relationship with Olga Sergevna. Should you become intimate with Madame *Prinkipia* and if she becomes pregnant, she shall be killed by same people who killed Olga Sergevna."

"Yes, you Polinkov always play for keeps." *Raskolnikov.* Ashley turned to leave.

"I realize you are now fearful of me. I am certain they have made mother out to be complete monster. And you think I am just as she?"

Ashley turned. "I assume, just like mother, you want complete destruction of Iskandarov."

"Yes, *Kitzi.* However, you are mistaken about one thing. Polinkov did not kill Olga Sergevna."

She's lying again. Tvarsch didn't register it. That simply means she believed her statement. "Very well, who did?"

She shook her head. "With murder and abuse of all Polinkovas over time, we would certainly be justified to take Iskandarova life. In this case, we are innocent. Same people who buried your father alive and made certain that daughter, Olga Sergeyvna, would not bear child with you."

"And who might these people be?"

"Rich and powerful in your country, same persons who abandoned your soldiers to Gulag. Do not imagine such abandonment ended with Great Patriotic War. Just last year, when our President, Mr. Yeltsin, visited your President, Mr. Bush, he told him American POWs remained trapped in Russia. Do you know what your government did? They said, after he left, Mr. Yeltsin had been misquoted."

"Yes, I remember something about that." While I can't really believe my own government could be against me, I can't dismiss it either. Iron Cage has become the ultimate irony. The kidnappers no longer have an interest in its suppression, only the victims' governments. "I assume you're referring to my father-in-law, George Farwell?"

"He is merely one of several in a very large web."

Not buying this. I don't think she would know the truth if it bit her on her lovely ass. "I am certain you believe what you are saying, but you are mistaken. It was KGB agent Raskolnikov who ultimately poisoned her. And very nearly me."

"Now that would be tragedy. I am certain Iskandarov have poisoned your mind against Mother."

"Well, she is not exactly giving Mother Theresa any competition for sainthood."

"Ah, you make joke."

"Yes, but I am willing to listen to anything you can say in her defense."

She went back to her chaise and pulled a red T-shirt from the satchel. *Covering herself means no distractions and she's going to be serious now.* "You came here to promote L'Enfant Initiative. I am seemingly only person here who knows importance of that to you. Best way for resuming your career." She waved her hand curtly. "No matter, you spoke of all parties in Balkans being guilty. No different here. You have again walked in during third act. Hear what I have to say and form your conclusions."

Ashley, arms folded, said, "Go on."

"Mother, poor peasant girl was born to terrible, horrible time. She knew of family's glorious past. But what good does that do you when you are starving? Her childhood, if it may be called something sounding so idyllic, consisted of learning how to stay alive." She began to pace, and her eyes shone, as she tried to conceal her anger. "She possessed strong will and pretty face, which could usually get her piece of bread and bed for night. She learned quickly and well, while forgetting nothing. When she rose to highest levels, she used her power to destroy Iskandarov as Iskandarov had tried to destroy Polinkov." She looked directly at him. "Have no doubt, had your father exercised power over her, he would have been as ruthless as she. Mother considered your father her property in partial compensation for all Polinkov serfs enslaved for centuries by Iskandarov. Immune to his charm, she humiliated him in view of his wife, to where he wished to die. She would not permit that. Mother kept him constantly on edge. Later, she helped make certain he remained buried alive in prison, knowing being deprived of women to adore and spoil him would be unbearable torture. Your father remained determined as well. When he reappeared here in 1976, she was done with him and did not wish him to charm any other women, as he had Cuban Rose whore. She resolved to kill him. After she did, as I have told you, Party turned on her and she was sent away to be tortured until she died."

Tvarsch tells me she is lying about father wanting to die. He wanted to kill her instead. "Now, when were you born?"

She studied Ashley, again brushing her hair away before smiling. "I am twenty-eight, same as mother when she began her rise. I understand what Iskandarov do not. Mother's brilliance lay in her using sexual power of Iskandarov to defeat them. To use seed of Iskandarov to empower new dynasty of Party leaders."

"Very well, then why did plan fail?" I want to see how truthful or realistic she can occasionally be.

"If I might digress, in March 1953 closest comrades of Stalin poisoned and ensured his most painful death."

"I know. What does this have to do with your mother?"

"Mother denounced Stalin's anti-Semitic Doctor's Plot, then in progress, as preliminary to going to war, just as Great Cleansings of thirties had been."

"Great Cleansing?" Give me a break. Mass deportations and killings are more like it.

"And that meant men closest to him—Khrushchev, Beria, Malenkov, Molotov and Bulganin, among others—would be replaced by younger men. After mother told them he would use his atom bombs against West, comrades struck first."

"I know about this conspiracy against Stalin, but I never heard anything as preposterous as this atomic war with West."

"Marshal Stalin told my mother, his only true confidant, of his plans. After Soviet victory, he would have been master of all Europe."

"I think not. First, your few nuclear bombs were quite primitive and may not have worked at all. Also, we possessed majority of nuclear weapons and delivery systems and if provoked, we would not have hesitated to use them. If this is true, Stalin would have ensured destruction of only Soviet Union."

"Not so. Stalin planned to preposition inconspicuous tramp steamers with atomic bombs in their holds, covered with lead shields, in New York and London, among other places. He would have made certain relevant persons knew of this when he demanded West Germany be demilitarized and, therefore, neutralized. If capitalists resisted, or if there was any deployment of bombers or missiles, he would give order to detonate." She brought her arms up in an arc over her head. "Bam! No New York." She smiled delightedly.

"Seems like clever, diabolical plan, so why settle for only Germany?"

"Stalin knew, like Bismarck, whoever controlled Germany, controlled Europe. Without their military to resist, great industrial power of Germany would soon be working for Soviet Union. With work of sympathetic or appeasing politicians, rest of continental Europe, except Britain, would soon have fallen into his hands, just like Hitler in 1940, but without war. Moreover, with Europe secured, who could stop Soviet dominance in Middle East, with all that oil United States and Britain required?"

"Why did she tell Khrushchev and the others all about Stalin's plan?"

"She knew plan to be madness itself. One slight miscalculation, on either side, world lies in ashes. She also knew, as you said, about bombs' lack of quality. Most importantly, she knew of outside world better from her contacts in Organs of State Security. She knew that new Eisenhower Administration burned with men just as zealous as Stalin. Men who would have been willing to sacrifice New York to destroy Soviet Union."

"So, your mother helped to prevent World War III?"

"That would be accurate. Does that not mitigate against what she did here?"

"Murder and torture can never be mitigated. But, if your mother was so powerful, why did she not seize control of Party herself?"

"In those days, such thing was impossible for woman. She always operated through men. She first approached enormously powerful Lavrentiy Beria, head of secret police, who very much liked Stalin's plan. Mother told this to Nikita Sergeyovich and his allies, who liquidated Beria at end of 1953." She shook her head. "Had not Brezhnev in 1964 ousted Nikita Sergeyovich, one of last true believers, Soviet Union would have long remained dominant in ideological struggle."

"You need me to be your Nikita Sergeyovich Khrushchev?"

"Sadly, situation for women in Russia has not changed. I prefer to think of you as my Lenin, creator of new order."

Ashley shook his head. "Only one problem. When Mother tried to harness power and magic of Iskandarov seed, she damaged both gene pools."

"Ah yes, but I am different from her and I have accepted your seed in way she never could."

"Interesting theory. Good. We both know where we stand."

"I know lunatic raised me. Iskandarov are equally so. They both look to past. Does it really matter you are descended from Great Alexander? You know you are Iskandarov. What else do you need to know? I look to future, more perfect one than we have had for long time. With your brains and my contacts, we can have successful coup and begin process of building better and stronger Russia."

Uh oh, again, this is Nata's pyordarsch prediction I must resist. "You are getting far ahead of yourself. First of all, Russian people would never accept American as their leader…"

"Wrong. You may have been born in America, but by birth you are half-Russian. I know you are Hidden One. This could easily be your task."

"Is that why your people have been trying to kill or kidnap me all these years?"

"We tried twice to bring you to us, like we had your parents. Had we succeeded when you were eighteen, with backing of Mother, you would have become Party leader twenty years ago with me at your side. And, like your father, have many children. With your knowledge of both America and Russia, Soviet Union would not only still exist, it would be prospering. But now instead, you should be fully prepared to join me in this venture. Because you are extraordinary as only Hidden One must be. And I have great plan for us."

"What, exactly, do you have in mind?"

"There was time, after civil war in twenties when progressive people around the world wanted to come and join new Soviet Union experiment. We were pioneering women's rights, new artistic creation, innovation and people's government like no other with worker's councils, where all could be equal. People were free in way they had never been. As journalist Lincoln Steffens said after visit here, 'I have seen future and it works.' After paranoid bureaucrat Stalin seized power, killed old Bolshevik rivals and all good in Soviet Union, he created Fascist police state cult of personality. And government had to keep people from leaving because they lived in great fear. You and I can recreate that hopeful time of before Stalin. We shall encourage those who can create and build. Those who cannot, we shall take care of. We can complete experiment Lenin started and even change world. Or, at least, significant and important part. With you as President of Russian Federation, we could sign genuine peace treaty with America. And once that is done, there shall be no stopping us in our quest for better world. The FSB shall be converted into national police force, like FBI. No more secret policemen pulling strings from shadows and terrorizing good people. We have opportunity right now. We must seize it before it is too late."

"Sounds wonderful. However, Gorbachev tried to reform Soviet Union and failed. Why would your plan succeed?"

"No, not mine, ours. He left too many party hacks in power. His program had little support from populace. But our plan to establish new working socialist state has great appeal and not just for Russians. Also consider, our Iskandarov-Polinkova union would be extremely popular as well. We would get rid of every law and decree that Stalin and his successors ever passed. *Tabula Rasa,* clean slate."

"You make it sound so easy."

"For someone such as myself who understands how state operates, it is. Yeltsin is trying, but he is following wrong model for Russia in democracy and lacks imagination. He can be easily overthrown. And may be in near future by reactionary forces. We must make coup before them. Because, if we fail, Russia shall soon revert to despotism and paranoia."

Her scheme's absolutely insane, but I get it. She genuinely believes all people can be equal. That has never worked because it goes against human nature. And I think of the tens of millions who've been slaughtered to make this idea real. But most importantly, I don't trust her. I sense all the hallmarks of a trap. Like her mother, what Svetlana Polinkova can't accomplish by force, she will achieve by seduction. "I am going to have to think about this long and hard. But before I do, I have some smaller questions for you. Why did you become involved with Joe Stevens?" Good. She's startled by my question. "According to Ambassador, your husband, he had Joe followed by Anghelina De laVega and he came straight to you."

"Ah yes—terrible Cuban assassin. All Joe possessed that I wanted was information. Our rendezvouses were our cover. I never bedded him. You were one I wanted. Why would I care about someone like him?"

"For starters, he was murdered. And Nick Stevens thinks I had hand in it."

"We were in process of forming alliance against Iskandarov when that little pompous shit who calls himself Sabreur Bleu killed him. That suggests you were involved. And New York City Police think so as well. You may have difficult homecoming."

"On what evidence?"

"Joe fucking your late wife. You certainly have motive."

"That is preposterous, and you know it. I could not care less about her lovers. She had lost all her appeal by then. Did you kill Larry Fischer? To refresh your memory, he was found in East River with *Juden* carved on his chest."

"While I did not kill him, I am responsible."

"But why?"

"If he lived, your legal firm would send him here in your place. That could not be allowed to happen. Your presence here, at this time, is essential for us to form alliance."

"Perhaps. And you think seed of Iskandarov is going to produce new generation of super-leaders?"

"This time with Iskandarov-Palaeologus cooperation, how can we fail?"

Ashley took a few steps forward, intently studying her. "Who is your father?"

She also stepped forward. "Vladimir, a rising star in *apparat* KGB, who, although somewhat younger than Mother, knew her support was essential. He knows of me. At this point, all I require."

It seems logical that her mother would have chosen from the KGB. However, why did she not just state his whole name? Perhaps that's all she knows. "I assume you are well connected because of your mother."

"Well enough." She ran her fingers through her hair and laughed, as she moved in closer to touch the side of his face. "Now back to you. As far as present Russian government is concerned, releasing Gulag diaries, assuming they even exist, would be tantamount to revealing state secrets. Thus, you would be Enemy of State. From experience of your father, you know what happens to such people. Very possible history could repeat." She held up her hand. "But there is good scenario."

"That is?"

"Cease your search for diary and join me. You are exceptionally intelligent man, very handsome, with great achievements, and you possess political perspective I totally lack. And again, since I am not your sister, we do not risk having idiot children . . ."

"Somewhat better odds, in any event."

"In all modesty, I am young and fertile, my genes are strong, and so we shall begin dynasty of very accomplished people and shall triumph."

"You make it sound so easy. But that aside, what are your plans for Annie?"

"It is easy, and pregnancy is key to my plan. Everything else is petty details, except Annie. She is young and close to my age. And one day, we shall become good friends and I shall tell her in detail our plans, which shall appeal to her."

Good Luck, Lana van Booben with Annie. "Tell me one thing, though. Is your near nudity for my benefit?"

She laughed as she removed her T-shirt. "Do you see any tan lines on me? No? That is because I have been sunbathing here ever since I was little girl and certainly have no bourgeois concerns of female modesty. I aspire to be simple and natural." She made a sweeping gesture. "But now back to matters of more import. Candidly, Iskandarov are in decline. They have no future, especially, should my realist half-brother disappear or be killed. This estate is virtually all remaining of their once vast holdings. That is why they are so solicitous of you. Had you nothing they desired, it is likely you should be long dead." She paused. "I understand you do not believe I am who I represent myself to be."

"You are so different from way you were in New York."

"It is you who have changed. I can be totally candid with you, now you are aware of your heritage." As she draped herself around his neck, he smelled her almond-scented breath, felt the hard crush of breasts and hips, but her actions and intoxicating perfume did not arouse him as it used to. She tried to kiss him, but he stepped back. *God, Bayta warned me it was dangerous to even kiss her. Get a grip.*

She laughed "You truly fear me like little boy. Very well, do not give me answer now. Think about proposition. Observe for yourself weakness, indeed, madness of Iskandarov. When time is right, I shall be where you are. I have turned my back on past. Are you ready to join me in creating new and better future?"

"You could start by being honest. Intuition tells me you have not been."

"I had forgotten about that. Another great asset for us." After removing her panties, she backed several feet away. "Compare my female perfection with Madame *Prinkipia*—branded, whipped and older." She shook her breasts. "You now cannot forget me…ever." She smiled wickedly as something black and slippery emerged from her vagina—a viper with large fangs and small red eyes. It continued straight up, its tail still inside her until its head was directly opposite his face.

"Right now, pet is here only for show. Single bite of venom and you go into eighteen hours of absolute agony as body slowly paralyzes. And then…you die. Of course, I have antidote, but best beg for it early because loss of voice is fairly quickly." She laughed and the viper fell to the grass and disappeared. "I shall return with pet—sometime. And I shall expect you to join me. Refusal would not be desirable choice."

"We both know you shall not kill me until you have what you want."

"Perhaps, but we both know you shall be mine and not your sister's." She walked over to her chaise, turned off the radio, picked up her panties and threw everything in her satchel and went into the Maze.

That was strange. I know she was playing music but after we began talking, I didn't hear a note. But that's the least of my problems. Ashley shook his head before sitting on the bench by the machine gun. She is so very idealistic. But her plan would never work. If she tries a coup, she'll be slaughtered. I must find Nata.

2.

Looking up, Ashley sees a descending bright light. Full-term pregnant Sainte Princess Xenia hovers just above him while her translucent wings slowly move.

"You have found place of martyrdom." When Ashley rises from the bench, she holds up her hands to show the deep ragged wounds the cross's spikes had made, just as *tvarsch* had previously shown.

The reality's much worse. "Hello, Princess I greatly admire your courage. But what did you do to deserve such horrible fate?"

"Today, I sent images to inspire you, but it was not my intention to have you overreact as you did. But that is to your credit because you reacted in most *un-avocat* way. I used to hold secret Orthodox worship services here. Second, I would not submit to violation by Polinkov. My unborn son Pyotr was husband Evahn's. That was why Pyotr was prevented from being born. I often stop here to relive my ordeal and ultimate triumph."

"How so?"

"From moment of kidnapping, Polinkov attempted everything to break me and could not. Crucifixion was to be my ultimate punishment. Major Polinkova would sometimes come to my cross at night with fire torch to watch me suffer. But I would not give her satisfaction. I never once cried out or begged for mercy from her or anyone. I remembered example of heroic ancestors who fought against staggering odds and prevailed. Your father, in particular, through martyrdom, brought down Devil's Lieutenant, Svetlana Feliksovna."

"I know she was evil, but…"

"Her privileged position in realm of demons is result of her being Satanist from early age."

"I had not thought about it, but she is in complete control of anyone in her shack. A fate I narrowly missed."

"Now to much more important subject. There exists metaphorical Tree of Traditions with many branches. More than you might expect, they maintain and protect ancient wisdom and are all interconnected and assist each other. They trace back to those who were thought to be gods. And in a sense, they were because they were so advanced—priests, warriors, magicians and, of course, kings and queens. They knew how to breed plants and animals for better results, so why not humans? They were much further removed from Iskandar than you are from him. It was through their influence humans evolved and continue to do so today. Your task and reason you have been hidden and protected all these years is to rejuvenate Iskandarov branch of tree. You must have Blood Union with sister Nata and begin new blood line."

"Wait, incest is universally recognized as sin."

"You can trust the word of sainte, there is no sin in Blood Union. And you shall not prevail in diary quest without Blood Union."

"But if she becomes pregnant, Polinkov shall kill her."

"Then you must protect her. And do not tell me you do not know how. You most certainly do. I remember your courage in Realm of Spirits. And no, I cannot help you with Svetlana

Polinkova dilemma." She smiles. "I know someone close to you who can. Ah yes, please bring out your icon of Sainte Elizabeta."

When he does, no light seeps around the edges. "What happened?"

Xenia glows. "I am sainte of Iskandarov, while Elizabeta is Russian. Therefore, I am now guardian as you today have taken large step to becoming Of Iskandarov. Now look again at icon and see my shining face and large golden halo."

"This is amazing and wonderful." Particularly after Elizabeta's failure at Bangkok.

"You are most welcome. Know had you kissed Svetlana Polinkova, her potion was on her lips and you would be overwhelmed, and she would not need snake."

"How can I defend myself?"

"You must evolve. Otherwise, only Iska with strong aura can protect you. I witnessed your conversation with Svetlana Polinkova. She knows if she can seduce and separate you from your kin, we are doomed. Thus, she shall try again until she succeeds or is destroyed. Do not ever fear death and know you are much loved and respected. I must go. I am needed elsewhere. *Das vedanya.*"

She flutters her translucent wings and rises to again become pure light and speeds away.

Ashley feels amazed and better. With Xenia and Bayta supporting me, how can I fail? And I know my ancestors had had similar support. Thanks to Xenia, I now more fully understand the importance of Nata.

3.

Back into the Maze, Ashley sat on a bench without plaques. Yes, Svetlana Polinkova was beautiful, smart and strong, not unlike Penelope when she was twenty-eight. And best-case scenario, my life with Svetlana Polinkova would be a repeat of the last eighteen years. And the worst-case scenario seems too horrible to contemplate. He thought about his father as Spencer Talbott, and all his affairs until he met Charlotte. She had purity and beauty that Spencer knew he could not live without and, in addition, a promised houseful of children. Most importantly, she offered a genteel domesticity that he did not know he wanted until he did. And Spencer was only thirty-three at the time. Back in the thirties, Angelina DelaVega Delgado, Spencer's companion at Havana's Chez Marianne, had started to lead him away from his old life. Then all of Spencer's bombing missions, and, especially, narrowly escaping death on the eighteenth one, had matured him beyond his years. Ashley rose and walked back into the Maze.

Now, a few months shy of his fiftieth birthday, Ashley wanted what his father had—the quiet, mature beauty and wisdom of a woman he could take care of and to whom he could totally commit. Incredibly, he had been changed in only a few hours in the Maze and now had the clarity of thought and vision he had lost. But how could a place of such cruel punishments and mass slaughter do that? He sensed, after a while, that it had not. Here, he had found the penultimate piece of his journey's puzzle. And Natalya would be the final piece. He had to find her, but because she was Iskandarova, his *tvarsch* would be useless. Aleks would know where she was. He seemed to know everything and was back at the dacha, probably having lunch. Ashley found a cracked-open door of a green concrete hut nestled in the hedge. The door had a faded 24 on it. Curious, he sensed the Maze was not finished with him. He carefully went down the narrow black metal circular stairs. At the bottom in a long concrete corridor were more circular stairways. To his left, a plate with 32 and to his right, 16. So, the first was eighth and last one would be 64. These numbers were duplicated on the stairs opposite in the corridor. Guards or whoever could be anywhere in the Maze to kill undesirables and quickly disappear to kill again elsewhere.

Following signs, he came to a large metal door. Opening it, a burly guard pointed his Uzi at him before smiling and said, "Major Cooper, princess was not expecting you quite so soon. No problem. I will take you to her. It is unfortunate about cuts and stained shirt. She has seen such reactions many times."

He entered a windowless room with Persian rugs, some faded and threadbare, carelessly overlapping at all angles. Icons, especially Sainte Xenia's large one, decorated the walls and Ming Chinese vases clustered in the corners. Against the far wall was a large display case with several elaborate clocks, smaller icons and ornate oriental antiques. Griffins, peacocks, and many lacquered boxes filled most of the available flat spaces. Four substantial black chairs with interlocking dragon tails formed a semicircle around a lacquered table. Overhead, a large gold chandelier with rows of miniature octagonal crystals, emitting spectral light, until they ended in the mouths of two intertwined snakes at the bottom. He smiled and shook his head at the room's over-decoration. *I'm a long way from Fifth Avenue.*

Princess Rini entered from another room, wearing a blue apron over a green dress and carrying a polishing cloth and a gold Maze plaque. "Greetings Brother Ashlei, welcome to *La Maison D'Or*. I am told during first Revolution in 1917, when outside was covered in gold-leaf, peasants tried to strip it all away. I am so glad you accepted my invitation."

The idea of a princess doing her own cleaning charmed him. After she left the plaque and cloth on the table, she enveloped him in her voluptuous softness and planted sisterly kisses on his cheeks. Her round face reflected a serenity Ashley had only seen in the deeply religious. After releasing him, she continued, "By soiled and wet shirt, plus cuts and red eyes, you have not reacted atypically to first trip through Maze. That is to your credit." She waved her hands joyfully. "I am delighted to see you again. Excuse me for being so evasive in Paris, but I did not wish to place you in any danger by revealing some things that you did not, at that point, need to know. Clearly, *tvarsch* found one of huts. I wanted to shine all of plaques before you went through Maze later today. You seem to have gone before we were ready." Her tone sounded mockingly scolding.

"Do you have Annie, I mean, Anastasia, with you?"

"She is with Verushka Sergeyvna in Cartvelian Caves. I understand your disappointment. But remember she has her own path to follow, just as you are now doing. You shall be reunited soon. And I know you shall appreciate changes."

"I hope so. Tell me, are plaques your idea?"

"Yes. Feodor witnessed all of horrors personally and he told me of them. While I had seen some, I was too young to have seen them all and I wished to preserve memory of our martyrs. I am especially impressed by faith of serenely beautiful Sainte Xenia, whose courage in face of death was especially inspiring."

"Yes, I saw her today. Magnificent lady."

"Feodor, in keeping her memory alive, showed us pictures and told us of her death. First time I ever heard of power of faith. To honor her memory and all others, I polish and restore plaques several times during year. It is least I may do."

"That is very good of you."

"It is my duty to Iskandarov. It was terrible time, but not unlike early days of our Church. We must never forget."

"No, of course not."

Rini invited Ashley to sit in a dragon chair, which felt comfortable. "We are in previous viewing room of Svetlana Feliksovna where she witnessed all horrors. We removed wall separating torture chamber, which also doubled as her indoor hanging room. This is now our Cartvelian Room, where, unlike very formal upstairs, we may relax and speak freely here. No listening devices can penetrate this room. Further down hall you came in is public execution space where her 'Game' was to execute any guards or anyone else she suspected of betrayal. I believe you saw that in one of sister Nata's *Andronyis*."

"Of all Polinkovs, why do you constantly use patronymic with Mother?" *Even though I know the answer, I want further confirmation and to change the subject.* Rini frowned and slowly shook her head. "To remind she was Devil's daughter because father was Feliks Dzerzhinski."

"Who ran Lenin's secret police before and during Red Terror. I thought he only had son and—"

"Devil cares not for sanctity of marriage bed. My grandmother, our other grandmother's servant, had his baby out of wedlock. Dzerzhinski took interest in his daughter. He burned with intellectual's love of humanity and contempt for people. He apparently recognized this quality in Svetlana Feliksovna." Feodor wheeled in a serving cart with a large silver samovar and began pouring tea over orange marmalade into the now familiar tall crystal glasses with silver bases and handles.

"Feodor, kindly tell Monsieur Cooper what happened in Maze."

He faced Ashley, bowed slightly and said in French. "Monsieur, this began after the breeding had stopped. The *zeks* and *zechkas* were told they would be liberated if they reached the Maze center undetected. They were then stripped and given an advanced start. The guards used the stairs you came down and made great sport of hunting them. Anyone who made it close to the center, found Colonel Polinkova's machine gun and killed those who thought they had earned freedom. To her, death was the only possible liberation for a *zek*. I know these things because I had the horrible task of assisting her. And for that, I shall forever be ashamed."

"Nonsense, Feodor. Someone had to bear witness to this horror. Besides, there were also the people you helped to escape."

Feodor bowed. "Thank you, Madame." Embarrassed, he left the room.

"Feodor's family has been in our service for many generations and he still regards anything but French as unspeakably vulgar, especially after Svetlana Feliksovna ordered him, on pain of death, to only speak Russia because she knew no more French than cat. Therefore, we accommodate him. Least we can do. Poor man remains so racked with guilt. As are we all. I do not know what I could have done to prevent any of this. Frankly, in those days, such thoughts never occurred to me. I was always good girl. I believed what Svetlana Feliksovna told me about Iskandarov being evil people deserving punishment. She told me I was not to be involved with any boys except Aleks and I obeyed." Her voice trailed off before she took a large sip of tea.

"Rini, you had to do whatever you could to survive to bear witness as Feodor has done."

"You are most generous." She sipped her tea before she rose. "Please remove soiled shirt. I shall attend to its proper cleaning."

"I'll just run upstairs and get cleaned up a bit and put on a new white polo and come back down."

"When you return, I shall help you find sister Nata."

"Great. I shall not be long."

NINE

Monday, 7 June 1993, Novo Ogarevo

1.

Ashley returned, cleaned up and refreshed to the Cartvelian Room. Rini had left but Natalya rose from a dragon chair, wearing a crisp ivory pleated blouse, tight black jeans and polished high-heeled boots, "I've been informed you desire to speak with me. And while I'm coming to trust you, please answer this first. Rini told me you met with Svetlana Polinkova this morning while she was trespassing in the Maze."

"I found her because *tvarsch* guided me there."

"And . . .?"

"And what?"

"And what occurred?"

"She tried to recruit me for the *coup d'état* your *pyordarsch* foresaw. I declined. Also, I needed information, which she had, and I got."

"Very good, but I've also heard she was naked or almost so."

"Yes, because she had been sunbathing."

"Remember, we're under Iskandarov Truth. And then?"

"This was her last-chance attempt to seduce me. My having gone through the Maze meant she seemed much less attractive and, at one point, I questioned whether I should even be speaking with her, lest I dishonor all our martyrs, especially here. She even tried to kiss me but when I refused, she produced her viper."

"She must've been furious with you to reveal that. I'm immensely proud of you and, after the Maze, you've changed and are becoming Of the Iskandarov. Any further sightings of Anghelina?"

"No. Although, even here, I expect an appearance. I believe she's satisfied and will now focus on the diary."

"Makes sense, anyone else I should know about?"

Ashley raised and kissed her, causing him to be consumed with warmth. His heart beat faster and his pulse quickened. At first, she resisted but then kissed him back hard. And after pressing together, the magic of their first kiss returned and their auras temporally grew brighter.

"You surprised me. I wasn't expecting that, especially, since our time is not yet at hand."

"I don't care. I had to kiss you after your long absence. I've realized we've kissed thousands of times or even more. And yet, how is that possible since I've known you for such a brief time."

"I've had the same feeling about kissing you. And I don't know how but the memory lingers. She gently pushed him away in order to look him up and down with love in her eyes. "We've much to discuss. Starting with your cuts."

"They don't bother me."

"While you wear them like a badges of honor, they trouble me. Even though they aren't nearly as bad as the wounds you had Friday. Now, please close your eyes."

Ashley sat in a dragon chair opposite her and, after closing his eyes, his skin tingled as Natalya slowly moved her warm hands from his face down to his shins. When finished, she sat in her chair, demurely crossing her ankles.

Leaning in, she quietly said, "I assume Bayta told you about me at your daughter's Ceremony. Good news, Annie's now an Iska. She'll tell you the details."

"Bayta did tell me and I understand what happened." I saw it but who sent the Andronyi? Nata, Bayta or someone else?

"I just spent a drunken night with six of my dearest sister Iskas."

"I believe you but now, I can't live without you and I'll fully commit to you when our time is right."

"Oh, my dearest one, you've just made me happier than I've ever been. And I pledge myself to you also when our time is right, which shall be soon. And in the meantime, we'll be building relationship bridges. I'm now ready to answer all your questions about me."

"What about our Blood Union? I need to know when."

"There are so many moving parts and they must occur in proper sequence. That's beyond our control. It's said, I think quite rightly, 'When men make plans, God laughs.' The union, primarily, is a test of faith, which we define in this case as 'evidence of things unseen.'"

She crossed herself. "Now, I should like to apologize about my conduct Friday. As I've said, it had been an extremely difficult and trying day. In the morning I took my two daughters to Mummy and her Iskandarov monastery where they wish to spend their lives raising their voices to God."

"A God who made them less than perfect?" *No point in delaying the inevitable.*

She stared at him. "How did you know?"

"Our father sensed that when he visited you during preparations for his Camp David Banquet. It's not your fault, you know. After all, it takes two to make a baby."

She made a fist with her right hand and forcefully struck her chest. "No. I'm the daughter of Sergei Dmitrovich Prince Iskandarov and Lady Charlotte Sternwood. All my children, regardless of the other donor, should be superior because of my blood."

"You, of all people, should know that mating with the Polinkov is, at best, unpredictable."

"I know. My twins have had their Ceremony and are officially Iskas but remain girls with their understanding of the world. Now, I was born on the twenty-eighth of May in 1956. Thus, I'm just recently thirty-seven. My time to become pregnant is getting shorter and I pledge I'll give you as many children as I'm able."

"You could give me no greater gift. I love you because you're a mature, beautiful woman who knows her mind, just as our mother was to our father."

"That's so wonderful. I was about to tell you that myself. But what of my bosoms?"

He laughed, "What of them?"

"I know you like buxom girls, like all the women in your life to this point—Olga, Penelope, Svetlana, Verushka. I recently discovered that even at seventeen, Mademoiselle Kyria Anastasia is larger than me."

"Yes, it's a great ego boost to be married to a buxom woman and to have her on your arm at a party to make other men jealous. That was my life in New York and The Firm, which was hyper-competitive, but that won't be my life here. I no longer need the boost."

So, you truly don't care?"

"Your bosoms are part of you and that's all that matters."

Tears ran down her cheeks. "This weekend, I thought I'd lost you forever and now...I can't live without you anymore." Natalya reached into her purse on the table, pulled out a light blue handkerchief and dabbed her eye. "I should like to tell you of my childhood."

"Only if you're comfortable doing so."

"That's not the question. If you're to fully understand me, you have to know this. And I assume Bayta and Aleks have told you parts. Here's the whole story. For a long time, Svetlana Feliksovna led me to believe she was my mother. She hated me and I could never understand why. Lady Charlotte, her maid, was wonderful to me. I didn't know at that time, she was my mother. I thought she was just another pretty noble lady brought from the Gulag. She would comfort me when I was lonely, which was often. When I was about five or six, Lady Charlotte revealed that she was Mummy and Sergei Dmitrovich was my father. I was conceived on the last night before he left on training for his Camp David mission in 1955. Mummy also stressed I was different from Aleks and Rini. She told our father about me during her nocturnal visits to him in the Gulag at Vorkuta. In addition, Mummy would tell me wonderful stories of the Iskandarov and about how I bore a proud heritage with the blood of greatness in my veins. She also told me I had a brother in America, and she knew a great deal about you." She paused, briefly looking at Ashley. "Our parents were so proud of you."

"I read about their loving feelings about me when I was in her womb. But how did our mother know so much about the Iskandarov?"

"She had learned some of it being in Bleu and our father taught her the rest. He stressed, early in their captivity, it was especially important for Mummy to know all the relevant information. In fact, my life depended on it. At that time, I also felt a great aching. I wanted to help the Iskandarov but had no idea how. One day, I noticed a very elegant lady here accompanying a general in the *Komitet*. You know this word?"

"Yes, the KGB."

"Exactly. She was his mistress. While waiting for the general and Svetlana Feliksovna to finish a meeting, the lady sought me out and told me her name was, Madame Elizabeta Petrovna Likhutina."

"Wait. That was the patronymic and surname of Sophia in Andrey Biely's *St. Petersburg*. A very high-risk name because the *Komitet* was well-read."

"Nevertheless, it worked for a long time. So thorough was her cover that not even Svetlana Feliksovna suspected for a long time. Further, I don't think most of KGB either read or understood that difficult book. The lady's true name was Elizabeta Mikhailovna Iskandarova and she immediately took a liking to me. Mummy approved of our relationship because she knew Bayta was a very heroic lady who helped some of the prisoners here escape."

Ashley decided not to tell her about Bayta's falcon flights. *I might, in time.*

"When I saw the blue falcon, I wished I could've flown away with you and gave serious thought to sending my *aminalus* to the falcon. But I was still needed at the Caves."

"How did you know what I was thinking?" *This is getting scary.*

"I recognized you because I very well know Bayta's tricks." She laughed. "But seriously, we're becoming a unity—where, in time, we will by mutual consent join our minds together. And no, I can't read your mind. I simply recognized your change of expression to something that was still unsettling you and the falcon was the most likely."

Not sure I buy her explanation. "Now, tell me more about you and Bayta."

"Bayta stayed at General Rianovski's dacha not far from here, and he was frequently away. She often came to visit me, and I visited her. Sometimes, we would ride our bicycles together through the beautiful woods to go swimming."

"I can see it."

"It was heaven. I was an outcast here. Aleks and Rini were all wrapped up in each other. I was just a little baby to them. I mean, they weren't mean or anything, but they had been ordered to spend most of their time together. Thus, I never held that against them. I was so grateful to have a friend in Bayta. She was so beautiful, as you likely saw in my photo gallery, but those pictures could never capture her flawless skin, shiny hair and was statuesque and always carried herself with great authority and yet ease."

"She told me she's exceedingly proud of you."

"You're most gallant." Natalya lapsed into silence. "You said Friday night you wanted to know everything about me. Is that still true?"

"Yes."

Natalya spoke so softly that Ashley had to lean closer. "As you might expect, things could not remain idyllic here for long. One day, I spent an incredibly joyful time with Bayta at her dacha. I walked home and fell asleep." The pulse in Natalya's temple began throbbing.

I know what's to follow. "Nata, if this is uncomfortable…"

"No secrets between brother and sister. You know of Chichikov?"

"Yes, a real slime bucket."

"More bucket of offal, I think." She shook her head and looked at the chandelier. "In fall of 1963, I was seven, hopelessly skinny and homely."

And I was beginning my sophomore year at Harvard, trying to forget my traumatic freshman experience. The pulse in her temple throbbed harder and to calm her, he said, "In your first *Andronyis*, you weren't the least homely, but even with your branding and whippings, I looked past that to see the real you—a cute girl. Just because Svetlana Feliksovna never admitted you were pretty and you didn't believe our mother when she, doubtless, told you, doesn't mean you weren't."

"I knew I was not."

"In any case, again, you needn't say any more about the *Andronyi* you sent me."

"No, I must tell you of my violation. Truth." She exhaled and closed her eyes. "That night, Chichikov, naked and drunk, tore off my gown, turned on the lamp, called me his 'little angel' as he got on top of me. I still remember the smell of vodka and tobacco on his breath and his body odor. And then, searing pain. Absolutely unbearable, but I dared not cry out lest he kill me. When he finished, he fell asleep on top of me and I was pinned to the bed all night as he snored drunkenly. I tried to get him off, but he was too heavy. Terrified, I wished to simply die. When he woke, he called me all manner of bad names and accused me of seducing him. He went to his pile of clothes, found his knout and began whipping me. I was screaming. Mummy came rushing in and tried to help, but he smashed her in the face with his knout. There was blood seemingly, all over. Certain he would kill both of us, I heard rapid shots and Chichikov fell over, dead. Brother Aleks shot him. Then, everything froze when Svetlana Feliksovna came from down the hall and took the machine pistol from him. She looked at Chichikov and shrugged. She patted Aleks on the cheek and said it was time he began acting like a man. She came over to me and said, 'You do not seem so high and mighty now, little princess.' She spat in my face, restraining my hands as her spittle slowly slid down my face, saying, 'Now you know real woman's lot.' She ordered Mummy to clean up everything, after which she would be expelled from the Institute as punishment for letting this happen. Svetlana Feliksovna ordered the Mongolians to dispose of Chichikov's body. When she left, Mummy was staggering as though drunken. I called to her and, seeing her face, realized she was, in all probability, blinded from his knout. I forgot about my own pain and found Aleks to help me get her dressed. We took Mummy to Bayta, who hid her for a while before driving her to an underground order of Orthodox nuns."

Natalya's face was wet, and her eyes and cheeks blackened from running mascara. Ashley stood and pulled her up to him before she buried her head in his chest and he felt her trembling, along with the welts on her back from Chichikov's knout. His rage trapped his tears. After a few minutes, she pushed herself away and looked straight at him. "Thank you. I am better now. You have my mascara on your shirt."

"Difficult day for white shirts." He smiled. "I would like to visit our mother."

"Certainly. We shall go tomorrow."

"No, I must go now."

"You are not properly dressed and both Anastasias remain in the Caves. Tomorrow, you shall meet them. We're expected then. Your daughter needs to talk further with her grandmother before the two of you speak."

"Why?"

"Be patient, please. All shall become clear tomorrow. Surely, after all this time, you can wait one more day."

"Yes, I can. What happened to you after all this? Were you in trouble for helping our mother?"

"No, Mummy was Chichikov's property. With him dead and Father gone, she ceased to have any value or interest to Svetlana Feliksovna."

"So, in a way, Chichikov did honor his bargain with our father."

"I should never use honor and Chichikov in the same sentence without a negative in there. He had no power to make any manner of arrangement. Therefore, when Svetlana Feliksovna expelled Mummy without papers, she knew very well it meant a long, slow death from starvation, if autumnal exposure didn't claim her first. Even though Stalin was dead, people still lived in such great fear. No one, she assumed, would dare help Mummy."

"God, was there ever a woman or a girl in this whole period here who was not raped, maimed or killed?"

"Rape, of both sexes, was Svetlana Feliksovna's way of maintaining order, of keeping everyone in their place. And of demonstrating to everyone that they had no power or worth."

"Incredible to fully see the corruption of absolute power."

"Such was the way of Svetlana Feliksovna. Perhaps, at first pass, it appears what occurred here was about sex, albeit in a most twisted form. But no. It was about her power to torture, humiliate and shame all. She orchestrated everything down to the minutest detail, with every punishment calibrated to extract maximum fear, pain and degradation."

"But how did she get people to do this to other people?"

"Ah, that was where she excelled. No one in her organization could ever feel safe. If she felt one of her guards not punishing her many enemies with enough zeal, he could well become tomorrow's victim. She peppered her organization with informers. Sometimes, she would arbitrarily pick someone for punishment. Thus, her underlings could never organize a rebellion. She had learned all too well the techniques of her mentor, Stalin." Natalya again looked up at the chandelier. "Placing it all in Russian context, for more than seventy years the inmates seized and ran the asylum, brutalizing all for a utopian future that could never be. Later, in the sixties, recognition that the terror had receded finally filtered down to the Ivans in the streets and was replaced by even worse debilitating cynicism and apathy while Russian paranoia remained. This, like some corrosive acid, destroyed everyone and everything it came in contact with and the ultimate result was the Chernobyl Nuclear Disaster in April of 1986. After that, the regime was doomed."

"Yes, but were you implying Svetlana Feliksovna orchestrated Chichikov's actions and all the rest?"

"While I should like to think she didn't have the power to humiliate me, blind my mother and have Chichikov killed, I know, in my heart, with just a rape suggestion to him, she did,"

"It seems improbable that she could control anything beyond your…violation."

"Perhaps. But in the end, it makes no difference. What happened, happened and I'm ultimately stronger for it."

"While I know very well the origins of our feud with the Paleologos, what keeps it going today?"

"Are you familiar with Orthodox time?"

"I'm not sure." I know it perfectly well, but I want to hear her version and help get her mind off the horrors she just described.

"It's true in Orthodox Christianity, time moves at a different pace than in the West. Russians hate Muslims and distrust the Jews and the West. All because in 1453, the Muslim Ottoman Turks conquered and sacked Constantinople, which, for more than a thousand years, had been the seat of Orthodoxy. They distrust the Jews because the Muslims tolerated them. Moreover, they distrust the West because the Roman Catholic Crusaders sacked Greek Orthodox Constantinople in 1204 weakening it for the Turks. To many, 1204 is yesterday."

"True, but it should be noted that the Crusaders also liberated the Holy Land from Muslim conquest. Does that not count for something?"

"Sadly, not much. The Patriarchy of Constantinople at Hagia Sophia Cathedral, built by Constantine the Great, was the heartbeat of Eastern Roman Christianity and, later, Byzantine Orthodoxy. Saint Cyril was sent from there to spread the true faith to our country and also to give us our alphabet. Jerusalem never had such status as that."

"I noticed you said they and not we."

"I think this is foolishness of the worst sort, even though I agree with Mother Church in most other matters. That is why your Bosnian initiative is, frankly, impossible. When Serbs are killing Bosnians, Croats and Kosovars, in their mind and on their lips, they're killing Turks in revenge for 1453 or their defeat to the Ottomans at Kosovo in 1389, which ended Serbian independence for almost five hundred years. Hence, Russians now see no reason to stop the Serbs slaughtering infidels, both Catholic and Muslim."

"I've encountered that all along the way. But I must try to make it happen." He sighed. "We seem to have wandered off the track on my last question about why the feud persists."

"My apologies. Our area of the Sakartvelo was only large enough for one noble family. We defeated the Polinkov back in the thirteenth century. They've not forgotten."

"You mean nothing else happened since then?"

"I do not wish to imply our victorious Iskandarov were somehow a line of philosopher-kings who ruled justly. While there were many great nobles, the hell of our Faustian bargain is that we have some who are neither genuinely great nor infirm. They appear to be superior but have some genetic defect which makes them unstable and, in some cases, monstrous. That is why we test all who would join us. The most notorious was Queen Xenia who, as she aged, believed bathing in virgin's blood would restore her youth. Sadly, she had the power to force many young serf girls to slowly drain their blood painfully and fatally into her tub. The victims were mostly Palaeologa…"

"That's at least, the second time you've used that name."

"Yes, I suppose it is. Their dynastic story is at least as true as ours. They, like us, Russianized their name, therefore, Polinkov is the proper usage. In the event, that was why Sainte Xenia, whose Maze plaque you couldn't have missed, was killed for her name in such a hellish way."

"I know her but didn't know she was killed for her name. She told me she was killed for being a good Christian."

"Very true, but had she been called Ivana, her fate would have been less severe because a name is enormously powerful.

Svetlana Feliksovna failed to take into account all the good we did for the Polinkov. Some of our rulers, through virtuous acts, tried to make life better for them. It did not occur often, but it did happen. Perhaps, she simply did not know. Or, more likely, care."

"Likely. And the Faustian bargain you referred to earlier is Iskandarov interbreeding."

"Precisely." She brought her fist again slowly to her breast. "I know about the unfortunate side all too well. I would have walked away from it all in an instant, and yet…"

"If you know all this, why do you still blame yourself for your daughters? I don't understand."

"I can't explain this rationally. Deep in my soul, I know I'm to blame."

"I'm sorry you feel that way. I wish I could convince you otherwise."

"We shall see. Moving on, when young, I would dance as a means of escape. In my vivid imagination, I thought myself Pavlova. Bayta told me dance was my Iskandarova gift. She asked Svetlana Feliksovna to sponsor me to the Vaganova Academy in Leningrad. Bayta was a formidable negotiator and Svetlana Feliksovna was intimidated by her. Do you know of the Academy?"

"I don't think so."

"It's the preparatory school for the Kirov Ballet. I went there at ten in 1966. It's perhaps the only reason I'm as sane as I am today. It was a revelation. Virtually all the girls there were tall and thin. I no longer felt like an oddity. And knowing that if I failed, I'd have to return here, I excelled in all my courses and dance. With Mummy still underground, Bayta would come to visit me and I spent at least part of my holidays with my mentor mother. She also helped me conquer my feelings of worthlessness and shame after my violation. My Iska Ceremony also helped greatly."

"How did Svetlana Feliksovna feel about all this?"

"As I said, she had never had any particular interest in me. I wasn't her child and she determined me too frail and my hips too narrow to breed. I was merely her sexual slave for many years and that's why she branded me when she thought she was losing me to Bayta. She assumed, in her ignorant way, if she wanted me sexually then so did Bayta, which wasn't true."

"Based on what you said, you've just made my case for your beauty."

She paused before smiling. "Yes, I did, didn't I? When a handsome man like you thinks I'm beautiful, I must be for him. While I can't wait to be with you, I know I must. Please be patient."

"I'm incredibly pleased you've realized that. Please continue."

"Had I not escaped to the Academy, my life here wouldn't have been pleasant, and likely, quite brief. When I was eighteen in 1974, I graduated first in my class and was accepted into the Kirov Corps de Ballet. And there was Svetlana Feliksovna bragging about how she had taken me in after my mother died and fostered my interest in dance. Truly nauseating. Finally, after all my arduous work, I was important enough to boost her career." She shook her head disgustedly. "Shortly after my acceptance, I met Bayta's nephew, Apollon Apollonovich Iskandarov. He was a Junior Lieutenant of Aviation stationed near Moscow. He was twenty and I fell in love with him. We carried on a clandestine affair with Bayta's knowledge and assistance. The first time, I saw all my ancestors. I know it sounds incredible…"

"No, not at all. I saw them with Olga Sergeyvna, I…"

"Did they speak to you?"

He shook his head, slowly and spoke wistfully. "No, they simply were there."

"Me neither. I'm told when Iskandarovs are intimate, their ancestors speak to the lovers." She shrugged. "I might have, at one time, dismissed such things as myth, but now, I don't know. Apollon was a Godsend to me. He completed my healing of the psychological damage Chichikov inflicted on me. I wanted his baby, but I knew it would also end my Kirov career. I'd fought too hard to get there. I had to become a principal. I stayed on the pill. All the girls were on it. I thought he and I had all the time in the world. We loved each other. I told myself that after I made principal, then we would get married." She sighed. "I achieved principal dancer. Soon after the celebration, Svetlana Feliksovna deported Apollon to the far north. I never saw him again."

"I believe your being on the pill caused you to only see our ancestors."

"You're right because, obviously, I couldn't get pregnant. Also, the Russian pill was so strong, even after stopping, it took an awfully long time for it to wear off. Anyway, the day after Apollon disappeared, Iosif Polinkov, a very handsome and heroic cosmonaut, appeared and said we were getting married. He did not need to tell me Svetlana Feliksovna ordered this, and I could not go against her or she would arrange for my dismissal from Kirov. Two weeks later, after all this, I had trouble focusing, thus, one night on stage, I broke my ankle. After a long healing and rehabilitation, I returned to the stage and received a standing ovation. Oh, I danced quite well, and the audience was most appreciative, but I realized I would never be as good as I was before my injury. The next day, I resigned."

Very understandable, she couldn't live up to her own lofty standards. I know the feeling myself but, unlike me, she doesn't let others determine her success. "Tell me what happened next."

"I thought a long time about that until I realized I was now free to be a mother. I could never feel the way about Iosif as I had about Apollon, but we went ahead when we were together, which wasn't very often. You saw the pictures of our mutual happiness on my wall." She paused. "I believe Svetlana Feliksovna had his spacecraft sabotaged and he burned to death on re-entry from orbit. I can't prove that. But when she realized Iosif and I were happy, it must have greatly annoyed her. And I'd also married him because I wished, in my naiveté, to begin to heal our inter-clan rift. I think that was another reason Iosif was killed because there could be no healing of the rift for Svetlana Feliksovna. In time, I was fine, thanks to Bayta and Mummy's messages she brought me. My experience with other men left me content to be a celibate mother."

"Tell me, if you feel able, about your daughters."

"Magda and Sonia have voices like angels with perfect pitch. Although they have trouble reading text, they can sing a score perfectly the first time through. When they compose, like Mozart, they write note perfect. Fortunately, they don't have to write lyrics as well. Magda learned how to play the piano in her spare time and Sonia, the organ. Our mother performed the baptism."

"You said they had their Ceremony?"

"Yes. All Iskandarovas do, regardless. It is a sacred trust. Although, I'm uncertain my girls fully understood it all, it was still lovely. Now they talk about making babies but without understanding the process."

Must be very difficult for you."

"Our mother told me today they seemed incredibly happy on Friday and seemed to fit nicely into monastery life. But it's still early. Forget that. Not something you should know."

"Forget what?" He smiled.

She laughed.

Nata again laughed at one of my jokes. This is the breakthrough I've been waiting for.

"If I might return to your religion, it's something I've wondered about. You and your half-siblings were obviously raised as atheists. How did you find religion?"

"Bayta told me the Iskandarov and the Church had been inseparable throughout the past millennia. One simply can't be a non-believer and an Iskandarov. Baptized first, I then told Aleks and Rini about it. They eagerly received the Blessed Sacrament from Mummy. We held secret services, very much like the early church. It gave our faith a strength those who have never been persecuted shall never know."

"Yes. But how do you reconcile your faith with incest."

"Incest is such an ugly word—images of a father seducing his young daughter and the like. The Church has no problem with us and has not for as long as any remember. I understand your discomfort with sister lovemaking. I also was initially repulsed when Bayta taught me about it. In time, I came to accept and embrace it. Truthfully, though, you were intimate with Olga Sergevna, of blessed memory." She crossed herself with three fingers. "And I suspect, Verushka Sergeyvna."

"You're right. No secrets. But I didn't know they were my half-sisters."

"Of course, you did. *Tvarsc*h knew full well. Now, again, I perceive the change in you since I left. I ask you to search your soul for the real reason you have a problem with our mating traditions."

"When I was young, I saw the results of incest and it made a very strong impression."

"No doubt. As you may have noticed, we're different. We've been doing this for thousands of years. You and I have excellent genes that need to be joined together to revitalize our bloodlines, which happens over time."

"Our father wrote to me about that so, I fully understand. But..."

"We still have time and we're close."

"There's something I need to ask you, but you may not like it."

"Of course. No secrets."

"About your ballet career. I know you worked hard and had the Iskandarova gift, but would that have been enough to get you into the academy and, ultimately, into the Kirov?"

"I take no offence to your question. My talent, gifts and work ethic qualified me. Svetlana Feliksovna's support proved important, although not critical. Not even Svetlana Feliksovna could have secured a place for Svetlana Polinkova." Natalya laughed. "She would be like the hippo ballerina in Walter Disney's *Fantasia*."

Ashley laughed and Natalya looked down at the crumpled handkerchief in her hand. "Thank you, I'm feeling much better now. I have much to do before tomorrow. I'll see you at cocktail hour." She vigorously kissed him.

2.

Because of Natalya's intense kiss and aura, Ashley could not focus and remained seated in the Cartvelian Room for another fifteen minutes inhaling her scent. Reluctantly, he went upstairs to shower. *Nata trusts me again and there can no longer be any doubt about her. When the time's right, we'll come together and have our Blood Union. Strange, today was the first time I'd seen her true self— a fascinating mix of contradictions. She has what I need. And so unlike Penelope with a pretty face and an aura, who seduced me when I needed a kindred spirit. No, that's unfair to Nata. She's pretty, even beautiful, in her own distinct way and greater than the sum of her parts. Yes, I once described Olga that way. And yet, they could not be more different. I can envision her dominating the stage at the Kirov with her quiet charisma, centeredness and abundant talent. And I'm sorry I never saw her perform.*

Still fatigued from the Maze, Ashley decides to nap before his shower and after removing his clothes and shutting the door, he falls asleep. He dreams about the evil witch, Svetlana Polinkova. *She can take her little Tatar babies and go to hell. Our affair's absolutely over.*

"Oh no, it is not. We shall continue on my terms."

Standing next to the bed, Svetlana Polinkova wears a burgundy silk robe. "You are prisoner, unable to move, for as long as I wish in mother's boudoir. Helpless to prevent revenge for your humiliating and rejecting me. Anyone who passes shall only see empty room. We have complete privacy."

"Do your worst because we are no longer able to mate successfully."

"And why might that be? Some babushka tale sister Rini told you? I do not believe. No matter. If I now wish to fuck you, you cannot resist. If Anghelina can rape you, so can I. And then Madame *Prinkipia* shall hate you because there is no way for you to wash off distinctive scent, much stronger than Cuban's, and it is proof you betrayed her after you knew who I truly was. Which means I win you back by default. We then go forward with our

plan, but you shall be puppet, not partner. And I would have access to wonderful seed."

"Knowing of what you are capable, Natalya would forgive
and heal me."

"Not so. She shall not let you anywhere near her to have
Blood Union. Soon, she dies of broken heart and Iskandarov are
doomed. Perfect revenge. I have different purpose now. I wish to
reintroduce my pet to you." She slightly opens her robe and from
her thick blonde pubic hair, a black viper emerges. "This is Ala-
na. I conjured her and first thing you shall notice is odor of decay
and death because I decided she is going to kill you."

About sixteen inches long, the viper has a long forked green
tongue and same large fangs but no eyes. After Svetlana closes
her robe, it slides onto the bed and slowly slithers around Ashley's body, coming closer each time. "I have also decided I shall
no longer reveal myself because you are no longer worthy of
such honor. As I have said, one bite and body slowly paralyze.
And then…you die."

Ashley senses the viper is more disgusting than scary. *Come
on, you slime, bite me. I can't bear waiting.* Almost as though
the viper hears him, he feels the searing pain from its bite on his
thigh and the viper heading toward his head.

"If you wish to say anything, you should do so now before you are unable. Your slow and ghastly death solves so many
problems for me and I alone can save you. Since you do not love
me, I shall not believe anything romantic you say." She laughs.
"I have proposition for you. I have demonstrated power. I shall
reverse if you agree to come with me."

"I am not going anywhere with you because I know you
fear Natalya's power. Even if I die, she shall know what you have
done. I do not fear death, which shall not solve your problems,
only increase them." Ashley has been slowly regaining his movement and now sits up.

"How? What are you doing? Impossible."

"I told you I have evolved beyond you, but you rejected
that. The bite hurt but I only felt slight tingling after that, and I

wanted to see what you would do. Your spell has worn off. Absent your sorcery, we might have, in time, come to a non-sexual accommodation. Most unlikely now. I used to think you were quite intelligent. Not so much anymore. Again, I am leaving you behind." *God, I hope I convinced her. The pain is pretty severe, but I feel no paralysis.*

"Next time, I need only to double dose, enough to kill elephant. Or conjure something for me even more fun. I know you are trying to hide pain. You have had mere sample of my power. I shall return." She picks up her viper and vanishes.

Ashley falls back on his bed and loses consciousness.

Later, he was floating and slowly opened his eyes to Natalya in her ceremonial robe. *She has yet again fixed my pain.* "Nata, I won't ask how you found me."

"I sensed Svetlana Polinkova had returned seeking revenge and assumed you were here. When I arrived, I saw the prominent bite mark on your thigh and knew what she had done. Did you have to tell her anything or give her information, so she'd release you? I'd be understanding, brother, if you did."

"I told her nothing of interest. And she didn't let me go. I used my own evolved power to defeat her. But she'll be back with something stronger."

"Then I'm extremely impressed."

"How can I repay you?"

She looked down. "Oh, I know of something." She smiled. "I'll see you at cocktail hour on the patio."

3.

After showering to remove the viper slime, Ashley, in slacks, polo shirt, deck shoes and blazer, went downstairs to the large stone patio outside the banquet dining room where he found Rini and Natalya under a brightly colored umbrella enjoying glasses of Bordeaux from a bottle on the table. As he came closer, he heard them probably speaking Cartvelian, so they were doubtless talking about him. Rini waved. "Brother, after you get drink from the bar, come join us." He smiled and poured himself a good full measure of the malt from the Isle of Skye he and Aleks had recently enjoyed.

"What have you ladies been speaking about in Cartvelian so I would not know?"

Natalya replied. "Brother, you have strong ego. We were discussing household details so Feodor could not hear us."

Ashley was about to respond when he heard machine gun fire. "Where's Aleks? I think Svetlana Polinkova is still on the grounds and she said she intended to kill him today. I must go to his aid."

Rini took him by the hand. "Dear husband, out on daily constitutional, is firing machine gun blanks at center of Maze, as he does every Monday afternoon, he is here during season to commemorate all our martyrs. As far as Svetlana Polinkova, she has made threats on him for exceedingly long time. He has threatened to shoot her when he catches her illegally sunbathing. As precaution, two of our Bleu guards are present when he fires. Sit down, he shall be along shortly."

"All right. As Nata has doubtless told you, Svetlana Polinkova was here earlier with her pet viper."

Rini said, "Yes, I have heard. While she is powerful witch, she is, except servants, alone at dacha. Should she do anything to dear husband, we would respond with great force. And she knows that."

Aleks joined them. "Brother, I am so glad you are uninjured. I was concerned." He lifted Ashley and enveloped him in one of his bear hugs.

"Svetlana Polinkova's spell did not work. I shall tell you about it later. I was concerned, after she failed, that she decided, as compensation, to act on her threat to you. When I spoke with her in Maze, she said if you, as realist, were killed, Iskandarov would fall apart…"

Aleks laughed heartily. "Cemeteries are full of people who underestimated Iskandarov. Besides, with evolved you and Nata on our side, we have nothing to fear. Now come, Ashlei. I have had grueling day. And you certainly have as well, and I see you already have your wee dram. After we have lovely dinner, we shall have show in sound room, *Bram Stoker's Dracula*, directed by Francis Coppola. We secured advance copy. Supposed to be brilliant and faithful to book. And then tomorrow, you and Nata can get early start for monastery."

Ashley turned to Natalya. "Does that mean you are staying here?"

"It only makes sense. We are much closer here to monastery than if we were at studio. You look considerably better than last time I saw you." Natalya dazzlingly smiled and kissed him on each cheek.

TEN

Tuesday, 8 June 1993, North of Moscow

1.

Next morning, while Natalya and Ashley were loading their luggage into her BMW 735i for the trip to their mother's monastery, she stopped, looked deep into his eyes and blushed before smiling, wrinkling her nose. *I don't remember if she has always done that. But damn, that wrinkling really touches my heart.*

Natalya focused her driving on shifting up and down over the twisting road, barely wide enough for two cars abreast, and through a thick forest of aspen, birch and conifer. *When I think about my mother, I feel both anticipation and anxiety. I still think of Charlotte as the beautiful redhaired uniformed English nurse whose picture I found recently while reading my father's diary. And before, the lovely and maternal lady in the flowing white nightgown on her nocturnal visits. But I also know her reality—a blind, scarred and unfamiliar stranger. When meeting my mother again for the first time in nearly fifty years, will any commonality remain, or will we awkwardly grope for polite words? I don't understand how tvarsch can't read her as it would any other non-Iskandarov.*

He did not understand why last night he dreamt of Olga Sergeyvna and not Natalya. His thoughts shifted to Iron Cage. Could George Farwell have stopped the Iron Cage decision, even if he had been inclined? Given the non-negotiation for Communist-held prisoner's policy, had there really even been a decision to be made? *That's the problem with history, people can only be judged by what they did, not by their intentions. If the atom bomb hadn't worked, then the Truman Administration's Iron Cage decision would have appeared brilliant when the Soviets assisted in the invasion of Japan, Manchuria and the rest of the Asian mainland. And perhaps after an extended war, we might've gotten our prisoners back.* He vowed he would shine a light on the some twenty thousand forgotten Allied POWs in the frozen Gulag. And among them, Sergei Dmitrovich and his fellow officers— the Lost Souls. *Had I been there, would I have had the strength to keep going when each agonizing moment held the possibility of horrible death in the next instant? Realizing the enormity of the task now before me, I've become more focused and relish the challenge. This is how I'll prove myself worthy to be Of the Iskandarov.*

Natalya gave a typically scatological Russian profanity as she slammed on the brakes.

"What is it, Nata?"

"Are you blind? Can't you see that creature in the middle of the road?"

He looked up and there was a huge bull moose watching them. "Amazing. I had no idea you have moose in Russia. I thought they only lived in my country and Canada."

"How provincial of you, Mister Cosmopolitan Attorney." She laughed. "You know, we also have rabbits and all sorts of other creatures, large and small." She smiled.

Oh my God, she's teasing me. Another breakthrough. "And I find you swear like a sailor."

She raised her hand to her mouth before saying, "Excuse me, it slipped. I hope I didn't offend you. It's just something I use sparingly for certain situations."

"I liked it."

When the moose finally sauntered out of the way, she quickly reached her cruising speed of one hundred thirty kilometers an hour.

She looked over at him. "Brother, since you didn't notice the very obvious—we're traveling at about eighty-miles-per-hour—were you thinking about our father?"

"Yes, but first, what's Annie still doing in the Sakartvelo after her Ceremony?"

"You forget, she's now Mademoiselle Anastasia. She visited our ancestral lands and toured the Caves. All part of her development as an Iska Lady."

"What does that mean?"

"Before her Ceremony, I knew she was suffering from a sickness. Sister Rini knew immediately what troubled Mademoiselle Anastasia, something many Iskas suffer from in adolescence. I also heard from Wisewoman Aunt Sonia, who knows such things, that Mademoiselle Anastasia so much wanted to come on this trip she suppressed her true feelings and pains until Yuri's death. Aunt Sonia knew the cure. You'll see, now she's much better."

But sister Rosalita who has *pyordarsch* helped her in New York."

"She did—to the extent of her knowledge. Think of Mademoiselle Anastasia's trip as, ah, post-graduate education."

"What keeps you going? That is, what or who do you believe in?"

"The God who made me and the Iskandarov. Without God, I'm dust. And without the Iskandarov, I'm a well-dressed monkey to the Russians. They despise me for my dark skin and hair and in Russia, if you aren't Slav, well, you're nothing." She sighed. "What do you believe in?"

"I believe in tradition, but without becoming its slave. And I believe in the Law, which is all that keeps chaos and anarchy at bay."

"Anything else?"

"I believe searching and finding our father's Gulag diary is the right and honorable thing. And if I must, I'll give my life to it."

"I'm impressed with your convictions."

"But?"

"What of God?"

"God is in the Law."

"Wrong. God is the Law, which kept anarchy at bay before human law was created."

"A very interesting perspective."

Natalya started to say something but stopped, shaking her head.

"You can tell or ask me anything."

"When I was a girl, under Svetlana Feliksovna's thumb, I never went with a boy to the cinema, not even later with Apollon Apollonovich. But last night when we were together in the dark of the cinema room, it was just as I had imagined. Chaste but extremely romantic with your dear arm around me, and I felt so safe. And later, when you gently kissed me and our lips were briefly stuck together, it made me feel pure again. When we begin our union, we shall both be virgins, our past gone."

"Sounds great but how do you propose to do such a thing?"

"As a healer I know how to do this. And I want to thank you for making this awkward time of our relationship easier."

I believe her. Since Natalya was in the highest gear, he held her hand and she smiled, again wrinkling her nose. "Now, if you say the words, 'I love you,' I want them to be honest and truthful."

I can say those words right now but, in her joy, she might run off the road. I'll wait for a better time. "All I can say is when those three words leave my lips, you can be completely certain they're honest and sincere."

She looked at him. "You said when and not if."

"Yes, I did.

She smiled before they fell silent, still holding hands until, when the trees became thicker and the road narrower, she asked, "Please watch for cars that might be following us."

"No one uses cars to follow at close range anymore."

"Perhaps in your world. The FSB, like all Chekists, want people to know they are being followed or, at least, under suspicion. Please watch for their Ladas or the *Mafiyah* drive Mercedes. They may have allied."

"All right, but I think you're being melodramatic. Why is the FSB interested in us?"

"The Polinkov, doubtless, are behind it, especially, a revenge seeker like Svetlana Polinkova, who's very well connected in the government. Prudence is never wasted."

"True on both accounts. In the meantime, I'm curious. Why did you send your daughters to the monastery instead of the Caves?"

"First, the Caves are mostly for the infirm. Second, they would be a long way from me, and I would miss them very much. Third, as I mentioned, since they learned about procreation at their Ceremony, they are, in your idiom, boy crazy. So, Mummy and the Iska Sisters can watch over them before they get pregnant. Depending on the man, any babies they have could be significantly better or worse than normal."

"Quite a dilemma."

"We'll discuss this further after you've been to the monastery. In the meantime, you need to know more about us. We came to prominence after the Golden Horde's conquest of the Kievan state in 1240. Our clan retreated, along with our Russian brothers and retainers to the Caves, then an impregnable fortress built on a flat mountaintop in the Sakartvelo. For several hundred years, we lived, launching raids against the Mongol. While the Mongol could not dislodge us, we could do little more than harass them. Finally, we were strong enough to raid their capital at Sarai-on-Volga. These raids were not without their own dangers—being killed was preferable to capture. Because the captives were herded to the Venetian colony of Tana, at the mouth of the River Don where it flows into the Sea of Azov. There, once sold into slavery, usually in Muslim lands, they would disappear forever. Except for the few who escaped."

"I'd have thought the Venetians would've helped their fellow Christians."

"We were Orthodox heretics in their Roman eyes. Unworthy of even pity, much less rescue."

"Before coming here, I never realized the animosity that existed between the two faiths."

"They would hardly even unite to fight the Muslims. I find it interesting, though, that Sarai-on-Volga is now Volgograd, formerly Stalingrad and Tsaritsyn. As a result of our retreat to the mountain, our blood remained pure from Asiatic blood and we became a symbol of resistance as the last free piece of Sakartvelo. The Iskandarov rallied the Cartvelians to the True Church against the Muslim Mongols during those dark days. The Iskandarov and the True Church have been intertwined ever since. In the minds of many, the Iskandarov is the Church."

Ashley's hand hit the dashboard. "Yes. So, this is why the purity of the blood is so important, besides maintaining Iskandar's genes. It's your, our whole claim to legitimacy, especially over the Polinkov, who presumably didn't fight the Horde."

"Exactly. Now, when Iska girls are taught the mysteries of the female, the union of brother and sister is held as the highest romantic ideal, same as love of a knight for his lady."

"That's the first time you've told me an Iska secret."

"This shall suffice for today."

"But what are Iskandarov boys taught about the mysteries of the male?"

"I don't know specifically, but generally how to be a warrior. Hence, the knight."

"Since you were there, I'd like to hear your version of Svetlana Feliksovna's killing our father."

"In 1976, I returned to Moscow from Leningrad, as St. Petersburg was then known. I stayed with Aleks and Rini, who were married. Since I no longer feared her, I helped Svetlana Feliksovna at the Institute with her elaborate preparations for the Hero of Camp David Reception. Later, when father returned, I was alone and overjoyed to meet him. He recognized me by my aura, pregnant as I was with twins. And we soon became involved in the most wonderful conversations. That night at the dinner, all of the political elites and wives were there, including Brezhnev. Svetlana Feliksovna entered in her uniform with a holstered pistol. She gave a lengthy speech, telling cynical lies about her role in father's release. And I watched father smiling because he had told me without sharing the details, he knew exactly what was going to happen. After Brezhnev pinned the Order of Lenin on him and father went to the lectern to deliver his speech, Svetlana Feliksovna shot him. Father made no effort to resist. At first, the still loud applause drowned out the pistol's reports. I ran to him on the floor, trying to do whatever I could. I wasn't unable to staunch the blood as he smiled and at peace, slipped away. I understood that the last Stalinist, the one who everyone feared, Svetlana, daughter of the Devil himself, was in custody. Placed in a psychiatric hospital, she never emerged. And have no fear, despite the lies I'm certain Svetlana Polinkova told you, Bayta and I were at the facility the day she was tossed her into a mass grave. With her death, there remained no one in the elite who genuinely believed in the Soviet Union. After that, its demise was simply a matter of time…"

"Still it's tragic that our father could not be around to see it."

"Remember, even one as great as Moses was not allowed into the Promised Land. Further, know that *pyordarsch* does not make me a fortune teller."

"I never thought that. In fact, I'm in awe of you all, even my own daughter, who has this gift. But it must be hard being extraordinary in a society so dominated by superstitions—atheist and socialist."

"It is hard. Around non-Iskandarov, I'm usually incredibly careful. Not bad advice for you, either."

"Definitely."

"Should the diaries suddenly appear here this very moment with no difficulty, what use would you make of them?"

He turned to her. "I'd get them published."

"You're certain?"

"The time has come to raid the Golden Horde." Natalya kissed him on the cheek. "I've come to understand the diary must be found and published. And I no longer care whose reputation is destroyed, even, perhaps, my own."

"Excellent, I wish to help you find and reveal them."

"Thank you. But, no."

"No?"

"I can't permit you risk your life. It's my fight."

"I make my own decisions. Sergei Dmitrovich was taken away from me as well as you. And I knew him as a real person." Natalya covered her mouth before saying, "Excuse me, that was uncalled for."

"No, you're correct."

"I know the land, where resources and allies are. Only with me do you even have a chance."

Ashley could hear the passion in her voice, but it did not persuade him. In any event, he would not let her risk her life, already in substantial jeopardy. *I must protect her.*

"I carry the Golden Horde analogy further. If you're captured on your quest, you'll fare only slightly better than our ancestors and you shall disappear. If you're by yourself, the odds of your capture rise greatly. Now, ironically, it's the quest for our father's diary that divides us, something he fervently didn't want. I know you fear when we come together and I'm killed, it shall bring back all those horrible memories of Olga Sergeyvna, of blessed memory." She crossed herself. "You must have faith we're meant to be together and we'll prevail."

"All right. I agree with you to an extent. Olga Sergeyvna's murder shattered me even more than I realized at the time. Had it not been for Ronnie and Monica, I'd still be a basket case."

"Yes, I, especially, understand."

"Good. One last question. Why wasn't I contacted in 1991 immediately after the demise of the Soviet Union?"

"Were Penelope still alive, do you think you'd be here?"

"Good question."

"Clearly, just as the death of Colonel Cooper proved a catalyst for others, your wife's death was one for you. And with Colonel Cooper dead and Verushka soon leaving, there was nothing, save your daughter and The Firm, as you call it, to keep you in New York City."

"You're substantially correct. But right now, there's something behind us. Looks boxy and slow so, it must be a Lada."

She looked in the rearview mirror. "And it's gaining on us. Buckle in."

Natalya again focused on her driving before turning onto another road. After making the turn, she slowed. "When I accelerate or brake, the Lada does likewise. In addition, they just made the turn. Hold on." Natalya accelerated and left the Lada in the distance before she turned onto a muddy logging trail. Ashley felt this was a risky move in a rear-wheel drive car, but they successfully came to a clearing with a large pile of weathered logs. They left the car amid prominent red paint on some trees. *The paint indicates this was originally a Gulag camp.* They hugged and he inhaled her subtle perfume. They heard the Lada's noisy engine long before they saw it in its full-speed pursuit.

Natalya whispered, "Such pathetic cars. No speed, bad brakes. They do have radios. When that car meets its counterpart, they'll turn around. We don't have much time and we must first visit the cemetery at the monastery. Bye the bye, I've decided I won't be joining you at the monastery. I'd just be in the way when you reunite with your daughter and mother. Instead, I'm going to lead the Ladas astray. Something serious is going on. I must discover what."

"I can't allow you to do that."

"This is not your decision. I'm a fully certified Bleu agent. We must now leave."

2.

The iron-fenced cemetery, built on a north-south axis and overlooking a pristine lake, was a square divided into four quadrants, with one hundred graves each. Ashley and Natalya walked hand-in-hand on the north-south path. She told him the quadrant to their right was the oldest begun in 1056 when the original chapel was finished. The Mongols had smashed all the quadrant's gravestones beyond repair. To their left, the headstones from the seventeenth and eighteenth centuries, and ahead on the right, the nineteenth century and on the left, the twentieth.

Turning on to the east-west path, they went about twenty-five feet to Sergei Dmitrovich's headstone with a black and white picture of him as First Lieutenant Spencer Talbott in his Eighth Air Force's flight suit. *Probably, the latest one Charlotte had.*

Visiting his father's grave offered Ashley a deep sense of accomplishment. He knelt before the headstone, bowed his head and said with conviction an Episcopal prayer for the repose of his father's soul. *I feel cheated for never meeting this man and I'm losing my composure.* He placed his hand on the headstone, trying to get a spark like he had tried in Paris with Olga. He received a strong vibration and heard in his head, "Welcome, Sergei Sergeyovich. We shall meet soon." *Today, I'm honoring a brave and honorable man, whose existence I didn't even know about until a few weeks ago. And I'm in a place tvarsch has known about for a long time, but for some reason, never revealed.* He rose and turning, saw Charlotte's tombstone and the familiar photograph in her nurse's uniform. "I thought my mother was still alive…"

"She lives." Natalya took his hands. "Our mother, now *Mere Superiore* Anastasia, is alive. Lady Charlotte died long ago. There's an empty metal casket in her grave across from father. He often communes with Mummy, especially at night. And when Mummy's journey is finally completed, their bodies shall lie here, and they'll be in paradise. After our father was shot, Brezhnev told me I could have father's s medal and his body for burial. While I thanked him, at the first opportunity I threw the medal away."

Ashley hugged Natalya. "Thank you, Nata. For helping mother. For bringing me here. For everything."

Eyes moist, she said. "You're most welcome. I know the pain you're feeling but now look around."

Coming slowly up from Charlotte's headstone was a younger version of Natalya in a white nun's habit. She sang, "Hello American Uncle Ashley, I am niece, Magda."

He turned around to Sergei's headstone when Natalya's other identical twin rose half-way and sang, "And I am niece, Sonia." Risen, the two came toward him and curtsied.

He smiled. I never realized I had any nieces or nephews. I'm with my other family. I already love these young women. He sang back, "Thank you for your lovely welcome."

The twins began giggling. He noticed that they appeared to be mirror images of each other. Magda had her short hair parted on the left while Sonia had hers on the right. *They certainly appear normal.*

Natalya said, "I must go now. This is the only turnoff from the main road for many kilometers. My twins shall escort you." Natalya kissed him and whispered, "My daughters know the way. They've played in these woods all their lives. They only know Russian. Wait, I hear a car in the distance. I must divert it."

"If we all get in, we can…"

"No. This road dead ends in a kilometer. Go now. I'll be fine. In addition, you and my precious shall be safe. She turned to her daughters. "We must hurry, my precious ones."

Ashley placed a small stone from atop Sergei's headstone in his pocket before going to Natalya, hugged her and said, "I love you."

She kissed him. "You've just given me the strength to go on because I love you as well. But I must hurry. Soon, we'll be together." She ran to her car.

The twins led him onto a wood chip trail through forest and he heard the BMW's throaty engine. W*hat if they kill or capture her? At least, she now formally knows I do love her.* He put on a brave front for the girls. Without looking at him, he heard Magda singing, "Uncle Ashlei, we go home. Uncle Ashlei, if you American then why you talk Russian?"

"Do you speak American?"

"We do not. But America must be close to Heaven. They have nun ladies there?"

"There is Russian Orthodox Church, Saint Sergius, in New York City, few blocks from where I grew up."

"Good. Maybe we go there someday."

"Maybe."

"You like Ma. You make baby with her?"

Magda slapped Sonia's hand lightly. "Not polite."

"Do not care. Ma wants baby. Uncle should make baby for her."

"Why, Sonia?"

"That is what two people in love do. We know. We have many ladies with babies."

This had quickly become much more complicated than Ashley had anticipated.

"We love boys and want them to make baby for us."

"Yes, we like boys."

Magda smiled at Ashley. "Is Mam'selle Ani your little girl?"

"Yes, she is my little girl." And hopefully, will be for some time.

"We like her. She is good lady, nice to us."

"I am glad."

He listened as they sang to each other. Their clean crystal sopranos are some of the finest I've ever heard. I feel sorry they'll never share their gift with the world.

"We think God is evil and deserves a good spanking. He should have made us perfect like Ma and Grandma Ani."

Before he could respond, he heard, "We are going to have babies, just like our ladies." Sonia smiled triumphantly.

"But mother said you are brides of Christ."

"Yes, but we want babies too."

"I do not think those two things can go together."

Sonia spoke. "Yes, they do. You will see. Now, I am bride of Christ. Da flied so high he could see God. One day, God decide he want Da to stay with Him. We marry Christ so we can see Da."

The story of their father's death certainly sounds like Nata. "That is good idea."

Sonia responded, "Yes, but we want to care for babies too."

"Well, that is good. Nuns often do that."

Magda stopped and pointed. "Look, Uncle."

Through the trees, there were three onion domes—one caved in, one a robin's egg blue and the gold middle one shone in the sun.

"This is where we live."

"With all ladies and babies," Sonia added proudly.

Magda yelled, "Aunt Rushka, Aunt Rushka, look who we bring!"

Ronnie stood in a clearing outside the whitewashed fortress of a building and waved.

Ashley thanked the twins for bringing him safely to the monastery.

Ronnie asked, "Nieces, are you ready for lunch? Later, I shall shave both your heads and we shall find real nun headdress for you. Then you shall be full Iska Sisters."

"Goody. We want donuts and jam." They ran into the building.

Ronnie said, "They've already forgotten about us. Don't take it personally. They can only focus on one thing at a time."

Yes, they spoke mostly about having babies. They also told me God needs a good spanking for making them inferior."

"Oh, I know those two only too well. That's not our God." She kissed him on both cheeks in the lovely French fashion and took his hand. "Come, we have much to discuss."

He tried not feel attracted to Ronnie, but her aura drew him, and he knew he must resist.

"Notice our ruined dome and the fire marks on the walls. A reminder of when the Mongols sacked the building several times and we won't forget someone could do it again."

3.

Ronnie led Ashley through a roughhewn unpainted door reinforced with two rusted iron braces. As they entered, light through a large stained-glass window in the wall above illuminated the room. They faced each other under the soft light. She wore khakis, a white blouse, low heels and sunglasses up in her black hair. I'm a swine—I desperately want to make love to her.

She crossed herself before saying, "I can't tell you how glad I am to see you again. So far, Russia has been a difficult place for you, particularly, Svetlana Polinkova yesterday. Aleks called me earlier with his report. Before we begin, I've some news from Paris. Nadia put up a brave front for you, but she has terminal cancer and won't live too much longer."

"I'm extremely sorry. I had no idea and really liked her. Such a courageous lady. So, you'll be taking over Bleu-Paris then?"

"Yes. While I get up to speed, Cosette will remain Director of Operations."

"Good decision. So, will you become a grand duchess when your mother dies?"

"Yes, but I haven't really thought about it. As you know, I'm not big on titles. Now, I've heard there are numerous people out to kill you. I also understand Anghelina is now pregnant by you. And keeps writing notes about the Gulag diary."

"She even bested Aleks' security last night but made no physical contact, only left a note on my bureau. As to the other, she caught me asleep and blindfolded, so I thought she was Nata."

"So I've heard."

"How come everybody knows everything?"

She looked into his eyes and gave a slight shrug. "Because for our survival, we must keep everyone informed. It's how we begin our day."

"Anghelina wrote that she was in *phygynaya* when she first found me, something you certainly know about."

"Ugh... She was in heat and had to get satisfaction. Does Nata know this?"

"Yes, but since she doesn't have it, I think it's hard for her to understand. Nonetheless, we're back together. Do you still have it?"

"As long as my estrogen levels remain high, I've my *phygynaya*, although at a slightly lower level. But enough of that."

Incredible. But then she's an Iska. She'll tell me about her pregnancy when she's ready. He put his hand on her shoulder and she placed hers on top of his, squeezing lightly. "Thank you. I know you're eager to visit Mademoiselle Anastasia."

"I'm also excited to meet my mother."

"And you will when she finishes leading the Sisters in prayer."

"Verushka, you're a person I know I can trust and..."

"To anticipate your question—Aleks, Rini and Nata are whom and what they claim to be. They don't need or want your money. It's not a con. No, it's all deadly serious."

"How did you know what my question was?"

"Ash, I've known you ever since you were eighteen. I think I've got a rather good handle on what makes you tick. Besides, if the shoe were on the other foot, I'd ask the same question."

Ronnie's tone was a bit flirty. She's my past and Nata, for as long as I have her, is my future. So, I must ignore her. Probably a test anyway. "Thanks, I understand about not reading Sergei and Dmitri's diaries before David died, but why not David's? I had so many questions while reading his diary. I would've given anything to ask him about a million questions."

Ronnie shook her head. "Your now stronger *tvarsch* knows the answers to all the questions you may have now and in the future." She crossed herself. "David was such a fine gentleman."

"I agree, but there's one question I've not gotten answered. Was David involved in the cover-up of Iron Cage?"

"He was caught between his protégé, Spencer Talbott and George Farwell. Although under intense pressure, he never acted dishonorably. And I know because since the late fifties, we'd been together working on getting Sergei released."

"OK. But why did David send Spencer on the Ploesti mission? He must've known it was, at best, a one-way flight."

"Probably, but David told me Spencer was one of the best bombardiers in the Eighth Air Force and he wanted the best teams he could assemble for such a critical target. You know most of the mission's details, but here's a key point you don't know. In the Bleu archives, I found there was a rescue operation, which had to be scrubbed. Because the airmen were not sent to a Romanian Army base, as original intel indicated. Rather, new intel found they were living with Romanian families spread out over too large an area to successfully rescue." She placed her hand on Ashley's knee. "Of course, the Gestapo and SS weren't consulted about their plans for the pilots, co-pilots and bombardier / navigators, who were sent to the *luftstalags* you know about. And in case you have wondered, before Alt Drewitz, these luftstalags were so well fortified and too deep in occupied Europe for any hope of a rescue."

"Good to know. It would've been worse had not the Red Army shown up early at *Luftstalag* Alt Drewitz."

"After the Iron Cage decision, the Prometheus Group destroyed all the evidence linking them with the decision and eliminating any loose ends who might appear, such as our father. George enlisted Charles Drew to be his man at the Firm and keep his name out of the decision."

"He has a conscience?"

Ronnie laughed bitterly. "Not the supreme narcissist George Farwell. No, he was angry that his decision was not only wrong but embarrassing."

"Yes. Such a revelation would definitely mess up his statesman image. And he'll crush anyone who messes with that. So, am I correct in thinking Ambassador Linus van Rouene was Mr. Phillips?"

"Since Sergei, as Spencer, had slept with virtually all the partner's wives, van Rouene set up a sub-group dedicated to making certain Spencer paid for his great insult to The Firm's partners. And Svetlana Feliksovna, ally of van Rouene, made sure he suffered even more. George was also involved in the decision to hand over our grandfather and many other Iskandarov to Stalin's executioners at the end of the war in Europe."

"Right. But why couldn't the Iskandarov or Bleu or someone have moved against George back in forty-five?"

"At that time, Bleu, almost destroyed by the war, was in no position to do so. Moreover, by the time we were, George had so thoroughly wrapped himself in anti-Communism that his assassination would have made him a martyr. As the Cold War waned, we increased the psychological pressure. Leaving reminders that we could harm him at any time we chose. After all, a man with a lot, has lots of worries."

"I remember he'd come over to the apartment some nights and rant about how his unspecified enemies were out to get him."

He shook his head sadly. "But why didn't he have me killed like Olga back in sixty-two?"

"He was warned not to touch you."

"Too bad Olga didn't have such protection."

"Remember the Polinkovs only wanted to kidnap you and Rand, not Olga."

"Because Rand's father, Harvey Jacobs, was still alive?'

"Yes. When your stepmother Patricia died while you were at Lawrenceville, we had your housemaster in Kennedy House watching over you. When you and Rand went to college, I asked sister Olga and her friend Corinne to guide and protect you both, due to the real threat of kidnapping. As you may remember in Paris, this cost Corinne her life during the kidnapping attempt on Rand after Nadia's Repast in the summer of 1962." She crossed herself.

"Undeniably. She's another courageous lady. Olga was part of Bleu then?"

"She was an agent of fortune, like David, an operative when needed."

Ashley smiled. "I thought when Olga was killed, Iskandarov tradition dictated her sister replace her."

She smiled. "Only if there had been a blood union. Besides, if you recall, I was married at the time."

"But you once said we had a special relationship."

"We most certainly did, and you remember very well how we pushed the boundaries, you naughty boy." She laughed, "Again, no blood union, no half-sister in your bed until she was single. Besides, now you have a full sister." Ronnie smiled. "Do you have a plan for the diary?"

"Don't I always? Have a chat with Aleks because there's a vital role for you along with our old friend."

"Will do. But sister Nata must help you with your task. And you must help her with hers."

"We've been working on that."

"Good. Now, although Bleu was watching you and Olga constantly, she slipped the coverage to buy the drug that killed her. Bleu's protection was as good as humanly possible."

"Why are you telling me all this now?"

"What I've told you today is what you need to know and resolve before you can finish your old life."

"Understood. You're certainly cold-blooded about Olga Sergeyvna, of blessed memory." He crossed himself in the Episcopal way.

"True, but that doesn't mean I didn't love her or not miss her now. I do, greatly. I can't imagine anyone actually buying street drugs from a total stranger. Especially when you know, at a minimum, you're a target of nefarious persons."

"Agreed. That was why I loved her. When I read about Spencer and Angelina DelaVega Delgado, it really struck me. Both Olga and Angelina lived their lives on their own terms, even though they were in serious danger. Angelina and her *Demoiselles de Joie* were absolutely scandalous for the time. Perhaps, even now. Yes, it was foolish for Olga to get pregnant, but she was a romantic. Besides, with *pyordarsch*, she knew and confirmed recently in Paris she was going to die on 15 May 1962. Only not knowing how."

"I'm impressed. Once more, you've surpassed my expectations. Not knowing sister's fate, we made elaborate plans to get her to Paris. *Mamman* Nadia when she discovered Olga was pregnant by the son of Sergei Dmitrovich was delighted beyond words. She knew Olga would be much safer in Paris. Olga's dismissal from Harvard was a ruse. She was tenured, after all and resigned. I remember you telling me long ago that you were appalled at the clothing she had on her bed the day you found her. That was part of a disguise along with a red wig, so she could avoid detection getting to and through the airport. The letter she left you while absolutely heart-felt and true was also a ruse. That's pretty much it. She had been using dangerous drugs long before you met her. Iskas don't use drugs because it reduces our gifts and because it's totally unnecessary. Going through her papers after she died, I found she went to Montreal to make love one final time with her mentor, Jean-Louis, a professor of history at McGill University. Then she planned to love you one final time before she died. Sadly, she was delayed getting back that last day and you found her already dying. I'd actually arrived in Boston several days earlier than you thought. I was shadowing you to keep you safe."

"Yes, I sensed someone was following me and knew whoever was friendly."

"That was a chaotic time but keeping you safe was then one of Bleu's highest priority and I had several other agents watching you. And, as soon your semester was done, we were all gone. I discussed moving you to Princeton with David. Much easier to keep you alive in a small town that a big city. But by the fall, things had calmed down so back to Harvard. Back to the present, beyond the Blood Union I think Nata would like to be formally married to you."

"And I to her."

"Fabulous. I also hear uncertainty in your voice."

"Because I've been warned that if we have a baby, Nata and baby will be killed like Olga Sergeyvna and my son."

"I don't think you fully appreciate the level of protection that's around you and has been since you arrived in Russia."

"I know that but it's not air-tight and exhibit one's Anghelina DelaVega. Well, Verushka Sergeyvna, what's Anghelina up to? I think you know her better than most."

"First, she's highly trained and very resourceful. She's also very strategic and patient to achieve her own long-term goals. I don't know whose side she's on in your struggle with George because she may not be on either one."

"I wouldn't be surprised. Candidly, of all the women I know, she's the one who really scares me. I mean that night at Nata's, she…raped me in such a cold-blooded fashion. There's no other word for it. She was quite experienced, and I admit I enjoyed it. But later I felt very uneasy."

"Perhaps that's part of your Iskandarov education."

"I don't understand."

"With any luck, I believe you soon will. Actually, she scares me too. I love her anyway."

"Last night, for some reason, when not thinking of Nata, I restlessly dreamt about all of Olga's life like I was watching a PBS documentary."

"That's something else you need to know about the flowers in the Maze. A Soviet biologist developed the nightmare rose. She injected the essence of a psychotropic drug into a white rose, the traditional symbol of pure love. People would be attracted to it, inhale the scent and anything they had repressed would be revealed. Problem was that it wasn't strong enough by itself to do much. But Svetlana Feliksovna brought thousands to the Maze. And it worked. The *zeks* were terrified of the horrible images the flowers produced. Some, who weren't murdered, died of their horror from suicide and heart attack. Most were just incredibly disoriented. Just as she wanted."

"I had a pretty rough time there yesterday."

"So I've heard. By the way, Aleks had more than half the flowers destroyed. The roses also tripped Olga's memories last night because you need to let those memories fade. I know you'll never forget her, but you need to focus on Nata. I've been flirting with you the whole time and you barely noticed it. You passed my fidelity test."

"Good. Look, you and Olga and David were the three people who really formed me. And you, especially, did an excellent job of preparing me for my life at the Firm…"

"Thank you, but again, you did all the heavy lifting. Finally, I think I've taught you about all I can."

"I doubt that. I still need you and your Bleu agent knowledge for my Gulag diary plan to work."

"Of course. I'll speak to Aleks later today." She paused. "I'm so proud of you. When you defied me three times at my cottage before agreeing to go on this journey, I was pleased. Because, in a sense I was your mother. To be a successful Iskandarov man, you need to be a warrior, not an attorney. And to be a warrior, you need to break cleanly with your mothers, especially your mentor mother, me. You completed that today."

"Again, I really can't thank you for all you've done. I'll always love you. Soon, I'll begin my life with Nata and you're going to Paris for Bleu. After I succeed in my diary quest, I want to help mend the rift between Bleu-Paris and Bleu-Russia. And with your cooperation, it should be fairly easy." He smiled. "I must keep sister safe when she's pregnant following our Blood Union. I'll defend her to the death."

"Romantic words for an attorney. In real life, you must stay alive."

"But, if I die, I'll bring George Farwell crashing down."

"Ash, you're of no use dead to either Nata or the Iskandarov. Because it has been foretold your children with Nata will be superior to restore the Iskandarov to their rightful place. You're in transition and it's hard but you must persist and be patient. There will come a time when you'll know what to do." She rose and took his hands. "Use what I've told you well. See you soon." They hugged before she kissed him on both cheeks and left.

He closed the door, feeling liberated and spontaneous like he had when Olga was alive. Just as his mother Lady Charlotte Sternwood had to die for her to become Sister Anastasia, so, Ashley F. Cooper, Esquire, had begun dying on the road to Sergei Sergeyovich Iskandarov. A loud metal door knocker startled him. "I think it's open."

ELEVEN

Tuesday, 8 June 1993, West of Moscow

1.

Annie Cooper entered, wearing sandals, a light blue off-the-shoulder silk gown with an ivory sash cinching her waist and a dark blue turban. She stopped about five feet in front of Ashley. "All hail, great father. Annie has said goodbye and girl's red hairs are gone. You see before you Mademoiselle *Kyria* Anastasia, Iskandarova Lady who shall have dark red or copper hair in future like Great-Aunt Bayta. Greetings..." Her voice broke and tears flooded her face as she ran to Ashley and during their long hug, he felt her shaking.

Wow. This is amazing. My little girl's all grown up and, most importantly, safe. My prayers answered.

They parted and studied each other. "Dad, why're you crying too?"

She even smells like a woman. "Because I'm so proud of you—confident, mature and graceful. And you look so beautiful and natural without makeup. And your adolescent black nail polish is gone replaced by a lovely scarlet."

"I don't need flattery. I practiced my Russian speech and had it perfectly. One look at you and I almost totally lost it."

"I won't tell anyone." He smiled. "Your Russian's improving. So, tell me more about the new you."

"I'm so happy because I discovered Yuri isn't really dead."

"How do you know? And, where is he?"

"Wisewoman Great-Aunt Sonia told me in the Caves, he's in Elsewhere."

I see but what's he doing there?"

"Um, he's hanging with other warriors and I'm planning to visit tonight. I've discarded Miss Chaplin's First Rule for Young Ladies, 'We are WASPs, thus, we do not show emotion, except behind a locked door.' I spent much time at my Ceremony hugging and kissing other Iskas and it was so liberating."

"Good. I rejected Lord Buckley's rules for young gentlemen within a year of leaving. In the real world, they didn't work. But tell me, where's my daughter, Annie Elizabeth?"

"She lives in your heart and I hope she always will."

"Count on it. I also hope a part of her lives within you." Ashley held her again, kissing her eyes and cheeks.

She said, "I love this little room where I meet with Aunt Ronnie, I mean, Verushka. It feels so authentically Russian with the plain whitewashed walls and, most of all, the spectral light coming from above."

"Ronnie left a few minutes ago. Yes, this spartan ambience helps to focus on what's important. But now, I want to hear, as much as you can, about what you've been doing."

"My gown is based on the classical Greek *peplos*, such as Athena might've worn. Customarily, it's worn for a week after the Ceremony in remembrance of the three Colchi princesses, Ilyrianaa, Aliannaa and Athaliaa. As an Iska noble Lady, a *Kyria*, this robe and sash denotes my status so that all Iskandarovs who see it will know as I search for a union-mate."

"I'd advise patience. When the times right, you will find each other." He nodded. "So, all the girls who go through the Ceremony have different titles when they're initiated?"

"Yes, there are six categories and *Kyria* is second to Aunt Natalya's *Prinkipia*, Princess. One day I'll have earned that."

Aunt Natalya? Of course. "Great, I'm very proud of you."

"Yes, as part of my liberation, I'm totally comfortable not wearing anything underneath, because, traditionally, the three princesses didn't. Don't get the wrong idea. I'm not wearing this to be sexy. I remain a proud virgin and will be until my marriage bed with my union-mate. Yuri will always be a friend, but he was my girl boyfriend. In Paris, when I wore the skimpy blue dress, it not only had significance for me being successor to Aunt Ronnie's future leadership at Bleu. Great-Aunt Nadia also was preparing me for my Ceremony. Further, being a girl, I had not mastered *pyordarsh*. Up to that point, it was an abstraction being about other people. Now it's so very real and I've expanded my abilities and finally understand and respect it."

That was a bit more than I needed to know but I'm proud of her candor. Our relationship just took a big step forward. "Oh, yes I knew very well how you felt about Yuri. You never forget your first love. But I'm also relieved you're in control of *pyordarsch*. But remember, what we have are gifts that we need to maintain, or we'll lose them, just like your mother lost her aura."

"Good advice. But I want to tell you about the Caves. Well, for the first time in my life, I've felt, these past few days, like I was really home. For my Ceremony, Aunt Ronnie and 'Lita brought me to the Caucasus Mountains, which are quite spooky with sharp peaks sticking up like cat's teeth. The Caves' main entrance is in a small valley and you enter through the ruins of a fortress. The floors are all tiled and well lighted. It's sort of like a luxury hotel. Among other things, that's where we attend to our less fortunate brothers and sisters. After my Ceremony in another part of the Caves, at first, I felt extremely awkward and uncomfortable there, you know? Like when you see a homeless person on the street." She took a deep breath and slowed her speech. "And this little girl, maybe five or six, comes up to me, smiles and takes my hand and leads me around. She had a clearly painful deformed right leg, which was hard to walk on and yet she did with no complaints. As I went around, hearing about the place, I understood I owed her and indeed, all them, so much. As we went deeper into the Caves, I felt a sense of peace, such as I've never known. It's a magic place, full of the most positive energy imaginable." She leaned over and again kissed his cheek. "I understand how my grandfather bore his great ordeals. His palaces were within and could never be taken away. My talent, my life is built on their backs. Also, I must tell you about Great-Aunt Sonia, Sergei's sister. She doesn't let her legs define her because she has transcended them. She goes around on an electric wheelchair and has the most beautiful smile and she's strong, yet gentle and very patient. She knew so many things and understood me and my problems almost before they left my mouth. She knew exactly what was troubling me—a lot of things I didn't even know about—tied in with *pyordarsch*. And I've also learned so much more about being Iskandarova *Kyria*. And then there's Grandmother Charlotte. I can't begin to tell you all the things I've learned from her. She, too, is strong and has endured so much to find here what she sought." She made a broad sweeping motion. "This is the place I saw in my vision back in New York, remember? And she's the nun."

"I know."

"Thank you for getting me started on this process. In New York and up on Quaker Mount, if you hadn't taken me where I needed to be before my Ceremony, I'm not sure I could've handled it." She smiled. "At Miss Chaplin's School for Young Ladies, now that I have my visions under control, I could go back and fit right in because I've the confidence to be my own person. But as I've said, I've rejected the rules and feel the need to pursue my education elsewhere. Either here or in Paris with Aunt Ronnie, sorry, Verushka."

"She told you about Nadia Mytrovna?"

"Yes, I'm so incredibly sad about her. I plan to go with Aunt Ronnie to her funeral."

"Good, you can represent our family. I'm going to be tied up here for the foreseeable future. And no question I've known about your struggles since you hit adolescence and how you'd go into your world-weary ennui to hide them. I could've helped you more but since I had to figure out *tvarsch* myself when I was about your age, I decided that was the way for you. And you've done it. I further suspect Aunt Sonia only gave a few direct answers and let you figure the rest out yourself." He paused. "I know something's still bothering you."

"You may think it's no big deal, but it is. I don't yet have a patronymic because I don't yet have an Iskandarov father and 'Ashleyevna' sounds ridiculous." She shook her head.

"I know. You don't just waltz in here from fifty years on the outside and join the Iskandarov overnight. And I'm working hard on that."

"With Aunt Natalya? Have you finally broken up with Lana van Booben?"

"Yes. On both counts."

"Dad, you've changed so much and it's so major a change, it's almost like you're someone else, but you're still you."

"Yes, and I don't think I've ever been better. But prior to today, ever since the airport, I've been terrified of losing you. I felt only slightly reassured when I visited you at the Metropol."

"Our little talk at the Metropol and knowing you were OK made my Ceremony tasks so much easier. Also, I remember feeding a morsel of meat to a certain blue falcon." She laughed.

"How could you tell?"

"He had your eyes. Flying's hard work. Don't worry I didn't tell anyone. Although I suspect Aunt Natalya knew. And she was still terribly upset about you. She told me what happened that night in her studio with Anghelina. And had I been Aunt Natalya, I'm uncertain I'd have believed your story either."

"Well, she and I are back together. And I swear, I'm innocent."

"I believe you because Aunt Anghelina's so amazing, she's one of the few people we know who could do that."

"Yes, indeed." Would it have killed Anghelina to reveal herself and then I could've been a participant? But if she had done that, would I have co-operated, knowing Nata was in the other room? One last fling before committing to Nata? No!

"You're still troubled by that and you must to rethink it. Aunt Anghelina could have any man by snapping her fingers. And she chose you. And not only that, you're the one she chose to make her pregnant. Because of Aunt Natalya, she probably knew if she asked you, you would've refused. So, she had to take what she wanted before she lost her chance. I'd say, cut her some slack."

"My, you've gained wisdom and you're right. But my future's here with Nata. We're making steady progress and should have our Blood Union in the near future."

"You really have changed. What happened?"

I fell in love with her. I want to protect, respect and adore her the way Spencer did Charlotte. I want to have children with her and spend the rest of my life with her, as much time as we have."

"Sweet."

"And?"

"I've been learning about Mom's *dhestovy*. And I now know exactly what she was going through."

"Are you trying to tell me you'll be going insane as well?"

"Not at all. Since I understand *pyordarsch* so much better, I now know the signs of madness. I mean mom's like our people in the Caves. She may have appeared normal like Queen Xenia of bath of blood fame, but they both had their deformities in their brains, not outside."

"Very interesting observation. It's always good to look at a situation from a completely unfamiliar perspective. Besides, you're concerned about your union-mate. Don't worry, you're one of the most beautiful Iska Ladies now. You can have your pick of whomever you want."

"Oh no, all fathers think their daughters are beautiful, even if they're not. I'll take pretty, but the man I'm looking for won't be swayed by such a superficial thing as that."

"Beauty is always a factor. After all, you may have to look at that person for the rest of your life."

"I can't tell you how much this trip has meant to me. At the Caves, my little friend pointed out a strikingly beautiful girl about my age. But when I tried to speak with her, well, she was in her own private little world, way beyond autistic. A few things different here and there and that could've been me." Ashley reached up and brushed a tear away from her cheek. She took his hand and gently kissed it. "One thing I've learned here is how fortunate and advantaged my upbringing has been. I owe the world, life, fate, God, whatever you call it, big time. I've now a chance to make a difference. How can I not repay such a debt?"

Ashley hugged her. "I hope that spirit will always remain with you."

"I know it will." She paused. "Oh, I had another vision. I saw a monument with a large piece of weathered coal, about ten feet high on a metal platform. It appears to be in a very barren place and it's part of your diary quest."

"It's probably in or around Vorkuta then. But why the long face?"

"It'll be very dangerous, even deadly, for you, if you go alone."

"Is this *pyordarsch*?"

"Yes. And I'll swear to its accuracy."

"I must do this. I couldn't live with myself knowing that my father's Gulag diary existed somewhere, and I was too scared to find it." *Add her to the list of my going with Nata.*

"I know, but I couldn't bear to lose you now when I feel like I really know the true you for the first time."

"I feel the same way about you. But now if I die, and I've no plans to do so, you'll at least have good memories of me."

"Please be careful."

"You know me. I always have a plan." He smiled bravely. In truth, it's only a partially formed one. Can't complete it unless I know more about Vorkuta and that info's very had to come by. "As you remember from the airport, I brought six thousand dollars with me for your birthday, largely to spend on your party and gifts. So, here it is. Happy Birthday and New Life."

They hugged as a nun walked in.

"Please excuse me. Monsieur Cooper and Mademoiselle *Kyra* Anastasia, come with me. Sister Anastasia now desires to speak with you both."

2.

The twenty-something nun Ashley and Annie were following was pregnant, but Annie did not seem to notice or think it unusual. They went through the side door of a large, whitewashed room with many pictures on the walls and two full bookcases. A spacious wooden desk was near the far wall with a rough-hewn round table with six wooden chairs to its left. In the room's center, a wide and dusty ray of sunlight cut across the stone floor from a high window shining on a tall, regal lady with broad shoulders in her white habit. Her black headdress had a veil partially concealed her eyes. Her face was pulled tight, presumably, after several surgeries. She said to the young nun, who was leaving and closed the door, "Thank you, Sister Marja Mikhailovna."

Ashley came closer. *This feels like a dream and yet, very real. But I can't feel my feet because it's as though I'm floating.* She held out her hands. He took her long, cool fingers and remembered her familiar lotion from her nocturnal visits. "Mother."

"Son." She ran her hands over his face and smiled, "I perceive you in my mind's eye quite well." She removed her hand from his and placed it on his neck and pulled him toward the curve of her neck, kissing him. Annie wept for joy as she hugged both of them. When Charlotte began speaking, her accent surprised him. *It reminds me of the superb Graham Greene film, The Third Man and others I've seen growing up. Because her speech sounds like it came from the thirties, forties and World War II, frozen by her captivity in Russia.* "Mother, it's so great to hear your English accent again."

"Jolly good and welcome finally. Come, my darlings, let's sit and chat." She walked toward her table.

"It's amazing to be here. Mother, you move so well unaided. How are your eyes?"

"By the mercy of God, Chichikov hit me from the right, thus, my left eye wasn't as damaged, and I see grey light and motion. The veil keeps my eyes covered more for aesthetic reasons than anything else."

Once seated, she said, "Darling Ashley, I wish to share a moment of which you are unaware. Back on 7 November 1942, your father, my recovered patient, had just asked me to accompany him to the Officer's Club at Wroughton RAF. Of course, I knew his true identity but had yet to develop any strong feelings for him. As we drank our whiskey and sodas, we spoke awkwardly, and I wondered if I'd made a mistake. The club's radio broadcast music through a large speaker. When Glenn Miller's *Moonlight Serenade* came on, he was up and took me by the hand to a small dancefloor. Someone turned up the volume and we danced cheek-to-cheek, as we used to say, and he was a marvelous dancer. It was at that moment I fell in love with him and, knowing I was ovulating, your birth became inevitable. When we stopped, everyone cheered and toasted us repeatedly because they could see we were in love. After the clamor subsided, he proposed, and I readily accepted. It was an absurd thing to do in the middle of a war, but I sensed if we didn't marry right then, we never would. And now, fifty years later, I've not a single regret."

"That was so charming and incredible. In one of Sergei's diaries, I read the two letters written when you were pregnant, and Spencer was about to leave for Ploesti—beautiful and tragic, knowing what would happen to both of you. Your last letter to Spencer especially, made me feel wanted like never before. And I realized he never read it before leaving on his mission. I suspect your sister Patricia pasted it in the diary when she came for his effects." *I'm trying awfully hard to hold back tears.* "When I was young, I loved your nocturnal visits when your sprit wrapped around me and I felt safe, warm, and loved and I'd hear your lullabies and encouragement in my mind. For a long time, I wasn't certain they were anything more than dreams. I desperately wanted them to real, because, in Patricia, I had a mother in name only. Recently, in our Quaker Mount attic, I found her possessions and read how her lover Colin's death over the English Channel in August 1940 broke her heart. Anyway, I forgave her and apologized at her grave for my unruly behavior before leaving the Mount."

"I wish you could have known her before the war, a brilliant and lively lady. In the twenties, she even joined Angelina's *Demoiselles de Joie* in Berlin and then Paris."

"Yes, Cosette told me but previously, I had already sensed that and, partially, is why I was searching in the attic for her possessions. I never read her collected letters because that felt like a violation. By the time you made your last nocturnal visits, I had *tvarsch* and knew you were real. I wanted to find you but *tvarsch* then was not yet powerful enough. I sensed from the start of my daughter's *pyordarsch* you had to be the nun she was seeing. At the same time, I didn't want to get my hopes up." His voice cracked and tears welled in his eyes.

Charlotte rose and came to him. "Let's have a little cuddle and let your feeling all out, my darling, we have loads of time." He put his arms around her and cried and shook as he felt her arms around him and her body's maternal warmth. Later, his chest aching, he looked up, seeing her beatific smile and felt better. "Please tell me how you came to be here. Nata has told me about Chichikov and how you got to Bayta. But how did you get to this place?"

"That morning, after Bayta's general left for Moscow, she bound my wounds and I remained hidden in the attic with Nata acting as lookout. But it was unsafe at the general's dacha because he unexpectedly returned that night and Nata and I had to remain very still and quiet because any noise we made would be fatal. Also, Svetlana Feliksovna could arrive at any hour, day or night. Had the general found me, he would have returned me and, possibly, Bayta to the Institute for certain torture and death. Fortunately, she knew the general would be staying away for several days and when I was up to snuff to travel, she and Nata brought me to an ordinary dwelling deep in a forest. As we approached, I heard hymn singing. But when I discovered I'd be staying in a make-shift nunnery, I thought my stay would be brief. I'd never been religious since I was a little girl. And until I joined my Sisters, anything but." She shook her head. "With abundant time to think and meditate, I eventually reflected on my life and realized

God had been testing me and my coming there couldn't be an accident. Despite my injuries, I still possessed visions and foresaw this habitation many years ago and proclaimed one day it should be ours. After the Bolshevik revolution, they stored grain in the Sanctuary. Later abandoned, the building fell into disrepair. The Iska Sisters realized the beauty of my objective and we focused our labors toward that. Truly, we are all equal here. Because of my visions, I'm Mother Superior but prefer to be called Sister. God knows that without my Ladies, I should long be dead. She stood, "All right then, let's walk, my darlings, there's much to see. My son, I would be honored to have you take my right arm."

When Charlotte led them from the room, on the wall there was a colored bas-relief of three women—Virgin, Matron and Crone. The plaque was surrounded by icons of men and women with thick gold halos and under it an incense burner with a residual scent. Xenia, Elizabeta and Vladimir the Healer stood out because their icons were larger than the others. On her office door was an Orthodox cross without title. He smiled and felt his mother squeeze his hand.

We'll walk in our cloister, a covered walkway around our courtyard where our Sisters tend our supplemental crops. Feel free to stop and examine any of our possessions. I appreciate, my son, you're having a certain amount of trouble with, shall we say, the metaphysical aspects of the Iskandarov."

"True, but much less than I used to."

"Permit me to remind you that Russia's a magical place, where the rationality of the West and the mysticism of the East merge into a Hegelian synthesis. A place where all is thus possible and where opposites co-exist, such as great cruelty and great beauty." She laughed gently and stopped walking on the brown-tiled cloister floor. "But now I'd like to relate how you came to be here." Charlotte reached into her habit's sleeve, held up a small ancient black leather book with gold trim and asked Annie, "Darling, please tell us the name of the volume."

"*The Second Decade,* the diary of my Great-Grandmother, Sophia Sergeyvna Iskandarova, Countess Kolchaka."

"Please begin on page forty-seven. Oh yes, darling, even though your father knows French very well please translate into English, my old brain isn't up to French anymore." Charlotte turned to Ashley. "I'm so proud of my granddaughter's French. You're to be commended."

Annie glowing with pride began:

5 May 1912

Yesterday, Mikhail and I hosted a gala Repast at
our Crimean Helicon Estate for one-hundred and
twenty notables. The ostensible purpose was to
announce I am expecting my second child. The
actual purpose, prior to the Repast, was to form
The Triad, a new clandestine organization to
monitor the situation in the Balkans. The Serbian
Black Hand {Union of Death} has championed
Pan-Slavism in such an inflammatory manner that
war with the Hapsburgs or the Ottomans or even
both is inevitable. If not properly contained, this
conflict shall lead to a general European war, given
the web of alliances among the Great Powers.
Count Mikhail shall lead the group of sixty to
surveil the Austrians from here and Vienna.
Brother Dmitri, with his entourage of five, shall
be our man at the Imperial Court at St. Petersburg.
And I shall be in charge of the Serbian / Balkan /
Ottoman group of fifty-five from our residence in
Odessa on Zimyava Street. Because it is only one
hundred and fifty kilometers from the Romanian
border, about as close as we can safely be. The first
task was for Dmitri to discover from the Okhrana
in St. Petersburg the true name of the Black Hand
leader, known as Apis {the Bee}. My second was
to send my sister Illyria Sergeyvna, the beauty in
our family, with her intoxicating bright blue eye
and shining black hair to Belgrad. There, she is to
use her prowess to find and seduce Apis in order to

discover what the Serbs are planning. And with her
visage and form, this should be child's play for her.

"I find this interesting as an historical insight into the activ-
ities of both Sophia and her husband, the Count Mikhail," said
Ashley. "While going through Dmitri Sergeyovich's footlocker
in our Quaker Mount's attic, I saw them in a hand-colored photograph on this day at their Repast. I'm also curious about Sophia's
sister. I've never seen her mentioned in any of the diaries."

"As Sophia predicted," Charlotte began, "Illyria was successful and continued her association with the Black Hand. Later, in Sarajevo in June of 1914, she witnessed nineteen-year-old
Gavrillo Princep of the Black Hand and his tragicomic assassination of the Austrian Archduke Franz Ferdinand and his morganat-
ic wife Duchess Sophie. After making her report amid the round-
up that followed, Illyria vanished. We now know she died in an
Austrian prison, despite the best efforts of The Triad to locate her.
When the first war began in 1914, we had to stop searching and I
don't think Sophia ever fully recovered from Illyria's loss."

"Thank you. Illyria sounded remarkably interesting."

"Quite so. The Triad's important. When David Cooper escorted Sergei, Sophia, and her agents to Paris in 1919, the American Secret Service thoroughly debriefed everyone before Sophia
formed anti-Bolshevik Bleu in Paris. Now, darling, if you'd continue your lovely translation on page sixty-three."

5 September 1914

I have just received word that Mikhail is not among
the prisoners the Prussians took after the disaster
at Tannenberg last month. Both he and General
Alexander Samsonov are dead, the latter by his own
hand. Good riddance, he was always a mediocre
commander. I shall miss Mikhail, Leila's true father,
who would never commit such a cowardly act. I shall
begin preparations for my period of mourning.

"Now, please turn to page ninety-four."

6 July 1916

Two days ago, I arrived in Petrograd, the former
St. Petersburg, because, I had calculated that the
Realm of the Spirits and demons would appear at
a small Orthodox church on the Prospect by the
Nikolayevsky Bridge. At the appointed hour, the
priest met with me and permitted me enter the Realm
of the Spirits.

"Please stop, my darling. I've heard, while In Paris, you
Ashlei ventured into the Realm of the Spirits"

"Yes, Countess Sophia summoned me and I somehow
managed to get through the realm of the demons to speak with
her. I don't think I've ever been more terrified. Frankly, I never
would've made it out without the help of Sainte Xenia."

"I was never there but I've heard such terrible tales." She
shook her head. "I commend you for your bravery. My darling,
please continue."

I met with Mikhail and he told me I must issue a
prophesy based on what he told me very generally
about the future. He told me my special gifts would
complete this. He asked how Leila was faring and
I told him well. And then about Sergei and said he
forgave me for my infidelity with Dmitri because he
now understood our Iskandarov customs. He also said
he was fine and quite content because he had died a
soldier's death. I thanked him and made my difficult
way back to safety in the church.

Ashley remarked, "In Paris, Cosette told me Sophia had
been to the Realm. I'm seeing where this reading is going. But
where was this Leila when David came to Odessa? There's no
mention of her in the diaries."

"Before the first war began, Sophia took her to Switzer-
land and enrolled her in a special school. She remained for the
next fifteen years before returning to the Sakartvelo with her
baccalaureate to attend her Ceremony at seventeen to become

your aunt, Mademoiselle Doctorat Sonia. Dear *Kyra* Anastasia, please continue."

> 31 March 1919.
>
> I had formulated my prophesy by early 1917, using a combination of tarot and pyordarsch to bring clarity to my task. With the chaos of the last two years, I had much more pressing issues to deal with. Now with S/M David Cooper, I have found the person who shall be the catalyst of my prophesy. I seduced him because he is full of potential and I need to form him into the man for this task. Dmitri is finally back from the Front and approved my plan. In short, early in the third decade, the Iskandarov shall have to endure an extremely dangerous time until early in the tenth decade. Then, David shall die at ninety-four and unleash momentous events that shall lead to an Iskandarov renaissance in the person of the Hidden One. Who must be kept ignorant of his heritage until David's death. Be aware-our enemies shall try everything, so this does not occur.

"Thank you, darling. Well done." As they walked, Charlotte said, "Now you understand, there's nothing you could've done. Once the time proved right, all the pieces fell into place. Your father, Seryozha, the diminutive of Sergei as his mother and I call him, was, like you, reluctant to assume his place and wanted to be a normal man. He thought he could escape the Iskandarov by running away from who he was. Thus, his masquerade as Spencer Talbott. But his fate would not be denied."

"Fate? What of free will?"

Charlotte smiled indulgently. "What of it, my son? You may think you've free will, but it's your fate being revealed. Once back in Russia, your father learned this and returned stronger than ever to the Iskandarov."

"Mother, do you have all the volumes of Sophia's diaries?"

"Yes. And you may read them whenever you're ready."

"Based on these entries and because I've not read any Iska diaries, I feel as though they'll complete my knowledge. Are there other treasures I should read or know about?"

"We have many such. And I hope you'll return here often. I hear the puzzlement in your voice."

Ashley liked how his mother was so attuned to his speech. "All right. I noticed Marja Mikhailovna who brought us to you was pregnant."

"Oh, yes, she's married to Captain Vladimir Alexeievich, in charge of the Bleu-Russia paramilitary station here. Everyone here is somehow related. The connections become extremely complicated. Thus, I largely ignore them. Vlad is a cousin of yours, but I don't remember how. Most importantly, remember the first Iska responsibility is to procreate. Also, I remind you that in Orthodoxy priests are allowed to marry. We've six married Iska Sisters and two who are not, expecting. And we have a nursery."

He turned around and became fixated on the eyes of a large icon and smiled in recognition of Sainte Elizabeta encased in a thick gold halo whose eyes appeared distant as the horizon to which she gazed. Her eyes had also promoted a most intimate and perfect peace. *Must be one of those meetings of opposites.*

Charlotte laughed delicately. "You've found the eyes of Sainte Elizabeta standing watch for the army of demons. And she is patron sainte of this monastery."

"Mother, I know because she was my patron sainte for most of my life, but Sainte Xenia replaced her in the Maze."

"Excellent. While we greatly revere Sainte Xenia, we kept Sainte Elizabeta as our patroness so as not to attract unwanted attention. Moving on, Nadia Mytrovna Andreyeva, when she married Seryozha knew him to be extraordinary. Because she knows very well what people need as opposed to what they think they want. And why she had to return him to his Russian roots. This terminated the marriage, not her love." She smiled wistfully and shook her head. "I, again, owe you a debt for abandoning you which may never be repaid. I must speak to this."

"No, Mother. It's all right."

"It's most definitely not. When I disappeared, I knew you'd be in the capable hands of the Colonel. Regrettably, as you have said, Patricia did not share his enthusiasm for you. And for that, I'm terribly sorry. I also regret Patricia naming you Ashley. I wished to call you Sergei."

"I would've liked that and when I was young, you called me Sergei Sergeyovich and that will be my name when the time is right."

"I must say I'm surprised with your memory. That was so long ago."

"Still on Quaker Mount, I used *tvarsch* to find my earliest memories."

"You're most creative. I've never heard of anyone using *tvarsch* through billions of memories to find a particular one."

"I had to know this and while painful and draining, it worked. But how did you manage to visit me?"

"We all have our distinct gifts. I've done this since I was a little girl. I had to let you know who I was I and that I remained alive. You always seemed incredibly happy to see me."

"Of course, but I really need to know how you came to me that way."

"Darling, you already are aware of the basics. The Iskandarov are one Tradition and the Sternwoods are a blend of Norse and Scot Gaelic under the Lord of the Isles. While all Traditions have basic similarities, each one has its own distinct gifts. People with visions are fairly common, however I could never do, oh what do you call it? Yes, *Andronyi*. My son, you're the blend of two great Traditions.

"Can Nata's spirit fly like you?"

"No. Although she has unique gifts and talents."

"I'm finding that. You said people can have visions so men can do it as well?"

"Of course. Although apparently not the Iskandarov. I believe that evolved so there would be cooperation between the genders."

"Mother, I just now realized I owe a debt to Patricia, because, in a way, she made me stronger."

"Agreed. As we've said, with the death of Colin, she became profoundly depressed but maintained her stiff upper lip so well that very few people actually knew the truth. But she gradually lost her Sternwood gifts."

"Like Pen. But what happened to you after my birth."

"Since you doubtless know my history with Chichikov, I begin as an RAF nurse. Bleu assigned me to your father, and I nursed him after his essential eighteenth bombing mission."

"Yes. I know all about that from his diary. But are you suggesting the eighteenth mission was preordained?"

"This was my best way to have met him, although I still mourn for all who died so this could happen. Just reflect on the consequences of my not meeting Seryozha. Or consider where we would all be had David Cooper not volunteered to be a typist and was killed like the rest of his mates. Or even consider what happened when Nata sent a garbled *Andronyi* to you and ended your engagement to Monica. You married an Iska and produced your lovely daughter. This is the way of the Three Fates. Seemingly unrelated events that absent any particular one, then, you and *Kyria* Anastasia never existed."

"I've been thinking about my whole life since my journey began and several times, I'm amazed I'm here at all. And now I fully know this is Fate."

"Precisely. Moving on, I attempted to remain aloof from Seryozha to hide my interest and curiosity. And because he was handsome, brave and dashing, I had my guard all the way up. In time, I discovered he possessed great humanity. And a child was never born with greater love than I had for you. On the day of your birth, Chichikov with his force, disguised as an RAF emergency team, appeared at RAF-Wroughton's base hospital to kidnap me."

"Yes, I've heard about your kidnapping from several sources."

"Indeed. It was reported I died after childbirth from 'complications.' As far as anyone knew, it was true. Only *Mamman* Sophia's clever work revealed the truth."

"Thankfully. Did you ever find my father in the Gulag?"

"In 1943, I began slaving at a Polinkov coal mine near Kaline, some forty kilometers east of here. I'd no idea where Seryozha was or even if he were alive. In the spring of 1946, Chichikov brought me to the Institute. I became the sexual plaything of Svetlana Feliksevna and him. It was two years later my nocturnal visits to you began and continued for about nine years."

"I never would've guessed you were in such pain."

"With Svetlana Feliksovna gone to fetch Seryozha, I also visited him at night in the Vorkuta Icebox and because of the two far-apart time zones, I could, after leaving you, wrap my spirit around him to keep him warm and helped him survive. Once your father arrived at the Institute, Chichikov, now with an audience, humiliated me in unbelievable ways, demonstrating his dominance over me in front of Svetlana Feliksovna, who proved her dominance over Seryozha. When we were alone, Chichikov could humiliate me in any manner he wished. I no longer cared. The guards at the coal camp had terribly abused me. But to see my beloved under the thumb of Svetlana Feliksovna, well, that broke my heart." Her voice trailed off and she shook as though crying but without tears. Ashley held her until it stopped. "Svetlana Feliksovna even went so far as to plant false information in Seryozha's training for Camp David, wishing him to fail and thus be killed in his attempt to wound President Eisenhower. She would be rid of him and cause the remnants of my heart to completely break. But Seryozha was too clever. Thinking back on that time, well, I've long ago forgiven Chichikov and Svetlana Feliksovna their transgressions. I've now been amongst the Iska Sisters thirty years because Nata was seven in 1963 when I was blinded. While not the life I'd have chosen, it has been a most blessed one."

Ashley hugged her and noticed other Sisters in their silent work on the courtyard crops. "Did you ever see my father again after he left for Camp David?"

"In 1976, I remained underground. Nata came to visit, even though it was extremely dangerous. She told me Seryozha was back at the Institute. I told her I could not allow him to visit me in such a state. Nata wisely said that my appearance would make no difference. After all his trials, he was no longer the handsome young flight officer. But he also thought I might still be angry about his children with Maria Civilli. I was not. After reassuring us, Nata began to arrange for our rendezvous. The date agreed on was the day after the banquet. I've pondered this at great length. At the time, I was obviously absolutely crushed by his assassination. In time, I realized the Three Fates were at work. Had we reunited, I'm certain I'd have left the Iska Sisters to be with him and all you see would have likely, never fully come to fruition. Thus, Seryozha's death proved I was where I was meant to be. But my love for him never diminished one iota and we often join our spirits together at night. By the way, I finally met Maria Civilli at the Iska Sisters Ceremony a few years ago and liked her immediately. Most importantly, you need to learn about the night before dearest Seryozha left for his Camp David training. We were permitted to spend the night together and had our Blood Union because I brought him with me as our spirits left the Institute and did everything in but a single night. Normally, the Blood Union is a process. Thus, had I not had my gift, our union would've failed."

"While I'm incredibly pleased you succeeded, I'd always assumed you had Blood Union with my conception."

"Think for a moment. I married Spencer Talbott who had turned his back on his clan. As to the Blood Union, I hear uncertainty in your voice. I'll merely say it was the most beautifully intense experience I've ever known. The memory of that has kept me going through all my trials. And, of course, the result was the birth of my darling daughter Nata." She smiled brightly. "However, as Seryozha prepared to leave, he apologized for having gotten me involved in this and handed me a small parcel, which he had hidden. The diary he had written about the Gulag and his experiences there. Tragically, Svetlana Feliksovna found and burned it."

"Yes, I know there's another one up north at Gulag-Vorkuta. But I don't know how to get there."

"You can't. However, Nata, being an official, can take you there."

"No. It would be too risky for her. There must be another way."

"I believe that's her decision." She placed her hand on his shoulder. "You need to cooperate with your sister and she with you. Your task's so daunting that even with both of you cooperating, recovering the diary remains extremely challenging."

"I'll ponder this further. Given the extraordinary adversity you suffered, tell me more about your survival."

"A person with a reason to live, lives. With no reason, a person dies. I've my vows. There's a great religious revival going on here and I'm pleased to play my small role in it after all those years of darkness. We've had our monastery restored to Iskandarovs after almost seventy-five years." She turned to Annie. "Before Chichikov, I was a lost soul in a land of plenty. I wandered, pampered and catered to through a life that truly offered nothing. I was, quite literally living on my drugs of choice, champagne and caviar. With Chichikov, I began my descent into a place I couldn't have imagined earlier. With your Grandfather, though, I experienced a bliss unknown to those who never knew the depths. If Seryozha brought me to the zenith, then Chichikov again cast me down into a deep despair. Through God's mercy, I survived and grew stronger in ways I never could've without my trials. When I came to the Iska Sisters, like early Christians, they were a persecuted minority. They took me into their sisterhood and helped me to find purpose and meaning."

"I fully understand, Grandmother."

"Mother, I'd like it if Mademoiselle *Kyria* Anastasia could stay here for a few days. I think she still has much to learn from you."

Annie mouthed, "Thank you."

"I'd be honored to have my beautiful granddaughter longer here with me. She'll be safe and there's still much we need to discuss. Don't you think so, darling?"

"I'd love to."

Ashley felt pleased about the deep verbal and non-verbal communication they had developed in their brief time together. *Very much like she had with Nadia.* Charlotte turned to him and asked, "What do you propose to do with the diary after you recover it?"

"I'd use it to expose Iron Cage."

"But why ever are you willing to do this for a man you never met?"

"I have a good sense of Sergei Dmitrovich and I greatly respect him. His diary didn't initially paint a flattering picture of him and, honestly, it repelled me. As I read more it was as though I was watching him mature into a real man. Now, my diary quest is also for me. I'd like to right a wrong or two. It's extremely easy to condemn the silence of others like the Germans who didn't resist Hitler or the Russians who didn't resist Stalin. I need to shine light on this dark corner of history."

"I'm extremely proud of you and your courage. But now may a mother give some long overdue advice to her son?"

"Of course."

"Loneliness is the great killer of people. You know you and dearest Nata are meant to be together. And it's especially important for the two of you have children."

"I know. Nata and I are waiting for our Blood Union." I'm again fearful I'll lose her like Olga. And I can't go through that hell again. Can mother tell I'm lying? I certainly hope not.

"You've given me and your daughter immense joy. But I know you had decided to go alone to Vorkuta before coming here."

Yes, I was seeking verification from the both of you because you matter so much to me."

"Thank you but ponder what I've told you. I don't want to lose you and that's precisely what will happen without Nata. And that's not enough either. You must have your Blood Union before going to Vorkuta because you will then become unified against the forces arrayed against you. Now, I know there are loose ends to tidy up before you fully commit to my daughter. Remember, you loved your half-sister, Olga Sergeyvna, because she was of the same flesh as you. Don't blame yourself for her death, it was preordained."

"Yes, her pyordarsch...and Fate."

"Trust me when I say fully uniting with your sister shall be glorious."

"I believe you."

"It was such a shame you had that long detour through the law firm and Penelope Farwell."

"I haven't been able to sort out my feelings about Pen. And I need to resolve that before..."

"What is there to sort out? You wasted no time falling into bed with Svetlana Polinkova. I don't condemn you, since you were unaware of who she truly was. Penelope, a lady of enormous potential, made many unwise decisions, which led her into the dark alleys of the soul. Something I know a great deal about. Largely, because she wasn't blessed with trials, she, or at least her soul, died many years ago. That's why you feel nothing for her now and why you feel guilty, which makes it difficult for you to do what you must."

"But that's what I don't understand. Pen was Iskandarova, so, why didn't we do better?"

"She was *dhestovy*. More importantly, she never wanted to be an Iskandarova, only a rich Farwell. And she, in her ignorance, thought she could defeat her *pyordarsch*."

"How do you know so much about Pen?"

"Through Verushka, I've been kept informed about you for a long time. Had I had a chance to mother you, I would have strongly opposed your liaison with such a defective person as Penelope." She shook her head and said, "You know of Queen Xenia?"

"Not the sainte but the historic queen?"

"The same person who possessed the ability to be a great ruler but difficulty in childbirth caused her to question her core being—her womanliness. When the same thing happened with Penelope birthing your darling daughter, she began a slow descent into insanity. Compounding that was her *pyordarsch* telling her when she would die, plus her knowledge you always loved Olga Sergeyvna more than her. Her madness was inevitable yet crept in so slowly as to be scarcely noticeable, except to Verushka, who saw her at greater intervals. Penelope's passing proved a blessing, giving her the peace always denied her."

"Not for long. She's now in the realm of the demons. And that's what I don't understand. She was insane and so, not responsible for her actions."

Charlotte laughed. "I've been waiting for a visit from our solicitor. When Penelope attempted to have Olga killed, she was not insane. What matters are her motives—envy and wrath—two of the Seven Cardinal Sins, thus, no mercy. And she never atoned for her sins."

"Mother, that seems very harsh. But will…?" Ashley heard running on the cloister floor and saw Natalya followed by a very tall man in a black uniform, who stopped beside Charlotte, touched her hand and said, "It is I, Vlad."

"Darlings, as I mentioned earlier, this is your cousin, Captain Vladimir Alexeievich Iskandarov, who commands our station of twenty-four."

When they shook hands, Ashley noticed his expertly tailored fatigues with a sky-blue beret and Bleu collar insignias and his firm handshake. "Call me Vlad."

Charlotte said. "Vlad, I assume the occurrence of some nefarious event justifies this intrusion."

"Yes, Mother Superior, Prince Aleksandr Sergeyovich's motorcade was intercepted and he has been kidnapped."

TWELVE

Tuesday and Wednesday, 8&9 June 1993, North of Moscow

1.

Within minutes of Captain Vladimir Alexeievich Iskandarov sounding the double klaxon, nuns, priests and paramilitary troops were walking briskly to their posts. Charlotte remained in the cloister calmly reciting in Russian a detailed list to her assistant, Sister Marja Mikhailovna, Vladimir's wife. Ashley, Natalya and Annie waited patiently. When Charlotte finished, she asked, "Dear Nata, just for my peace of mind, who was it again who confirmed Aleks's kidnapping?"

"Mummy, Aleks's assistant, Grigori, in the motorcade, confirmed it to Rini, who called on my car phone soon before I arrived. Cousin Vlad ordered our lock down just as his counterparts had locked down the Institute and the communications center at Saint Vladimir the Healer's Church."

"Excellent. Grigori is a good man, nonetheless, my heart's heavy over this kidnapping business. Even though we're not related, I still love Aleks. He saved my life."

"Me too, Mummy."

"And I as well—for saving my life in Bangkok," Ashley said, "Mother, I don't understand this Bleu paramilitary station. I've only met Bleu agents."

"My son, that is true of Bleu-Paris. But these men are Bleu-Russia. You probably read in one of the diaries how my leaving Bleu for all this caused the rift with Paris. It had been a long time in coming. After the war in June 1945, with our intelligence network substantially destroyed, we realized we needed an army for protection against Stalin and the Polinkov. Thus, intel gathering became secondary to survival. Grand Duke Alexei formed the group from our returning soldiers in the Red Army..."

"Iskandarovs were in the Red Army?" Sister Marjah Mikhailovna led eight other young nuns, moving quickly past him.

"Stalin decided, as Lenin had in the civil war, he would accept good officers of any political belief. However, our men and women quickly disappeared in May 1945 to train our troops before they could be purged. Thus, although officially paramilitary, they're well trained. This station along with many others shall remain open as long as the political situation remains unsettled. Now, darlings, I know both of you wish to help rescue Aleks, but Cousin Vlad's an excellent officer and I'm optimistic they'll liberate Aleks." She smiled. "I'm incredibly pleased the two of you are working together. Let's make our way to our armory to pick up the kits Vlad has prepared for you."

They came to a blue door in the far cloister wall. Both Anastasias remained in the cloister as Natalya and Ashley went downstairs. Before entering the intercept room, Ashley heard the clatter of telexes and printers, and felt surprised with nuns without headdresses wearing black baseball caps with a red X under their earphones. Seated in swivel chairs at long desks decked out with multi-band radios, large reel-to-reel tape recorders, electric typewriters, and multi-button telephones, they remained busy. Ashley pointed at a curtained-off ten-foot area and gave Sister Marja Mikhailovna a questioning look.

"Sisters are well trained to take over from troops in emergency. And behind curtain is new triangulating computer, which can monitor up to ten vehicles at same time." She went to another door, unlocked it and led them into a roughly twenty by twenty red brick room with steel gray cabinets on all four walls.

From a specific one, she took out two blue travel bags. "Two standard issue Beretta 9 mm. 92SBs with thirteen shot magazines and ten extra clips for you both, two Uzis and communication equipment. Sadly, we have no current maps for Vorkuta. We are in contact with Princess Rini who is negotiating for husband's release. We now know where he is within ten meters because shoe transmitter is working well. We have also picked up two Ladas heading this way from Moscow with three people in each. Be careful when you first leave and God bless your Majesties."

"Thank you, Marja Mikhailovna, for all your help," said Ashley.

She smiled for the first time. "You are most welcome. But before you leave, I wish you to see one of prize possessions we keep securely down here." She showed them a snake-handled silver sword under glass in a corner. "This is sword of Iskandar, gift he gave to princesses."

Ashley said, "That is incredible. I did not see it at Iskandarov Collection Exhibition in New York."

"We did not send complete collection because some, like this, are too fragile to travel."

"Thank you so much for showing it."

On their way upstairs, Natalya said, "All Bleu field agents and soldiers have a transmitter in one of their heels. I do, and Feodor installed them in your shoes while we were at the cinema."

"That should come in handy."

Back in the cloister, as Ashley went to Charlotte, Annie was frantically writing in her leather-bound diary.

"Mother, I'd like to go on the record…"

"Again, I am most certain you should love to join Vlad in rescuing Aleks. Now, show some humility and let the professionals handle this. You've your own tasks."

Annie hugged Charlotte after Natalya asked, "Brother, do you have anything Iskandarov with you besides your Sainte Xenia icon?"

"Our father's cigarette case. Why?"

"I'd like to have Mummy bless it to protect us on our journey and to establish our common bond."

"Great idea."

"Ashley, I'm well pleased this case has found its way to you. I always thought it so romantic when Seryozha would take out two of his Lucky Strikes, tap them on his case before putting both in his mouth, lighting them and handing me one. I came to enjoy his cigarettes in the fleeting time we were free together." She sighed and looked at Annie. "Everyone smoked in those days."

"Yes, so I've read. It's still a lovely story, Grandmother."

Charlotte smiled as she held the scratched and bullet-dented metal box in one hand and guided by the scent of incense, took it over to a burner. She opened the case and held it over the smoke for about two minutes before bringing it to her nose and smiling. "Excellent." With her free hand, she made the sign of the cross over it and said some words in Greek before returning it to him. "Now, darlings, I'd like to relate a vision that came to me recently. I could see and I was deep in a large cave with Iskandar, shining brightly, in the middle. There were thousands of small lights circling him, coming and going. As I came closer, I became a point of light going into him. And when I emerged, I was young again in a beautiful wood and I saw Seryozha, smiling, as I ran to him." She smiled ecstatically. "So, you know, darlings, death is not the end."

"Mummy, as wonderful as that is, I hope you have much more time with us."

"Of course, Nata. You understand, though."

"Completely."

"Well now, there you have it, darlings. I'm so delighted the two of you shall work together to recover the diary. There's really nothing more for either of you to do here. As you heard, the bells have tolled fourteen. Nata, where have you chosen?"

"Larissa."

"Jolly suitable. Godspeed to you both. I shall be here to welcome you home. Now, I must lead a prayer vigil for Aleks in the chapel."

Natalya and Ashley hugged their mother and Annie before Natalya led him to a red door, which opened to a lighted tunnel. Once inside, he spoke softly, "I'm truly delighted to see you.

Frankly, after you left, I was worried that you could just as easily be the captive everyone's concerned about."

"While I appreciate your sentiment, I again stress I'm not the helpless maiden you imagine. I outran both Ladas before doubling back on another logging trail."

"I know you're extremely capable but with two Ladas pursuing you, that would be four Chekists. Bad odds, even for you."

"Perhaps, but we've a much larger problem—the two new Ladas with Moscow-based *apparats* because their cars are much faster and travel in tandem. Most likely, our morning chase was a prelude to the kidnapping and I'm certain whoever's in the new Ladas mean to arrest us. Further, we must assume they aren't FSBs on brother's payroll. They've official sanction and doubtless will first go the Institute and then here."

"I assume you've a safe destination in mind."

"I certainly do."

Even though the tunnel went further, Natalya went up a metal ladder to unlock a manhole near the parking lot. When Ashley came out, four armed guards escorted them to Natalya's BMW.

2.

After taking a call, Natalya scanned her rear-view mirrors. "Rini says those new Ladas are about two kilometers southwest of us. The three triangulators at the Institute, monastery and St. Vladimir's have been monitoring all Lada's positions all day and a key reason I was able to lose them earlier."

Ashley looked back and saw no one else on the road. *The trees here are much bigger than this morning and closer to road so, it feels sort of claustrophobic.* "Good to know. But what's the situation with Aleks?"

"Rini said if Aleks signs a document renouncing your L'Enfant Treaty, the abductors say they'll release him. But he won't, unless you give him permission."

"And if I don't?"

"Exceedingly difficult to predict. They may torture him into changing his mind."

"Who is this 'they'?"

"Likely, the same group we encountered at the Metropol and my studio."

"Have they made further demands?"

"I'm certain Rini would tell me everything. Our default in a situation like this is that it is a Polinkov operation. And we must assume, at a minimum, Polinkov are aware of this and will use it to their advantage."

"So, the kidnappers could release Aleks only to have him shot or re-kidnapped by the Polinkov."

"Possibly but be assured Vlad's force will make sure that doesn't happen."

"What's your best estimate of how likely they are to release Aleks if he complies?"

"Kidnapping in Moscow is as common as being robbed in New York City—serious and possibly, life-threatening. Thus, having achieved their goal, the kidnappers don't want to make a bad situation with us any worse."

"What do you propose?"

"Were I a better person, I'd say let Aleks be a martyr to the cause of peace in the Balkans and preventing a wider conflict. However, in my heart of hearts, I know…" She paused. "Please don't take offense but I fear even should your initiative be implemented, nothing of substance should come of it because of Orthodox time, among other factors."

"I appreciate your candor and I've the same doubts. We in the West have a conceit we can impose peace on peoples who want to kill each other and have been doing so for hundreds, if not thousands, of years. Such as the rest of the Balkans, the Middle East, and Ireland. And many other hot spots."

"I know fully what L'Enfant means to you personally, to Europe and the world. I know your inner struggle. I'll support your decision either way."

"If we've even the faintest hope of getting Aleks back, we must try. Because, had it not been for his courage in Bangkok, I'd be dead or kidnapped to the Institute. Moreover, absent Aleks,

Chichikov who doubtless also had his service Tokarev pistol, would've killed you and our mother. So, I'm in his debt three times. Therefore, tell Rini I release brother from L'Enfant."

Natalya punched in a number on her car phone and said, "*Ad.*" And, after nodding, hung up. "That was Cartvelian for 'yes'. It's in God's hands now. I know principles are important to you. Family should be even more so. As you said, had it not been for Aleks then Mummy, Bayta and me and possibly Rini, should likely be lying, forgotten and unmourned, in an unmarked mass grave somewhere in the woods." She shook her head. "We're still in danger from multiple groups. Rini reported that the new Ladas are going east on this road and closing on us."

"What's your plan?"

"Just like this morning...make sure you're belted in."

When the tandem red Ladas came into view, Natalya, in the right lane, let them get within twenty feet of her. Ashley turned around and there was a blonde and brunette in the cars' passenger seats. Turning back, he was not too surprised that the large bull moose had appeared in the left lane. After Natalya surprisingly accelerated past the moose, it stopped in the right lane and the Lada, unable to stop, hit the moose in its long legs so it landed on the hood blocking the windshield. The driver lost control and collided with the other car and they both hit trees. The moose charged into the woods while all six people ran from the Ladas just before both vehicles exploded into flame.

"Had I not witnessed that...no, I'm not sure I believe what just happened. I mean the moose falling into just the right place to cause the crash and then getting up, seemingly, uninjured. I'm sure it was an exceedingly difficult piece of sorcery to produce such a thing. Am I right about you?"

"Again, I'm merely a healer. I couldn't do that—ever. However, a *grande sorcière* could. And I only know one. The last time we saw the moose, it took me awhile, but I recognized he was a Bayta conjure and we'd see him again."

"Bayta told me she would protect us until our union." Ashley laughed, shaking his head in amazement and then he and Natalya lapsed into what was, given the circumstances, a comfortable silence.

Oh my God, I'm receiving an Andronyi. He smiled as it finished and relaxed. He enjoyed her car's fine ride and Natalya's precise focus on high-speed driving until she downshifted for a turn onto a muddy road, slowly driving before coming to a stop in front of a two-story log building. Out of the car, a woman of colorful clothing and indeterminate age greeted and affectionately hugged Natalya, "Welcome again, *Prinkipia*, to my inn."

"It is good to be back, Larissa. This is my friend, Ash." Natalya gave her the car keys and Larissa smiled, "Another high-speed chase?"

Natalya nodded as Larissa ushered them over the freshly cut grass to a stone patio and a square wooden table and two chairs. As she left, she told them she would have the car moved to the barn and have their luggage brought to their room. Ashley looked around at the other couples having lunch but sensed no alarm but remained alert. *Somehow, I recognize all this from when it was in much better shape.* On the table, which still had traces of gold from a long-past elegance, he felt around his chair's right side until he felt *SII* but could not remember what the first two letters were. Next to it was another *SII* with a heart between them. *It'll come to me.*

Natalya looked at the birch and aspen forest some ten meters equidistant from both the patio and back of the building. Ashley breathed in deeply the clean, fragrant air and felt the warm sun on his face, relaxing him.

"It'll be safer to speak English. Larissa claims she's the granddaughter of Larissa Fyodorovna Antipova. You know, *Doctor Zhivago's Lara.*"

"How, even in Russia, can one be descended from a character in fiction?"

"You're so literal sometimes. She's the granddaughter of the lady who inspired Monsieur Pasternak. In fact, he carved his initials by your left hand. And there are many others on different tables."

His hand felt the Cyrillic *BLP* and smiled.

She fixed her gaze upon him. "You've been acting in a most un-*avocat* fashion."

"Since I can't return to The Firm due to my failure on L'Enfant, I feel I'm no longer even an attorney."

"Nonsense, you can work wherever you like."

"Perhaps, but once you've been a partner, no, a senior partner at Gules, Or, Argent and Drew, there's really no other place to go. Because virtually everything else is a giant step down."

Natalya raised her hand to her mouth. "Oh, dear God, I had...didn't know." She reached for Ashley's hand and squeezed it. "I'm all the more impressed by your decision about Aleks."

"Perhaps I've been an attorney too long anyway."

"I'm certain a man of your gifts will have no trouble finding any position he desires." She smiled encouragingly.

"Not interested because I've a plan almost worked out."

"Share?"

"Not yet. Still some loose ends." I really hope she can't tell what I'm thinking.

"I'm curious. I know you've been worried sick about your daughter's safety and now, when you have her back, you allow her to stay with someone you hardly know."

"At the monastery, I knew from Annie's reaction, Anastasia was my mother. After the moose incident, I had a vision of Charlotte and me. And I knew."

"Yes, I recognized your expression when you received it. And I also knew it must have been a most intimate moment between you."

"Charlotte suckling newly-born me with her serene expression, filling me with love and nourishment."

"Oh my God, that's so incredibly beautiful."

"Indeed. It was sent by our mother, but she said she couldn't do an *Andronyi*."

"She can't but that doesn't mean she can't send visions. Different Traditions, different gifts and names. This was her way of thanking you."

"I need to watch you Ladies, you're worse than a whole firm of lawyers when it comes to parsing facts and truth."

"It's only until you become fully Iskandarov. Let's forget about Aleks for a while. He's been kidnapped before, he's no novice and knows how to act. Right now, I need your complete attention to answer a most important question. Why do you wish to join the Iskandarov? And think very carefully before you answer."

"I understand the importance of the Traditions. I believe in the mission of the Iskandarov—to preserve and enhance our Tradition and support others to bring progress to the world. That's fine, but I not only fully accept I'm the Hidden One, I understand why. I could've been hidden anywhere in the world, but it was New York for a reason. Dmitri Sergeyovich had sent Sergei Dmitrovich there and, in his diary, felt strongly he should've stayed there. Colonel David Cooper raised me there as an American liberal. I believe in freedom. Our whole Fascist thing has to be discarded. I understand why, out of necessity, we were that way. But the world has changed, and we need to so as well. Royalty and aristocracy are also done, and we should abolish our titles. *Prinkipia* Natalya. I've no intention of accepting 'prince' as a title."

"Are you teasing me again?"

"I'm serious."

"Your proposal for us is rather radical. You'll face a lot of resistance."

"I'm counting on it."

Before he could reply, Larissa came out with a tray of large platters of meat, cheese, raw vegetables and fruit, dark bread, and in the middle, a carafe of chilled vodka with two glasses, and Natalya's car keys on the right side. They ate quietly and it was a while before Ashley carefully sipped his vodka, leaned forward and took Natalya's hands in his. "Nata, I think you're fabulous. I wish I'd met you a long time ago. But what I want, in this case, doesn't matter."

"Oh? And what does?" She downed her vodka and poured another.

"I must find and publicize Sergei Dmitrovich's Gulag diary. I've a primary obligation to him and all the others who perished in the Gulag. It may cost me everything, including my life. Or the life of someone I care about...Annie or even you. Therefore, after we eat, I'm going to leave you. You'll be safer with your family."

"First, you can't walk or drive to Vorkuta. Only by train. Second, you lied to our mother—a Holy Lady. You agreed we would search together. Don't you realize that's a major sin? You're now damned, so you better stay alive for a long time." She bit angrily into a radish. "Perhaps, there are some women who'd be scared off so easily. However, I don't belong in their ranks. I believe to the center of my being these horrors must be revealed. It's part of my atonement for the actions of my stepmother, the most odious Svetlana Feliksovna, for all the Iskandarov who perished so horribly at the Institute. Besides, you can't leave me because you know nothing of the geography or even where the diary is, beyond generally at Vorkuta. Such ignorance would only speed up your permanent trip to the realm of the demons."

Ashley slammed his fist on the table. "Nick and Drago are after me. They don't care a whit about you."

Natalya's voice remained calm as people began looking at them. "They stand just as much in my way."

Ashley downed his vodka before standing and leaning across the table. "You do not understand. I have gotten myself into something way over my head. I am probably not coming back alive. Therefore, I must make preparations for Annie. She's safe for the present with her Grandmother. I need someone to be her guide through the maze of life. I want that person to be you. She's going to need you alive."

"As much as she'll need a live father. Sit down, you're causing a scene. As one man alone, you'll have nil chance against the formidable forces facing you. We've allies you'd never find. We're here because this is a safe place from which to begin." She gestured broadly. "Look around."

Ashley closely observed his surroundings. The two-story log building with its wood, grayed by age, also had several homemade patches. The windows were not completely straight and had distortions in their glass. "Here? It doesn't look all that safe." *I know this building, just not how.* He sat.

"This inn's so normal it has never attracted suspicion. It's been a haven for free thinking people since the mid-nineteenth century. Monsieur Pasternak came here on several occasions to read the Lara poems when they were banned, and after that, he carved his initials on this table as an act of defiance."

"It's certainly historic and courageous. But after lunch, I want you to leave me at a railroad station somewhere with instructions on whom to contact."

"Your daughter's now a full Iskandarova *Kyria* and you need to start referring to her by her proper name. You can't continue to cling to Annie in either sense. That girl no longer exists. Besides, our entire clan will support her and even let her make some mistakes. Thus, I'm not essential. Besides, Russia needs you. Much more importantly, I need you. Russia should manage, as will Mademoiselle *Kyria* Anastasia." She bit into a hard-boiled egg.

"No."

After washing down the egg with vodka, she asked, "But why not?"

Ashley filled his glass and downed it. "Because you'd be too big a distraction." He poured a refill.

She arched an eyebrow. "I don't think I understand you. Perhaps you could explain in Russian?"

Ashley finished his vodka. "Simply, when I'm with you I can't think clearly. Also, my fear returned this morning after you drove off to lure the Ladas away. I was deadly serious when I said you could well be the hostage we were speaking of. Or something worse. You'll be killed for bearing our children and I can't shake it. In a sense, my freshman year at Harvard never really ended, the pain of Olga Sergeyvna endures to this day. Our mother says we should be together. Verushka and Rini say we should be together. Even my *Kyria* tells me we should be."

"And all we women are crazy?" She shook a scallion in a circular motion before eating it. "I told you the night we first met I've what you need to be whole again. That's what they all know." She shrugged. "I don't know. Perhaps men can't see such things." She leaned back in her chair. "One time, when I was young and here with Bayta, we heard Boris Leonidovich Pasternak read his poem, *A Fairy Tale* about a knight rescuing a maiden from a dragon's lair. He doesn't know who the maiden is, only that the dragon is torturing her. He goes into the lair and does battle. He's wounded and falls from his horse. His horse tramples the dragon as both animals ultimately kill each other. The knight revives and rescues the maiden, but he has lost so much blood in the battle, he collapses. She revives and, seeing the knight's blood, assumes he's dead and swoons. And it continues until they both die, never having known the other. That can't be our fate."

"Of course not, but…"

"Despite your protestations, you're still thinking like an *avocat*. And I understand your reluctance to move on. But you must." She sipped her vodka. "I confess that despite my bravado, I need your protection from our enemies. You have a Beretta. I assume you know how to use it." She looked at him. "Hello, are you hearing me?"

* * *

Ashley—naked, young and in great shape—arrives in a strange place. A man who appears to be Sergei Dmitrovich carries a sword and shield, and wears sandals, bronze armor over his shins, chest and shoulders, beneath it a linen tunic. "Welcome, Sergeval, to *Thurnane*, the repository of all *tvarsch* wisdom and knowledge. I am Prince Serzak, your stepfather. We are here to commemorate the eighteenth birthday of Iskandar. Phillip II of Macedon, his demanding father, challenged him to fight to death a giant Thracian, like David and Goliath. Combat was witnessed by his tutor, Aristotle. We know Iskandar triumphed to become Alexander III of Macedon. Had he failed—gone and forgotten. This is why we challenge our young men at eighteen to combat another giant. If successful, they become adult warriors. Remember, if you are not a warrior, you are dead and no Blood Union. Today, your mother Athaliaa and her Iska Sisters shall witness your combat as shall I along with many other notables. Your sister Nazillaa is fasting, praying, and meditating in hopeful preparation for your union." Serzak hands him his short sword and a heavy three-foot diameter bronze shield. "You are the third to be tested today. The first two were killed. Good fortune." He disappears.

Guided by *tvarsch,* Ashley comes to the outside of a circular black marble building. There is a snakehead on his sword's handle, and he walks through a dark corridor into the bright sun and a round sandy arena and estimates it has a twenty-foot diameter—no place to hide. The sand is extremely hot, burning his feet, but parts of it are wet and blood-soaked from the defeated so, he stands there. The arena benches are full, and he is announced as Sergeval to the crowd and many cheer. Ashley, parched from the sun, feels the beginnings of dehydration. After being announced, naked Shakuraley enters with his trident and net. He loudly announces he will sodomize this pretty boy before killing him—just as he did with the first two. He is muscular, very tall and, even at a distance, smells terrible. The giant charges, roaring and yelling, but does not break Ashley's focus and he uses *tvarsch* and quickly steps aside cutting Shakuraley's side but, in return, is cut on his chest. Ashley blocks the trident with his shield, cutting the giant several more times while keeping away from Shakuraley's net. He realizes they are in stalemate and the longer they are, the better for the giant, because Ashley is bleeding, and dehydration is setting in. Ashley retreats and goes into a crouch taunting Shakuraley. Furious, he charges using his trident as a triple lance. Ashley smashes his weighty shield into the monster's knees, hears breaking bone and cartilage before he stabs his sword into Shakuraley's soft underbelly, and blood spurts everywhere. Ashley cuts his sword into Shakuraley's neck and head until the monster disappears. The men cheer and call out, "Welcome, Iskandarov warrior, Sergeval." He remains on the hot sand, badly bleeding and dehydrated, and has no idea what to do. He sees someone who looks like Natalya in her flowing Greek *peplos* robe coming toward him. He is soon floating while she heals his wounds. "There, my beautiful son, love and pride from me. I have not only healed your wounds but liberated you as well."

Oh my God, this must be Athaliaa the Colchi princess. "I do not understand."

"To become a warrior, you had to overcome your fear of Shakuraley. Use that to overcome your other fears and you shall this afternoon be rewarded beyond any dream."

She's identical to Natalya except for no Orthodox cross. "I shall look forward to it."

"Remember, I conceived you and Nazillaa with Great Iskandar. Nazillaa had her Ceremony last year and you and she shall soon have your union. You shall see me later." She disappears.

* * *

Back at the table, Natalya said, "I was afraid because I nearly lost you—forever. Instead, you're now an Iskandarov warrior and your aura—which has been dimming since I've known you—has regained full force. Just in time for our Blood Union. But such time is limited. Thus, you must decide whether you truly are Sergei Sergeyovich Iskandarov who'll commit to his sister this day and never stop until the stars fall from the sky. However, if you still feel you aren't able, then you may have my car to return to your world." She downed her vodka before tossing her key ring on the table. "Know that your sister will be ready to begin our union. I need ten minutes to prepare. Ask Larissa which room. Then, tomorrow, we'll go together to resolve a great injustice." She rose and walked toward the inn.

He knew Ashley F. Cooper, Esquire, Gules Senior Partner had died in the arena. After his decision on Aleks had wounded him. I'll take my rightful place, my birthright, where I should've been all along. But God, this is scary. Get a grip. If you leave now, all you've been through to get here will be for nothing. But if we fail to achieve union, insanity and death. He noticed the fob on Natalya's key ring—an orthodox cross with a small crossbar above the axis and further down, a slanted crossbar. In the middle was that mysterious squiggle shaped like an unfinished circle. A hand-hammered gold oval encircled it. The way it caught the light captivated him and he stared for some time, feeling a deep sense of well-being. He put the keys in his pocket and went to find Larissa. She smiled, revealing her perfect white teeth. "Prinkipia Nata in the room at top of stairs, middle one best." A smile reflected pride in her English. He thanked her.

3.

After the bright sun, Ashley's eyes gradually adjusted to the room's semi-darkness. It smelled of kerosene and he felt uneven wide wooden boards that creaked as he walked. The ceiling slanted down at a sharp angle from the center, making the room feel small and intimate. Natalya's eyes had a dreamy glow and she stood with hands on hips beside a large bed. For the first time, she revealed her Ceremonial off-the-shoulder blue gown with a white sash. Strangely, she also wore thick gray socks. As he approached, she said, "We convene to celebrate our original conception by Great Iskandar and Princess Athaliaa and our first conception after your combat. I am daughter of Athaliaa and see your eyes glow, but I no longer perceive Ashley Cooper. Rather, you are warrior Sergei Sergeyovich Iskandarov who sacrificed career for sake of brother because he understands importance of family. You know making love to your sister is not incest but mark of respect to all those who suffered and perished, so you could have name and blood of Iskandarov. Also, mark of respect for me, you know there can be no love greater than between sister and brother. Last night, although tempted to come to you, I did not. Rather, I purged and repaired myself, so I am with pure white sash like Princess Athaliaa. You are my first man and, as is traditional, my virgin blood shall be on sheets in morning. And when Athaliaa last healed you, she restored you as well. I pledge fidelity to you forever."

"I am warrior son of Great Iskandar. I place my hand over your pristine womb, which I swear to fill with life now and forever. I also pledge eternal fidelity to you—my first but last woman." *I've a memory of saying and receiving similar words several times before, but I can't remember from where.*

"We shall soon recommit ourselves to each other. Please permit me to remove your clothing." When finished, she appraised him. "Yes, you are very much as I saw you in dream. But your scars, hallmark of warrior, remain. Today, I now completely reveal myself to you as I truly am. Something I never fully revealed to even husband or lovers because I no longer feel embarrassment for imperfections."

She untied her white sash, undid her gown's shoulder clasp and let it fall to the floor. *Her aura's so bright—much more than Olga or Ronnie's. And she still has her cross around her neck.*

Still in socks, she continued. "Welcome home, brother, you make me happy as sunshine. Because you can see ugly branding, I shall now stand back to reveal scars and ridges of my back." After slowly turning around, she looked at him quizzically.

"I believe finally seeing actual wounds have hurt me far more than you. No question, you are most beautiful woman I have ever seen. There are no flaws, only glow of aura. Welcome back, dearest sister." Ashley took her in his arms and explored the peppermint scent of her mouth and inhaled the aroma of her skin—her natural bouquet—extremely soothing and arousing all at once. He gently kissed the three-C branding on her left breast before turning her around and tonguing her whipping scars and ridges— and a feeling of serenity consumed him. As he continued, an excitement, an electricity, gradually replaced his serenity. Ashley turned her back around. While still the trim dancer of youth with her olive skin, rounded hips, strong legs and firm breasts and again her tufts of dark armpit hair, the years had enhanced and matured her beauty.

* * *

With the heavy curtains pulled against the White Night, the bedside kerosene lamp shone dimly in the dark and warm room. They lay, bodies still encased in each other's sweat and the strong aroma of sex. Natalya's head rested on his thigh, her normally beautifully coiffed hair damp and disheveled, in some places clinging to Ashley's skin. She slept, but Ashley, although exhausted, wanted to prolong the moment, which he knew could never be surpassed in this life and he felt truly at home and connected.

When Natalya stirred, her scars looked like snake tattoos. At this angle, they resembled vipers slithering over muscle and bone. She raised her head slightly, eyelids heavy and said softly, "I think we shall need lot more practice." She laughed, rolled his spent penis along the hollow of her cheek and softly kissed it. "Thank you, dear Brother."

"I confess confusion. You said, you were daughter of Athaliaa. After my combat, our mother Athaliaa, after healing me, implied I would impregnate her tonight. So, who was I making love to? You or her?"

"That is extremely complicated. As our union progresses, you shall learn many things that shall amaze you."

"OK, simpler question. What about socks?"

"While I appreciate your indulgence of other disfigurements, I refuse to expose you to ballerina feet. They would, surely, send you running out of here in instant, disgusted."

"Remove your socks."

"No."

"You cannot hide them forever. No secrets."

She looked at him for a while before pulling them off and made a face as she did.

"Bring them closer."

When she resisted, he spun her around to kiss her feet.

"Are you insane? Feet are disgusting."

"Do they hurt you?"

"Merely embarrass."

"Your feet are result of honorable and demanding profession. There can be no shame in that."

"Hmm. I never thought of them like that. All right, why do you accept my scars and branding?"

"I saw them shortly after creation in one of your *Andronyis*. Svetlana Feliksovna, as you have told me, had power to kill you at any time. Weighing some marks on your body against not having you at all—no contest."

"Perhaps I underestimated you. No, that is untrue. I underestimated Ashley Cooper and not you, Sergei Sergeyovich, Iskandarov warrior. You possess, in addition to everything else, great wisdom and compassion. That just makes me love you as I always have."

"You know, Ashley truly existed in vacuum. I do not know if there is male equivalent of *dhestovy*, but he was certainly one apart. He lived life in limbo, neither Iskandarov nor Cooper. When I sat down with Ronnie at cottage, seemingly long ago, I vaguely sensed this day would arrive."

"Indeed. We shall become unity again and whatever I can do to help, I shall."

"As shall I."

"Excellent. I now most definitely want you again."

Ah, proverbial offer I cannot refuse."

* * *

In each other's arms, Natalya said, "We are getting better." They both laughed and hugged. "We shall scale even higher heights. This night, you took me to sexual places I had never been before. Truly, I never even dreamed such delights existed for woman. And I cannot thank you enough."

"What is so amusing?"

"It is nothing."

"Come on, you can tell me."

She whispered conspiratorially, "Do you know what Russian foreplay is?"

Ashley shook his head.

"Man tells wife, 'Brace yourself, Tatiana.'"

Natalya burst out giggling. Ashley felt annoyed with her girlish behavior until he realized this was probably the first time,

she had ever shared a risqué joke with a man. He laughed heartily. "Took me moment."

"All right, but what are you thinking?"

"Why has no one searched for our father's diary?"

"We have been waiting for you. Had you never come it never would have been revealed."

"Why is that?"

"Because, except for me, you genuinely care about this
more than anyone. However, I could not go by myself. That is
why we must work together. We shall achieve full union in fortnight and then seamlessly work together, unity."

"I believe you, but, beyond the obvious, why do you also
care about diary."

"At height of Terror, there were some twenty-eight million
people in Gulag. There is scarcely family in Russia who does
not know someone or have relationship to it. Because there were
relatively few Westerners in Gulag, that is why story is of limited
interest abroad."

"No doubt."

"Please tell me more about your plans for Iskandarov."

"As liberal clan we shall grow and prosper. Thus, there shall
not be, as some have longed for, Iskandarov political revival. My
daughter once told me our father and grandfather prevailed because castles were inside them, not outside. That shall be basis
to facilitate reform. We have much to teach world. Since we still
have enemies, I wish to restore Bleu-Russia's ties to Paris, either
with Nadia or Ronnie. I wish to reform our clan but not whole
of Russia. Not part of mandate. Finally, I know my first task as
Hidden One with you must be diary."

"Love, that is extremely exciting. Clan needs reform and I
am confident majority shall approve. Now, my beloved, it is time
to rest." He reached over to turn off the light and, in the darkness,
listened to her breathing, soft and rhythmic, until he could no
longer resist sleep. *Tomorrow, we begin our quest.*

4.

They awoke simultaneously around midnight.

Natalya still naked, sat up. "We, for security, now speak English. I had an experience when Athaliaa's Consort, Serzak, made love to me shortly after my first Ceremony. It was so sweet and beautiful."

"Yes, I made love to Athaliaa quite soon after my combat and it was fabulous, just like making love to you. I thought we had a prohibition against that."

"You met Iskandar after that, didn't you?"

"Yes. When I opened my eyes, I saw in a large silver plate on a wall I was Athaliaa, which confused me, having recently impregnated her. At eighteen, I thought this night was still my first life visit to *Thurnane* and I initially felt uneasy being a woman. My *pyordarsch* finally told me I was further back in time to when we were conceived. I began to relax and knew this was another Iskandarov test, one I absolutely had to pass. I began to feel excitement when Iskandar arrived because he was you in larger male form. He kissed me before carefully removing my gown. Our lovemaking was utterly amazing as I felt incredible sensations even before I orgasmed. When we finished, I knew I was pregnant. I asked to make love once more and this was even better than before."

"I'm so proud of you. I know there are many men who couldn't do such a thing. But you, so confident in your masculinity, would have no problem. And I so enjoyed shooting my seed into you…twice. A matter of fairness and balance. It's also important because we now are reminded of what our union-mate goes through. And that, in turn, makes us better people and, yes, lovers. You're right. This was a test for both of us and you're only pregnant in *Thurnane*."

"I know. It's a shame that not everyone can experience this. It reveals so much that is mysterious to us."

"Absolutely. And seeing you as Athaliaa who had some battle wounds was important. Thus, I need to heal my disfigurements because I no longer need to be reminded of my triumph over Svetlana Feliksovna."

"As I've said, don't do it for me."

"Precisely why I'll soon do it. You've accepted me as I am."

"I confess I had an experience without you."

"I'm not surprised. Tell me more."

"It began after impregnating Athaliaa. I was in Babylon and Prince Serzak and Athaliaa ushered me into a completely empty hot green marble room open to the sun. I actually smelled Iskandar before I saw him. He was drenched in a pungent oil he said was for his many wounds. Also, his clothing smelled of sweat, blood and body odor. I assumed no one would dare tell him he smelled bad. To be fair, he told me he was just back from battle. I remained standing while he circled around me, giving me a running commentary on my life, the good and the bad. And he knew everything. He asked me a series of questions. Did I remember being there before? Did I remember any of my previous lives? Did I remember being a woman as well as being a man and a warrior? And as all these memories came back to me, he had morphed into me. I was looking at myself as he welcomed me back. He acknowledged I'm the Hidden One, as others have been throughout millennia." Ashley sat up and looked around. "And Nata, that's why you've brought me to this building and room. It was here I birthed our grandparents—Dmitri and Sophia— in 1885 when I was Sonia Ivanovna Princess Iskandarova and you were Sergei Ivanovich Prince Iskandar. We had been touring in the area when my water broke, and we quickly came here where Natasha Ivanovna was the chief Iska midwife. I was back the following year to birth Illyria and Feodor. I know about Illyria and the Serbian Black Hand. But I remember now after graduating from college, Feodor was a naval officer. During the Russo-Japanese War of 1905, he was a junior officer on a cruiser that was blown out of the water at the disaster at Tsuchima Straits in May. I also remember that their birth was extremely painful, but they were two of best-looking babies I've ever seen. I also remember early on all the lovemaking with family members..."

"But only after they were adults from Ceremony or combat."

"All right, but I don't remember why this was done."

"Understandably. It was the aristocrat Ladies who were doing all the work while the gentlemen had all the pleasure. It was by no means preordained that Iskandar's *Ulimos* commands would be carried out or even succeed. And that's why Athaliaa and her Iska Sisters, their children and descendants had to take such extreme measures in the early years after Iskandar left. By the time of our birth the next year, the three Colchi mothers knew what they must do—have as many babies with pure Iskandarov blood as possible. The sons of Iskandar had to fill every available Colchi adult womb with twins or else our *Ulimos* would have failed. Athaliaa had recently taken Prince Serzak as her consort, not husband, to help produce those many twins with her and others. After my Ceremony seventeen years later, since you were still considered a child, I began my first twins with Serzak and the following year, after your combat, you made me and Athaliaa pregnant with your younger seed and our family soon had my two sets of twins. When our eldest daughter, Xaliaa, had her Ceremony, you impregnated her and she delivered her first twins about the time our eldest son, Dalion, had his combat. He then impregnated both Xaliaa and me. And as our many twins came of age the process, as ordered, continued for seven generations, two-hundred-ten years."

"Why is an Iskandarov generation thirty years?"

"That was life expectancy when we began, and no one has since changed it. Not surprisingly, only a very few complained or refused because everyone else knew the importance. I had fifteen pairs of twins between the ages of seventeen and thirty-eight, when I died after successfully birthing my last pair. I didn't especially enjoy being pregnant almost non-stop, but I knew why I was doing it."

"Interesting. However, I remind you that we men were not just making babies. No, we were defending the Colchi Ladies from many external threats, sometimes, at great cost. After you died, I was heartbroken. I tried to remain celibate. But after the mourning period, two young Iska cousins and widows—Gamella and Doria—arrived at my door. Their late husbands were officers in my command, so I had to take them in. Since the three of us slept in the same bed, they were both soon pregnant. This continued for five years until I was killed in battle. And according to tradition, Dalion and his brothers continued, as they came of age. When I was again born, I was a female and, thanks to you, seemingly birthed a ton of babies over several lifetimes. Do you have any memories before Iskandar?"?

"No. We six, along with Ilyrianaa and Aliannaa's twins, are the creation of a demi-god. Iskandar also left many other children in the known world who created their own Traditions. Some succeeded and some failed."

"Yes, I remember visiting some of them to give advice about succeeding. I also remember our first blood union about 150 B.C., shortly after we moved to Sakartvelo. And it was under Queen Thaliaa, who looked like Verushka, that the Code of the Iskandarov had been formalized a year earlier. And that was the end of impregnating anyone outside the union."

"True. But it still occasionally goes on in various forms but only between adults. So, I've heard. I would remind you that your affairs with Olga and Verushka come awfully close because they were two of your three mothers and no one rebuked you."

"I never thought about it that way. But I take your point. And I'm glad Verushka is pregnant."

"I'm glad you're glad. I loved it when we went back the seventy-six generations to Iskandar and Athaliaa seeing and hearing the congratulations of our ancestors, having only seen them before."

"Yes. I had the same reaction."

He pulled her hand up and kissed it before she continued. "Here's what all this means today. Our father bore eight children with four non-Iskandarovas—Nadia, Charlotte, Svetlana Feliksovna and Maria Civilli. Our father told me the day before the Institute Banquet why he had done so. His task was to inject new blood into our line, as must be done from time to time in the seventy-seven generations since Iskandar and the Colchi princesses. And we must carry on and I've good news. I'm pregnant with twins."

They shared a soft, lingering joining of lips. "That's wonderful news." Ashley pulled her to him and said, "We must make sure, just in case you're not pregnant. Besides, it's my turn to shoot into you."

She laughed as her nose wrinkled. "Fair is fair."

THIRTEEN

Wednesday and Thursday, 9&10 June 1993, North of Moscow

1.

Ashley Cooper, not quite awake, heard, "It's me." He felt her mouth around his early morning erection before she swung around so her well-trimmed and almost opaque pubic triangle was in his face and, delighted with her familiar scent, used his experienced tongue.

Afterwards, she whispered, "You taste so good and I adore your scent."

"As do I, yours. It's no mystery how we've become so intimately compatible in such a brief time." They kissed, each with their scents on their lips and falling back to sleep in each other's arms.

* * *

They reawakened in a light room and stared into each other's eyes as though there was nothing else in the world except soft ethereal music seeping in. *I recognize* Enya's *Caribbean Blue, but I don't know whether it was coming from another room or from my mind. Whatever, it's so perfect.* Ashley said, "Back in 1970, Sinatra did an English version of Antonio Carlos Jobim's *The Wave.* There were two lines I didn't entirely understand until now. *When I saw you for the first time was half past three. When your eyes met mine, it was eternity.*"

"That's so beautiful. I know the song and that gives me shivers. Hold me tight and never let go."

When they held each other, Ashley's heart beat faster. "My God, I love and adore you."

"And I love you with my whole heart."

They kissed again and Ashley, accessing her thoughts for the first time, could feel her love for him. *I know for certain we can truly read each other's thoughts but only sometimes.*

When Natalya reluctantly broke their embrace and headed toward the bathroom, Ashley said, "Nata, unless this eastern light's playing tricks on me, your scars and ridges are gone."

"Don't be silly, they can't be."

"Look for yourself in the mirror."

When she did, tears flooded her cheeks and she sat down on the bed unable to speak for several minutes until, "I didn't do this."

"Who did it then? I certainly can't. Although I wish I could."

"Well, if you learn how, you could start with my branding and my awful feet."

"I noticed your branding is a bit lighter and your face seems younger. You appear no more than thirty."

"All your gray hair is gone, and your face looks younger as well."

Ashley went to the mirror. "You're right and I've lost weight and added muscle. What's going on? This has never, as best as I can remember, happened before."

"I honestly don't know."

He went back to the bed and examined the bottom sheet; covered with a granular substance he recognized as skin cells. "We've shed our skin in bed."

"Amazing. I don't know if this is now complete or continues. You're perfect, so I think you're done, but I'm certainly not."

"You don't need a thing." He looked at the sheet further down and there was, as she had promised, her virgin blood. This will be her year zero, a new beginning. Gone are Chichikov's rape, her first husband and even, what's-his-name? Yeah, Apollon what's-his-face. Even, in a sense, her twins. Last night, it was amazing that at thirty-seven, she had the tightness of an eighteen-year-old virgin. And this is also year zero of Sergei Sergeyovich as I continue to shed Ashley Cooper. It'll take time and I won't ever completely lose him, Last night, I was, as well, a virgin. Goodbye to Pen, Svetlana, Ronnie, Anghelina and all the others I slept with. Further, Annie now has her patronymic.

"You have seen my blood on the sheet. That is my gift to you. We are the People of the Blood because that is our most precious possession."

"I remember now. You've given me your sacred blood. Thus, my gift to you is the life now growing in your womb." They kissed tenderly. "Nata, I've three things I want to discuss. First, as Sergei, I've chosen my diminutive—simply, Serje."

"Serje and Nata, I like it. However, I've never understood how a diminutive can be the same or even longer than the name. Mine's Natasha, birthday of the Lord, with seven letters same as my name and has a similar meaning. It's a Christmas name because, despite my late May birth, Mummy wanted the most Christian name she could 'in this atheist wasteland.'"

"Love it. Second, yesterday, on your key ring, I saw your Orthodox cross with the squiggle in the middle."

"That squiggle, as you call it, is the Cartvelian letter, *ini,* or I. Absolutely not something we share with outsiders. Throughout history because of this cross, many Iskandarov perished. And during the Stalin interlude to be caught with it was an automatic ticket to the Gulag or, after extensive torture, a bullet to the base of the skull. Torture not to elicit information but rather a renunciation of both God and clan. And now since you are Isk, and I used the term before without explanation, we say *Ulimos* rather than clan, which means, 'All People of the Blood and our World.' You'll receive your cross when you join the Church."

"Great. Now, third, I don't know the etiquette on this…"

"Serje, we are now union-mates because it is a once in a lifetime joining and takes precedence over marriage. Thus, I'm now your wife and you're my husband. And one day, as a mere formality, we'll have the Wedding Ceremony at our monastery before the *Ulimos*."

"I'd like to make it official."

"Then I need to tell you the history our religion. Our Colchi ancestors, long before Iskandar, worshipped the universal creator God, *Aleph*—the double-A. That's why all our ancient women's names end in the double A, meaning 'daughter of Aleph.' With the coming of Christianity, we were able to merge *Aleph* into the Orthodox God. But when the Bolsheviks seized power, the Russian Orthodox Church became compromised. Thus, we returned to *Aleph*. And this continues as we adjust to the revived Orthodox Church. Thus, our churches, such as Saint Vladimir the Healer are traditional, that is to say pre-1917 Orthodox and open to all. But our monasteries, as you must've noticed, are only Iskandarov *Aleph* and closed to outsiders."

"Yes, it's coming back to me. *Tvarsch* tells me I need to go for a run to learn more about *this*."

"While you go on your run, I'll do my yoga. We both need to have some private time now. But when you return, we can soak in the huge wooden tub in our bathroom. Before I messed up my feet, I used to run on trails through the woods and there was a plain wooden bench in the middle of the forest. You should seek it. And I laid out your running attire on the table over there when I rose early to watch you sleep until I had to try that new way to welcome and wake you."

"And it was so special—something incredibly intimate. But as far as my clothes, I can certainly do that."

"I know but it's my pleasure to help and take care of you. Now, you run, and I'll see you soon."

2.

Ashley, in a green T-shirt, shorts and running shoes, but without his Walkman, ran easily on the pine needle trail on a beautiful morning through the birch, aspen and conifers. He loved the forest's aroma and chirping birds, all of which brought back happy memories of summer camp in Maine. He felt he could run forever and followed the path deeper into the denser and darker woodland. Coming to a fork, to the right the trail continued before turning sharply. *I'm certain it loops back to the inn.* To the left a muddy trail and he sensed it was the way to the bench.

After about a half hour, he comes to a clearing and sees the bench with a sparkling stream behind it, running into a water lilied pond. He kneels by the stream to scoop up several handfuls of water to relieve his dry throat before rinsing his sweaty face.

Going to the bench, he sees Bayta this time dressed in a black gown with a rose sash. "Exceptional greetings be upon you Sergei Sergeyovich of Iskandarov and union-mate to lovely daughter, Nata. You are to be commended. You have fully liberated Nata and made her bold because she would never have dreamed of initiating such truly intimate acts."

"My, dear mother-in-law, you have become quite voyeur."

"Ah, This one of your famous jokes, yes?"

"No. It is just..."

"I know, but you are mistaken. It gave me such delight to witness two of you becoming unity because, in her doing that, I sensed no shame, hesitation or guilt. And felt her fantastic joy for you both."

"Yes—everything was our first time. Giving her pleasure provides me such happiness. And greetings to you. Now, why are you dressed? You were very pretty naked."

"Thank you. Today, I and all others you must meet shall be gowned because we all have serious mattes to discuss."

"Were you bull moose yesterday?"

"Yes, I conjured it and it was play of children."

"No doubt and thank you for timely intervention. I did notice all six people and moose survived."

"I have never killed anyone without cause. I knew nothing substantial about four FSBs but Anghelina and Svetlana's time is not yet at hand. Now, we must speak of important matters. You are still basking in glow of your union and that is how it should be. You know where you are but not why. I am here to refresh your knowledge about our God. *Aleph* was first letter of our ancient alphabet. Have you ever wondered how if both sexes are made in image of God, then that God must have male and female aspects? *Aleph* does. His Triple God aspects are Husband, Warrior and Sage. Her Triple Goddess are Virgin, Matron and Crone. First two are what you would expect. But Crone is complex because in West, it is term of hostility for old woman. Here, we value her as Wisewoman, counterpart of Sage. She is wise because she retains her monthly blood and instructs children, grandchildren, and great-grandchildren about being honorable women. Just as Sage teaches his male descendants about honor, duty and responsibility. Both of these also have concealed identities. Not to be confused with your Hidden One. This is because there are times when male is ascendant, and female becomes concealed. Or female is ascendant, and male is concealed. In either case, concealed one does not disappear. Or sometimes, male and female are in balance. Now that you are joined with Nata, you are also here to learn more about female mysteries, using sharp powers of observation. But first few basic tenets. *Aleph*, like God, is eternal and everlasting. But *Aleph* is also balance of opposites, for one cannot exist without other. This is what Olga Sergeyvna was trying to teach you. As I said before, you must learn to live in balance. Not just male or female. But more that you shall discover because you must find where you are between poles. And remember, balance can shift on daily or even hourly basis. This shall take time, but when you achieve balance, you shall be happy. And when you and Nata find your mutual balance point, you shall be unity. When you have achieved that, you shall not only know female mysteries but understand them. And Nata, who now knows and understands male mysteries is already adjusting to you." She pauses. "I have told you what you require about *Aleph,* but there is much more for you to learn in these woods. Yes, before I forget, I shall not be going with you and Nata on your quest. Because you must strengthen your union together."

"I understand, as does Nata."

"Remain on bench and you shall, perhaps, learn more. Good fortune." She disappears.

When the birds stop singing, Ashley knows his next test is about to begin. *All right bring it on whoever you are. I'll handle it.*

Soon, he hears the voices of Natalya's twin daughters singing a complex arrangement of the Beatles' *All You Need Is Love*. As they approach, they are dancing, wearing white gowns and golden sandals. Closer, they have glowing silver demon eyes. "We hate you, Uncle Sergei. You and Ma are perfect because you stole from us. We will have revenge on children you make with Ma."

"I warn you. I shall allow no such thing to happen. Our children with your mother are vitally important to Iskandarov…"

"I am Magda, elder. And when they are born, you will ignore us, tossing us aside like garbage."

"Not at all. You are both fully-grown Iskandarovas and your contributions are particularly important to Iska Sisters of monastery. Further, I was wrong. No reason why you cannot have babies like other Ladies."

"I am Sonia. Ma abandoned us there so she could be with you. We want more than babies, we have revenge when we kill your children." They turn and lift up their gowns to reveal their naked buttocks and together say, "You son of shit." before running away on the trail.

What the hell was that? They're supposed to be at the monastery and that's a long journey on foot. And how did they get those demon eyes? Does Nata know about this? At the monastery, they certainly put on quite a show of innocence for me.

His thoughts are interrupted when he sees Anghelina, arms folded, in a bright red gown with a blue sash standing before him. "Ash, or should I say Sergei? Your aura is much brighter now and made finding you so much easier. I saw the two of you resting after fucking last night so I left no note. Also, earlier you obviously recognized me in the red Lada."

She has regular eyes, but she doesn't seem wholly real, as though I'm only seeing her protus. And, because she's Iskandarova, I can't learn anything more. "Yes, thanks for your discretion." Damn, beginning to feel like we made love in Grand Central Station last night. But if so, we've nothing about which to be ashamed. "Sister, what is on your mind?"

"We are expecting you in Vorkuta soon and you remain under my personal protection. But Sister Natalya does not. And, after we win, I plan to persuade her to renounce her Blood Union. If she agrees, she goes free. But if she refuses, I shall torture her until she either agrees or dies. Then, just as it should be, we shall have our union."

"You must know it is incredibly difficult to break our union."

"However, you are still in the vulnerable stage for about another two weeks. And, no question, I shall break her."

"If you do any harm to Natalya, count on it, we shall never have union."

"We shall, whether you wish it or not. After all, I am also carrying your child and Iskandarov custom and tradition gives me the right to take her place in the union after death. I know Sister Ronnie has told you that several times. Besides, look at me. I am better for you than her. I am younger, stronger, more beautiful and much better lover with what I learned from Mother Maria and Grandmother Angelina. And also, I can protect you better than her. You are not getting any younger and over time you shall not be able to defend yourself from your many enemies. Look at all the security systems I have bested."

"You leave out two key facts. First, you virtually raped me to supposedly get pregnant. Second, I do not love you."

She laughed. "I did not hear any complaints when I was fucking you. Second, you married Pen and we both know you did not love her."

"I am not inclined to repeat that dumb mistake. I love Nata and our love is our protection."

"We shall she how that works when I have Natalya begging me to kill her to end her horrible pain, I shall inflict on her as you witness it. The pain you suffered after Sister Olga's death shall be nothing in comparison because I shall not grant her wish to die but continue increasing her pain. I cannot wait to have you both captives after you fail in your so-called quest. It is impossible for you. If you change mind and not go, I shall leave both alone...for a time."

"I have heard and read that your mother Angelina was such great and good person. What happened to you, Anghelina?"

"You should know by now not to believe everything you read. Early on, she was a Rose, who killed many people and later, executed many as a Commissar in Cuba." She loudly laughs and vanishes.

Tvarsch tells me she's lying about Angelina. Also, I'm in the Realm of Triple Goddess, and this is part of our Blood Union after the Aleph teaching. I remember seeing that picture of the Triple Goddess in Mother's office. Now, only the Crone remains, and she'll be difficult.

Turning his head, he sees the Crone all in black with a large hood sitting next to him but facing away. When she speaks, it is as though she is speaking to herself. "I shall die on morrow, or was that yesterday? I have lost all of family, all children and grandchildren because I have fallen altogether outside of time. I still have painful P branding on chest. I do not recall who inflicted it—Poles, Polinkov, Soviets, French with *putaine or* Germans with Panzer? Whoever they were, they shelled monastery before killing all men and repeatedly raping and branding all Sisters and me. They then killed my Ladies and I was only one spared." She turns toward him, but her hood partially obscures her face, except for deep furrows around a wizened mouth. "Monsieur, I am *Mere Superiore* with no convent or monastery, no lands, nothing. Who are you? If you are here to rob me, do not bother, I have no purse." She looks down. Her voice is slightly familiar but does not sound right.

"Madame, I am Iskandarov and, if I may, I am here to help you."

"That is kind of you, Monsieur, but you are far too late. *Pyordarsch* has turned on me and I cannot separate all my lives from each other."

"What was name of your monastery?"

"Sainte Elizabeta."

"And who was *Mere Superiore* when you first arrived?"

"Sister Anastasia followed by Sister Marja and then me. You ask far too many questions. Most improper for us to even be speaking. Good day to you, Monsieur Iskandarov."

"Please, before you leave, one more question."

"Very well, but then I shall leave. My time is at hand."

"What is your Iskandarova name?"

"*Prinkipia* Anastasia Sergeyvna." She vanishes.

"Annie, come back!" Why does someone want to inflict such horrendous pain on me? I wish I knew whether this madness will actually happen to her. I must find out. He yells, "Why are you doing this to my daughter and me?" But he only hears breeze through the trees and not a note from the birds. Bayta returns. "I think you have learned important lessons today from all of these women—three phases of Triple Goddess, Holy Trinity, if you wish. Because number three represents stability and balance."

"I have never heard that before."

"Three is minimum number of legs to make stool stable. Like three phases of sacred moon, Virgin is crescent phase—new beginning. Matron is half-moon—maturity. Crone is full moon—completion and death."

"I wish I understood Nata's twins and even Anghelina."

"You shall, in time. When you saw daughter, as she said, *py-ordarsch* had turned on her, result of trying too hard to prophesy. And that is your fault."

"How so?"

"You have been pushing her ever since she was girl to excel. And in future she feels need to be even greater prophetess than Great-Grandmother Sophia. You might say she wanted to run before she could crawl. I do not think I need to say anything more."

"But I certainly do. I have long stressed she should always strive to be extraordinary person I know her to be. Not to encourage her constitutes, in my mind, child abuse. Secondly, I have always stressed problem-solving with her. She is Iska lady and I shall not intervene. She is quite smart and shall discover, on her own, solution for problem."

"Ah, you are no longer attempting to hold on to your little girl. I know you would like that, but you have attained wisdom not to. Thus, I am impressed. Good fortune." She smiles before disappearing.

Tvarsch internalizes what Ashley has learned and he resumes running and is soon on a boardwalk as the overhead trees almost block the sun until he hears a familiar voice. He sees Sainte Xenia in a black hooded robe and feels her soft, liquid hand in his as she leads him through the forest to a clearing, where he sees a ruin through the trees.

"Why are you not pregnant today?"

"I am spirit of powerful Queen Xenia." She removes her hood, smiles and reveals her demon eyes.

"What do you want with me?"

"Yes, my alter ego, sainte told me that you are trusting soul."

"I repeat my question."

"You are brave as well. You cannot defeat me even though you are warrior."

"Frankly, I am not impressed by you or your threats. But I sense you are merely testing me, like everyone else seems to be doing. Why have you brought me here?"

"I have power to take you to realm of demons…forever. I am descended from Ilyrianaa and because, in past, you and I have had children many times, that is my right by custom of Blood Union."

"Do not be absurd, your alter ego, as you say, would rescue me in instant."

"You do not yet understand rules and our protocols. I am Xenia as much as she is and if I take you, there is nothing she may do. After all, how can I take you away from me?"

"As you must know, I am in union with Princess Natalya, *sorcière*. She shall come for me."

"Even if she does, she cannot defeat me because I remain powerful queen and *sorcière*." She smiles. "Now regard me. Am I not more beautiful than your princess?"

"I know all I need to know about beautiful demons thanks to my late wife. Now, tell me why I am here, or I am leaving."

"You are most impatient. Besides, you would never find way out of forest."

"Of course, I would. Boardwalk is only about ten meters behind me."

"Not so. You are no longer in Realm of Triple Goddess. Your princess cursed this land and you do not know how to release her spell."

"You are not making any sense." He looks around. Oh my God, she's right. The land has changed. Get a grip.

"Think. You know more than you suppose. Follow me, I want to show you my estate and tell its history. This shall be of great interest to you."

Ashley joins her on the path through the woods to what had been the ruin, which is fully restored as a large and elegant cottage.

"Here, year is 1603. I am queen and this is cottage on grounds of my huge estate where I bathed in blood. As Princess Xenia, I was first born thus, I would become queen when mother died. I had two siblings, boy named Vladimir, who is now you and younger sister, Alexandra, who is now Natalya. You and I, according to Iskandarov tradition, began mating after my Ceremony and your Warrior Trial. The following year, Alexandra, after her Ceremony, joined us as well. I became jealous of her. You and she had rapport I could never match. After bearing more children with you than she, I tried to enhance my beauty. Hence my tub. One day, when I was fresh out of my bath of blood and was parading naked, you said I looked ridiculous."

"Oh my God, I remember now. 'Sister, you may possess great physical beauty, but, at your core, you are horrible person and no amount of virgin blood or anything else is going to remedy that.' I took Alexandra and her children to Moscow. Both you and Alexandra were *sorcières* and this led to stalemate in our war for control of this part of Russia."

"Yes, war for fifteen years, against background of Time of Troubles and finally support of Tsar Michael Romanov was needed to defeat me. You personally cut off my head. I shall have my revenge on you and *Prinkipia*." She reveals her brutal neck scar as she disappears.

Trying to find his way back in the dense, dark forest, naked and pregnant Sainte Xenia descends in front of him. "Congratulations, on your union with Princess Natalya, Prince Sergei. Or should I say 'Serje?'"

"What just happened?"

"I again rescued you despite what she said. If you recall, queen has always possessed unreal sense of her abilities. You are now true Iskandarov, thus, I may reveal true self." She transforms from blonde to silky black hair, contracts her womb and wears a white gown with purple sash. Ashley checks her eyes. *Good, she's still an angel.*

"I appreciate your confusion. I show myself in diverse ways to different people. You have become comfortable with public me. And sometimes, I shall still present myself that way. I am dressed in ceremonial robe because I do not want you distracted. First, I want you to remember what happened when you and Natalya worked together. During that horrible fifteen-year war when thousands were killed, Natalya, as Alexandra, improved her sorcery, while I, as older sister remained confident of being superior one. That, no question, was why I lost. When you killed me, as you now know, I was sent to realm of demons. Now, unlike Gulag, which is purely punitive, realm seeks to redeem. After three centuries, in your time, of torment, Sainte Elizabeta came to me and told me I had been redeemed. I was most fortunate because there are spirits whose crimes are so heinous, they can never be redeemed. By grace, I was given second chance and knew, in this new life, I would die young. You know rest, and that is my tale of redemption."

"All right, I know you want to talk about something else besides beauty and vanity, but before you do..."

"You certainly have changed these past days. I know you want to speak about your daughter. First, when it comes time for her to take over Bleu-Paris from Verushka, she may, as is her right, decline. And, instead, become *Mere Superiore* of monastery after both Anastasia and Mara Mikhailovna die. You witnessed what may happen next. Bayta has given you solution of balance. Mademoiselle *Kyria* Anastasia needs to find hers just as you are doing. She then may be exceptional in what she decides to do because, in process, she learns some humility. Her persona as Cone was from different life."

I never thought about Annie having past lives. "Does she ever learn to prophesy?"

"When time is correct, she may. Or not. Now as to what you experienced in Realm of Triple Goddess, first two women are quite possible. However, your daughter's future is too far distant. It is simply reminder of failure and one possible outcome. Now, I am here for another reason. You know only part of my story. As you are now of Iskandarov and have greater understanding, it is vitally important you know more about me as Queen Xenia. I should like to add to what my alter ego told you because she is usually superficial. When princess, from early age, I was told by everyone I was extraordinarily beautiful, I believed and became perfectionist. As queen, I would inspect our serf maidens every year and very few who were perfect and beautiful became my attendants. It was mostly imperfects who had their blood totally drained into bath. Even after you and Alexandra left for Moscow, I continued promenading naked and bloody around castle feeling beautiful. And who would dare say I was not? Serf girls were no more than objects I owned. It never occurred to me they might be human."

"Amazing. But why are you telling me all this?"

"You are already so very overconfident about your quest because Princess Natalya is joining you. I tell all Iskandarovs my cautionary tale after their Ceremony or Trial. I was seduced by my many gifts, which is their downside and my downfall. Most of Iskandarov I tell are young and lack wisdom. You have wisdom and experience, but you shall soon face in your diary quest going against such power as you have never experienced. And look at you, again made so confident by your union you thought you could handle mud trail. Have I not advised you, as did Countess Sophia, to be humble? Embrace being underdog to prevail. I wish someone had warned me back in 1603, when I began to live my delusions. Finally, when you and princess go on your quest, I shall not be with you. That would tip balance too severely in your favor and I shall let you make mistakes to help you learn."

"Do trials and tests ever stop?"

"No. As queen, I had none and look what occurred. But let me tell you of aftermath of that war. Yes, you and Nata, who had fought beside you, had won, but you lost your souls in process. Slaughter, famine and destruction had made both of you numb, which meant, you were even crueler to serfs than I had been. Until about five years later they rebelled and sacked manor house. You both fled with precious little but your lives."

"The serfs were Polinkov then?"

"Yes. And memory of all our cruelty became prime reason for Polinkov cruelty to us once they seized power."

Orthodox time again. Nothing is forgotten and nothing is forgiven. "Then what happened?"

"Sainte Elizabeta appeared and told both of you to go to nearby monastery and join order of flagellants who wandered year-round in countryside begging for food and shelter. You both joined scourging each other's backs and chests with whips and knouts, eating whatever you were given in hovels where you stayed. In time you both were restored to grace but in 1648, after you became lost in blizzard you both froze to death. This knowledge is what you need to become good and just ruler of Iskandarov. Let us say that to this point you have received rather sanitized version of Iskandarov history, although your father hinted at truth several times."

"I fully understand. But does Nata know what I am experiencing here?"

"Only in same sense you knew of daughter's Ceremony. And I chastised Bayta severely for allowing you in blue falcon to even witness part of it. We have our laws for exceptionally good reasons, worked out over millennia. In that spirit, I cannot apologize ever enough for starting war and, especially, my monstrous actions against serfs and all who died in war. Please forgive me."

"You ask me to forgive you when my crimes were much worse than yours? I do not understand."

"As I said, you received grace long before I did. Besides, two of you with memory of your previous lives want to do good for *Ulimos*."

"My wife Penelope had Olga Sergeyvna, of blessed memory, killed and is now paying penalty as you did. I hated her passionately when I first learned of this. But then I learned truth of *dhestovy*, which caused her madness, and I knew you, as queen, suffered from same condition. You saved my life in realm and have been immense help in my journey. I simply cannot hate you for something that happened over three hundred years ago. And I know I speak for Nata on this as well."

"Thank you. You show great wisdom in rejecting Orthodox time, which is to be expected in man like you. Since you can forgive me, you should be able, as well, to forgive Penelope. If you do, I shall release her from realm of demons."

"I forgive her."

"You show compassion. I shall go there immediately and release her into paradise." She paused. "Know well, this is not only land under curse you may encounter on your search for Gulag diary."

"I expect Vorkuta is cursed."

"It is, but that is man-made curse. No, what I speak of is not human curse." She smiles, removes her gown and hugs him, which is unforgettably like being surrounded by swirling warm water. As she moves away, she adds, "You need to seriously ponder what has happened on this alternate trail. I shall simply offer you, Good Fortune." She spreads her translucent wings and is gone.

Oh my God, I was Saint Vladimir the Healer. I never healed anyone. He looks down at his running shoes filthy and caked in dried mud. Reality has returned.

3.

In front of a full-length mirror, Natalya was in a full lotus position floating about a foot off the floor. "How was your run and what did you learn in the Realm of the Triple Goddess?"

I'm not surprised she can float. "That I was Vladimir the Healer. What a farce..."

"Not so, after the war, you helped heal the wounds and brought the factions together. Our bad period lay in the future."

"I've also changed, and I'll tell you all when we're in the tub. I hear water splashing."

"I'm glad because while you were gone, I sensed you were enduring something difficult."

"Come on, stop admiring your naked self in the mirror."

"I'm simply checking that I do my poses correctly." She stood, gently floated down, and took Ashley by the hand to the tub where she quickly undressed him

In the hot, steaming wood tub, neither one said anything for several minutes while adjusting to the water. "Anghelina said our brighter auras made it easier to track us. Don't worry. They'll obviously know when we're in Vorkuta. Where else would we go to search for the Gulag diary? How big's Vorkuta?"

Natalya thought for a moment. "About 140,000 but declining."

"A lot bigger than I expected. Who'd want to live in such a hellhole?"

"During the Post-Stalin Period, many people were offered special incentives such as double professional pay and pensions to come there. And they did. Now, with the collapse of the regime, they can't leave for a variety of reasons. And most of the time, they aren't even paid. Except the coal miners. But they've begun striking because their pay is sporadic."

"Amazing. Look, I also encountered your twins." After telling her about them, he ended with, "They were speaking, not singing, their threats. What's going on?"

"You're saying my daughters raised their gowns, showed their naked *derrieres* and made threats against us? And used such terrible language. I've no idea where they learned such words. I'm terribly sorry. I sent them to Mummy who could cast out their evil spirits."

"Evil spirits? Seriously?"

"That's much easier than saying their Iskandarov blood is weak and hasn't conquered their Polinkov side. Even though a good man, husband had pure Polinkov blood. It's a rare occurrence, but also, we're currently in full moon when my girls' Polinkov blood gets a majority over ours. They'll soon return to normal and we'll eventually cure this. Besides, I'm not even certain they know they're doing it."

"Nonetheless, it was quite disturbing."

"I know all too well." She shook her head. On a happier note, I know you must've seen Sainte Xenia who told you about her life as queen. She does that to all Iskandarovs after our Ceremony or Trial."

"She's not protecting us in Vorkuta."

"I'm not surprised."

"I'm not either. Still a lot to do. I also told Xenia I forgave Pen. And she flew to the realm to take her to paradise."

"We can't condemn a madwoman. And I now also have memories of when we were horrible persons."

"Especially Queen Xenia. I now remember she was as ignorant as one of her serfs. And as queen everyone lived in mortal fear of her ignorance and stupidity. Even when we were making babies, she always seemed aloof from it and us. As though she had something more important to do."

"Yes, and her hurtful aloofness from me, as though I were one of her attendants."

"Yes. One thing I found curious. When Sainte Xenia changed, her hair went from blonde to black, what she called her true self."

"Of course. Russians expect blonde angels. She, like all Iskas, is descended from the three dark haired princesses. Each sister has their own characteristics. As Athaliaa, we may interact with Ilyrianaa the eldest or Aliannaa the middle sister. Or perhaps both. In your life, unusually, you first interacted with Aliannaa, as Olga Sergeyvna. She was creative, smart, charismatic and loving. After her death, you interreacted with Ilyrianaa, your Ronnie, the mentor and wise one, until finally me." She paused. "Strange. I never even thought about how my daughters will react to our superior children, but of course, they'll feel threatened by them. When we return, I'll reassure them of my love and, hopefully, yours as well."

"Good plan." I seriously do not want to drive stakes through the hearts of nieces in some terrible future.

Natalya gave him a curious look and he wondered if she had just read his thoughts, but said, "But now, it's past time to get clean. She pulled him up and thoroughly washed him with a large bar of gray soap. "Now, it's your turn to clean me everywhere."

After washing her, Ashley told her about Anghelina's plan to break their union.

Natalya replied, "You know, virtually everything she said is true—younger, prettier and more sexually experienced."

"I don't care. I love you, not her."

"Oh, I know. But she doesn't truly know me. While I'm not as powerful as Bayta, sister would be foolish to underestimate my powers. She'll be the one to beg for death."

How about I get them to stop threating to kill each other. But I suspect with this family that might be a good deed that would never go unpunished. "Let us just relax in the warm soapy water for a while." Ashley lifted her foot out of the water. "Look, your right foot is fixed and, probably your other one is as well."

"Oh, dear God, thank you so much." Her composure broke and she sobbed and shook as Ashley held her until it passed. "Now, I can run with you. I want see your feet."

"Nothing wrong with my feet."

"In case you missed it, your feet are a mass of callouses and scars." She lifted his feet and studied them. "Ah, much better. I'm sure you'll be more comfortable running now." She looked down. "Sadly, my left bosom remains blackened by her C-3 branding. That's what I really wanted fixed, even more than my feet. I know it doesn't bother you, but it certainly does me. At *Kyria* Anastasia's Ceremony, while none of the Iskas said a word, I still felt like a freak and very unfeminine. I hate it when other Iskas feel sorry for me."

"I think you should be patient. Your branding is much worse than your other wounds. Give it time."

"You certainly have changed. No longer the oh-so-busy New Yorker now advising patience. But now we'll dry each other off and you can prove to my satisfaction my branding doesn't lessen your love for me."

FOURTEEN

Thursday & Friday 10 & 11 June 1993, in Transit and Vorkuta, Komi Republic

1.

Later that morning, Ashley and Natalya descended the Larissa Inn's stairs and he smelled flowers and looked around for the source. Every table in the restaurant area had a bouquet in a large vase, bursting with fragrance. At the bottom of the stairs, a smiling Larissa met them, wearing a multi-colored dress with her hands clasped lightly and led them to their table with a beautiful view of the forest. Before seating them, she said softly, "Congratulations, *Prinkipia* Nata."

"Thank you. I am so excited."

Larissa looked deeply into Ashley's eyes. "I offer very great congratulations, *Prinkip* Sergei."

"Thank you, Madame."

She kissed him on the cheek before leaving.

Ashley asked, "What does Larissa know about our union?"

"Nothing specific, only that we had it."

"How?"

"She knows more than most about Iskandarovs but is most discreet. Also because of our argument and my retreat followed by you going to our room. Not an uncommon occurrence. You know, sometimes, men are reluctant to give up their Iskandarov Magic to attract girls and only commit to one woman."

"I've lost my Magic?"

"Only for this lifetime. You no longer need it and given your recent troubles with Anghelina and Svetlana Polinkova, it's actually a blessing. You hardly require it to attract women. I've always wondered if the Isk magic actually exists or is just a confidence builder fathers tell their sons."

"Perhaps."

Seated side-by-side, they drank orange juice already on the table before Larissa returned with two steaming cups. "Strong English tea with cream. And *Prinkipia* Nata, I am preparing favorite breakfast as celebration."

"Oh, how wonderful. Thank you."

After she left, Ashley asked, "Beyond the obvious, why is Anghelina trying to break our union?"

"There are women who try to break a new union merely for sport."

"Incredible. But why is a new union fragile?"

"You can break our union any time in the next fortnight as could I. Sometimes people discover they've made a mistake and haven't found their true union-mate. It's a safety valve and doesn't mean they won't have another union with the right person in this life."

"I'm not going anywhere without you."

"Nor I without you."

Larissa announced, "Two large plates of wild blueberry pancakes
with freshly churned butter and our own syrup and sides of bacon. *Bon appetit*."

After his first bite, Ashley said, "This is fantastic. I don't think I've ever had better."

"This is the meal Bayta and I used to have here. Like the café where *Kyria* Anastasia had her Ceremonial banquet in Sakartvelo, this also is Iska-owned for many generations, as you remember. And we still employ a midwife for emergencies. Looking for something more luxurious, few tourists come here but there are numerous Iskandarov present for our union. Bleu-Russia holds quarterly meetings here in an outbuilding in the woods. But now we begin our quest...together. Right?"

"Right. You know I just realized we didn't have dinner last night."

Natalya smiled. "Of course, we did—we had a banquet of love. But now we must focus on getting to Vorkuta. As I've said, while foreigners are allowed to go there, they're not allowed to buy tickets. And, actually, it's even difficult for an ordinary Russian not living there. And you know that there's no road going there either. We could fly on one of Aleks's two jets but because of his kidnapping, both will be in use. That leaves the train, the most reliable way to get there. The trip lasts about thirty-six hours from our local Yaroslavl Station. I'll use my government credentials to get us on the train. The train has few compartments and they usually fill quickly. If we go back to Yaroslavsky Station in central Moscow, we can get a compartment, but it'll be harder to get you on the train than at Yaroslavl."

"How do you know so much?"

"I've been doing research, including speaking with several people who have done this." She smiled. "After all, I knew you were coming."

"If we don't get a compartment, what's left?"

"We sit in a day coach and sleep in a fold-down bunk with a privacy curtain. If we make the noon train, it'll be for one night."

"Noon, it is." Ashley did not believe her about Aleks's jets because he sensed she had an ulterior motive for the train, and it was important. "Is there at least a dining car?"

"There's a car where they serve food. But not a dining car as you must be used to. We buy vouchers for food and drink along with the tickets and that includes a bottle of vodka at our table for each meal."

"Stoli?

"No Stolichnaya. Lower your expectations. We're not going on the Siberian Express."

"If I'm with you, I can live on love like I proved last night."

"Flatterer. I can tell you're holding back something."

"I had a brief meeting with Annie yesterday. I wasn't going to mention it, but…"

"Wait. You saw her as Crone? That must've been so extremely difficult for you. And, of course, you wished to protect her. But, remember in the future we must share everything to make our union strong."

"Even my feelings?"

"Oh yes, especially those. Now tell me more about your seeing Annie as Crone."

Ashley related what had happened and what Bayta had told him.

* * *

After concealing their Berettas and communication devices in their luggage, they realized they would have to leave their Uzis locked in Natalya's trunk. She had said earlier it would be madness to leave her car at the railroad station because, in short order, it would be stripped. Thus, Larissa drove them in her Volkswagen Minivan to the station in downtown Yaroslavl, a larger station than Ashley expected. When they arrived, Larissa told them to call her for pick-up when they returned. After thanking her they went to the ticket kiosk. But when Natalya asked for two tickets to Vorkuta, the clerk's eyebrow raised as he intently studied them. Ashley read his face—*Fancy people don't go to places like that.* When she produced her government credentials, the clerk, now obviously nervous, offered to give her the tickets and meal vouchers. He also apologized about the lack of compartments. Natalya refused his offer and paid him in roubles from her currency roll. The train was scheduled to leave shortly, and they hurried down the platform, toward a relic of the Tsarist railway system, a coal-stoked, steam-spouting, smoke-belching survivor of a lost time.

They went first to their sleeping car, which was full of what they took to be miners, most of whom were somewhat drunk. A man called out numbered bunks while looking for the right man.

All the men were smoking Makhorka tobacco, filling the air with a thick stink.

Ashley spoke loudly, "Men, father was *zek* at Vorkuta back in forties. We are going there to honor him and his sacrifices. Wife is government official sent by boss to report on conditions there and he shall take action to improve them. She would like to interview all of you."

A voice responded, "And I would like to interview all of her as well." This caused the men to laugh rowdily.

The man reading out the numbers asked, "What are your names?"

"We are Sergei and Natalya Iskandarov."

The man persisted, "Who are you truly? Iskandarovs are myth. Or, at least, completely purged by Stalin."

Natalya responded. "You doubt we speak truth?" She pulled out her credential. "Here is proof. Your union boss may come forward to examine it."

A tall middle-aged balding man with a slight slant to his eyes stepped forward. "I am Georgi Grigorovich, coal union leader of Team VR 24. We are returning from week holiday. At this point, I am missing one of comrades. While I wait, I examine your identification." Natalya handed it to him, and he examined it and her picture closely. "Ah, yes. Natalya Sergeyvna Iskandarova, were you formerly ballerina with Kirov?"

"Yes, I was. Why?"

"Many years ago, on holiday, I saw you dance in Leningrad day before I heard you broke ankle performing your exceedingly difficult and complicated maneuvers. It was unforgettable."

"Thank you, Georgi Grigorovich. I am honored you remember."

"Of course." He turned to Ashley. "What was father's patronymic?"

"Sergei Dmitrovich. Although Russian, he also was called Spencer Talbott."

"I never met him, but predecessor told me about Spencer Talbott, Americanski flier along with group of other soldiers.

Very brave and upstanding men." He turned back to his men. "Comrades, these are two exceptional fine people. We must protect them from FSB stooges on board. Pass the word to all, they are under personal protection." He turned back to Ashley and Natalya. "Welcome aboard I will have all my men speak to you."

"I would like to take notes. Will that be acceptable, Georgi Grigorovich?"

"Of course, Natalya Sergeyvna. Please join us in dining car this evening for some fun. In meantime, if you require anything ask one of my men."

"Thank you, Georgi Grigorovich. Your hospitality is much appreciated."

"Of course, Sergei Sergeyovich. I should like to speak with you later. Comrades, let us leave and give our guests some privacy."

After the miners left for the day car, Ashley saw they had one of thirty-two upper and lower bunks, sixteen to a side separated by a three-foot aisle. Almost all with miner's duffel bags on them. Under each lower bed, there were two large, numbered lockers for luggage and valuables. Natalya told him not to trust the old, weak locks. But since their suitcases had sophisticated inter-locking devices, they used the lockers to keep them out of sight. Ashley surveyed the car and found toilet and washbowl rooms at both ends of the car. Fortunately, their upper bed was in the middle, as far as they could get from the already malodorous toilets.

The day car was virtually ignored in terms of maintenance and cleanliness, with sixteen rows of patched double-cloth seats facing each other on a stained and worn wood floor. *Definitely superior to the cattle cars used to haul the zeks up to the Vorkuta camps.* They sat in forward-facing seats and stayed vigilant, despite their reception. A rotund woman in a dark blue uniform and round green hat paused to study them carefully. About to speak, she saw two large miners facing her, she moved on. They thanked the miners before Natalya whispered, "She is clearly FSB State Security and trouble for us. She shall return when we are more vulnerable. Ignore her."

By the late afternoon, the trained stopped for an hour in Velsk before proceeding through the Arkhangelsk *Oblast*. Georgi Grigorovich welcomed them to the dining car and sat with them. Just as in the day car, there were sixteen tables on each side separated by a six-foot worn linoleum aisle. Someone had tried to clean the large windows on either side giving a somewhat better view than the day car. From the extremely limited menu they ordered some sort of sausages heavily spiced with garlic along with cabbage and potato pies. Ashley reached for the table bottle of vodka.

Georgi Grigorovich said, "This is made in North Korea. Be very careful with it."

Ashley nodded and when he drank, it felt like it burned off the first layer of his throat and digestive tract. He also knew, because he did not have any anti-acids, he would have serious indigestion later.

"Please excuse my men, they are trying to extract every final drop of alcoholic happiness they can before we return to our subterranean existence for job formerly done by *zeks*. My men are rough but good hardworking comrades. Now, if you please, tell us about yourselves. Starting with you, Sergei Dmitrovich."

They told him their life stories. When they finished, Georgi Grigorovich said, "So, Sergei Sergeyovich you are American. I would not have known from your accent. Kindly tell me truly about your country. I distrust what government has been telling us for years"

Ashley told him a great deal about the States and with Natalya answered all of his many other questions.

After eating, the miners began singing drunkenly and some did Cossack dances in the aisle—shooting out their feet while squatting with their arms folded and shouting. Some drunks just fell over trying to do this and laughed loudly. But Ashley, sticking out among the miners was scanning the car for non-miners. A few thugs in suits looked like *Mafiyah*, but they could also be FSB. Because of her magic credentials, Natalya was not bothered by any of this and he began to relax enjoying the impromptu show. At one point, one of the miners stood up and began playing a weather-beaten violin and his enthusiastic gypsy music brought cheers and laughter to the car and even more miners began filling the aisle with traditional Russian singing and dancing and falling over. And some were outstanding. *I like this very much.*

Georgi Grigorovich asked, "Madame Natalya, I should like favor."

"Of course."

"Have you ever danced to balalaika?"

Not in long time. You wish me to dance for you and men?"

"Yes, I would love to see your routine I saw many years ago."

"Of course, my husband has never seen it. My love, please help me off with my boots. This shall be fun." After her boots, she took her socks off and undid her blue denim skirt. *Fortunately, her white blouse goes far down.*

The balalaika and a squeezebox player and the violinist reported to their leader and Natalya sang her basic music. Georgi Grigorovich stood, "Comrades, clear aisle and be seated. Famous Kirov ballerina, Madame Iskandarova, had agreed to do her most famous routine for us. It was hard enough to do on stage, much less on moving platform. I ask you to be silent, and she is able to concentrate."

The men cheered and clapped when the music began. Natalya stood on their table and leapt onto the floor and on her toes, which she called *en pointe*, went down the aisle gracefully before coming back the same way. Natalya, ran, leapt, which she called *jeté*, with legs horizontal and spun so fast she almost seemed to disappear. It seemed to Ashley the two of them were the only ones in the car because she was clearly dancing for him. Her final leap nullified gravity and then she stood regally smiling, arms straight up and on her toes. After a moment of silence, the room burst with applause and she again went down the aisle blowing kisses to all. Georgi Grigorovich stood to greet her return. "Madame Natalya, I wish I had large bouquet to give you. You are even better than I remember."

She smiled and kissed his cheeks before falling into Ashley's arms as he gave her a big kiss. "Nata, I had no idea. That was magnificent."

The kisses caused the miners to laugh and shout while she dressed. She stood in the aisle. "Most pleasant night to you all." She bowed again and took Ashley by the hand to their sleeping car, as she whispered, "I've never wanted you more. I feel insatiable."

"As am I after that performance. But you should have told them you know how to float."

"And spoil my mystique? How do you think I made principal at the Kirov so rapidly?"

"Makes sense to me."

* * *

In their confined upper bunk, their Berettas under the pillow, the thick wool curtains on the aisle left Ashley in total darkness. Swirling particles appeared before his eyes as he stared into the void while listening to Natalya's smooth breathing. The swaying motion of the train coupled with the sounds of steel wheels on the narrow-gauge tracks soothed him. The noisy hissing of antique steam heating did nothing to warm the bunk and it was too hot to sleep under the blanket and too cold not to. The mattress's moldy stench mixed with unknown odors kept him awake. The air retained sour food aromas and he could occasionally hear some revelers singing in another car. The group in his car, having passed out earlier, snored drunkenly. The garlic churned in his stomach and he could smell cheap vodka and tobacco mixed with the wafting stench from sloshing toilets and miners' body odor.

The train had, yet again, stopped and he now understood why it took so long to get to Vorkuta above the Arctic Circle in the northeast corner of European Russia. The way Natalya had described it, he was not all eager to get there. He heard gunfire, followed by raucous laughter. He heard Xenia in his head, "Sergei Sergeyovich come to me." Closing his eyes, he left.

Ashley felt Natalya wrapping herself around him as he wondered what had just happened. It seemed he had been away for a long time and yet was back in almost an instant. When he felt soft kisses on his eyes, he smiled, and, even though he knew Natalya could not see it, she could sense it. She snuggled with him as they closed their eyes.

2.

After a modest breakfast of tea from the day car's communal samovar and breakfast bars Natalya had brought, Ashley sat alone because she continued interviewing miners elsewhere. He wore jeans, a red T-shirt under a brown leather jacket and black boots, watching the train lumber through the tundra. The train had left the shadowy forests of yesterday behind, as they had moved into the vast barrenness of the Polar Regions and passed a few villages with small brightly painted wooden houses and steeply pitched roofs to keep the snow off and people in relatively light clothing. Looking out the dirty right-hand windows were the northern Ural Mountains—the division of European and Asiatic Russia—rising up out of the vast white and brown emptiness. Ashley realized Natalya's reason for the train—to show him close-up the conditions under which their father and others had labored. His heart ached sensing his father had worked under much worse conditions with much less clothing than the people outside. He so admired the inner strength that had kept Sergei Dmitrovich going.

Natalya, dressed in a pleated, high-neck white blouse and blue denim skirt extending half-way over her shiny black boots, returned to her seat. "Conductor told me we have arrived in Komi Republic. This section of railroad from Kotlas, great deportation rail center for Gulag, was built by *zeks* beginning shortly before World War II. Solzhenitsyn wrote, 'beneath each tie, two heads were left.'" She crossed herself. "Fortunately, for us, our father arrived after completion of railroad. For *zek*, prisoner of state, even minimal rights he once had as Soviet citizen were stripped away. And in Vorkuta, ninety-nine kilometers above Arctic Circle many died of insanely freezing weather or from starvation rations with no fat or protein and also terrible diseases. *Zek* was little more than piece of meat for enjoyment of various sadists, either criminals, *urkas*, who ran barracks, or camp guards themselves. Or both and even other *zeks or zechkas* might kill someone to get their sleeping pallet or clothing or even better tools. Official position was you had three months of use. After that, you could be discarded, not even close to completing your sentences of ten to twenty-five years. No doubt key to Sergei's survival was Lost Souls, all those officers and men from German POW camps who banded together to watch out for each other and terrified *urkas*." Ashley continued staring out the window, trying to imagine building anything here. This rail bed, covered in wildflowers, was built up some ten feet from the brown wet ground. But everything, even those flowers, seemed hostile. Natalya told him that when the weather turned warmer, this area would be a swamp. He said a silent prayer for all those anonymous victims of Stalin whose bones they were riding over right now.

"Before track was finished, *zeks* who built this perished, their bodies were thrown into pile of rubble and dirt which was built up for the track beds. Afterwards, they were stacked like so much cord wood by side of tracks. When thaw came, they had thin layer of soil shoveled over them. As bodies decayed, their bones stuck up through soil. Local Komis did nothing because these zeks were Russian and Enemies of People. It is only recently they have given some proper burial. Nonetheless, do not be surprised if you still see some bones sticking up." She stood. "Excuse me, I still have many miners to interview."

After she left, Georgi Grigorovich joined him and said, "Come, let us take walk."

As they went through the cars toward the back, they spoke of nothing of importance until, going through the compartment car, they came to the last car, guarded by a large man. Georgi Grigorovich said, "Checko, let friend see who is in car." He turned to Ashley, "Look for yourself."

This modern compartment car seemed out of place and inside, young Asiatic schoolgirls appeared to be on holiday. When he tried to open the door, it was locked. "I do not understand."

Georgi Grigorovich said, "Then come with me and you will."

He led Ashley back to the other compartment car and knocked on a door before entering. Natalya was sitting at a table by the window in the light and sunny room, talking to an Asiatic woman who wore a short black leather skirt, fishnet stockings and a bright red blouse with a plunging neckline. She was short with a brown complexion, dyed blonde hair, braless, heavily made-up, and reeking of strong perfume.

"Serje, this is Zareeka, who has proposal for us."

"This is about schoolgirls locked in last car. Right?"

Georgi Grigorovich said, "Sergei Sergeyovich, let us sit on bunk and discuss this."

"All right but let us stop being formal. I am Serje to my friends and my wife is Nata to all hers."

"I am Georgi to my men and friends. Now Zareeka, please tell our friends what you have in mind."

"I am from Tashkent, Uzbekistan and when I was young girl was brought by Government to Syktyvar, capital of Komi Republic, where I was learning to become seamstress. About ten years ago I was abducted at fifteen from there to Vorkuta. You can see what I am is future of those girls."

"Who abducted you?

Georgi answered, "I am strictly coal and am not in *Mafiyah* group who does this. As result, I am not rich man. But my mother was Uzbek and thus, my bond with Zareeka. You and Nata are people we have been waiting for."

"Go on."

"Girls in last car are inspected virgins and at midnight will be auctioned off to highest bidder."

"That is horrible." Ashley looked over at Natalya, who asked, "Zareeka, you told me you have plan."

"Yesterday, I was ordered to help get girls on train and I saw three Uzbeks among thirty-two and I had idea to rescue them and spoke with Georgi because I heard you were on train. And I felt stars had aligned."

Ashley said, "Perhaps. How much are you seeking?"

"One hundred thousand roubles."

"That is lot of money. Tell me more."

"You and Nata cannot go to whore's house. Only Georgi and I can. We buy three girls with money before auction." She paused. "Do you think I dress this way because I like? As I said, I am seamstress, but whore to survive. With rest of money we go to Syktyvar much nicer place than here. I buy good seamstress shop where girls apprentice and we live."

Ashley asked, "What about your pimp. I don't think he shall simply let you go."

"I had one once, but he was killed, and I freelance on train and Vorkuta. I go anywhere within Komi."

Georgi added, "And I would go with her to protect them. I am tired of coal. There are many opportunities for me there. And once we have enough money, we will marry."

"You have certainly given this great thought." Natalya looked at Ashley who nodded. She reached into her pocket. "Very well, here is one hundred fifty thousand roubles."

Zareeka replied. "Thank you, Nata, but I only need one hundred."

"I know, with the extra money buy better shop and get married. I highly recommend it."

After joyful hugs all around, Georgi said, "We do not know how to thank you..."

"I speak for Nata, no need, both your rescue, happiness and joy are reward enough."

* * *

After they left, Natalya turned to Ashley. "Satisfied? At least three girls go free, Zareeka becomes seamstress in better place and gets married too. She is genuinely nice person who deserves break. We spoke extensively from when she found me in another car and brought me to her compartment."

"That is money well spent. I knew early on, Georgi had something on his mind. I wish we had enough to buy them all. And yes, today, I feel same way I did when I read in David Cooper's diary about being in Paris after World War 1. He gave Charisse, his 'pretty Belgian Oo-la-la girl', his bedmate, good portion of poker winnings, thus, she could start over because Germans had destroyed her home. And like Zareeka, it was more money than she had ever seen. In other words, I feel terrific."

"Me too, my love. We did best we could. We could not possibly buy every girl without causing riot at bordello auction. But now, we have something to discuss. Where did you go last night? As we are becoming unity, I felt your absence."

"Sainte Xenia, even though she said she was not coming with us, had some things she forgot yesterday. I listened as she told me things I already knew, but here is really interesting part. I asked her how Queen Xenia was able to leave realm of demons to be in forest, because I thought she was trapped in realm. Xenia replied that because forest is cursed, queen may come to it but no further. Also, there are certain portals around world that, if not properly secured, shall allow demons access to our world. She was not making idle chatter."

"I have heard such tales before but am skeptical."

"Frankly, having been to realm, I believe it. Xenia also told me something truly horrible. When draining Polinkova serf maiden's virgin blood into bath did not produce results queen desired, she began abducting young Iskas for bath. This was after we left for Moscow. While Polinkovas were never real to her or even considered human she felt same about Iska maidens."

Natalya said, "That is horrible. It reminded me that, after serf's rebellion, we joined order of flagellants, whipped each other and lived on charity. We were finally forgiven after we froze together in 1648."

"I especially remember that. When snow began, we found hut and while naked began to whip each other until we were both bleeding profusely. I took you in my arms, our blood mingled, and we kissed final time before freezing together."

"I do not think I have ever loved you more than when we kissed then."

"Indeed. It was so intense We could have found shelter, but, instead, decided to collect our reward in paradise. Xenia also said we shall soon face such power as we have never experienced, and this shall be true test of ourselves and union. Shall it hold under tremendous stress? Also, she shall let us make mistakes in process to help us learn."

"We shall be ready when time comes."

* * *

Natalya put her head on Ashley's shoulder and slept. *I'm tired as well but know I must remain awake and alert. It would not take much to pay a miner to kill us.* He passed the time between watching the scenery and surveying the car, fore and aft. The *Mafiyah* passed their seats more often than seemed necessary, and, although they paused to give both Natalya and him the once over, they said nothing.

With the monotonous scenery, he took Aleksandr Solzhenitsyn's *A Day in the Life of Ivan Denisovich* from his jacket pocket and reread in Russian about being a *zek*.

Looking up, the FSB woman now in a suit studied him. "Why you on train, foreigner? You have no business in Vorkuta. When you arrive, you report at local FSB office for fingerprinting, interrogation and deportation. I know who you are. Do not try to avoid what I tell you." She smiled slightly. "Next time, I not be so pleasant. Yes?"

A group of Georgi's miners had gathered behind her, shouting obscenities and insults, which drew more miners until they had her effectively cornered her and she yelled, "You hooligans are disgrace, you must respect authority of FSB."

A short man yelled, "Fat ass, what are you going to do to us? Send us to mines at Vorkuta. Now get your shit ass out of this car and do not bother these fine people again. If you return, you will end up having very unpleasant time. We greatly outnumber you, lazy bitch. Comrades, take her away and give her lesson."

After the miners led her away, the short man said, "Your Honors, Georgi has told me we are to escort you out of train to prevent any further problems. Where are you staying?"

"Hotel Beria."

"Good. Close to station. We heard what you did for Georgi, Zareeka and the girls. We are in your debt forever. Plus, with Georgi leaving soon, I will move up to boss." He winked, smiled and left.

Natalya, awakened by the commotion, said, "You must ignore FSB orders to report to headquarters. If you do, you shall not be leaving there anytime soon."

"But how can I avoid them?"

She kissed him on the cheek. "You know how. Now, please tell me what you are hiding from me. Your temple is pulsing."

"I was waiting for appropriate time to tell you."

"Now is as good as any. I am not going anywhere."

"I remain concerned about Anghelina's plans to break up our union by either forcing you to renounce it or even killing you, so she and I can make new one."

"She is young and very foolish. It is very much harder to do that than she knows. And even though she is trained assassin, I, *sorciere,* may have to kill her."

"I have absolutely no desire to make union with her. I might kill her as well."

"See, that was not so hard. I did not break or anything." She laughed. "I have been thinking further about your proposal for *Ulimos*. Remember, we have been nobility for millennia. For less than seventy years have we been Fascists. I know there are many of our people who are tired of having to explain about that. But I am uncertain how they shall feel about democracy, alien concept in Russia."

"Then, it is overdue to start. Excuse me, I need to stretch my legs."

At eight, they ventured back into the eating car for another round of the same food and very carefully drank the vodka—the only beverage available. The miners were very somber, and Georgi was not among them. They smiled at Natalya and Ashley but seemed reluctant to speak until a young man came to their table. "Excuse me, please, Madame Iskandarova, but I have never seen anyone dance like you did last night. I never forget it. Thank you greatly."

Before they could even ask him his name, he quickly left the car. Ashley smiled. "Must have been hard for him to even speak to you. I guess now you are celebrity."

Natalya shook her head and finished her vodka.

In their seats a half hour later, they passed tall barbed wire fences with armed guard towers. *I wonder how many politicals remain in that prison?* Snow began to turn darker until soot black. Huge coal processing plants belched black smoke that for a few minutes entirely blocked the sun. It only cleared when they came to the outskirts of a city, an ugly scar on the land with poorly made grimy and stained reinforced concrete structures, which became more numerous the further they went. He saw no trees worthy of the name, only green and black shrubs and dirty melting snow in pools of murky water. Every so often, strands of barbed wire stuck up from the snow. The onion domes of churches he had seen in virtually every other Russian city were completely absent.

Natalya said, "This is Vorkuta. As they say, 'Welcome to Sovietland where last Soviet state still exists.'"

* * *

Miners began to reluctantly gather their belongings. Vorkuta was still, literally, the end of the line. The thirty-two Asiatic girls in red and green plaid uniforms came through the car under the supervision of two large men in dark suits. Natalya turned away, her eyes wet with tears. Ashley put his hand on her shoulder. Natalya barely spoke above a whisper. "As you know, poor girls are ones we spoke of. I know we are making dent, but this happens all over Russia Federation. Girls with dowries are great expense for poor family. Even though *Mafiyah* bought them for pittance, it was fortune to families. Besides, had father refused, *Mafiyah* would abduct them."

"Still there must be something else we can do."

"Any further action now would be unwise. Vorkuta is totally corrupt. We cannot afford to cause any trouble. At minimum, if caught, we could be sent to one of prisons we saw on way here. People do not easily emerge from such places. We must do our business, be as invisible as we are able and leave quickly. I feel your anger, I am pained more than you know because who knows better than I what it is like to be girl violated by smelly, drunken man? Again, simply because I do not want Tatar blood in veins of my children does not mean I care any less about these girls. They are all creatures of God."

He whispered, "I still feel we must try."

"I know you speak truth. But I also know you are very tired, as you were when we first met and are not thinking clearly. And I owe you great thanks for giving me opportunity to rest while you watched over me."

As they put on their parkas and joined the mob, Ashley felt for his 9 mm.Beretta in his parka's inside pocket. Natalya squeezed his hand and whispered, "Our enemies only understand force. Beretta is in holster, affixed to top of left boot."

A phalanx of miners, led by Georgi and Zareeka, surrounded them. They slowly made their way off the train and through the dirty blue and white cracked cement station. They plowed through a horde of aggressive prostitutes soliciting everyone, staggering drunks, obvious *Mafiyah* soldiers and a few uniformed officials. At the Hotel Beria, the phalanx circled around Ashley and Natalya until they were with Georgi and Zareeka and went into the coal-dust encrusted building in the Stalinist concrete style. Above them, a burned-out and sooty window on the second floor had been fire-bombed.

Inside, Georgi spoke, presumably Uzbek, with the desk clerk. The only word Ashley caught was "commissar."

While a porter gathered their luggage, Ashley and Natalya, among kisses and hugs, wished their friends well in their new venture. They followed the porter through the narrow corridors, buoyed by Georgi having told them that they would well taken care of. Neither had any idea what that meant.

FIFTEEN

Friday & Saturday, 10&11 June 1993,

Vorkuta
1.

After a peaceful night in their beautiful room on the Hotel Beria's Commissar Floor, Natalya and Ashley, casually dressed, took the private dining room elevator to the rear of the ground floor. Entering a large plexiglass dome, the Maître d'hôtel greeted and led them through a patio garden to a table with a snowy tablecloth and a vase of fresh roses. After he left, Natalya said, "Oh my, what lovely garden and gurgling fountain in center."

"And water coming down outside from top of dome to wash off coal dust into moat. And I feel freshly pumped-in air. This oasis of privilege is our friend Georgi Grigorovich's thank-you. And he has more power than he told us."

"To his credit, I sensed he was honest person who has great influence but little money."

A waiter dressed in black except his white butcher's apron took their order and brought them tea from the steaming samovar by the door. Soon after, they were eating scrambled eggs, ham, buttered rye toast, fried potatoes and fresh-squeezed orange juice.

Natalya smiled, "You have no idea how precious and rare this orange juice is. And now we have had it twice in two days. This has to be good omen."

"From your lips to God's ears."

Between sips of tea, Natalya said, "I feel so clean. Last night's shower was better than what either I or brother have. Perhaps we are in wrong business." She laughed. "Seriously, did you notice how terrible regular rooms are? Especially horrible breakfast alcove in shabby lobby we saw last night. As George Orwell wrote, *All animals are equal, some animals are more equal than others*. Especially here in Sovietland."

"Yes, *Animal Farm*. The Soviets seemed to have adopted that as universal rule. I had opportunity on train to speak with Georgi further yesterday afternoon. He really revealed a lot about his father and *Mafiyah*. Father, Grigor, was part of criminal gang, *urka*, here in Gulag Vorkuta. After being temporarily released by Stalin from Gulag, he fought in Red Army during World War II. When he and his comrades returned to Vorkuta in 1945, they waged war on those *urkas* who had not fought, whom they called *suki*, bitches. The Bitch War was nationwide and lasted until 1953 when *suki* lost. By end of that war Grigor was *Vor*, literally, 'Thief' and made man and had group within larger *Mafiya*h organization. He did not say, but Georgi Grigorovich, despite denying it, is obviously *Vor*. FSB are not allowed in here."

"Good. I did not know that history, but I remember in seventies under Brezhnev, *Mafiyah* allied with *nomenklatura* bureaucrats and, after paying large bribes continued their illegal operations."

"But of course. You know, ever since I began my journey last month, I have been told I must be humble. And I never understood term as you use it. In her nocturnal visit, Sainte Xenia was kind enough to explain it, 'knowing where you fit in universe.' I have been pondering this since."

"I would say rather than universe, *Ulimos*. Right now, you know who and where you are but not fully where you are going. It is lengthy process."

"I know very well." He looked at his watch. "It is now nearly nine-thirty. We need to rendezvous with Verushka and her team at ten in Lenin Park. But the hotel has no maps, even on our floor, as though they are state secrets."

"I think everything here is. I knew you had plan but why Verushka and her team? I am not objecting, merely curious. I though our quest would be just us."

"Being in Bleu-Russia, she has been here before and knows lay of land but knows nothing about disposition of diary or place of monument. Nonetheless, good person to have on our team because of vast experience and is lethal with many weapons. I assume she knows where Lenin Park is."

Ashley looked up and Alex Dragovitch was standing over them, dressed in a black leather jacket over white T-shirt, jeans and black boots. "May I join you?" Without waiting he sat opposite them as the waiter appeared to take his order.

"Hello, Drago. I would like to introduce my wife, Natalya Sergeyvna."

Natalya smiled and extended her hand, which Dragovitch shook. "I have heard great deal about you, Alex Dragovitch." She smiled. "I am Nata to friends. Thank you for helping husband recently. How may we help you today?"

The waiter arrived with Dragovitch's tea and pastries.

"Please call me Drago and congratulations on your recent marriage. Sadly, I am here in Anghelina's absence to remind you that time is running short."

"We know. Husband and I were going to begin when you arrived."

"Then it is fortunate I found you." He reached into his jacket and pulled a map from his inner pocket. "This is current map of Vorkuta and I will be shadowing you at distance to make sure nothing or no one interferes with your search. But at some point, I must leave."

Ashley sipped his tea. "Thanks for map, we certainly can use it but..."

Dragovitch put his hand up, "Ashley, you have no idea how dangerous this city is. I have stayed at the Beria many times, thanks to George's connections with Genovese Family in New York. But once you leave this oasis, be on your guard at all times."

"Will do and where might our George be right now?"

"In flight to Moscow."

"And where might my friend Nick Stevens be?"

"Still in Moscow."

Natalya looked around the garden at the other diners. "I was concerned. No one appears to be giving us slightest notice."

"All right, Drago, we accept your most kind offer."

Natalya smiled brightly at him. "Please excuse while we study map."

"What are you looking for?"

"Lenin or, perhaps, Victory Park."

"Yes, it is known by both names depending on how long you have been here. It is not far. I will escort you to Lenin Street, five-minute walk. You will go down street to park. Now, this place became quite prosperous in the late Soviet period. And the people hate Yeltsin for destroying it and there are many devoted Communists here."

"Thank you for warning."

"I require ten minutes and I shall meet you and Serje in lobby."

2.

About twenty-five minutes later, after Dragovitch left them on the wide boulevard of Lenin Street, Ashley and Natalya, wearing boots and parkas, studied Dragovitch's map which showed Victory Park but no monument to Stalin's victims. They had walked to the boulevard because, unlike virtually every other Russian city, outside the Beria, there were no eager guides waiting with cars. While they wanted to walk hand-in-hand, they knew it would unwise.

Today, the city was experiencing a heat wave of almost 8 degrees Celsius or 46 degrees Fahrenheit. Walking toward the park, the melted snow made the streets wet and slippery and filled many potholes with dirty water, which passing cars had no problem splashing on pedestrians. Ashley had become accustomed to the White Night in Moscow, but here, the twenty-four hours of daylight with no twilight made time almost meaningless. He hoped he had told Ronnie 10 a.m. If he had misspoken, they would either have to go on alone or hide in the hotel all day.

The park in the center of the city was muddy and garbage strewn. Nevertheless, Lenin's statue still had fresh flowers and overhead worn red banners extolled the people to "Build Future Together." Ronnie had not yet arrived, and they sat on a bench near Lenin, discussing what to do if she did not show up. A number of disreputable people wandered around and it surprised him when an elderly man in shabby clothes approached them. "Good day, I see you fine people appear to be lost. May I help you?"

Ashley studied the man before speaking. "Yes, we are looking for monument to Stalin's victims."

"That is most dangerous to be seeking. I admire courage. Continue on Lenin Street past where it ends and follow trail to monument."

Natalya spoke, "Thank you so much. May I offer you reward?"

"Thank you, but that shall not be necessary,"

Natalya reached in her pocket and pulled out a five thousand rouble note. "For your church then."

"Thank you and good fortune."

After the man left, Ashley said, "He had foreign accent and seemed sort of out of place. I was wondering if he had been deported from Moscow Airport like they threatened me with."

"We have underground church here, Saint Vasili's. Among other duties, they meet deportees at airport and bring them to church, heal them, give them money to get home and repatriate through St. Petersburg."

"And Kaha Antonovich tells them when plane shall arrive."

"After his release, Aleks shall soon file charges against Major Iganiev and confederates. They shall soon be residing in Komi for exceptionally long time."

"Excellent, could not happen to nicer people. Seriously though, I have been watching two skinny young men with shaved heads armed with long knives and wearing identical black nylon jackets, jeans and boots, who seem to be heading toward us."

When they arrived, no one spoke until Ashley said, "All right, comrades, what do you want?"

One stepped forward, "You foreigners who give whore money for nothing on Moscow train. And you give more to old man. Give us and we leave you alone."

"How did you hear about us?"

"Have comrades on train."

Natalya added, "We gave both of them roubles for exceptionally good reasons. We are not accustomed to giving people money for nothing. Because if we do, there shall be no end to requests."

"I give you good reason, lady, better than others. Give us money or we kill you both. No one here will help or care."

Ashley said, "We are not scared by knives. You probably do not know how to fight with them."

"Yes, I do. Learned in army in Afghanistan and taught younger brother. We are lethal."

"That is hardly impressive." Ashley smiled. "Right now, behind you are two ladies with Berettas aimed at back of your heads."

"Best you can do is that? I was not born yesterday."

Ronnie and Rosalita moved their Berettas to the nape of both necks. Ronnie said, "Drop knives or we shall without remorse blow heads off."

The young men dropped their knives. The older said, "Please do not kill us. We are sons of miners and are hungry. Meant no harm."

Natalya with her Barretta in hand, said, "Meant no harm, really? What are your names?"

"I am Nikolai Carbone and younger brother is Nikita."

"I am surprised you have Italian name."

"Grandfather Luigi was POW here, *zek*. He was artist in Venice who admired Mussolini even after his death. In 1946, he was travelling in northern Italy and was caught in war between

Fascists and Communist partisans. Partisans captured him as Fascist spy and sent him here. When camp closed, he married Russian woman and had three children. Father is also artist when not in mines. He and Luigi have several sculptures in area. We do not want to be miners but having tough time leaving this place. There is no work."

Ashley asked, "What do think we should do with these two?"

He heard a familiar voice behind him. "I vote for clemency."

Ashley turned toward his best friend Randell Speers and noticed his white Episcopal clerical collar under his parka "Rand. What are you doing here?"

Randell smiled and put his arm around Ronnie. "She called me you were in serious trouble. I came immediately."

Turning to Rosalita, wearing a fur hat over her parka, Ashley asked, "'Lita, what brings you to end of earth?"

"I have come to talk some sense into sister's head. If Anghelina does not listen to reason, I shall kill her. That only way to erase shame she has caused both Civillis and Iskandarov." She patted her right-side pocket.

"Thank you for coming, all of you. We can certainly use all help we can get." He turned to Nikolai. "Georgi Grigorovich is friend of mine and if you cause any more trouble, you shall be reporting to him. However, I am going to trust you both. We need guides, you need money. Agreed?"

"You can trust us. We know city very good."

"Pierogi shop down street. Here is food money. You have fifteen minutes to eat and return to guide us."

Ronnie bent down and picked up their knives. "I shall keep these. Go." They ran down the street.

Randell said, "Ash, or should I say Sergei? This may not be end of world, but you can certainly see it from here."

"Yes, we always had such great adventures when we were young and now, we are about to begin new one in place we never thought we would ever be."

"Count me in because for first time in many years light has returned to eyes. I was going to ask if you were sure about all this. But no need. You are clearly Sergei."

"Yes, Rand. With wife, it is like I am finally home. Please call me Serje."

"Happy to, Serje."

Ashley turned to Natalya. "This is my oldest friend."

Natalya bowed her head as she shook hands, "I know all about you and long-standing relationship with Serje. And yes, I was mystery woman at diplomatic reception so long ago." She smiled, "And now, Father, I am honored to finally meet you."

"And I, you, Madame Iskandarova. Verushka has told me great deal about you."

"Please, Father, I am Nata to my friends."

"I am Rand to mine."

"Oh. I could not possibly call holy man by first name."

"Try it, you might like it." Randell smiled.

Ronnie said, "Here we are just like we planned at monastery." She shook her head. "What are we looking for, beside diary in this God-awful place?"

"Kyria Anastasia saw in vision monument to Stalin's victims somewhere around here. And we are trying to make sense of clue father gave me, VL-19-5. Monument is key to clue."

"As you know, I have been here few times before. Since V is obviously Vorkuta, L could either be map coordinate or, most likely *lagpunkt*. That is, sub-camp. At one time, there were hundred and thirty-two of them. Sometimes these lasted, as needed, for long time or only one season. Nineteen could be *lagpunkt* number. As for five, probably numbered building."

"That helps greatly. However, if there were that many *lagpunkts* we could be in for long search. I suspect Nikolai and Nikita can help with that." He looked at his watch. "They should be back soon. While waiting, everyone come together, and we'll go over plan."

After they finished, the young men returned. "Boss man, where you want go?"

"To coal monument for Stalin's victims."

"Very interesting but dangerous. Follow us, please."

* * *

They passed open-fronted bars with raucous music blaring and out front scantily dressed women promised amazing delights if they entered. Inside, drunken men heavily groped waitresses in revealing costumes. Nikita said, "Places are *Mafiyah* gyps. Girls only want men with money. Drinks are watered and if you have lot of money, they drug drink. I have friend who woke up next day, stripped naked in alley somewhere." He shook his head. "All women here only want money, me and Nikolai are out of luck. If we could go to Moscow, things would be different there, good jobs available."

Natalya said, "You do respectable job for us and we shall see what we can do to help you."

"Truly?"

"It is all up to you."

Further along, around the elaborate Party Headquarters— another oasis of privilege— several flags flapped in the breeze with blue, green and white bars, which Natalya said was the Komi Republic's. *But most of the white bars have a gray tinge.*

The group later passed non-descript stores with almost empty windows and Ashley said, "I sense we are being followed and not just by Drago." He turned but saw no one. *Our enemies are either exceptionally good or a mind-figment.*

They continued in silence, until Natalya whispered, "My love, there is something you should know about father. Why he surrendered to Svetlana Feliksovna."

Ashley whispered back. "I thought it was Icebox."

"That was enough to get him to Institute. There, Svetlana Feliksovna learned Father would bear any pain she could inflict. Naturally, weakness was Mummy. Svetlana Feliksovna had them stripped. And she held blowtorch and threatened to burn Mummy's vulva."

"Damn her, would she have followed through? She certainly had will to do such monstrous action. But tactically, destroy mother's sexuality and bitch has no power over father."

"She did not. This finally broke his resistance. I do not mention this capriciously. We may find ourselves prisoners in similar predicament. They can torture me in any way they may devise. No matter my screams, do not give them what they want. They may kill me but then I shall be with *Aleph* and shall wait expectantly for you to join me when your time is at hand."

"Is *pyordarsch* telling you something specific?"

"Not exactly but, given with whom we are dealing it is reasonable possibility. We must be prepared for anything."

"If positions are reversed and I am recipient, do not give them any satisfaction. And I shall die with your love warming my heart. And I also wait for you to join me."

They started to kiss but thought better of it. Despite my bravado, it would crush my spirit to see so much as a slap on Nata's face. To dispel the blowtorch images, Ashley focused on his surroundings. Vorkuta reminds me of Pittsburgh before being cleaned up. With everything sooty, not even the sun can dispel the omnipresent gloom and hopelessness.

Having walked away from the center, there were numerous empty vodka bottles along with massive amounts of garbage in white plastic bags thrown away during the winter. Piles of slag coal appeared without any apparent reason. Similarly, railroad tracks sometimes with large locomotives parked, or, perhaps, abandoned ran in all directions.

Later, they passed the dirty reinforced concrete multi-story buildings he had seen from the train. Some of the apartments were occupied but many were empty. A block further, a brick coal processing plant rested on concrete supports almost twenty feet high. It was the best constructed building he had seen but seemed abandoned. Overhead, high power lines loudly buzzed and spat on the way to somewhere beyond the south horizon. When they passed a large field on their right with many four-foot poles, Natalya laughed and stopped. "I laugh at hypocrisy. Father said most of dead *zeks* were routinely tossed into mass graves. But under these poles, were people of some importance buried in wood boxes. Each pole had number on it, ranging from AA00 to

V99. And after latter was used, the next pole went back to AA00. Now, have no fear, Chekists in Moscow still have complete personal data on person under each pole."

Ronnie asked, "But what about hypocrisy?"

"Family or relatives of V99 would be told of death and proper and correct socialist burial. To remind them Communists were so much more civilized than barbaric Nazis who threw their victims into mass graves or burned them. Punishment had been personal, not attributed to specific group, like Jews, and person was buried as comrade."

Ronnie replied, "And of course, there was no mention this person should not have been here at all, except for falling afoul of Stalin."

Ashley explored a nearby numbered pole—GG-24 and shook his head. "Not even a picture of the deceased."

The paved streets ended, replaced by muddy trails atop formerly strip-mined uneven brown tundra. Among the sooty snow, mushrooms and wildflowers sprouted in melted areas. As they went on, barbed wire remained clinging to posts or small trees.

Nikolai pointed out one of the original camps with the barracks still in use. The guardhouses had cement and barred punishment cells. "What we see on side of buildings, Grandfather told me, are iron cages. Unlike Icebox for major crimes, *zek* could be sent to small cages where they squatted in fierce weather. Guard decide length and not uncommon for guard to forget *zek*. Many died for most minor reasons."

Ashley said, "Good to know what iron cages actually were. Camps had rules for everything. Solzhenitsyn, in one of his books, related in his camp there was rule *zeks* would not work on any day camp thermometer showed equivalent of minus forty Fahrenheit or colder. But camp thermometer was broken at minus thirty and never repaired."

As they walked on, Ashley felt horror at an Icebox's metal door hanging open, revealing its barren concrete interior. He shuddered as he imagined his father in there at the mercy of the cold and crossed himself. They continued past several abandoned wooden barracks, which were sinking slowly into the tundra.

Further on, they came to several pink barracks with small terraces added where people still lived.

"Me and Nikita and I live in barracks with red stripe on roof over there with family. Not very good but no rent either."

Great, they must know this whole area exceedingly well.

After walking through this ring of camps, Nikita drew their attention to a statue on a four-foot riser of a skeleton mining coal with a pickaxe. "Grandfather made this as protest. Big bosses always want more coal than anyone can dig. Miners said you never get to Heaven or Hell until you mine your quota."

Ronnie and Natalya studied it together before Ronnie said, "It is actually exceptionally good but chilling. Your grandfather was artist."

"Maybe I give you tour of his work."

She smiled. "After we finish our tasks here, I may take you up on that. What do you say, Nata?"

"Something to look forward to."

* * *

They found the monument on a hill with the three-foot lump of weathered coal, wrapped in barbed wire, atop a twelve-foot silver-colored base. After going up a stone path leading to its large concrete slab, there was a fresh wreath and a plaque dedicated to Stalin's Vorkuta victims. Ronnie, Rosalita and Nikita searched the area for any clues, while Ashley, Natalya, Randell and Nikolai searched the monument. Natalya let out a loud gasp and Ashley ran to her. She stared at a blanched skeletal arm and hand sticking up, which had graffiti.

"Lady, not be scared," said Nicholai. "Look around, there are twelve sets of real arms and hands reaching out, trying to touch monument. This was Grandfather's contribution, which he made of real bones."

"I understand it now. Many bones here for his art. What perfect symbol for horrible place."

"What are you doing at subversive place? Demand papers." A tall man in a gray suit with a white shirt and dark blue tie, held up his FSB State Security credential. *Well, isn't this just damn perfect, busted by the FSB. The Chekist alphabet soup continues even after the demise of the regime. What else could possibly go wrong?*

"Who are you?" Natalya held up her government credential and paused to let her question sink in on the surprised security man. "As you can see, I am Madame Natalya Sergeyvna Iskandarova, Executive Assistant to his Honor Minister Aleksandr Sergeyovich Iskandarov. This is my colleague, Ashley F. Cooper, Esquire, noted international attorney from New York City. Along with other members of my research team, Reverend Randell Speers and Verushka and Raisa Sergeyvna Iskandarova. I feel certain you know our guides, Nikolai and Nikita. We are here to gather information about conditions in this hellhole. His Honor is extremely interested in welfare of people of Vorkuta and this report we are gathering shall produce major legislation to help poor wretches stuck here. That is all you need to know." She paused and made a broad sweeping motion. "Vorkuta is literally crawling with *Mafiyah* and you, stupid imbecile, are interrupting mission. Now leave us. I have your name, Captain Yuri Iprovich Malenkov, and if you do not want assignment that shall make you look back fondly on this one, you shall never appear in my sight again. And have no doubt I shall make that happen."

"Madame, if you are on mission, why are you all here instead of speaking to citizens of Vorkuta?"

She held up her notebook. "Taking respite from mission to see reason I volunteered to come here. Father was *zek* here in forties until NKVD Colonel Svetlana Feliksovna took him back to Moscow, where in 1976 he became Hero of Camp David and was awarded Order of Lenin by Secretary Brezhnev."

"As you say, you are well connected. But attorney Cooper is not allowed here and yesterday on Moscow train was told to report to FSB upon arrival. Do not know legal status of research team but am positive they should be of interest to us."

Ronnie stepped forward. "We are staying at Vorkuta Hotel after arriving by jet this morning at Vorkuta's airport. Where credentials were approved."

Natalya spoke. "Attorney Cooper is under my protection as well His Honor's. His participation is crucial to report and has no obligation to report to anyone. I suggest you forget about us if you wish to have future. Am I clear?"

"Do not appreciate being bullied by you and elite friends. I may return with larger force. Or not."

"Or not?"

"Yes, it is well known you are giving away money."

"I shall not offer you bribe. Money was for liberation of three girls from *Mafiyah*. Had you not been bribed yourself, you could have arrested men who brought girls here."

"Perhaps, do what you have to do and leave by tonight. Am I clear?"

"Quite."

Malenkov smiled as he left.

Natalya spat on the concrete slab. "I do not trust that bastard one millimeter. FSB shall return later with more agents. Therefore, we should take one more look around before our time expires."

As the seven of them searched, Ashley returned to the skeletal hand that had frightened Natalya. Squatting, among the graffiti, he saw the VL-19-5 neatly written on top of the hand with two marked skeletal fingers pointing east. As he rose, Ashley heard a familiar sound overhead—the unforgettable wash of a helicopters' rotors chopping through the air. He recognized a sleek and lethal Soviet Mil Mi-24 helicopter gunship flying low and fast toward them leaving litter and smoke on the ground in its wake. The gunship was also known as "Crocodile" because of its camouflage. It was heavily armored and had a Yak-b Gatling gun in the front bubble turret, which, once in range, could kill them in an instant. The gun fired a short blast to intimidate and when the gunship reached the monument, its undercarriage barely cleared the coal lump. Ashley and the others had spread out and were flat on the ground as dust and smoke rained down on them. They drew their Berettas. *Like me, they must know it's a futile gesture, but, at least, it makes me feel better*

The helicopter rose to about one hundred feet and slowly circled the monument three times. Since there are red stars on the sides of the gunship, I doubt the FSB would send such an expensive machine merely to take us back to their Vorkuta headquarters, although, perhaps, to Moscow. Wait, I see 'Croc' in English on the port door. So, this belongs to George, always bragging about Croc and how he stole it for around twelve million dollars. A pittance to him and what a fantastic way to entice reluctant customers, suppliers and anyone else. Are they going to kill us or warn us to get searching?

Nikolai and Nikita moved away from the group as the gunship began its descent with the rotors stirring up dust and debris causing heavy coughing. It landed fifty feet from the monument with the Gatling gun actively scanning the group. When the rotors stopped, the port door opened and Dragovitch walked toward them. "I hope you enjoyed demonstration of what Croc can do. We are deadly serious and hope you are as well. Anghelina will be here briefly. She is leader of group because George trusts her. He wants Gulag diary and has allowed her great discretion in achieving goal."

Anghelina DelaVega gracefully descended the gunship's steps, wearing dark glasses, a dark blue suit and hose, a white high-necked blouse, red running shoes, and had no apparent weapon. Approaching, she spoke directly to Ashley. "You've assembled quite the team. All of you have seventy-two hours to find the diary and with so many of you, that shouldn't be difficult."

Ashley asked, "What if we find it?"

"If you hand it over, all of you'll be free to go."

"And what if we don't find it?"

"That depends on the circumstances. Best scenario for you is if you can prove it doesn't exist."

"You must know how hard that will be."

"I never said your task would be easy."

"You lie, *puta nigra! Besarme mi culo, perra!*"

Ronnie placed her hand on Rosalita's shoulder. "Calm down, please."

"I won't. My sister's a disgraceful traitor. I've nothing further to do with that *puta*."

"While I don't blame you, right now she appears to be holding all the high cards."

"I still won't speak to her."

Ronnie stood in front of Anghelina, both intensely studying each other until Ronnie turned. "Nata, 'Lita, please join us." Only Natalya joined them before Ronnie spoke. "Anghie, I'd such hopes for you just a few years ago after your Ceremony. And now, look at you. You're dressed like some junior corporate climber. Red running shoes? It makes you look like a clown. Matching blue heels, girl. And on top of that, as 'Lita said, you're lying. Once George has the Gulag diary, he'll kill all of us without remorse. As elder Iska, I declare Iskandarov Trust. Agreed?"

Anghelina and Natalya nodded. After Anghelina looked over at her sister and shook her head, the three women cautiously came closer together.

Anghelina said, "George wants you searching for the diary because you're the most likely to find it. But then whether you find it or not, you all become the loose-end he so hates."

"Then fundamentally we've no incentive for finding the diary."

"Precisely. To him, you're already dead and it's only a matter of time. To encourage you, I've a proposition. To me, you have your three days and a good chance to survive if you find the diary. Or, I can promise you a quick death right here from my Gatling gun and save you the trouble of searching for something that may or may not exist. If, after the allotted time, you have no diary because you've discovered it doesn't exist, unless you have absolute proof, why then, we kill you all."

Ronnie shook her head. "You're going to have to do better than that. You should know Iskandarov don't fear death in any form. Now, let us take care of something else. You owe Natalya an apology. You know what for."

Natalya had been studying Anghelina. "Yes, it's time we formally met. What do you have to say for yourself?"

"You're very pretty. But I'll not apologize because I've done nothing dishonest. Had I found you and Ashley in bed together or with some evidence you had sex that evening, I would've left after delivering my note. But the fact that you were not lovers led me to believe he was available, plus I was in *phygynaya* and desperately needed relief that Ashley, being the only Isk around, could give me." She paused. "This has caused you great upset and for that I do apologize."

Natalya replied, "We are sisters and there must be trust between us. We are also physically similar. I too know what it's like to be a tall, gawky flat-chested girl and how you must always prove your femininity to yourself and others. I also know what you're about here. I have a counter proposal. But first I accept your apology because I smell we are all pregnant. Am I correct?"

Both women nodded and Ronnie said, "This brings up an interesting point of Iskandarov principals—it is strictly forbidden to kill either pregnants or their husbands. So, Anghie, are an Iska or not?"

Anghelina turned to Natalya, "Before I answer, I'd like to hear your proposal."

"Personally, I believe the diary no longer exists. I believe our father and others, wrote it. But after he left Vorkuta, the camp guards burned it. We have one final lead we are in the process of following. If that's a dead end, we'll be on a flight back to Moscow very soon. And now, since Sergei and I have had our Blood Union, you would be most foolish to try to separate us. I also know from *pyordarsch* you'll soon meet someone special."

Anghelina took Natalya's hands in hers. "Very well, I agree, but you must report to me afterwards. If you find the diary doesn't exist and swear that under Iskandarova Truth, that will be all."

"And you'll spare our lives?"

"I'm a free agent and, despite everything, I remain Iska. If the diary no longer exists, that's all. Then George is safe from any unpleasant revelations and, as well, all of you are safe. He rightly fears me because, while is powerful in the boardroom, he is physically weak, and I can force our agreement on him. You are Iska honor bound to diligently search for the diary. Now, we must seal this with an Iska kiss."

They all kissed each other. The truce-making over, Anghelina and Dragovitch returned to the gunship, which took off.

Ashley left the others and came to Natalya and said, "Do you believe Anghelina shall honor agreement?"

"Absolutely, as you must have heard, she accepted my counter proposal under Iskandarov Trust and will spare us under our principals. And the penalties for violation of those are severe."

"Despite our situation, you seem happy."

"Yes, because having spoken under our Truth, Anghelina told me I was very pretty. I now believe you when you tell me. I smelled that Verushka's pregnant with twins like Anghelina."

"I know, but how's pregnancy even possible for woman of sixty-four?"

"Iskas have extended fertility, usually until sixty-six."

Since Ronnie must not believe in Nata's "meaningless intercourse" either, she took her last chance at motherhood and damn the risks.

"And I believe you're the father."

"You angry?"

"No. When it happened, you didn't know I actually existed. We are unique sisterhood, not only of Iskas but also daughters of Sergei Dmitrovich. Back in time of the three princesses there were two seasons—raising crops and war. Latter to destroy former. Sisterhood began when every war season half of all men over eighteen left to fight, while other half stayed in fortress outside Caves to protect food and Iskas. Those pregnant or with children lived that season deep in Caves by a thermal pool and waterfall. This is now the *haram* site with the Iska Ceremony Hotel by the pool."

"Interesting. But I watched you extremely carefully with Anghelina. When you began your counteroffer, I clearly saw her surprise. I think she has long felt you were weak and that was cause of midnight incursion. No more."

"Thank you for telling me all these things. I also hope you heard that George fears Anghelina and she implied, at some point, she may kill him."

"Yes, I've suspected that for long time. Now, we need to get on with our search. Before this interruption, the VL-19-5 clue was written on the skeletal hand over there with two fingers pointing east."

Later, after leaving the monument, some were still coughing, when Nikolai spoke, "This has certainly been eventful time. Thank you for including us. Me and Nikita know where location is. And after seeing all your courage, we are honored to take you there."

They passed the collapsed and ugly monument to the first coal mine shaft dug back in the thirties at Rudnik One. *I know Rand feels depressed but he's doing an amazing job of hiding it. He's always counseled me so, now I can return the favor. We'll speak later when I can get him alone.* Ashley smiled at the thought of helping Randell. *All my life, he's been there for me. Especially the summer after Olga died and when I was uncertain where God wanted me to be just before unexpectedly making senior partner and so many other times.*

The wind blew harder carrying debris along with a sour smell from some unknown source. They soon found it—a squalid and forbidding single story stone building dug into the tundra. The weathered wooden door had a peephole and two little completely barred windows. It reeked of blood, death and horror. Later, Ashley passed a tall wooden guard tower and four barbed wire fences strung from small birches. *I wonder why the camp had such measures because there was no place for a zek to find freedom after escaping into the vast tundra.*

Three hundred yards ahead, as they left the second camp, stood a row of ten cottages built on a slight hill. Nikita said, "Here we are, and number five is third from right."

SIXTEEN

Saturday & Sunday, 11 & 12 June 1993,
Vorkuta and North

1.

Nicholai and Nikita led the group to the ten cottages, which they said were former Vorkuta camp guard's houses about twenty-five feet apart. *About half of them have been abandoned or torn down and only a few seem to be currently occupied.* Number five was an unpainted wooden building about thirty feet square and had a small porch on the front where an elderly man and woman sat drinking from tin cups.

Coming closer, the man's sharp gray-blue eyes under thick gray eyebrows, reflected either madness or genius—or both. Ashley felt warmth in his chest, which ended abruptly when the man looked away. He smiled at the man's eclectic clothing—a Red Army fur hat with a red star, a black T-shirt under his USAAF fleece-lined flight jacket, which had two silver Captain's bars and an Eighth Air Force patch on his left shoulder. And last, Soviet cargo pants with his bloused air force flight boots. His gray beard hung from his chin to his waist and swayed in the wind. The woman wore a green high-necked blouse under a tattered red shawl and black boots. Her long gray hair, parted in the middle, fell into her lap.

The man spoke Russian with a baritone Carolina drawl. "Nicholai and Nikita, you seem to be staying out of trouble today. Thank you for bringing guests to us."

Natalya smiled at the two young men. "Thank you for bringing us safely here. Here is ten thousand roubles for each of you. We may call on you again."

"We thank you for your kindness and really interesting time. Good fortune on whatever is happening." They turned and left, smiling and joking.

The man smiled, rose to his full height of over six feet, and continued in English. "I'm Harvey Jacobs, and this is my wife Carmella Civilli. Welcome all, we've been expecting you. Before Spence Talbott left here with that crazy woman commissar, he told me to expect the five of you on 11 June 1993. I greatly trust Spencer's predictions." He first looked at Ashley before focusing on Randell. "Welcome, my son with the clerical collar."

"I'm Randell Speers, an Episcopalian rector in Manhattan." He came forward.

Harvey grinned, "When I graduated from Harvard in forty-two, I'd been accepted at General Seminary in New York for the autumn. Spence and Mac were my good friends. They were enlisting in the Army Air Force and I had to go with them. I was accepted to pilot school. You know the rest." He paused, seemingly, remembering. "It never occurred to any of us that we would not be coming back from war. I even asked the seminary to keep spot open for when I returned. Obviously, my enlisting was the hinge of my life and especially for all of us Lost Souls."

"Margaret told me a great deal about you. She remarried in 1955 and died last year. My stepfather is also gone."

"I do not need to tell you what great lady and mother Margaret was. And your stepfather must have been a good man to marry a lady with another man's child. I was with Margaret at an RAF hospital for your birth shortly before Ploesti. All these years later, miracle, here you are. Stop and think how improbable this is."

"Good thing I deal in miracles then. I am Rand to my friends."

"All right, Rand." He looked back at Ashley who again felt the warmth. "You, the tall one with the broad shoulders, must be Spence's son, Sergei, because you look so much like him."

"Major Jacobs, you're right. I'm greatly impressed by your faith. I am Serje. And this is my wife Natalya Sergeyvna Iskandarova. Like my father, you and your crew received posthumous promotions."

He shrugged as he took Ashley's hand into his large, calloused one. "I thank you for telling me, but such things belong to a life that barely seems real anymore. I assume you saw my message at the monument, even though you had Nicholai and Nikita."

"I sensed you wrote it, but thanks for the confirmation."

Carmella had gone to Rosalita and after hugging, they were soon deep into Spanish conversation.

Natalya surprised Harvey with a hug. "I am greatly honored to meet you, sir. Survivor of Stalin and the Gulag. I am Nata to my friends."

"It has not been a great honor to be here but thank you. I greatly appreciate your sentiment…Nata."

Ashley added, "My step-father was Colonel David Cooper, who recruited you three for Ploesti and died this May, an exceptionally fine man…"

"I never thought he wasn't. And, of course, I knew him. He didn't have to raise you, but it was a debt of honor." He shook his head. "It is strange because rather than going to seminary, I met a number of Russian Orthodox priests in the Gulag and they taught me their ways and beliefs. You might say I am a wandering monk and mystic. Or, saner version of Rasputin. One reason I survived here. That and knowing you would come."

Harvey turned to Ronnie. "You're Verushka, one of Spence's daughters. I've seen you before, but never spoken. After the last time you were here, I asked around and you're with Bleu-Russia and Paris?"

"I am. Pleased to finally meet you. My father told me great deal about you. That's our sister Raisa speaking to your wife."

When Harvey appeared confused, she continued, "She is one of two twins our father had while in Cuba with Maria Civilli."

"Interesting. I didn't know anything about that. Since the other girl is not here, I suspect there's trouble."

"You could say that."

"I know why you're here, searching for something personal. Please come into our cottage. We have much to discuss over tea and who knows, maybe some moonshine, which we Carolinians know something about."

"I am Carmella Civilli, Harvey's camp wife. I would be pleased to meet all of you shortly, but please excuse us while I go for a stroll with my grandniece and get acquainted."

Damn, I'd completely forgotten back in New York I told Maria Civilli I'd look for her aunt and here she is. "Carmella, your niece Maria asked me to find you and we should talk at some point, although Rosalita probably knows more than I do."

"*Gracias, Senor* Iskandarov." She turned and arm-in-arm with Rosalita walked away.

Natalya asked Harvey on the way in, "Would it be all right if I took some notes on your conversations? I've brought a notebook and pen."

"Wouldn't bother me a bit, Nata."

Once all were seated, Harvey began, "I came here with your father and many others. What ever happened to old Spence, anyway, besides Cuba?"

Ashley replied, "It's a long story." He detailed his father's odyssey and by the time he had finished, they had all consumed several tin mugs of tea with a bit of moonshine for flavor and to ward off the chill.

Harvey shook his head. "Damnedest story I ever did hear. But knowing Spence as I did, I'm not surprised." He whistled and shook his head. "I guess I should explain to my son about Car."

"That's as good a place to start as any."

"She was a firebrand and fought for the Loyalists against the Fascists in the Spanish Civil War. She married a Russian commissar she met in Madrid in 1937. He got her out of Spain in 1939 before Madrid fell to Franco. I don't recall his name, but he was important in the defense of Moscow back in *Barbarossa.* By the end of the war, he had risen up pretty high. Then in 1947, Stalin ordered that all Soviet citizens could no longer marry foreigners and made it retroactive. So, this guy divorces Car even though they had a couple of kids." Harvey shook his head. "She was kinda friendly with...Lina Prokofiev, the wife of the composer. Well, next thing you know, she and Lina are arrested as spies and sent here. Car was originally Spence's camp wife, that is, he protected her in the camp from guards, *urkas* and other *zeks.* I was truly enchanted by her dark intense eyes. Most of the *zechkas* had shaved heads and looked like hunched-over walking skeletons with dull eyes. Not my Carmella, even though bald as a billiard ball and thin as a post, she walked erect with sense of purpose and a light in her eyes. Because she was a Communist and knew why she was here, unlike most of the *zeks.* She had left Madrid before it fell. She should've died defending the city." He sighed. "We helped each other survive. In 1956 Khrushchev closed the camps. But I was still an Enemy of the People. The bureaucrats wouldn't give me an internal passport, not even the lowest grade, called wolf. The official reason for not getting one was the Lost Souls didn't exist. We were never on any camp records because the Germans never reported the Ploesti crews as PWs to the International Red Cross because we had embarrassed the Reich. But we all had numbers just like the rest of the *zeks.* The bureaucrats conveniently ignored that in my petitions. On the other hand, as a Communist, Car was able to get any kind of passport and could've gone to South America or the better parts of the Soviet Union. But even if I could've somehow gotten out, I knew the Americans wouldn't let me return. And, frankly, I wasn't eager to go back to the country that betrayed all of us. Some of the guys tried. No cigar. All sent back. But Car decided to stay with me. We found this cottage and continued our relationship. The Chekists have been guarding both the train station and the airport since before the camp closed. Vorkuta remains a big prison."

Natalya rose, took Harvey's hand and said, "If you wish, we can take you with us. Anywhere you'd like to go. Brother Aleks can get you any documents you'd need."

Harvey smiled. "That's very kind of you, Nata. This is where I belong. I've been dead to my people for almost fifty years now." He shook his head and took a sip of tea. "No, this place was hell on earth but it's our home. And I owe it to my buddies to stay. The ones who made it and those who didn't."

Ashley said, "Since you know why we're here, will you help us?"

"As best as I can. The diary is a pretty complete record of Vorkuta and the troops from the war, Korea and Southeast Asia, most with name, rank, hometown, service number and any personal information."

"Since you're using present tense, the diary still exists?"

"As far as I know. You see, it's not here. Safe, but a ways away." He paused. "Do you know about Mac Goodwin?"

"Your co-pilot on both *Beauty* and *Jezebel*. But when he bailed out after Ploesti his parachute didn't open and he was killed."

"Not quite, I've no idea how he survived because he'd never talk about it. Your father never knew that Mac and ten other Allied officers who'd been in a different *luftstalag* arrived here after he left. They were a mixed lot of Americans, Brits, French, RAF Poles and two Italians."

Ronnie asked, "Was one of them Luigi Carbone, Nicholas and Nikita's Grandfather? We've recently seen a bit of his artwork."

"Yes, his works are a great comfort to all of us. Now, Mac called the men, his council, of which he was the leader. In the spring of 1971, he told me that he and his council were going to steal two trucks and head north along with some weapons and supplies they'd already stockpiled. He wanted to take the diary and told me it was the only way to protect it because guard's searches were becoming more frequent. That night, they escaped. I didn't hear from him until fall 1973. He and his council were having a Christmas party. I propeller snowmobiled up to his place because there's no road. He told me they barter with the Komis for what they need, and hunt, fish and forage for the rest. They left here before we were made Soviet citizens and began to receive a small pension, which we supplemented with odd work in town."

Randell asked, "They went north? I didn't think there's anything of significance up there."

"You're largely correct. We always said the camps up there were in the Valley of Death."

Ashley said, "I'm not surprised. But is Mac still alive? And how do we get to him?"

"As far as I know, he is. I've access to a fishing skiff and we'd have to go against the current on the Vorkuta River, which is strong this time of year and then slog over wet or still frozen tundra. Weather's unpredictable right now, the river still has ice floes and might be frozen solid at some points. The boat's big enough that we can't portage. And we'd have to start walking on the ice from there. And this time of year, that can be an extremely hazardous proposition. I can see by y'all's clothing you've come prepared for harsh weather."

Ashley said, "Sounds like a lot of fun. I'll do it."

Natalya added, "Wherever my husband goes, so go I."

Randell and Ronnie both said they were coming. Carmella, who had earlier returned from their walk, said, "'Lita and I have to find my other grandniece, Anghelina and knock some sense into her stupid head. One way or another, the three of us will be here when you return." The two women left while Ashley said to Harvey, "I sense there's a good bit more you're not telling us about where we're going."

"I need to tell y'all what we're getting into. I won't sugar-coat it. I doubt you've ever been to a stranger or more dangerous place than where we're going. As I said, this was not of Spence's doing. Had Mac not taken the diary, all I could show you would be ashes. But now, Serje and I need to talk...alone. While we're gone, I'd like y'all to really think deeply about this journey. If you feel you can't or won't do it, let me know when we get back in a while. No shame if you don't go."

After leaving the cottage, they did not speak until they were a distance away. "Ever since David Cooper died, I've been in some bizarre places and my life's been threatened on several occasions, but I must find and publish my father's diary. And if I'm killed, I'll at least have gone down fighting. But with Nata's many talents, I'm confident we'll be successful."

"I wanted to speak to you about that. I've no doubts about your sister Verushka's credentials. I know Nata's your dear wife, but she seems frail. Can she make the journey?"

"People often underestimate her physical side to their regret. She's much stronger than she looks and is pure Iskandarova, as well as a long-time Bleu-Russia agent."

"Let me be clear. I'm not going to babysit anyone. I'm your guide, that's it. Spence told me you and your group had to search for the diary yourselves."

"I understand."

"I thought you might be angry."

"Not a bit, I've been tested ever since David died. This will just be another test. No more, no less."

"I like the cut of your jib, young man. We'll get along famously."

"I'm worried about my old friend and your son. There's some great hurt within him but he won't show it."

"Noticed that as well with his trembling handshake. As his father, it's my responsibility to get to the bottom of this. You've got enough to be concerned about."

"We'd best get back to the others and be on our way."

2.

Harvey, now in a sturdy parka, steered the skiff's small outboard motor while Randell sat next to him, speaking quietly. Ashley sat in the bow, which smelled strongly of fish and gasoline, watching for any hazards on the Vorkuta River. On the middle bench, Ronnie and Natalya were to report anything Ashley missed. On the left bank, Harvey pointed out the whitewashed concrete barracks, coal processing and administrative buildings for *Rudnik One*, the first mine from the early thirties. It had been a massive and expensive failure and completely abandoned, the vegetation slowly recovered the buildings. *At the English Sunday Lunch, Aleks told me Vorkuta was a complete economic failure. Even with slave labor, it never turned a profit and was an important reason Secretary Khrushchev closed it in 1956. Stalin probably didn't care about the economics because Vorkuta and other camps were meant for getting rid of political undesirables, either real or imagined. And for him that was invaluable.*

Further upriver, they passed around Harvey's moonshine jug to ward off the river's frigid wind. Ashley, after a few good slugs, felt his innards burn, but not as badly as from the North Korean vodka and he did not feel the chill half as much. Everyone seemed in good spirits, especially Natalya who kept laughing with Ronnie. They had both said they were looking forward to getting away from "horrible Vorkuta and into pristine nature."

Ashley partially agreed with their assessment—the land had a primeval beauty but with an undercurrent of danger. Being relatively safe in the skiff could end abruptly with one miscalculation. *Then we'd be trying to get back to Vorkuta and I don't like our chances.*

There were small and large green scrubs, but no trees. He also saw and heard the wildlife—reindeer with bells and their herders, who waved as they passed by, a few bears, wolves in packs and birds, some of whom sang. Ashley called out a partially submerged ice floe and Harvey navigated around it. Ashley looked back at Natalya and Ronnie who were now covered in blankets over their parkas. Harvey was not and Randell chose not to be either. Ashley, with nothing to prove, happily wore an old and thick cream wool blanket. They passed a few small, riverside communities, but on the whole, the riverbanks stayed virtually untouched by civilization. Harvey told them they were now in no-man's land. Except for the outboard motor, Ashley enjoyed the silence of the incredible vastness of the Russian Polar Region.

Ashley called Harvey's attention to fog up ahead. "We'll keep going as long as we can see, and y'all start searching for a flat place to beach the boat. If we can't see, ice floes, if large enough, could easily sink us. But don't despair, the fog won't last long, but will be very cold.

After beaching on smooth river stones and with tundra about six feet above and in front of them, Harvey left to reconnoiter. They huddled together in their blankets in the middle of the boat and passed the jug around taking larger swigs. The freezing fog became so dense they could barely see each other. The crunching moans of the river ice, broken by unseen howling wolves, were the only sounds besides their chattering teeth. Time seemingly stopped and Ashley felt the others shivering under the blankets. He began trembling and remembered the line, *When the minutes turn to hours* from Gordon Lightfoot's *The Wreck of the Edmund Fitzgerald*, about a huge iron ore ship on Lake Superior battered and sunk by massive waves in a November storm. His teeth chattered even more, and he felt sleepy. He had to stay awake and yelled to stir any who might be slipping away. They were all yelling. *Would we freeze to death only to be eaten by wolves?* Soon, he heard different voices calling to him, but they sounded distant as if from down a well or a cavern. He could smell everything and even taste the fog and his blanket. His senses were overwhelmed.

Ashley felt her peppermint kiss but could only smell her scent. She was hugging him and rubbing his back before she squeezed him. He had no idea where he was or even where he had been. He felt the cold, wet air he was breathing and realized he was shaking. Natalya kissed him again and although now able to open his eyes, everything stayed blurred. She told him to open his mouth and he felt moonshine warming his throat and spreading down. As his vision cleared, the Artic sun shone overhead and he heard Natalya, "Serje, my love, what happened?"

"I don't know. Remember feeling drowsy and shaky. And then heard all these voices in my head."

"Did they sound happy or sad?"

"No, they weren't talking, they were screaming in agony. Oh my God…"

"Yes, we're in the realm of the demons."

"I know. Sainte Xenia warned we could face cursed areas on this trip. And here we are."

"Being gone, Harvey left the small area of fog and began reviving us. I insisted on reviving you. It's all right. My husband lives."

Back among large ice floes and hard sheets of ice along each bank narrowing the ice-free channel, a light fog also impaired visibility. They had a number of close calls with floes as the temperature dropped. Harvey said they could not rule out a spring snowstorm. *How can anyone possibly live here without going insane?*

After several hours of slow progress, they docked at a well-built stone pier on the left riverbank. Once on the pier, Harvey said, "Listen up carefully. Mac told me it's always warmer here in the spring and we'll encounter areas of permafrost. As the name implies, it is always frozen and is the layer under the tundra. The melting snow has no place to go, leaving the tundra wet and boggy and it's like trying to walk on a trampoline. It takes practice, so follow my lead. We will see animals, so keep your firearms handy to scare them away."

Natalya asked, "How far is our destination?"

"It's a ways. But at least we don't have to deal with tall mounds of snow such as we've seen."

As they walked with their weapons and provisions on the wet tundra, another fog rolled in from the river. Ashley took Natalya by the hand to help their balance and Randell did the same for Ronnie. After a while, the four of them found a measured rhythm and the labor of walking began to warm them under their parkas and blankets. Ashley focused on trying to walk as surefooted as Harvey over a lot of moss on the tundra with other small plants breaking through it. He dimly saw a caribou quickly moving on its wide hooves, which acted like snowshoes. *But where there's caribou, predators can't be far behind.* A large polar bear in front of them focused on the caribou, ignoring them. The bear glowed and Ashley could not understand how such a bear could be so far from an ocean and not hunting seals. Then, as quickly as the bear came, it disappeared into the foggy distance and he did not hear the sounds of one animal eating another. But he heard wolf howls, which gave him shivers, and he could barely make out their shadowy forms. He did not sense any immediate danger because the wolves seemed to be only observing the new people arriving on their land. He heard an owl hoot as if in confirmation.

The fog lifted and they were on dry tundra in the midst of several stone buildings along with the footings of former buildings. It appeared this had once been a thriving community. There were elevated two-inch-tall stone paths connecting the buildings which continued toward the snow-capped Urals in the far distance. Ashley went to a small cemetery with eleven black gravestones in a pristine row. Someone had taken the time to carve the names, ranks, nationality, lifespan and either a cross or star of David. On three, the date of death remained blank, Mac's included. He was extremely surprised that Major Francois Landfear, Ronnie's first husband, whom she thought long dead, did not have a date of death. *If he's really alive, I know Ronnie would be ecstatic to see him. I wonder how anyone could be buried in the tundra. Oh, I get it, these are only monuments. But why did Mac's council stay here? I believe this far north there were fewer border controls and with their vehicles they probably could've made it to Finland. But then what? They'd be in limbo between the U.S. and Soviet Union.*

Randell joined Ashley and said prayers for their souls before Ashley turned to a large single-story stone building on a hill. The front room had curtained windows, and a set of rooms with high square windows that led into another large room with small colored glass windows and, lastly, a windowless room.

I've got a theory why was this built here instead of closer to the river. He went toward the house as Natalya and Ronnie stopped and Natalya said, "We're going to protect Rand from any dangers."

"Dangers? Aren't you two being a little melodramatic?"

"Not after we saw those wolves tracking us. We're both much better shots than he."

"Maybe you can get him to open up about what's bothering him."

"Just before we left Aleks's this morning, he got a phone call, one of several, and he hasn't been the same since. I'll do my best to find out more."

"And?"

The two women conferred before Ronnie said, "Beyond being in the realm, there's something about this place that isn't right. And Harvey knows what it is. From the moment we saw the totem polar bear, I was scared…"

"Me too, and you're right."

"And Ash, you still want to continue your search?"

"Of course, I do. We're first and goal from the four. The diary, if it still exists, is likely in the main building. After we find it, we're back on the river and on our way to Moscow. Harvey agreed to go with me into the building." Natalya and Ronnie kissed him on his cheeks.

Ashley joined Harvey on the building's stone porch with a Russian message in chalk on a smooth surface by the front door:

> They used to come only at night, but now they come
> at all hours. I keep windows shut and heavy curtains
> drawn. They cannot smell, so, as long as I remain
> inside, I am safe. I have always taken diligent care of
> my council, but now they are gone. I wait expectantly
> for one foretold. Mac. 5/6/92

Ashley turned to Harvey. "I've known we're in the demon realm since the freezing fog. I know because I was recently there."

"You're braver than I thought. Here's the truth, the Komis have lived here forever. Long ago, they discovered a cave under this building they said was inhabited by their evil god *Omool* and they made sacrifices to appease him, which sort of worked. When the missionaries started coming in force in the sixteenth century, they discovered this was a permanent portal to Hell. Soon the Russian Orthodox Church was involved and built this house and church over it with a secured door to keep the demons locked in. There were twelve monks here with a maître on a rotating basis to make sure the door was always locked and to convert the Komi. Mac's father was a monk and he claims he was born here. That's why he wanted to get back."

"How were Mac and his council persuaded to live here for almost eighteen years?"

He had learned the secret from his father who also told him wonderful stories about *L'Eglise de St. En*, the Komi's god of good, which is the church's official name, but nobody, who's not Komi, calls it that. That's all I know. For a number of reasons, I haven't seen him since Christmas of ninety."

"Well, we should find out what's what."

Ronnie joined them, "After the last of his comrades died last spring, why didn't Mac ever leave this isolated place?"

Harvey replied, "As he wrote, he was waiting for Serje here to accept the diary."

"I've always known I should've come to Russia sooner. I..."

Ronnie placed her hand on his shoulder. "Serje, don't say that. You had no way of knowing."

"*Tvarsch* should've told me. Mac sounds like a fine officer and I was looking forward to meeting him. We must focus on the diary. I sense Mac hid it well since there are, and have been, others looking for it."

"I know you're Spence's son because, like him you know things other people don't. And frankly, you're a little strange, just like he was. No offense."

"Not at all, in fact, coming from a man who knew him so well, I take it as a compliment."

Natalya and Randell joined them at the entrance.

3.

Once inside the dark house, Ashley felt and commented on the warmth. Harvey replied, "The monks fixed up thermal heat. One less thing to deal with."

They opened the thick curtains, and everything appeared to be in order in the wood-paneled main room—pictures and paintings of the monks and maîtres on the walls, many books in their cases, a wooden table set for two with unlit kerosene lamps and matchboxes next to them. And there were two comfortable sofas opposite facing, one green and one blue. *Probably, colors of the monks' order.*

Harvey called for Mac as Ashley went down the hall where six monks' cells on both sides were furnished with single beds, made with military precision. The walls were bare of any personal touches, likely confiscated earlier. Natalya said this made them eerie, as if no one had actually ever lived here. Ashley in the maître's bedroom and office was shocked by a mummified body in bed—skin like parchment, wearing only boxers. Ashley noticed his wooden desk with a green chair was clean, except for an ashtray full of Russian cardboard cigarette butts, stub pencil shavings and next to it, an air force flight knife. His clothes looked dusty hanging in an exact order in his open wooden armoire. He studied an ancient area survey map on another wall for useful information but aside from some obscure markings, there was nothing. Ronnie examined the body and found a letter written in pencil, "Serje, this is addressed to you." She handed it to him, and he read it out loud:

> Sergei Sergeyovich, my name's William Macpherson
> Goodwin, known as Mac and I've been the keeper of
> Spence Talbott and Harv Jacobs' Gulag Diary since
> 1971, awaiting your arrival. What I'm about to relate
> is something I've never told even my comrades. My
> father Grigori Ivanovich Gutvenov was a Russian
> Orthodox monk and maître of this church from 1898
> to 1921, when the monks were forced to evacuate

it. My mother, Sister Tanya, lived in this room with him and it's where I was born in 1919. The Church dates back to the sixteenth century and was built over a portal to Hell, where, prior to our monastery, the demons could come and go as they pleased. My father saw to it that the portal was always locked so no demons could escape. In spring 1921, a delegation from Moscow arrived to announce that we had lost the civil war with the Bolsheviks and to take us to Finland until "things returned to normal.

Of course, they never did, and we left for Boston, Massachusetts. Once there, Father left the order and became a financier George Goodwin, my mother became Lilly and I became William Macpherson. We were trying to be good Americans and worked hard to improve our English and civics. Nonetheless, father told me wonderful tales about the monastery. Some pretty fantastic. I joined the Army Air Force right after graduating from Harvard. On the Ploesti raid, both Spence and Harv thought my parachute had not opened and I had been killed. It partially deployed and I landed in a lake. I was banged up and Romanian soldiers found me on the bank and took me to a hospital. After recovering, I was sent to a PW Camp. Liberated by the Red Army, I was ultimately reunited with Harv after Spence was sent to Moscow with that female commissar, Svetlana something.

We survived Vorkuta, but even after the camp closed, we still could not leave. It was better than before but nothing to write home about. In spring 1971, some of the guards thought that if they killed the prisoners, they could go home or somewhere better. Scuttlebutt said they were focusing on PWs. I still don't know if these guards had official sanction or not. But they also knew we were stuck there and very vulnerable to the terminal settling of scores. It was time to get out. I and ten of my comrades stole two vehicles and supplies and headed north. A Komi chieftain told me that the demons had been on the loose for more than fifty years and took me to the tribal elders. I made a deal with them. I knew from Father how to reseal the portal. In return, as they had done formerly, they would make food and supply shipments to the monastery in the spring and just before the long winter. We also hunted and foraged. For almost sixteen years, this worked very well until the winter of '91-'92, which was longer and more severe than any in memory. By late April '92 we were still snowed in, except around the monastery, which we had kept dug out to the barn and the winter showed no sign of ending. We were also extremely low on food. A month ago, Major Landfear, our negotiator with the Komi, died of a virus he had contracted from them. A few days ago, Lt. Barkley opened the portal to Hell, yelling, "I'm coming to you, Teresa." The demons escaped and I was too weak to close the portal. In addition, because my memory's going. I couldn't remember how to do it. The demons have the house surrounded and I can't get out. I've not eaten in days. With the return of the demons, our deal with the Komis is over. I'm too weak now to get up. Even if I could, I'd just be delaying the inevitable. I'm the last. I know you'll come for the diary. Good Luck."

Randell spoke. "What courage and faith. I wonder how he knew we would come."

Ashley winked at Natalya, who smiled and said, "We need to get into the sanctuary. I'm positive that's where the diary will be, and the portal must be close by." She paused, looking around. "But first, I didn't see any demons outside. I wonder where they are?"

When they found the sanctuary, the door was locked. After a fruitless search for a key, Ronnie said, "I don't know what time it is, but I'm hungry. This has been an extraordinarily long day. Nata, will you help me make supper?"

The two women left while Ashley, Harvey and Randell continued searching.

When they returned to the main room, the curtains were drawn, the kerosene lamps lit, and the food, which they had brought with them, was on the table—reindeer stew, potatoes, onions, carrots and several bottles of Russian beer they found in a cupboard and glasses of moonshine.

After eating in silence, Ashley said, "I confess I'm stumped. Unless we can find how to unlock that door or break it down, we can't get the diary, and all this has been for nothing."

Randell said, "Perhaps, there's a back door to it from the maître's room."

Ronnie said, "I searched the room thoroughly, even his desk drawers, and didn't discover any keys or doors. And I'm assuming the sanctuary's rather large, given the size of the door."

The moonshine and beer, the day's labors, and the comfort of the couch, made everyone drowsy and the lamp's glow had dimmed.

* * *

An unfamiliar woman's voice says, "You are in our ante-room to meet your guides who shall help you navigate and, if worthy, you might yet make it to your paradise."

When Ashley looks up in semi-darkness, he sees a young woman in a black robe with a red sash. She wears bright red lipstick and her light brown hair is done in a forties retro style. She seems familiar but cannot remember from where. He looks into her silver eyes. "Whoever you are, you are a demon."

She smiles. "Silver eyes mean nothing. We may be demons but that does not make us evil. Right, Harv?"

He replies, "I have been intrigued by Iskandarov cosmology and have studied it extensively with the monks I know. While it is true there are some spirits with silver eyes who are reasonably good, for the most part, they are evil. Margaret, my son Randell told me you had died. Because I have not seen you in fifty years, I do not know what kind of person you became."

"Rand, please come to the defense of your mother."

"I would say she was quite a good person for as long as I knew her, so I do not understand how she could possibly be a demon."

"Excellent. And look whom I bring." Corinne Duval, lean and sleek and also in black robe with a silver sash appears. "Hi, my love. I have missed you so much. And I have such fond memories of our time together. Especially our two weeks in the summer of 1962 in Paris before I was killed after Nadia's Repast defending you from the Polinkov kidnappers. I think you owe me something."

"Such as?"

"Come with me."

"I might, but first, I must see Monica and Deborah."

"Monica and your daughter Deborah are safe and happy. I shall take you to them."

Randell is so overcome he cannot speak, and tears flow as he trembles. Ashley comes over to support him from falling. "Rand, why didn't you tell me?"

"Serje, Monica and Deborah went over a guard rail yesterday on a rainy night on Quaker Mount and were killed. I have always loved Monica, but like Olga and you, Corinne Duval has always had a special place in my heart."

"I know. That's perfectly understandable."

"Corinne, at this time I shall not be coming with you. Serje still needs my help and my father and I still have much to discuss. When everything is settled, then I might."

Major François Landfear with good spirit eyes appears in his uniform, speaking French. "Veronique, my beloved wife, I have been patiently waiting for you here, after escaping the Gulag. Did you not notice I was one of Mac's council? Why did you not attempt to liberate me?"

"I did and cashed in every chit I had to find your whereabouts. My sources told me you had been murdered in the Gulag."

"That is what they tell all inquiries. You should have dug deeper. Had you paid Marcel, he could have liberated me."

"Yes, of course, I could have done so and you would be released, and we could have been together all these years. Except he was a scoundrel I did not trust. I loved and still do love you. Why did you not contact me sooner?"

"Look at my eyes. I only recently died and had great difficulty finding you, since you were moving all over. Now, please come with me."

"Where do you wish me to go?"

"To my old room here."

"All right, when this is done, I shall find you."

"Excellent." Major Landfear disappears.

Natalya stands and asks Margaret. "Who are you truly? I am Natalya Sergeyvna Iskandarova, *sorciere*, my counsel is Elizabeta Mikhailovna Iskandarova."

"Yes, I know of her. But she is not here, and you think I should fear you, a mere sprat of a girl?" She laughs.

"You still have not told us who you are. What do you fear?"

Ashley rises. "I do not think you are being wise. And I do not believe you are Harvey's wife and Rand's mother. Thus far, you have only brought pain to our group…"

"I am powerful Komi witch Yoma-Baba." She becomes stocky in bright and mixed blue and red silks with a yellow turban and a large gold chain around her neck.

This is strange. I expected her to look Asiatic and yet she appears European.

"Pain? You want pain? Do you hear those loud screeching and breaking sounds? They are ice floes crushing your wooden skiff against the stone pier. You are trapped. I know why you came but now you have a higher priority—to simply survive. This is no place for mortals. We have ranged freely here for millennia. But have no fear. We are your saviors and I came to right a great wrong. All five of you today have either married or are living with the wrong person. I know Natalya and you have the blood union. A problem to be sure. One we can solve with Olga Sergeyvna."

Olga appears in a black robe with orange sash. "Ash, you have done well, and I am proud of you, my star pupil. But now you have reached the end of your journey."

"Not so, because if you were really her, you would understand why we cannot get back together. And you would call me by right name."

"Of course, we can reunite."

"Even if you tried to force me to disclaim my union with Nata, I shall not. You are my past, she is my present and future. And I would choose to spend eternity with her in limbo than with you in the Realm of the Spirits. This is not personal. I would say that any woman who tried to break our union. Besides you told me in Paris you are a drifter and not in the Realm. I do not know who you truly are, but your imitation is terrible. Be gone."

She vanishes and Junior Lieutenant for Aviation Apollon Apollonovich appears to Natalya. "Cricket, I have been patiently waiting for you."

"We had a mad affair while I was with Kirov and I thought I loved you. But now, I shall always choose my Serje over you or anyone. I have matured and want more than just an affair. I am now a totally different person, as we all are. Besides Serje and I have been joined in previous lives. We are close to becoming a unity. Be gone."

Apollon leaves and Yoma-Baba smiles. "I have good news for you all. You are not truly trapped here. Why? Because you are all dead. You froze to death when I sent the ice fog to entomb you. Your bodies remain in the boat downriver on the shore. As a courtesy, the wolves and bears shall not eat you, yet. Your choice is simple. Either you come with your guides and spend eternity with them or remain here in eternal limbo—neither in the Realm of the Spirits nor the demons. Oh, that look on your face, Sergei, is not what you were expecting, correct?"

Natalya speaks. "As a *sorciere*, I know well the difference between life and death. I assure you all, we are not dead. Yoma-Baba has placed a spell on you, which I soon shall lift, and then defeat this nefarious witch and her schemes."

"This young witch does not have your best interests as I do. Do you not appreciate what we are offering? A chance to reunite with your lovers who were so cruelly torn away from you by forces beyond your control. Is that not right, Veronique, Ashley, Harvey, Randell, even little Natalya?"

Harvey adds, "If you were Margie, I'd say I loved you when we were married and were serving together in the war. But for the last fifty years, I have fought a different war along with Carmella for most of it. We belong only with each other. No place for a third, like you."

Yoma-Baba responds, "I tried to offer you all a relatively easy solution to your problem of being stranded. We shall leave now but when we return, your arrogance shall be gone, and you shall beg to go with us. Deep inside, you know I am right, and that knowledge shall rise and take you over entirely. In the meantime, each one of us shall appear naked only to the one they shall guide to give you a preview of what we offer."

The demons privately reveal themselves.

Ashley is amazed when Penelope appears just like the night he proposed. "Pen, what are you doing here? I sent Sainte Xenia to rescue you."

"She wanted me to give up my swinging life with the demons to be with a bunch of Bible-thumpers and miss goody-two shoes? You have got to be kidding me. No, I tried disguising myself as Olga, your Russian whore. Your bigamous Russian witch, Natalya, is the real devil here. Remember, I too am Iskandarova and remain your wife. You are not permitted to have another one. Come."

Ashley and Penelope are in hot bituminous air beside a black broiling river and on the far bank an extremely tall mountain. Demons are flying around them, ready to attack him, when someone gives the order.

"Since you are dead, I most certainly am allowed a new wife."

"You forget. You are dead and I remain your wife."

"I am not dead. I survived being mortal in the realm before as you remember. No matter. Why have you brought me here?"

"Yoma-Baba and your Russian witch are doing battle as we speak. Yoma-Baba will kill her with no more regret than crushing an ant. As I foresaw—once your witch is dead you will be mine forever."

"Dream on. Now, why are we here?"

"The Komi people, to whom the gods gave this land, believe at death you must swim this river of molten pitch in front of us and then climb that mountain to reach paradise. If you fail, only torment."

"Why would I want to go to a Komi paradise when I can go to an Iskandarov one?"

"This is your only option and I sense your witch is dead. Yoma-Baba killed her faster than expected. Therefore, I claim you according to Iskandarov tradition. You are dead and we will return to my realm apartments where I once invited you. And if you do not please me, I will send you to my old friend Svetlana Feliksovna...forever. In return she will give me such power as you cannot even begin to grasp."

"I believe that Svetlana Feliksovna is an old friend of yours. Two peas in a pod. However, I do not believe that Natalya is dead. Your *pyordarsch*, such as it was, was pretty shaky. If Nata is truly dead, there a number of Iskas who have a stronger claim on me than you."

"Perhaps, but I am here, and they are not."

"You have no standing to claim me. You have been Penelope all your life."

"Of course, I have. What of it?"

"That is your girl name. To have standing, you must have an Iska name. You would have received it at your Ceremony on your seventeenth birthday. And I distinctly remember in 1961 on your birthday we were at the Drew Estate for a party. In bed together, we went further than we ever had until you stopped me after the first time, you promised me 'tonight would be the night...'"

"Yes, I was testing you to see what would happen if we did not."

"You never could lie to me very well. Since you have no standing as an Iska, I will not be going anywhere with you."

Her voice changes. "You cannot defeat me. I am Yoma-Ba-ba in the form of my servant Penelope. Through her, I will kill you for defying me."

Before Ashley can speak, all the wounds and even the ringing in his ears that Natalya healed have returned.

"You are returned to being Ashley Cooper, no longer Sergei Sergeyovich. As for your pain, I simply undid your wife's spells."

"How can you be here when you are supposed to be fighting Natalya?"

"I can easily overwhelm you both at the same time. Now turn around and look in the large mirror."

Ashley sees he is rapidly ageing.

"You are now one hundred years old. Your last punishment is my keto fire. It burns but does not consume. After one hundred years, it only stops when you suffocate. Enjoy my horrifying pain."

When Yoma-Baba leaves, the invisible fire burns and weakened, he nearly falls into the river of pitch. The fire's too intense to embrace. I thought perhaps the pain would lessen as I become accustomed to it, but that's not the case. I must endure as best I can.

Penelope, in her regular voice, says, "This is so wonderful. Yoma-Baba has promised me when you finally die, you'll finally be mine forever." She laughs and sits down to watch.

I can see I'm getting younger and now I'm getting smaller. How can I fight this? Soon, I'll be dead.

The fire abruptly stops and a large hand grabs Ashley by the neck. A new voice says, "You are coming to me."

SEVENTEEN

No Time, No Day, North of Vorkuta

1.

Pavel Chichikov wears his RAF flight officer's uniform and Charlotte in a gray gown lies in a hospital bed. Ashley is a baby in Chichikov's large, powerful left hand squeezing his neck, while his right wields a stiletto. "All right, faithless whore, your choice, I'll either strangle your little bastard or cut his balls off."

Oh my God, he's about to kidnap mother. I've got to do something. At least, I've no burns or wounds. And I don't begin to understand what just happened in the realm. I must focus on another damn test.

"No, Pavel, for once in your life, demonstrate some compassion." Her speech is slurred from a birthing drug. "This is none of your affair. We both know you can't father a child and I've longed for one."

"You slag, who do you think you are giving me orders in your posh voice? How about I castrate your bastard and let his blood wash over you?"

"I should think the RAF Police know you're here and are coming to capture you. Put my son down gently and I shall not scream for one minute. Time for your escape. Therefore, I'm your only hope. You leave now…"

"I don't negotiate with shitefull whores." He takes out a syringe case from his coat and sticks a long needle through her gown into her arm. "Now you won't be able to scream, much less move. Fuck him. I don't give a shite about your little bastard. The footsteps you heard are my team dressed as doctors and nurses. We'll roll you out of here on a gurney explaining you've got postpartum complications and we're taking you up to London. But you're really going with me to where you'll pay for this."

Chichikov wheels Charlotte and before leaving, carelessly tosses Ashley onto another bed. *Damn, he almost missed, and I would've fallen on the hard floor. If I cracked my head open, I'd be over before I began.* Ashley is in pain until a nurse picks him up. "Where's your mummy, little luv?"

He hears outside, "Patty, I couldn't have gotten here any sooner. Yesterday, I lost thirty aircrews to a buzz bomb in London. The next wave attack on Ploesti. Gone."

"I know you are terribly busy, but it was important for me to be here for Charlotte. And now I sense something terrible has happened."

Oh my God, that's David and Patricia and this confirms she had some Sternwood form of visions. Patty? Who knew?

The light goes off. "Thanks to *tvarsch* you have first memory. Now what lesson do you take away?"

"Whoever you are, I am Sergei Sergeyovich Iskandarov."

"You most certainly are not. You and Princess Natalya Sergeyvna have, like children, only been playing house. You have yet to earn honor of such name."

"I disagree, we are union mates and..."

"You are failing in diary quest because two of you still not seriously working together. Now, please answer question."

"Bayta, is that you? You sound different but you obviously rescued me when you said you would not intervene."

"I shall let Nata explain after we have finished."

"Of course, you defeated Yoma-Baba and cancelled her spell and..."

"We are not here to talk about that. Answer question."

"I do not know for what you seek."

"Your reaction. In hospital, less than hour old and think you must do something to save mother. While I understand instinct, you were even more helpless than her. Why do you still feel it important to be hero?"

"I do not know, especially now I am warrior. I shall think hard about this."

"Your being hero has caused you to be in this terrible predicament." A candle lights on a wooden table with two chairs in a cave, revealing that both the adult Ashley and Bayta are naked.

"Where are we?"

"We are where we need to be. I am acting as Matron for Triple Goddess. Therefore, do not resist me. Refuse and you shall lose."

"How do I that?"

"You have been taught well by some of best minds in your world. But because of strong ego, you were not always listening as carefully as you should have because you thought you knew better. And even worse, you thought you could do everything yourself. From missing soccer goal at Harvard through countless episodes to now your dilemma accessing diary. This is who you truly were and remain. If you stay as you are, you shall fail in diary quest, you shall no longer be Iskandarov and union shall fail. And then you might as well be dead."

"What do I need do to prevent that?"

"You have all knowledge you need to succeed. You were recently told what to do, as Olga Sergeyvna did long ago. Think."

"Balance?"

"Go on."

"I need to be in balance. And clearly, I am not."

"In realm, you have become seriously out of balance."

"Shall you help me?"

"Progress. You actually realize you need help. Thus, we must expand on concept of balance. It is not merely male and female but encompasses all opposites. Foremost, you must learn to balance your rational and mystic sides and most essential love and hate. Have you even thought about balancing Ashley and Sergei or *avocat* and warrior? You need to do this before becoming grand duke. That is not right for you, Chieftain of *Ulimos*. You must learn to be like Aleph—meeting of opposites and keeping them in balance. Back to basics. Normally, female aspect, *aminala* is in balance with around seventy percent *aminalus*. But you pushed *aminalus* to ninety-four-point-two because of being in extreme fighting mode. You cannot succeed in task without *aminala*. Because *aminalus* must be reduced now after fighting demons. Right now, Natalya's *aminalus* is extremely high to fight powerful witch Yoma-Baba. Should Natalya win, balance shall be restored. Just as yours must be. When you are both restored to mutual balance, you shall succeed."

"Because we shall be able to work together as countless people have told me?"

"Obviously. Is your fighting done?"

"Not quite. How do I kill Penelope?"

"You cannot. Like all spirits, she is pure energy and cannot be destroyed. However, I believe you know something you have forgotten." She stands. "I almost forgot. Madame Anastasia forgives you for lying. She understands why and you are restored. Now, take my hands." A lightning-like current rushes through him before she says, "We are in balance now. Remember, you have nothing to prove. Good Fortune." She disappears.

I wasn't sure I was going to survive that current but I'm now better. Time to get back to Nata.

* * *

In the main room of the single-story building with the heavy curtains fully drawn and kerosene lamps set low, Natalya, in a flowing white nightgown ran to him. *Thankfully, Bayta triumphed.*

"Oh, my love, I had no idea where you were, and thought I had lost you forever." Since you are naked, I shall be as well. I would like if everyone could see me. She removed her nightgown and smiled, "Look, I'm completely cleansed of my bosom branding and finally free of Svetlana Feliksovna."

"Amazing, I'm so happy for you and us. That's certainly something to celebrate. And we should. Where's everyone?"

"Harvey and Randell are talking in one of the monk's room, while Verushka is entertaining Major Landfear in another." She took him by the hand down the corridor. "Everyone decided we should have Mac's room. Rand and Harvey took Mac's body to the barn where he was shrouded with the others. Ronnie helped me make the bed with the relatively clean sheets she found."

* * *

Natalya said, "That was, as expected, so wonderful. And I feel as though I'm whole again. Once we return to my studio, I warn you I may be "topless" for a long while." She laughed. "And you've changed again. And you seem almost happy, despite our circumstances. Where have you been?"

Ashley told her about their mother in the hospital, Penelope with her threats and Yoma-Baba and her keto fire.

"How dreadful. How did you get away?

"Bayta..."

"Not quite. She and I cooperated to defeat her. As a result, her spells were broken, which I assume saved you."

"Thanks then. But I find it bizarre that when I left the keto fire I was precisely where Bayta wanted me. And..."

She smiled. "You must learn to relax into the bliss of not knowing because there are things that simply cannot be explained and must be accepted. And I know that shall prove extremely difficult for you."

"Not so much. Tell me more about Yoma-Baba?"

"Bayta and she are ancient adversaries."

"But Bayta told me she wouldn't be helping us here."

"She's been observing us and defeating Yoma-Baba was too tempting to pass up."

"I'm glad. Thanks to her, I'm back in almost complete balance."

"Because of her, I am as well. You know, I'd never given that any thought about your first wife remaining with her girl name. How strange for an Iska."

"She never really was. I must ask you how you feel about the realm?"

"As I've told you, *Aleph* is the meeting of opposites. We also, obviously, believe in demons, and understand their existence. So, they must have a place to exist."

"Tell me more."

"Without evil, there can be no good. Even the demons are fulfilling *Aleph's* role."

."Was Stalin doing *Aleph's* work as well?"

"Interesting question. He made Russia a great nation, but by evil means—killing off his rivals and most of the best and brightest people or suppressing their ideas, he also laid the groundwork for its destruction. Here we are a mere forty years after his murder and his regime is gone."

"Amen. I now want to tell you more about why I left my life in New York. When Ronnie challenged me to discover who I actually was, I reluctantly accepted, but when she said we could try to have union, I was sold. At that moment I knew you were the one missing from my life."

"I've dreamt about us being together for a long time. But I wouldn't have you think I was easy. Thus, I resolved to play what American women call, hard to get. Although that night when we first kissed, I almost melted in your arms. However, the time just was not right."

"Now consider this. Even though the time was not right, had you submitted to me then, we would've been spared a load of grief."

"Perhaps. But our trials have made our union stronger and better. As I once said, the union has so many moving parts and they must occur in proper sequence. That's beyond our control. Finally, I needed to maintain my feminine mystique." She laughed before falling silent. "I'm afraid I've some awfully unwelcome news. "I don't fear dying but when Harvey went out after the demons left, he confirmed our skiff was destroyed. Thus, it appears we're trapped, and we may die here."

"Nonsense, with us working together, we'll beat this. But

now it's time to sleep." They kissed and worn out by their day, quickly fell into a deep sleep.

2.

Sound asleep, Ashley smelled coffee and, at first, had no idea where he was until Natalya kissed him and said, "Let's get dressed and get coffee before it's all gone."

They walked hand-in-hand into the main room. Everyone was already up and drinking coffee. There were some biscuits for breakfast. Randell smiled. "You were certainly making a lot of noise last night."

Natalya smiled, "We were doing a scientific experiment to confirm we're alive. We are, so you must be too."

"Touché, Nata. Serje, how're you doing? We were worried."

Ashley told them first about his mother and Chichikov. "But I still wonder why, when it really mattered. the nurse left her alone like that."

"A B-17 had crash-landed on the base and it was all hands-on- deck."

"Thanks, Ronnie. I feel better knowing, having read Spence's account of his crash- landing after their eighteenth mission."

Ronnie asked, "Harvey, I've been thinking. Are you aware of any outbuildings besides the barn that could be a garage of some sort?"

"No, Verushka, besides if such a building existed, we would've seen it by now."

Ashley replied, "True, but I think Verushka's on to something. They must still have the two trucks they escaped in. So, we should do a more comprehensive search of the barn and its surroundings. Rand, you should stay here with Ronnie to keep the demons out. And, as we search, Nata will protect the rest of us."

* * *

About an hour later, they returned, and Ashley reported, "We found, I'd estimate about two hundred shrouds in the barn's crypt. Aside from that, unless someone knows how to motorize wheelbarrows, there's no transport in there until winter. Their trucks are gone. We only found some snowmobiles and one propeller driven snowmobile on skis."

Natalya smiled. "Oh my, Bayta had one, called an aerosledge and we were laughing merrily while propelling across the snow."

Harvey added, "We had one and that's how we got here in the winter."

Ashley smiled. "Harvey, tell them about the huge padlock to the empty room we found."

Harvey laughed. "This is one of the triumphs of Soviet manufacturing—the one kilo lock holding a large chain over the entrance. I saw a number of these locks at Vorkuta. Now, you may ask why on earth anyone would want a two-pound padlock. First of all, it looks formidable, but isn't. Secondly, it was the only kind available. Some bright factory manager realized since he could not meet his weight quota with small locks, he would only made these. He met his quota and he and the workers all got their bonuses. The idea quickly spread. That no one wanted such a monstrosity was never a factor. And, even then, you had to queue to get one."

Ronnie said, "I've seen them before but didn't know the story."

Randell asked, "Now, are we stuck here without the skiff?"

Ashley replied. "Not necessarily. I've got the germ of an idea. But first, let's go to the portal room."

Natalya asked, "You're not proposing we go through the realm to escape to another portal?

"No, even with our gifts and icons, we wouldn't get far. But I do need your cooperation."

She smiled. "Of course."

Ashley explained his plan, so when they arrived at the open portal, the wooden door was reinforced by three horizontal iron bars like the realm entrance he had seen in Paris. Natalya went to the right side of the large Orthodox cross facing the portal while Ashley stood on its left.

Ashley opened his Sainte Xenia icon, "I've got no light."

Natalya responded, "I don't either. What are we going to do now?"

"The time for cooperation has arrived." They sat cross-legged opposite each other, holding hands.

"We must be a unity and if we deeply focus, we can seal it." They closed their eyes and focused so hard, they were shaking. The door refused to close. "Keep on it, Serje, focus more."

With a slam, the door shut, and Ashley heard it lock.

Randell said, "Amazing. I don't know how you did that, but the cross is vibrating and glowing and I noticed the squiggle midway up. Nata, what's this on the cross?"

Natalya smiled and sat with her legs around the cross, palms pressing it and eyes closed for several minutes. When she released it, she remained sitting, "The maître who placed the cross here was an Iskandarov and this is the center of a network of Orthodox crosses to contain any demons who escape. All the demons outside, locked out of the realm, will slowly wither to nothingness without a way back."

Ashley asked, "How did you find out all that?"

"Using *pyordarsch*, I was able to go back to the founding of the monastery in 1587. But like your *tvarsch* search for Mummy, it really taxed me to my limit."

"You all right?"

"I'll be in a moment."

Ashley rose. "We're still not in the clear. After we find our father's diary, it's a long way to Vorkuta, much less Moscow. Anyone have any brilliant ideas?"

Randell said, "I believe strongly, if the diary exists, it has to be in the sanctuary, probably in, or near, the altar."

"Why?"

"Based on Mac's letter you read so eloquently, I know he would've mentioned it if the sanctuary had been desanctified when the monks left."

"Then the diary, for maximum safety, will be in the most sacred spot, the altar. But the door's locked, remember?"

"Yes but think about this. Since the demons couldn't enter the sanctuary, why have it locked at all? The monks required daily access to it. I believe with the portal closed and the crosses activated, the sanctuary is now open."

Upstairs, they entered the sanctuary and Ronnie and Ashley went looking around the altar for an opening of some sort, but it was solid oak.

"Well, I suppose we could tip it over to see underneath."

"Sergei Sergeyovich, this remains a consecrated altar. We can't just go tipping it over."

"Natalya Sergeyvna, I'm sure God won't mind if we…"

"My love, I cannot allow you to commit such a blasphemous act."

"I'm not going to leave it tipped over."

"I know. But it isn't there."

"How do you know?"

"Rand's theory's correct but the place is incorrect. Climb up to what you know as the pulpit, from where the priest speaks."

Ashley climbed the stairs to where he had a splendid view of the room but saw no diary. He looked under the lectern and found a box. He opened the box and found the diary. He stood, controlling his emotions, and asked, "Nata, how did you know where it would be?"

"I knew from recent *pyordarsch*." She went over to Randell. "I just wish to clarify something, being a *sorciere* doesn't mean I'm not a good daughter of the Church."

"Never doubted it for a moment."

"Thank you…Rand."

"You finally did it. And you weren't struck down by lightning."

She shook her head. "Now, you're teasing me too?"

"Life with friends would be very boring without humor."

Ashley, still in the pulpit, said, "How true. Mac wrote he was born in 1919, so he was in his seventies when he died, but he looks a good twenty years younger, so knowing there's no time or space in the realm, he didn't age at all while here. We can assume the same for Mac's council. But the question remains, what happens after you leave here? Do you keep it or do the years catch up?"

Natalya said, "Perhaps, we've been here for twenty years in the outside world, or twenty minutes or even twenty seconds. And, as far as I know, no way to find out until we leave."

Back in the main room, they all sat on the couches thinking about a solution for their next problem until Randell stood, "Dad, would you join me? I want to see if the network of crosses is properly working."

"Of course, son. We'll begin by the river."

"This will take some time. Don't worry, we'll be fine."

When even Harvey hugged everyone before leaving, Ashley knew what they were doing, but after proper consideration, said nothing. After they left, he began looking for a letter, which he eventually found and returned to Natalya and Ronnie. "I found Rand's letter. He and Harvey won't be coming back. Rand wants to be reunited with his family. And now he knows with the demons contained, he will, with Harvey as his guide."

Ronnie asked, "But what about Carmella?"

"Assuming we get back, I expect to see her and Harvey the shaman back in Vorkuta. I sensed in the skiff yesterday his guiding Rand was what they were talking about. And they didn't want to leave without sealing the portal and finding the diary. That's the gist of his letter written last night." He sighed. "I can't believe Rand's gone. I've known him all my life. He was so wonderfully wise, and I knew I could count on his support. Look how far he came this time."

"Obviously, I didn't know him well, but I definitely liked what I saw. I'm terribly sorry for your loss, my love."

"Thanks, Nata."

"Ash, I fondly remember the two of you, along with Monica, were inseparable when you were young. The three of you always getting into trouble for something or other. But you all were always such great kids. Ronnie dabbed her eyes with her light blue handkerchief and rose to dab Ashley's eyes as well.

Natalya joined them and took out her light blue handkerchief and they all hugged and cried for some time, until Ronnie said, "We are family. Nothing to fear. You are safe." Just as she had told Ashley in Olga's "pad" back in 1962.

Ashley smiled. "I'm surrounded by Bleu agents. I've nothing to fear." With his face still wet, he sat for a while before speaking. "Harvey left us a clue before he left. The river."

Ronnie shook her head. "OK, how do we get anywhere without a boat?"

Natalya jumped up. "Of course. It's so obvious. Brilliant, my love."

Ronnie smiled. "Absolutely brilliant, Serje. We can go downriver on the ice by the shore and then an ice floe."

Ashley replied, "Right. But I'm uncertain about the dangers."

Ronnie asked, "How so?"

"Since we don't know where we are in our world, once we leave the realm, all the ice might have substantially melted or the river might be frozen, after the relatively short summer or we could get caught in a snowstorm and freeze before Vorkuta."

Natalya added, "Despite my bravado earlier, we still don't really know if we are alive or dead in the outside world. Thus, we may not be able to leave the realm."

Ashley asked, "Verushka, it's probably none of my affair, but when you die…"

"You're right, it's not, but I understand why you ask. David's now with his first wife, Gwenneth Drew, who died in childbirth."

"Yes, I remember that from my eulogy of David, and she was also Charles Drew's older sister."

"When my time comes, I'll be with François, who came to me last night to start making up for all the time we could've been together." She went over to the window. "We now have a bigger problem, and I don't think we may be going anywhere for a while."

Ashley asked, "Why not?"

"There are several hundred spirits outside. Can't tell, from here, whether they're evil or good."

A man in an Army Air Force captain's uniform comes through the locked front door, "Greetings. I am William Macpherson Goodwin, but all my friends call me Mac. And I have been observing you, Sergei, Spence Talbott's son, your wife Natalya and your half-sister Verushka. First of all, I was impressed by your collective ingenuity in finding Spence and Harv's diary but, especially, in closing the portal."

No silver eyes. Ashley replied, "Thank you. I sense you have more to say, but there is something we must know first. We would all like a better explanation of why you came here."

"You know the basics from my letter. My original plan, after our escape in 1971, was to close the portal and then make our way to Finland and seek asylum. From there, we thought we could return to our respective countries."

"What happened to change your plans?"

"Three things. First, we knew Vorkuta would send out an alert to all stations about our escape, and we decided we would hide out here for a year. As for leaving the country, we had two routes, a northern and less northern. And they both had serious problems we could not overcome. I shall not bore you with the details." Mac shook his head. "Had the winter of '91 not been so long, cold and snowy, Major Landfear and I could have greeted your party. Veronique, I feel as though I know you the best from what François told me."

"Thank you. But now I am curious about all the spirits outside. I am not certain I understand what is happening."

"The spirits of all the monks and nuns who died here have lingered, not having been released from their vows. Each time the portal is shut, more of them can leave. About half of the monks and nuns are here to take a close friend to Heaven, just as Harv took the Reverend Speers. The last group from 1926 must remain until they are relieved."

Natalya said, "Mac, we do not know about this group, only your father's group who left in 1921."

"The Church decided that the situation had returned enough to normal that a new group could be sent here to close the portal and insure it continued and be left alone. They did so until they were discovered by geologists searching for other coal beds besides Vorkuta's. Unfortunately, the geologists had a military escort who killed all the monks, except Maître Igor Igorevich, who was taken back to Vorkuta for interrogation and subsequently killed."

"That is terrible, but not unexpected. When we return to Moscow, I shall ask the Church to send a new group."

"Thank you, Natalya. But that leads to my next point. And that has to do with your status. You are in limbo. You can either go directly to your paradise or you can try to get back to Harv's skiff and hope your bodies are still ones you can revive."

Ashley spoke. "How long have we been gone from the outside world?"

"Hard to say. Based on what I know of such matters, I would guess between two to six weeks. Obviously, I have no idea about the condition of your bodies by the river."

"Thank you for your candor, Mac. I sense you shall be leaving us soon."

"Very good, Sergei. I had a special girl who said she would wait for me when I enlisted. She has recently died, and I intend to seek her out."

"Well, best of luck to you then."

"And to you all, as well." Mac smiled and disappeared.

"Since we don't know how much time we have left to find our bodies, we need to leave now."

3.

Ashley found a waterproof Soviet military backpack for the diary as they quickly gathered up their belongings and pistols. After another difficult trek across the soggy tundra through the thickening fog to a place downriver where the shore ice was strong enough to support them, they walked together in the icy wind, which had blown the fog away. A large stone Russian

Orthodox cross on a ridge made Ashley think of Randell. He smiled but also heard wolves calling close by and soon, he saw the snarling pack. They were large wolves, hard to stop with just pistols. *Oh, for those Uzis now.* They came closer, eyes gleaming. *Damn, these aren't normal wolves.* Ronnie stood before them and when she howled a she-wolf call, they stopped. After a second one, they fled. Ronnie rejoined Ashley and Natalya, who asked, "What did you just do?"

"Oh, it's part of my *phygynaya*. Not a big deal."

"Yes, I remember a time…"

Ronnie said, "Ash, I'm sure you do. Now, let's just drop it."

Natalya hugged Ronnie. "Thank you for saving us, yet again." They kissed in the Iska manner meaning Natalya had told the truth.

"Not to interrupt you two fine ladies, but I think we would be safer on an ice floe away from more wolves and bears. Keep your weapons out and let's find a suitable floe."

Later, a perfect floe came by and they jumped on and floated down river. Fog reappeared and they silently drifted, hearing the cracking and breaking of the ice and the howling and scuffling of wolves and bears they could not see. Ashley said, "I'm concerned, here we are blind in the fog and we may not see anything until we reach Vorkuta and that would mean we're likely dead or soon will be, having missed the skiff. I also can't tell how thick the ice is under us and it could simply break in two right down the middle or it could melt enough to sink us, and, with all our equipment, we'd drown."

"Serje, you're so cheerful."

"Not so, Nata. I just want us to be prepared for anything."

The cracking noise came closer and they moved away about two minutes before the ice spit. "Come on, we need to move closer to the right bank. I sense we're close to where we need to be."

They had to leap from floe to floe, not knowing whether the new floe would support them. But in the fog, they could not split up. Each one had to keep the other two in sight at all times to make certain no one had drowned. *If we're really dead, we couldn't drown, but I'm not foolish enough to test that.* Sometimes, to get to a new floe, they had to go backward or just jump laterally. Their clothes were getting wet and froze in place.

The fog abruptly lifted and Rosalita steered another skiff. Hey, she's wearing a Mets baseball cap over her shaved head. How NYC!

Once aboard, Ashley asked, "'Lita, how'd you ever find us?"

"Anghelina isn't the only Civilli who knows how to track people by their auras. You've been gone about a month. Today is July fifteenth. And you've grown an incredibly good beard."

I had no idea. I didn't have it just a few minutes ago.

Natalya said, "Ooh, I like it. Makes you look like a Cossack. And she then began to squirm. "I'm beginning to show my pregnancy as does Ronnie and I'm very uncomfortable in these wet clothes."

Rosalita said, "Do the best you can. Aleks' jet will be at the airport to take us back to Moscow." She turned, "Keep the beard, Ash. On the day after you left, I was able, with Carmella's help, to track you to Harvey's beached skiff before your auras faded. We protected your bodies as well as we could. I knew you weren't dead because I could intermittently track your auras. I assumed you were in one of the realms. And there's good news. I persuaded sister to convince George, Nick and Drago to come with me in his helicopter and when it hovered low over the skiff, George was delighted you three were dead and more so after I told him you hadn't found the diary. I said I would properly bury you. They all, including sister, flew back to New York the next day, after a raucous celebration at a Vorkuta club George knew about."

"That's good news. But what did you tell them about Rand's body not being in the boat?"

"He had volunteered to get help with Harvey, and they disappeared on the tundra. They bought that. I also see your waterproof pouch and the diary in it. Congratulations."

Ashley told Rosalita where they had been and by the time he finished, they were almost to Harvey's skiff. Ronnie said, "I believe, based on what I know of such things, our bodies in the other skiff are in suspension. That's the good news. But this is going to be complicated and there's no assurance we'll be successful. If our bodies are not handled exactly right, we'll likely be dead. Plus, there'll be a period of confusion as we sort out what each of ourselves know. Coupled with that, we were in the realm before the freezing fog. But since we closed the portal, I don't know if the realm exists here anymore."

"Verushka, how do you know all these things?"

"Nata, I've had a long life and learned many things that didn't seem to be important at the time, but, unexpectedly, became useful."

Ashley said, "We came out of the realm when my beard and your bumps appeared. Yoma-Baba's protection of our bodies has expired. We need to hurry."

* * *

Rosalita sped the motor as much as she could and landed her skiff next to Harvey's. When the three of them got out to examine their bodies, Ronnie said, "God, I look horrible."

"As do I, Verushka."

Ashley said, "If you two ladies are over your vanity, Verushka, are we OK?"

"I think we have an even chance. First, we carefully move our bodies from the skiff to the shore."

After moving the bodies, Verushka asked, "Now, who wants to go first?"

"I thought we'd all go together."

"No, Nata, it has to be one at a time in case anything goes wrong."

Ashley said, "I'll be the guinea pig."

Ronnie continued, "Lie next to your body and focus like you did at the portal."

Ashley closed his eyes and felt the chill of the river stones through his parka as he passed into a brightly lit place and saw his alter self. They began rapidly swirling around each other, gradually coming together until Ashley was uncertain which one was him—the one from the realm or from the boat. He lost consciousness before coming around still on the stones and vomited thick red and beige liquid. *Must be what's left of my other self but smells terrible.*

"My love, are you all right?"

"Well, I've been better. But is there only one of me?"

"Yes."

"Good, but there's all sorts of stuff swirling in my head. But I do have moments of lucidity, which are slowly getting longer. Just let me lie here while I sort it all out."

Natalya went next and he watched her levitate before disappearing. She was gone a seemingly long time before reappearing and reluctantly vomited the same liquid, leaving her face pale.

Ronnie came to Ashley, still lying on the ground. "I may be too old to stand the strain of this and, potentially, I could disappear, never to return."

"I'll watch you as best I can." Ashley unsteadily sat up alarmed when Ronnie was gone much longer than Natalya. Of course, I've no idea of how long I disappeared. Damn, I can't lose Rand and Ronnie on the same day. I'll be completely lost. Especially, if I lose Nata. 'Lita, I'm concerned about Ronnie. She's been gone a long time."

"You, Serje, of all people, should know how tough she is. She'll be fine."

When Ronnie appeared, she seemed very confused and lay quietly but did not vomit. Ashley helped her into the boat before helping Natalya. "Sorry to take you second, love, but I'm very concerned about Verushka."

"I don't know but I suspect her age and *phygynaya* are the problem. I'll try to watch her, but my head's still spinning. I think I'll be all right if I can just sit back in the boat."

Back in Rosalita's skiff with Harvey's in tow, Ashley reached down to pick up the knapsack, looked in and smiled. "We were successful in our mission for our father's Gulag diary."

Ronnie shook her head. "I've still no memory of how we did that."

"No matter the how, here it is. And in the days to come, I expect our memories will sharpen and we'll know what actually happened."

Ashley asked Rosalita, "Where's Carmella?"

"She's been so incredibly helpful. Although she failed to convince sister to change her mind, she still made an extraordinarily compelling case that sister should repent and rejoin us. I believe, at some point, she will. I've a theory about what sister's doing, but I'm not yet ready to share. My great-aunt also told me so many wonderful stories about Spain, before and during the civil war. She and Harvey should be waiting for us at *Rudnik* One. And I assume Reverend Speers died in the realm."

"Sadly, he sacrificed himself so we could leave and that made this a terribly expensive journey. He turned to Natalya. "You were not exactly honest with me about why we were the only ones interested in finding the diary."

"True. But we finally truly worked together and are that much closer to a unity. Had I shared what I knew about it being be exceedingly difficult, would you have come with me? Because, if necessary, I would've gone alone."

"You know damn well I wouldn't have let you go by yourself. You would've failed just like I would have had I gone alone." He smiled. "You know that was our first frank conversation. I guess we're really married now."

"We must be careful. Even though we've been gone for a month, given our two days in the realm, I don't know if we've met the Fortnight Rule to finalize our union. While we are nearly a unity, we may still be under attack to break it."

"We'll be careful. But, as long as I have breath, no one's going to."

4.

On the journey back to Vorkuta no one spoke, busily trying to remember everything. Until Natalya removed her gloves, unzipped Ronnie's parka, placed her left hand on Ronnie's abdomen with her right supporting her back and elevated her a few inches above the skiff. She ran her hands over Ronnie and gradually brought her down to her seat. Ronnie opened her eyes and smiled weakly before vomiting over the side. Natalya smiled and zipped up Ronnie's parka. "You'll be all right. And you haven't lost your baby."

Ronnie, based on her history, will probably have another difficult delivery and she might die of complications. I hope I can help her prevent that. Ashley wanted to bring both Harvey and Carmella back to New York. Harvey could do TV ads for the diary book and Wow! when people see how fit Harvey is, the Gulag diet will be the next big thing. But then his thoughts turned back to Randell as the finality of his death struck Ashley hard so that he shook with tears under his parka and blanket. Beside the loss of Randell's sage advice, there was no body to bring back for his New York funeral. He remembered their last two Wednesday tennis matches at the Racquet Club. And especially, Randell's lob at the same time as Natalya's first Andronyi arrived, causing him to lose. And also, at their last match, which he had won, he regretted it should be fueled by such a useless emotion as his anger at being adopted.

He heard in his head, Do not worry. You shall not get rid of me, your conscience, quite that easily. With Nata, you no longer really need me. If you do, you know how to contact me. Greeting from an incredibly happy Speers family.

He smiled. Randell was right about Natalya. His thoughts turned to Ronnie, who seemed to be reviving as Natalya watched over her. *These Iska Sisters are really something with their intense loyalty to each other.*

An hour later, with all three feeling almost normal, Rosalita docked the skiff at the base of the ruins of *Rudnik One*. Walking up, within the ruins large trees protected from the wind had been breaking the concrete and returning this blighted place back to nature. And the obviously sloppy and cheap *zek* labor made the tree's task all the easier. Harvey and Carmella were standing by one of the ruined whitewashed barracks. After Rosalita went to Carmella, Ashley said to Harvey. "How is it you're here? I thought…"

"I can tell you found it. I told you I was a wandering Orthodox mystic. Like you, I know and do many things other people
don't. I also know you want us to return to New York to help
with the diary publication. You may contact me, as needed, but
there is no need for us to be in New York City. I know you'll
be successful in this as you were in your mission. In fact, your
diary search will be child's play compared to getting published
and creating sales. Car and I are needed here and where we must
remain. Good fortune to you in this venture and in all to come."

"So, thanks for all your help."

"You all did the heavy lifting. Oh yes, Car asked me to give
you this letter for Maria Civilli."

"Of course, I'll be happy to deliver this." They shook hands
and Ashley watched them walk away, arm in arm.

The four of them went to find Nicholai and Nakita before getting
their luggage from Rosalita's hotel, where she had gathered it all.

5.

When they tried to board Aleks's jet, a suspicious guard began
questioning everyone until Natalya, still uncomfortable and
angry, flashed her credentials and bullied him in submission.
Once on board, Natalya and Ronnie hurried to change into their
nightgowns to be more comfortable. After flying over the camp,
the blight of Vorkuta was disappearing. A black river with some
ice floes cuts a broad swath through swampy and muddy tundra,
punctuated by blotchy lakes. He thought about all those, Russian
and foreign, who labored and perished here—this would be the
best weather they would ever have, bogged down in the swamp.
After silently saying a prayer for the repose of their souls, Ashley
looked down at the backpack. The truth would come out and all
those men, the Lost Souls and the other POWs, would finally be
recognized. Done properly, it would also be enough to destroy
George Farwell's reputation. On the other hand, the national
animosities their publication would likely raise might be the
death knell of the L'Enfant Initiative. Ashley began reading:

29 April 1945

Today, I begin this journal in the absolute belief that,
in the fullness of time, these words will find their
way into the hands of the man for whom they are
intended. Moreover, he will understand its meanings
and take action. I have no fear of detection. I have
been taught well in the art of concealment, among my
other survival skills.

My name is 1st Lieutenant Spencer Talbott, USAAF.
And these are my bona fides. Service Number 12-
267-349. In my last assignment, I was bombardier/
navigator on the Consolidated B-24 heavy bomber,
'Jezebel', attached to the 44th Bomber Group from
Eight Air Force, along with my skipper, Captain
Harvey Jacobs, Service Number 12-117-783. And
co-pilot First Lieutenant, William, 'Mac' Goodwin,
Service number, 12-129-694. We had flown eighteen
missions in our Boeing B-17 Flying Fortress,
'Bounteous Beauty' before catching hell coming
back from Frankfurt. After getting out of the hospital,
Harv, Mac and I volunteered for special assignment
on 'Operation Tidal Wave', the first Ploesti Romanian
Oil Refinery Raid. We were shot down over Romania
on 1 August 1943 and Mac was killed. After escaping
from several luftstalags, Harvey and I were shipped
to Luftstalag IIIC, 'the highest security stalag.' near
Alt Drewitz, approximately eighty kilometers east
of Berlin. Earlier this year, unlike some of the other
luftstalags, the Krauts did not evacuate us westward.
Scuttlebutt had it that the Gestapo was going to
execute us. However, the Red Army arrived there
sooner than expected. The Reds told us we would be
repatriated, like other Allied PWs, through Odessa
in the Crimea. The Reds gave us new Air Force
uniforms and fed us before we marched off east to a
railhead. As we left, I heard small arms fire before the

camp was set afire. At the time, I thought nothing of it. Now, I know that it was significant.

For the past week, we have headed east, by train, foot, barge, or whatever was available. For the past two days, we have traveled in a cramped cattle car with crude bunks, but not toward Odessa. The guards are on platforms outside the cars, supposedly, for our protection, since Nazi units and Fascist partisans are still operating in the area. Cannot say I believe the Reds' good intentions because through the cracks in the car, I can see the sun is rising to our right. That means we are now headed north. Odessa is southeast from Berlin. Anyway, I am extremely uncomfortable being in Russia again. So here I sit on the straw, amid the stink of waste and unwashed bodies, wondering where the hell we are going. We have had endless debates about this. Perhaps, it is a detour because Russia is still pretty torn up from the German invasion. Or, a new port of embarkation has opened in the north, possibly, Murmansk. Nonetheless, going north makes me nervous. That is where Stalin reportedly has his worst slave labor camps. I cannot shake the idea we are traveling into a lair of absolute evil and will ultimately come to the final ring of Hell. Nevertheless, there is no way out. While it is hard to believe Stalin would just kidnap Allied PWs and send them to the camps, I do not put it past him either. To most of the guys here, Stalin is 'Uncle Joe', our gallant wartime ally and liberal reformer. Because of my father, I know what a brutal, paranoid bastard he is.

My father is a colonel in the Waffen SS, hopefully, he is still alive. We did not spend as much time together as I would have liked before the War. The Struggle took precedence. I have no seen him since he came to interview me at the Luftstalag III-B, near Furstenberg, Germany, and tried to get me to enlist

in the Waffen SS. Told me I could be in Paris the
next day with my first wife, Nadia. She had come to
visit me as well and was even more beautiful than
I remembered. God, it was tempting, but I have a
responsibility to my buddies, my adopted country
and especially to Binkie. A guy I met in one of the
luftstalags told me we have a son. He is with Colonel
Cooper and his wife and they have named him Ashley
Cooper. Nadia confirmed this and told me Bleu
knows Pavel Chichikov, Red operative, kidnapped
Binkie. I must find her. We will have a normal life
one day. I swear it. I must regain the faith of my
family. Below, I have listed the bona fides of every
man in our group. And if worse comes to worse, I
will record the stories and bona fides of every PW I
encounter. I also name those who betrayed us. The
blood is Iskandar. May he speak within you.

Ashley felt as though his father had been right beside him. *I
now know his whole story.*

When Natalya returned from visiting Ronnie and Rosalita
while Ashley read, he said, "Since separating from my alter-ego
and losing that horrible-smelling liquid, I sense I've evolved."

"Yes, I sense that as well. But will you still love me when
I'm big as a house with twins?"

Ashley laughed. "Of course, I will. Unlike you, I think naked pregnant women are the epitome of God's creation. And you
look so sexy with your bump in your gown, I'm having trouble
restraining myself."

"I'm extraordinarily pleased. Now that I'm one, I agree
about pregnant women one hundred percent."

"Good. Now, is our union complete?

"Like us, it's never finished..."

"I know that. I meant is the fortnight time of our union
completed?"

"That's a very interesting question."

Ashley looked up at the pilot who told him Aleks was calling.

When he returned, Natalya said, "You look like a white sheet. What happened?"

"Aleks is safe and had a call from George who had my daughter kidnapped. Aleks is trying to confirm this. For her safe return, he wants the Gulag diary. I'm not amazed he knows we're alive and have the diary."

"This must be the work of that FSB bastard Malenkov, who has kept us under surveillance. We should've been more vigilant coming back on the river."

"Yes, no doubt George had the skiff under surveillance. Now, some good news. Aleks executed his kidnappers and so his renunciation of L'Enfant is void. And that gives me an idea." He looked at his watch. "We have about an hour of flight left and time to begin developing our plan."

"Before we do. I have confirmed that we're past fortnight. No one, not even we, can break our Blood Union. You're stuck with me."

"Great. I can't think of anyone I'd rather be stuck with. So, let's discover our plan." *And now begins the inevitable and final clash with George.*

She nodded, and they melded their minds together as a unity, and not speaking to maintain privacy, Sergei and Natalya formed a suitable plan by the time they landed.

Acknowledgements

For helping to make this book possible, I would like to thank my friend Ian Graham Leask and my wife Julie for their unwavering support. Also, Gary, Susan, Mike and Josh at Calumet Editions, and Nicholas at Oakheart Productions.

About the Author

NORM MITCHELL has lived in Minnesota for thirty-five years, longer than New York City, where he was born and grew up. Early on, he developed a love of history, especially that of Russia, Germany and the Balkans. And that, along with writing, has been his lifelong passion. He graduated from Tulane University in New Orleans, Louisiana, with a B.A. in history and a minor in philosophy. He has travelled extensively in North America, Europe, and the Middle East with the Air Force. His last book, also published by Calumet Editions, was *The Hidden One*, the first book in the *People of the Blood Trilogy*.